ROB HARRELL

Top Shelf Productions
Atlanta/Portland

Published by
Top Shelf Productions
PO Box 1282
Marietta, GA 30061-1282
USA

Publishers: Chris Staros and Brett Warnock.

Visit our online catalog at www.topshelfcomix.com.

First Printing, July 2013.

Printed in China.

For Bur

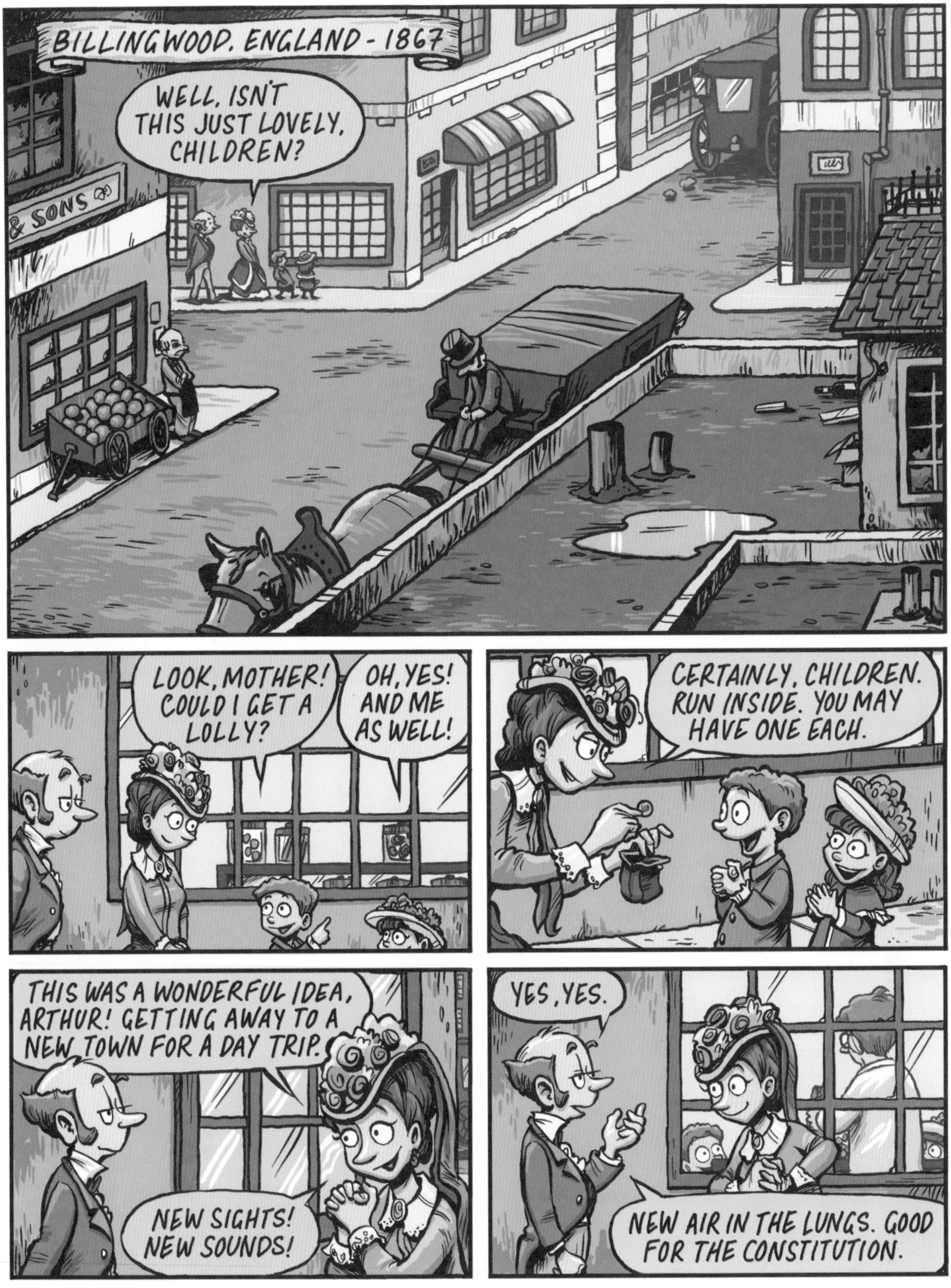
BILLINGWOOD, ENGLAND - 1867
& SONS
WELL, ISN'T THIS JUST LOVELY, CHILDREN?
LOOK, MOTHER! COULD I GET A LOLLY?
OH, YES! AND ME AS WELL!
CERTAINLY, CHILDREN. RUN INSIDE. YOU MAY HAVE ONE EACH.
THIS WAS A WONDERFUL IDEA, ARTHUR! GETTING AWAY TO A NEW TOWN FOR A DAY TRIP.
NEW SIGHTS! NEW SOUNDS!
YES, YES.
NEW AIR IN THE LUNGS. GOOD FOR THE CONSTITUTION.

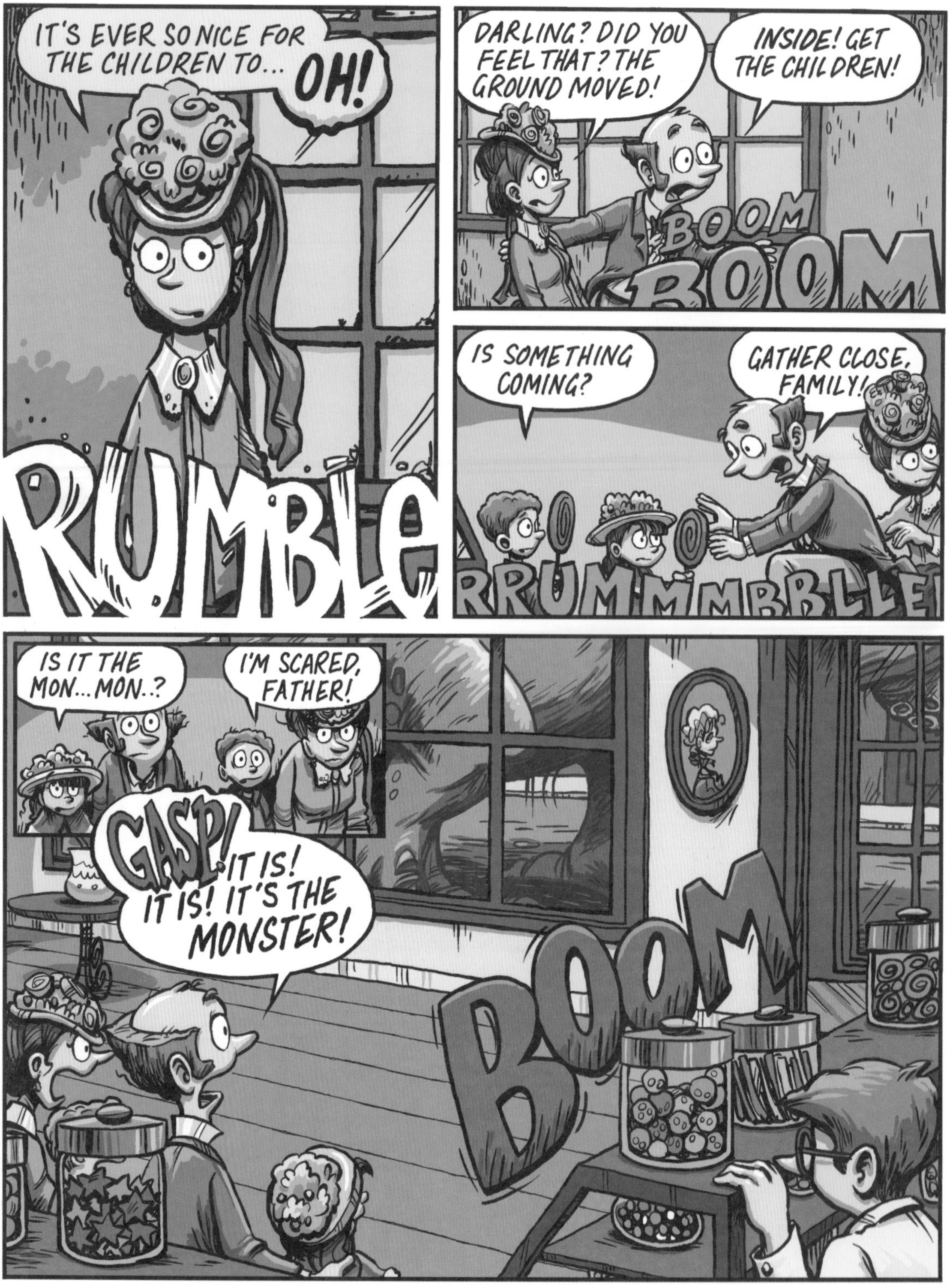

IT'S EVER SO NICE FOR THE CHILDREN TO... OH!
RUMBLE
DARLING? DID YOU FEEL THAT? THE GROUND MOVED!
INSIDE! GET THE CHILDREN!
BOOM
BOOM
IS SOMETHING COMING?
GATHER CLOSE, FAMILY!
RRUMMMBBLLE
IS IT THE MON... MON..?
I'M SCARED, FATHER!
GASP! IT IS! IT IS! IT'S THE MONSTER!
BOOM

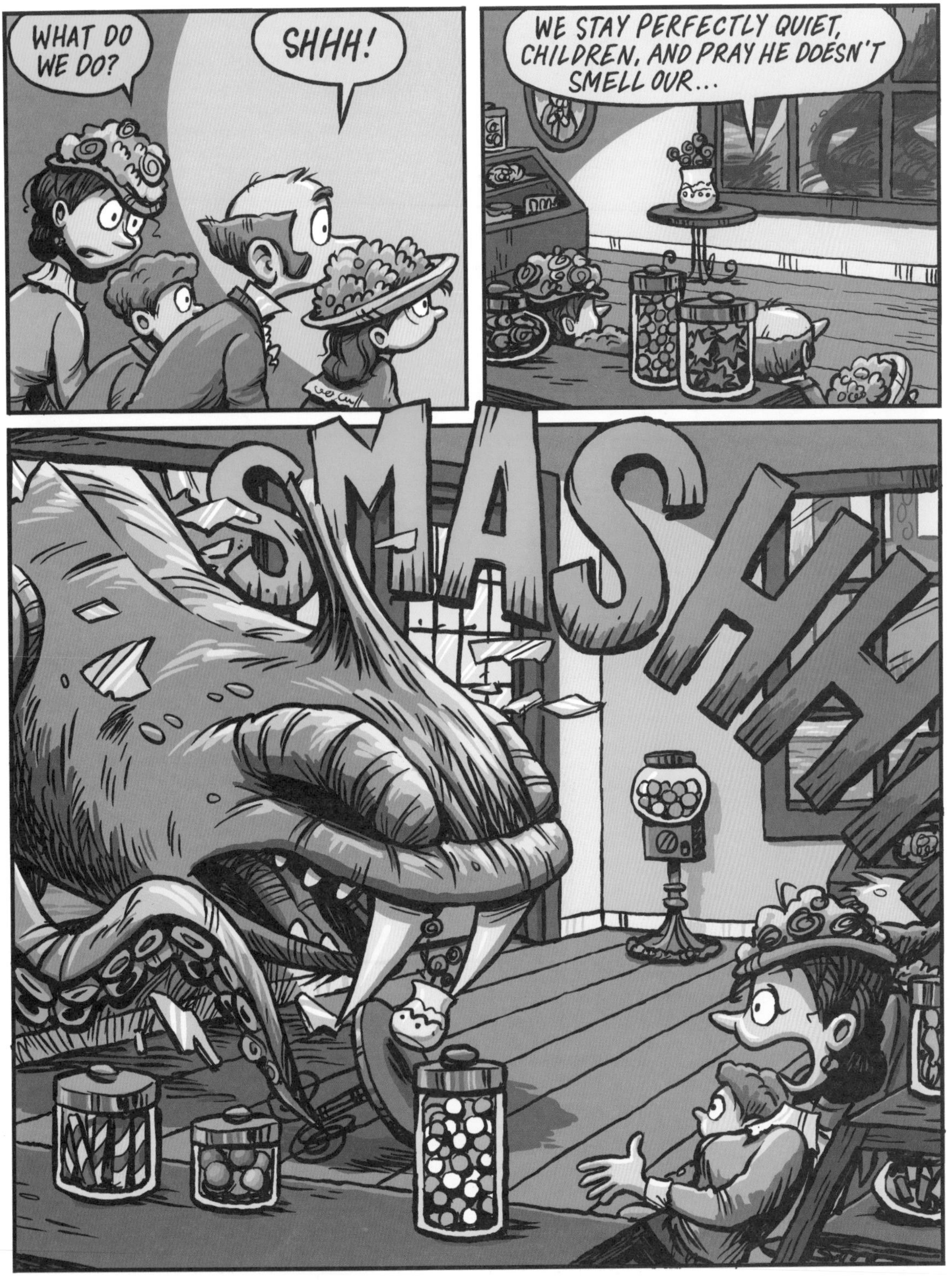
WHAT DO WE DO?
SHHH!
WE STAY PERFECTLY QUIET, CHILDREN, AND PRAY HE DOESN'T SMELL OUR...
SMASHH

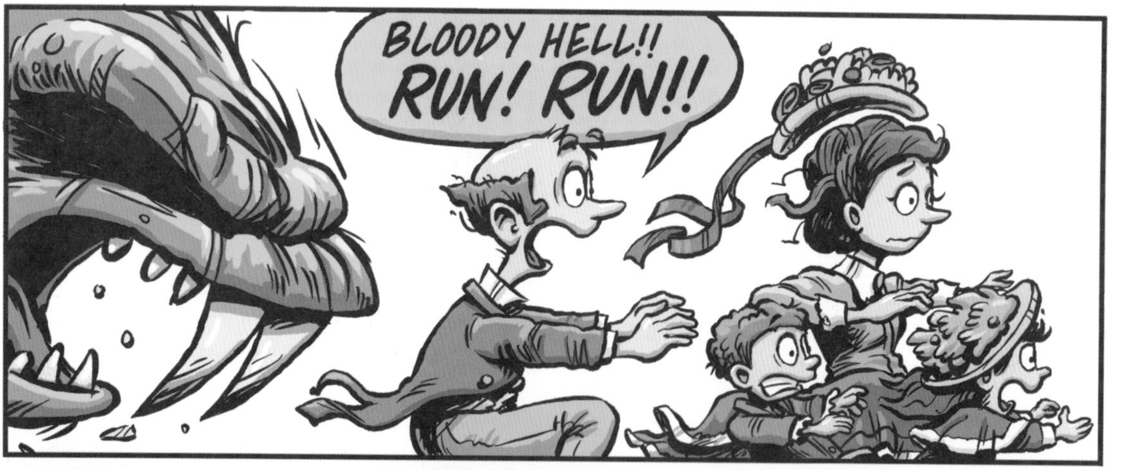
BLOODY HELL!! RUN! RUN!!

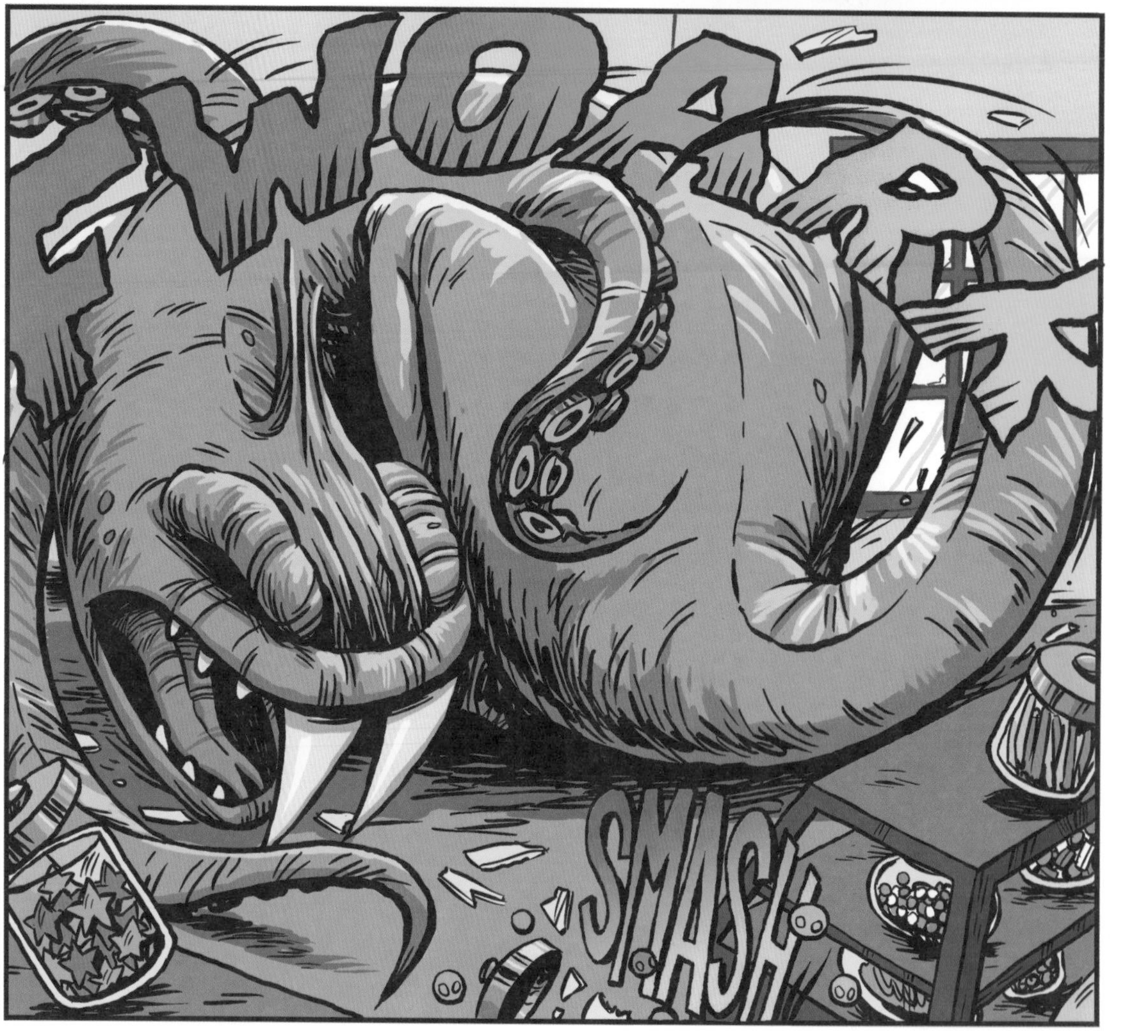
WOAAR
SMASH

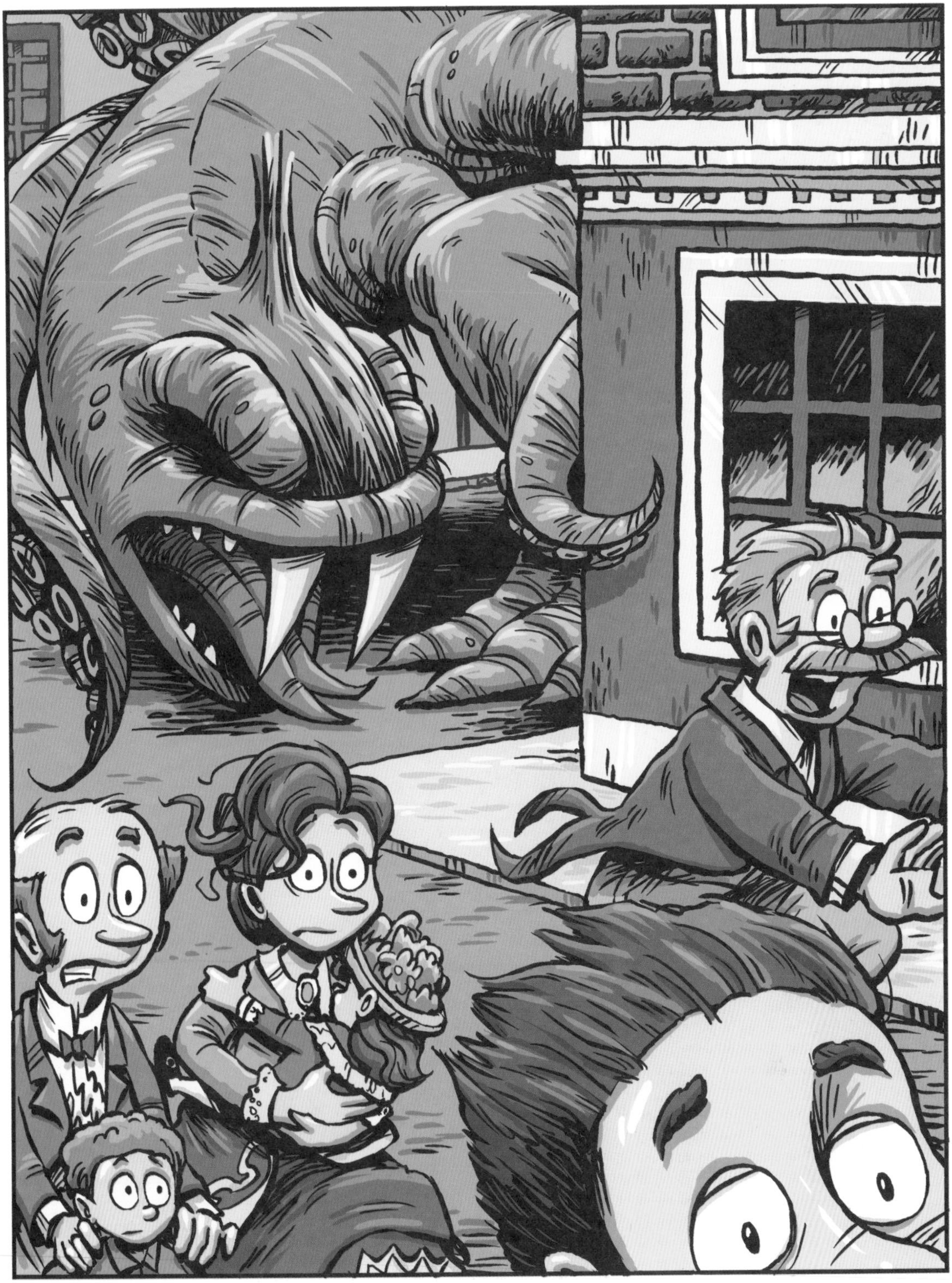

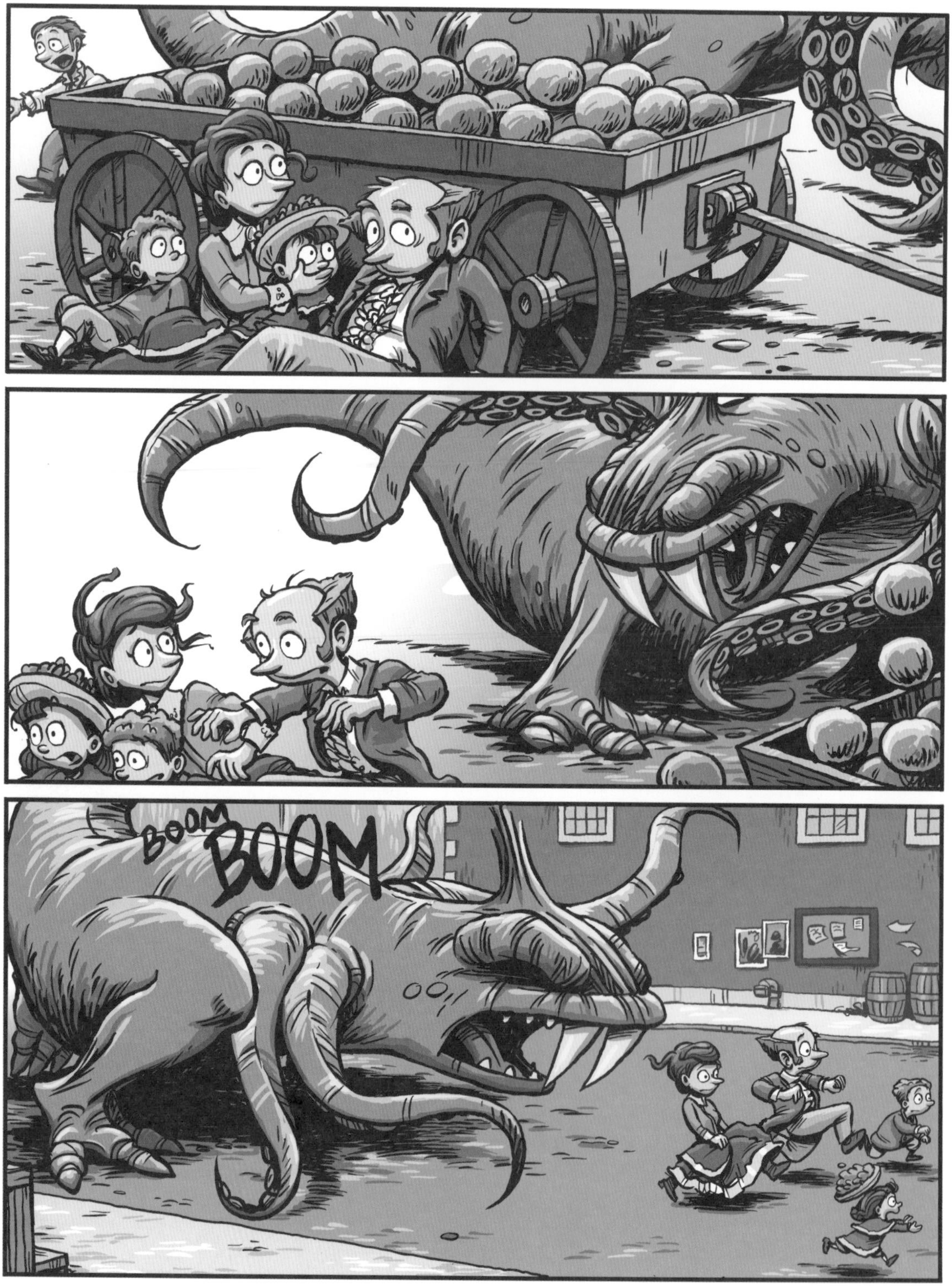
BOOM
BOOM

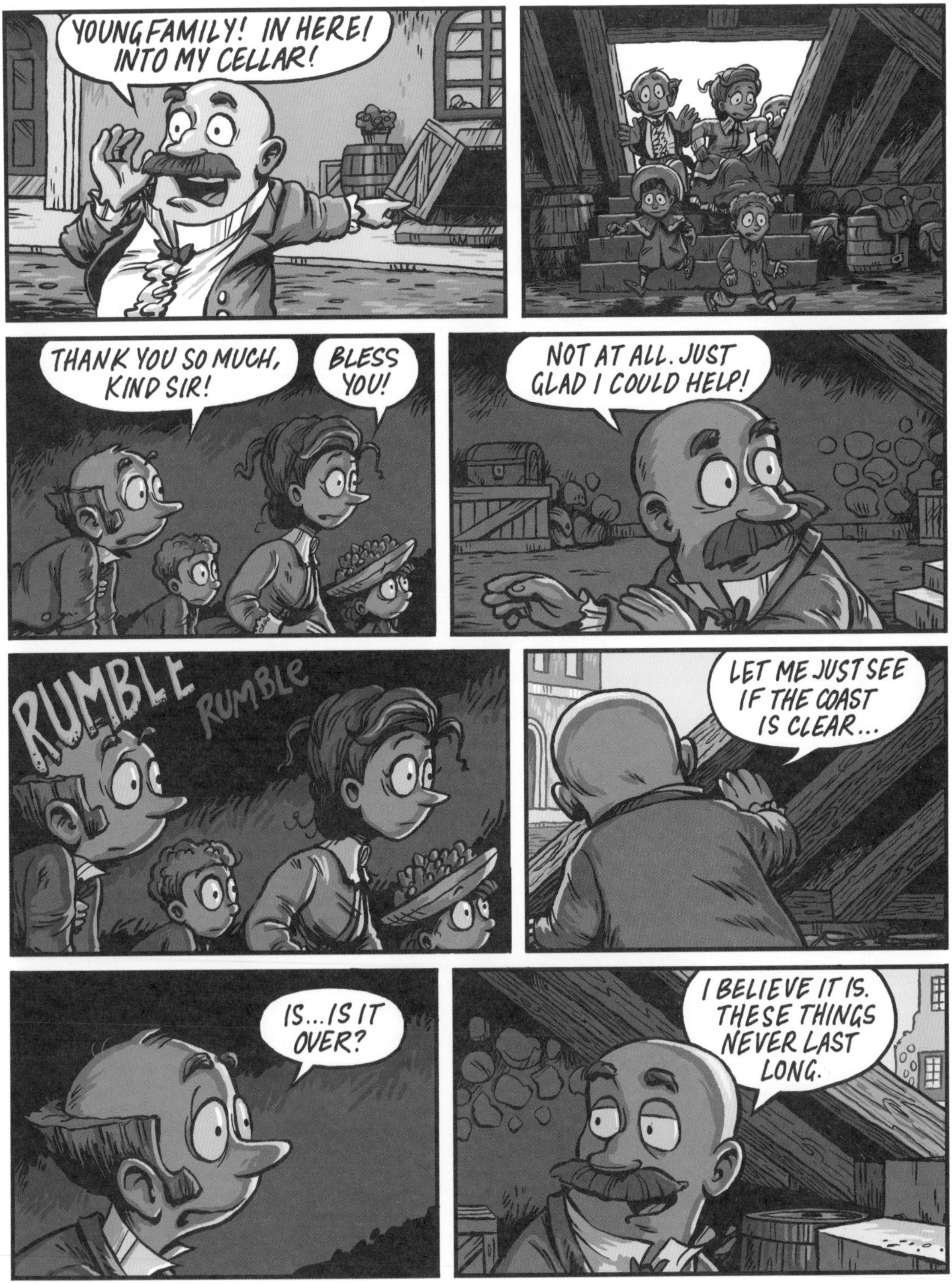
YOUNG FAMILY! IN HERE! INTO MY CELLAR!
THANK YOU SO MUCH, KIND SIR!
BLESS YOU!
NOT AT ALL. JUST GLAD I COULD HELP!
RUMBLE
RUMBLE
LET ME JUST SEE IF THE COAST IS CLEAR...
IS...IS IT OVER?
I BELIEVE IT IS. THESE THINGS NEVER LAST LONG.

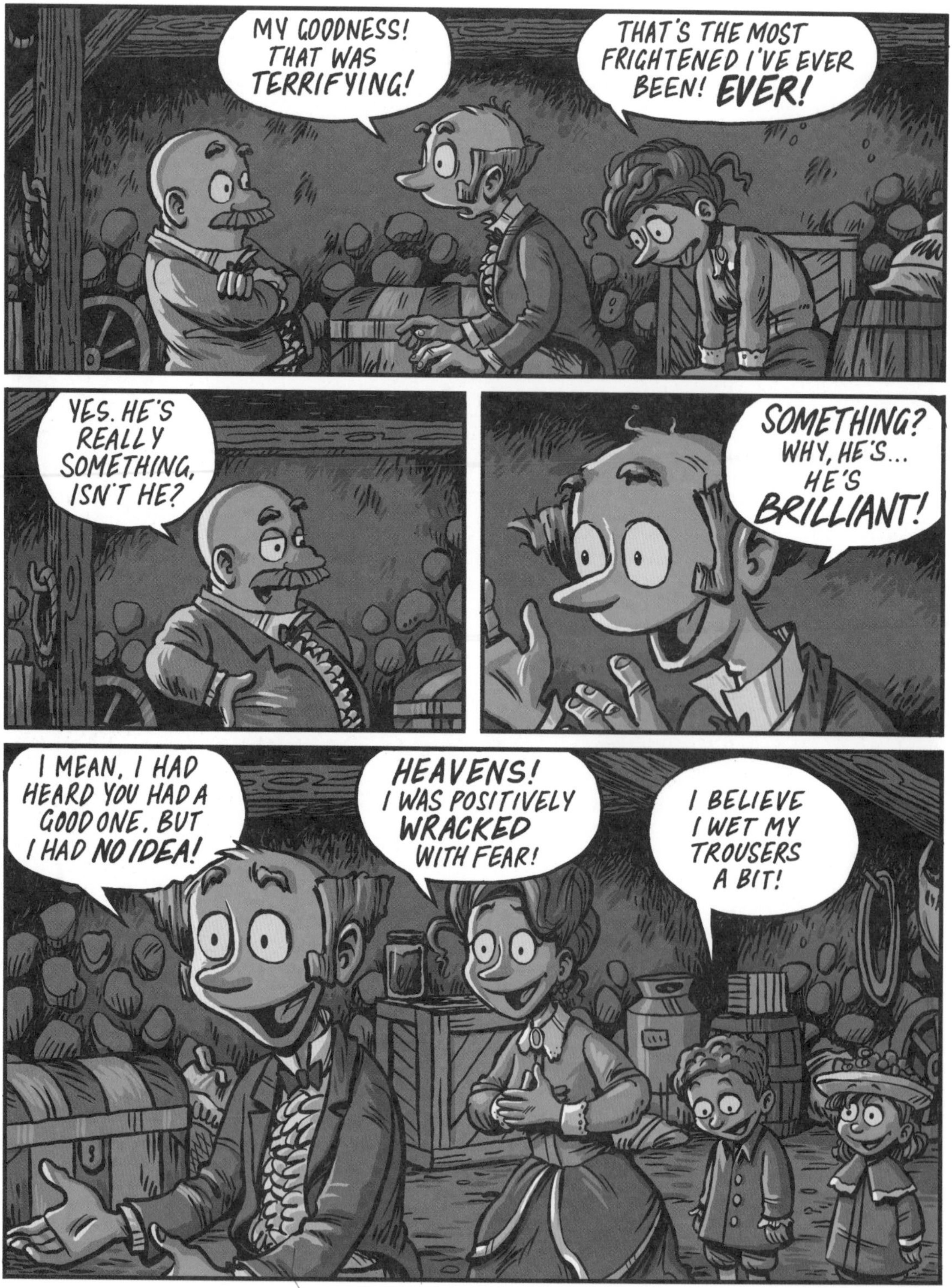
MY GOODNESS! THAT WAS TERRIFYING!
THAT'S THE MOST FRIGHTENED I'VE EVER BEEN! EVER!
YES. HE'S REALLY SOMETHING, ISN'T HE?
SOMETHING? WHY, HE'S... HE'S BRILLIANT!
I MEAN, I HAD HEARD YOU HAD A GOOD ONE. BUT I HAD NO IDEA!
HEAVENS! I WAS POSITIVELY WRACKED WITH FEAR!
I BELIEVE I WET MY TROUSERS A BIT!

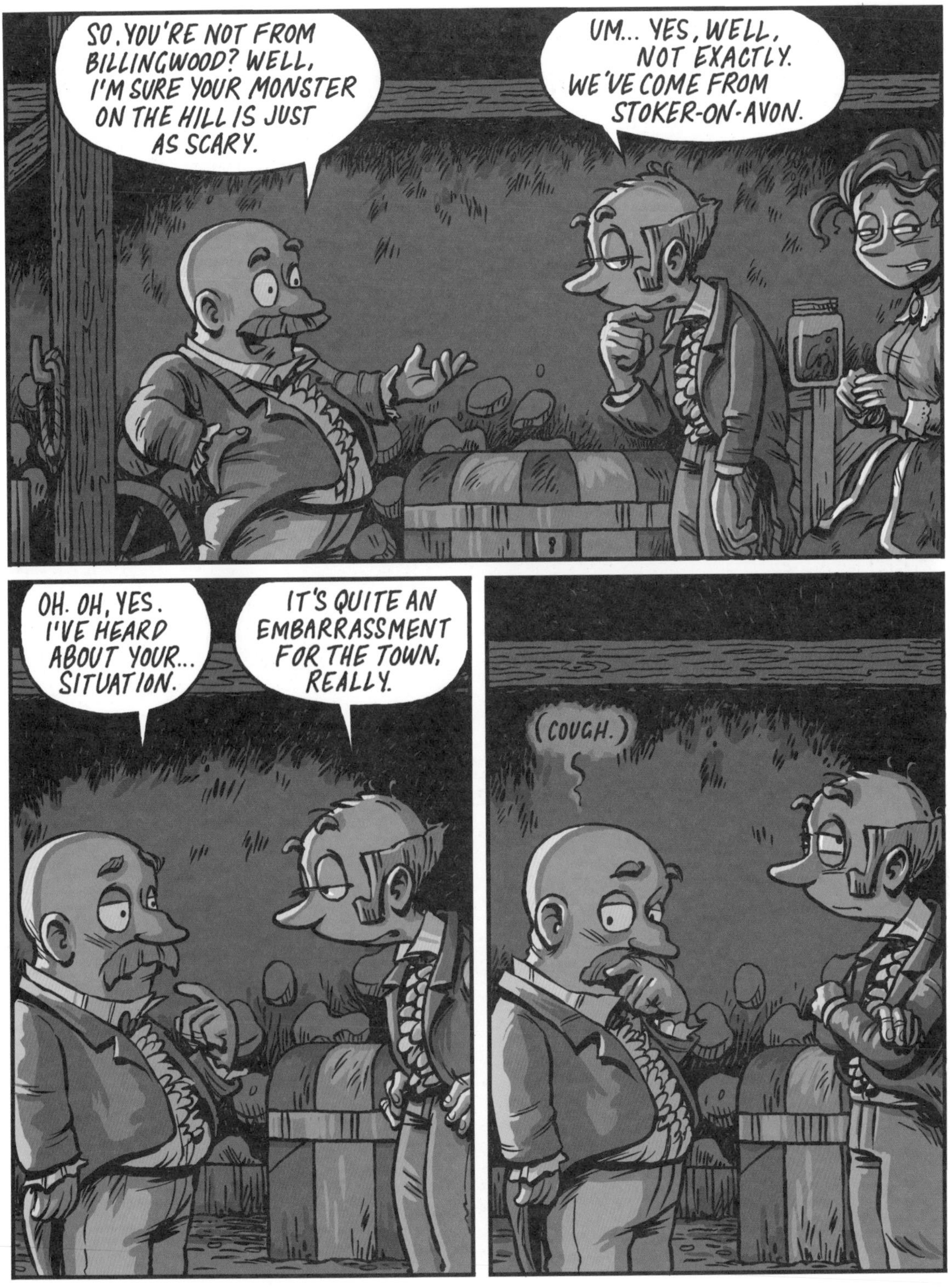
SO, YOU'RE NOT FROM BILLINGWOOD? WELL, I'M SURE YOUR MONSTER ON THE HILL IS JUST AS SCARY.
UM... YES, WELL, NOT EXACTLY. WE'VE COME FROM STOKER-ON-AVON.
OH. OH, YES. I'VE HEARD ABOUT YOUR... SITUATION.
IT'S QUITE AN EMBARRASSMENT FOR THE TOWN, REALLY.
(COUGH.)

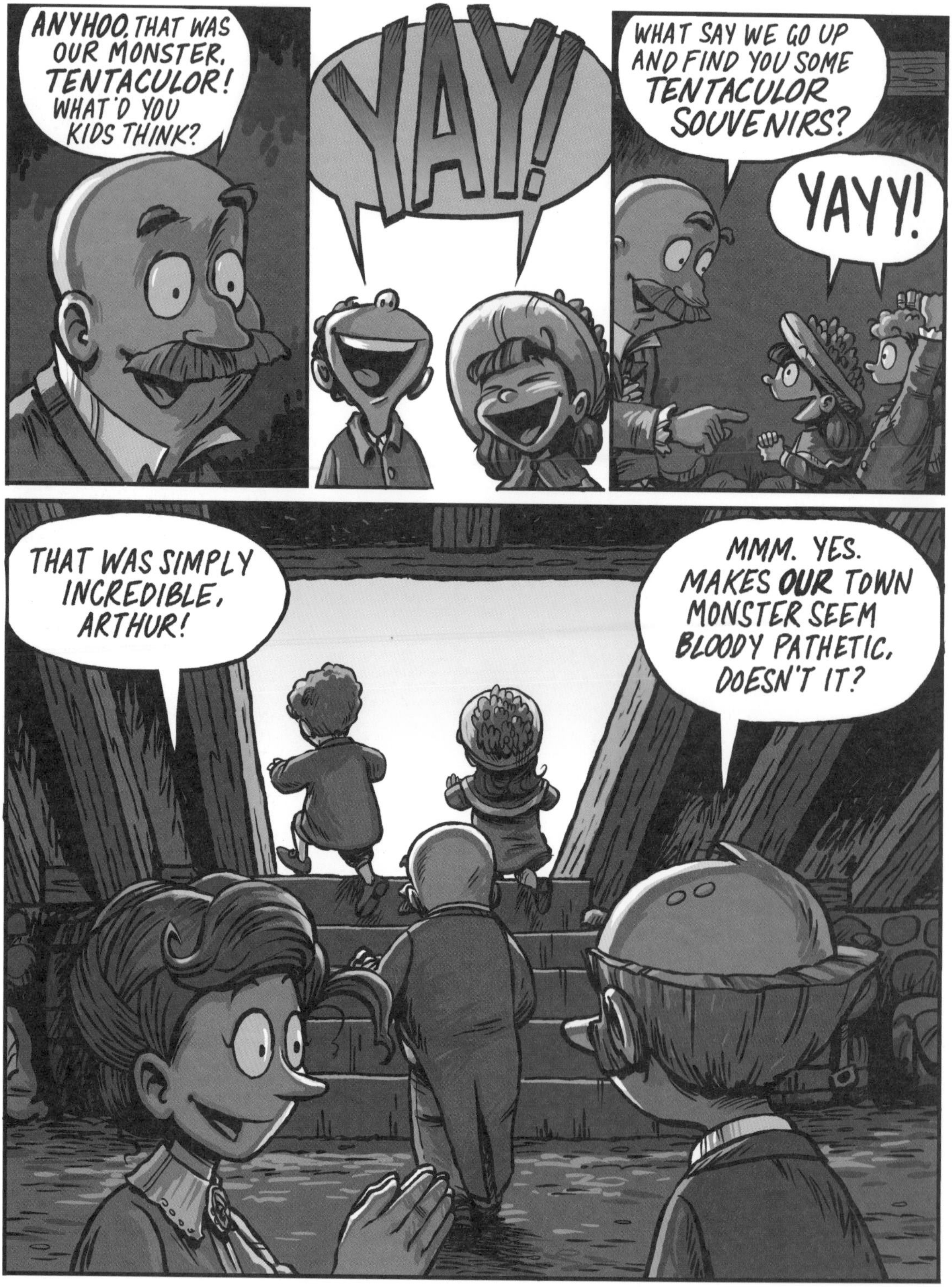
ANYHOO, THAT WAS OUR MONSTER, TENTACULOR! WHAT'D YOU KIDS THINK?
YAY!
WHAT SAY WE GO UP AND FIND YOU SOME TENTACULOR SOUVENIRS?
YAYY!
THAT WAS SIMPLY INCREDIBLE, ARTHUR!
MMM. YES. MAKES OUR TOWN MONSTER SEEM BLOODY PATHETIC, DOESN'T IT?

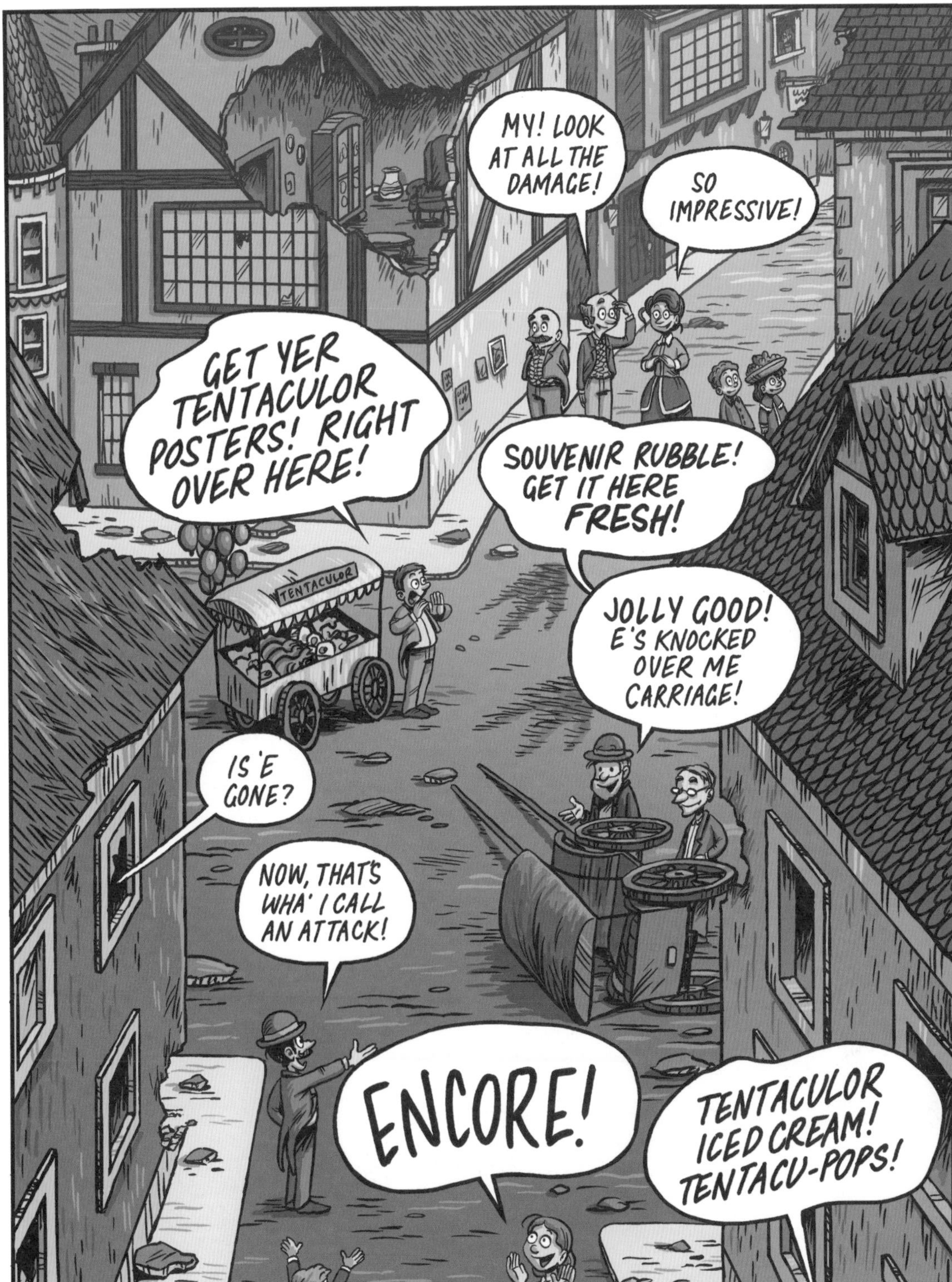
MY! LOOK AT ALL THE DAMAGE!
SO IMPRESSIVE!
GET YER TENTACULOR POSTERS! RIGHT OVER HERE!
SOUVENIR RUBBLE! GET IT HERE FRESH!
TENTACULOR
JOLLY GOOD! E'S KNOCKED OVER ME CARRIAGE!
IS 'E GONE?
NOW, THAT'S WHA' I CALL AN ATTACK!
ENCORE!
TENTACULOR ICED CREAM! TENTACU-POPS!

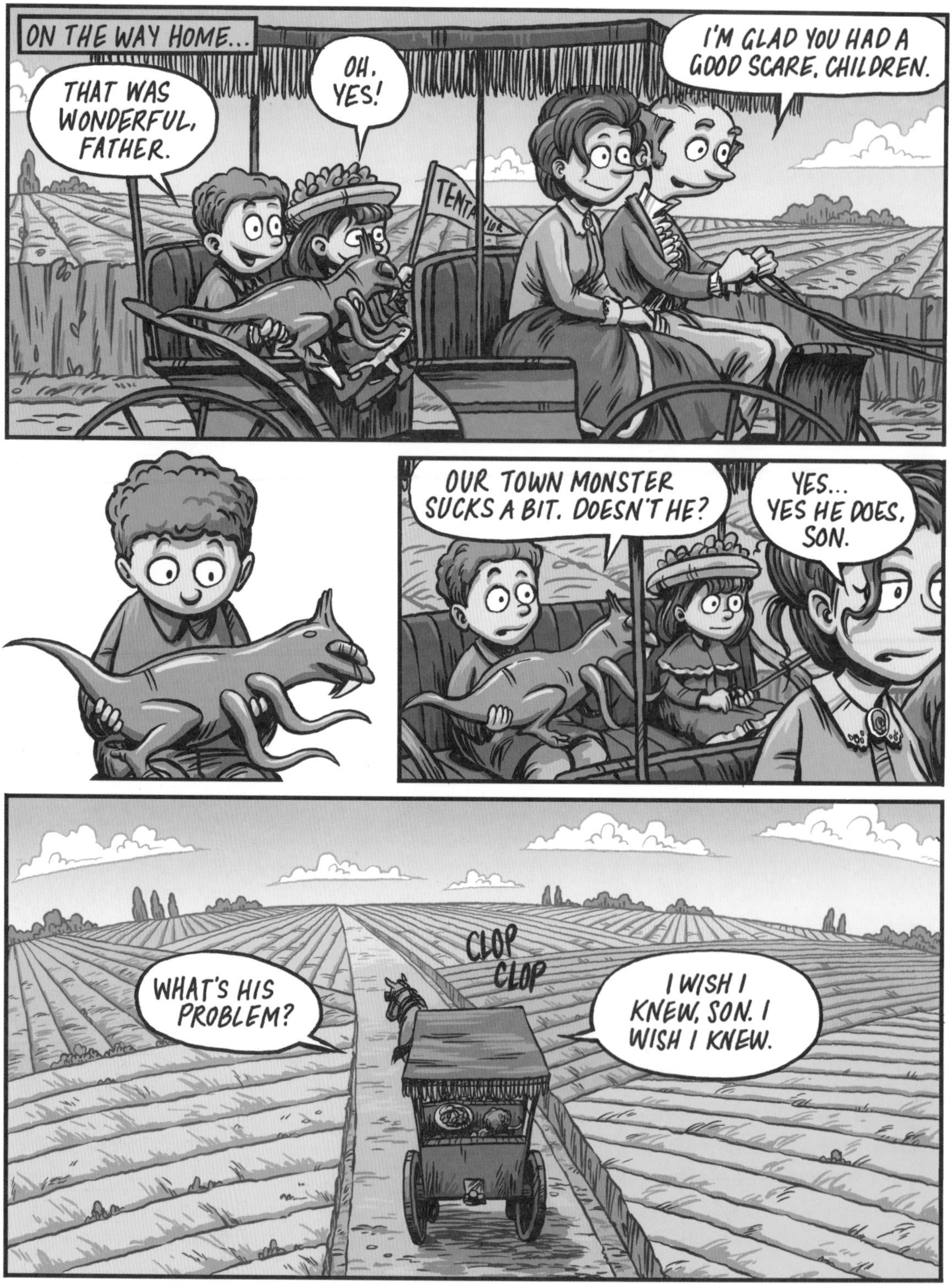
ON THE WAY HOME...
THAT WAS WONDERFUL, FATHER.
OH, YES!
I'M GLAD YOU HAD A GOOD SCARE, CHILDREN.
TENTA...
OUR TOWN MONSTER SUCKS A BIT, DOESN'T HE?
YES... YES HE DOES, SON.
CLOP CLOP
WHAT'S HIS PROBLEM?
I WISH I KNEW, SON. I WISH I KNEW.

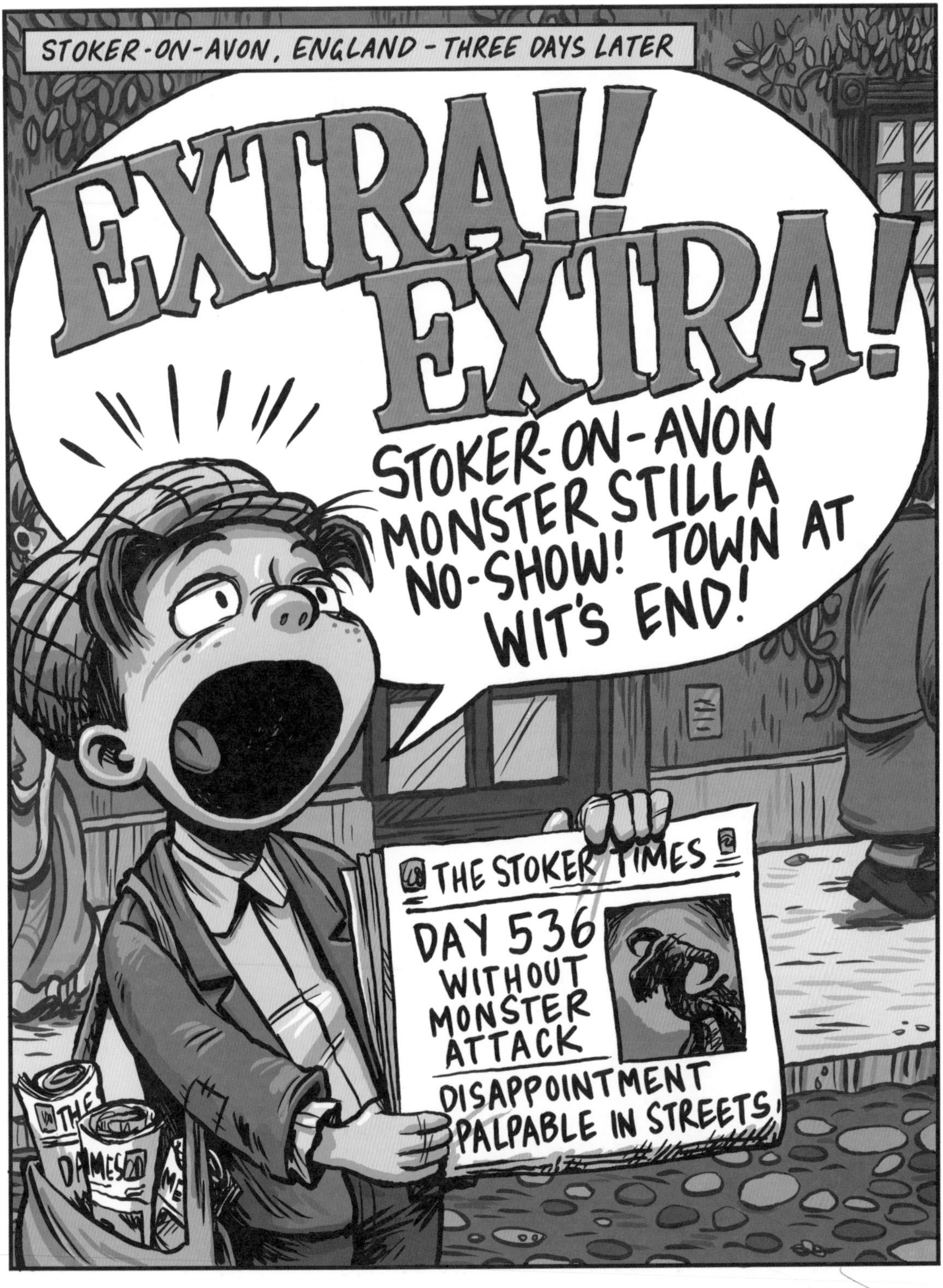
STOKER-ON-AVON, ENGLAND - THREE DAYS LATER
EXTRA!! EXTRA!
STOKER-ON-AVON MONSTER STILL A NO-SHOW! TOWN AT WIT'S END!
THE STOKER TIMES
DAY 536 WITHOUT MONSTER ATTACK
DISAPPOINTMENT PALPABLE IN STREETS

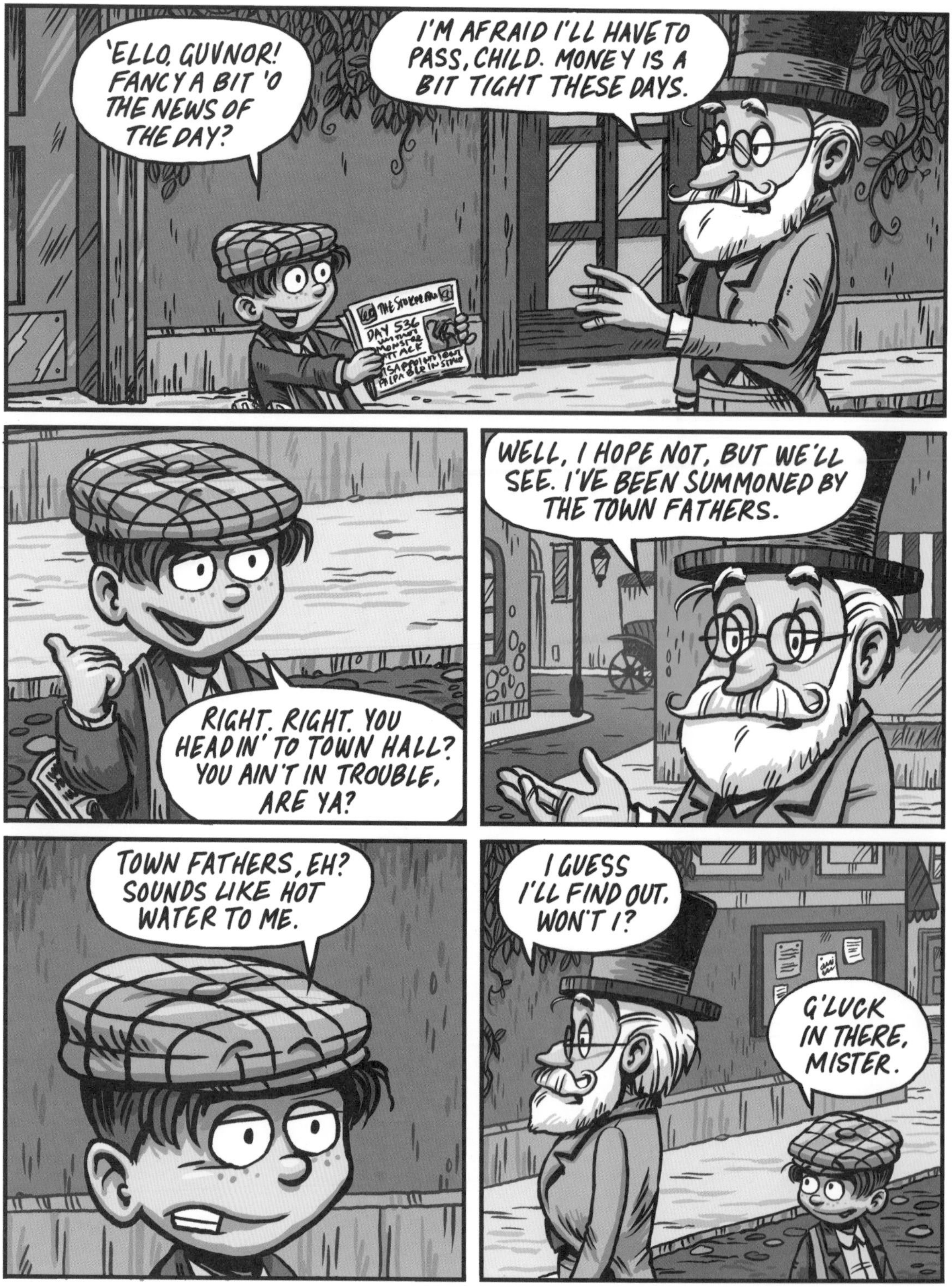
'ELLO, GUVNOR! FANCY A BIT 'O THE NEWS OF THE DAY?
I'M AFRAID I'LL HAVE TO PASS, CHILD. MONEY IS A BIT TIGHT THESE DAYS.
RIGHT. RIGHT. YOU HEADIN' TO TOWN HALL? YOU AIN'T IN TROUBLE, ARE YA?
WELL, I HOPE NOT, BUT WE'LL SEE. I'VE BEEN SUMMONED BY THE TOWN FATHERS.
TOWN FATHERS, EH? SOUNDS LIKE HOT WATER TO ME.
I GUESS I'LL FIND OUT. WON'T I?
G'LUCK IN THERE, MISTER.

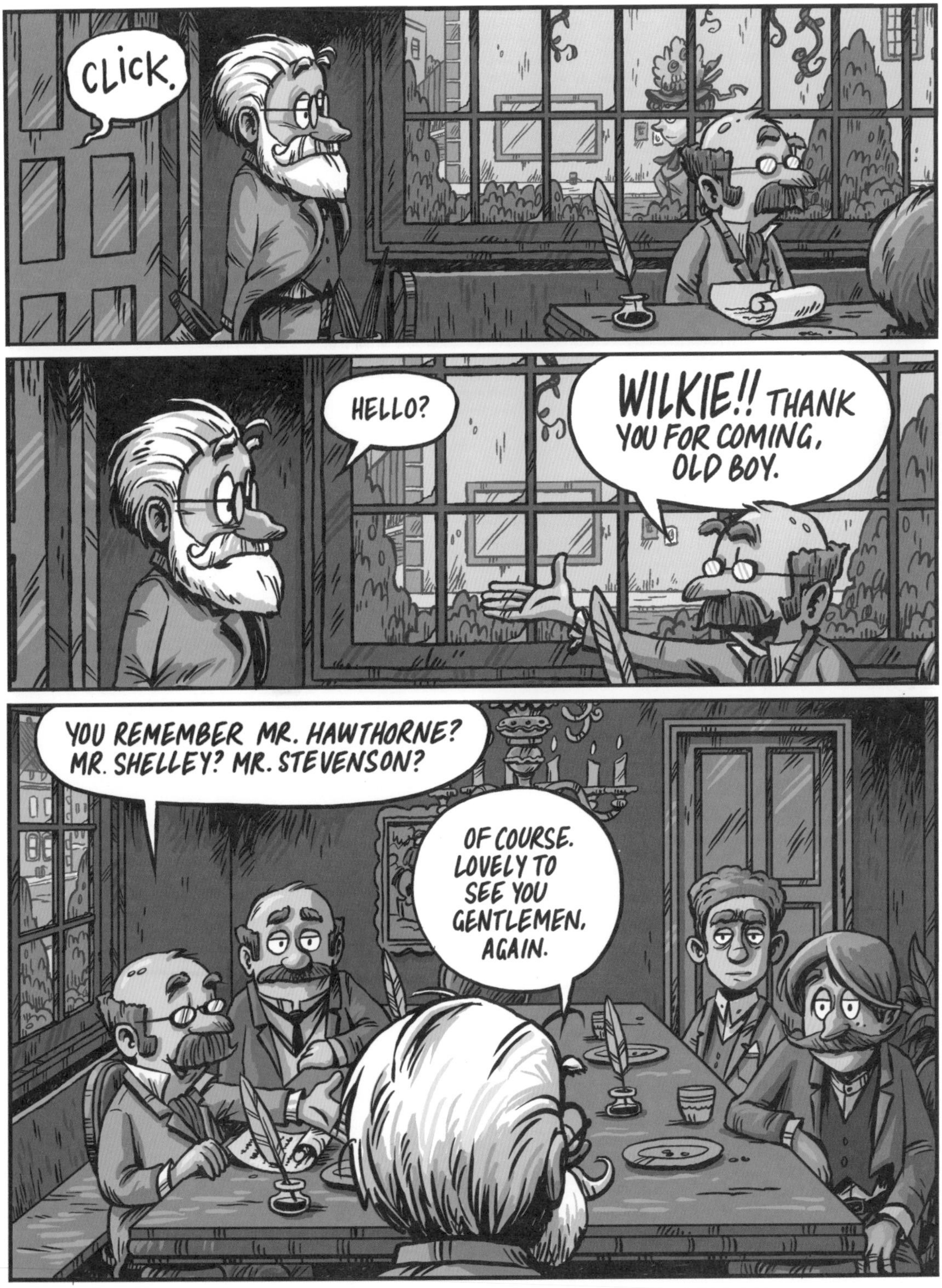
CLICK.
HELLO?
WILKIE!! THANK YOU FOR COMING, OLD BOY.
YOU REMEMBER MR. HAWTHORNE? MR. SHELLEY? MR. STEVENSON?
OF COURSE. LOVELY TO SEE YOU GENTLEMEN, AGAIN.

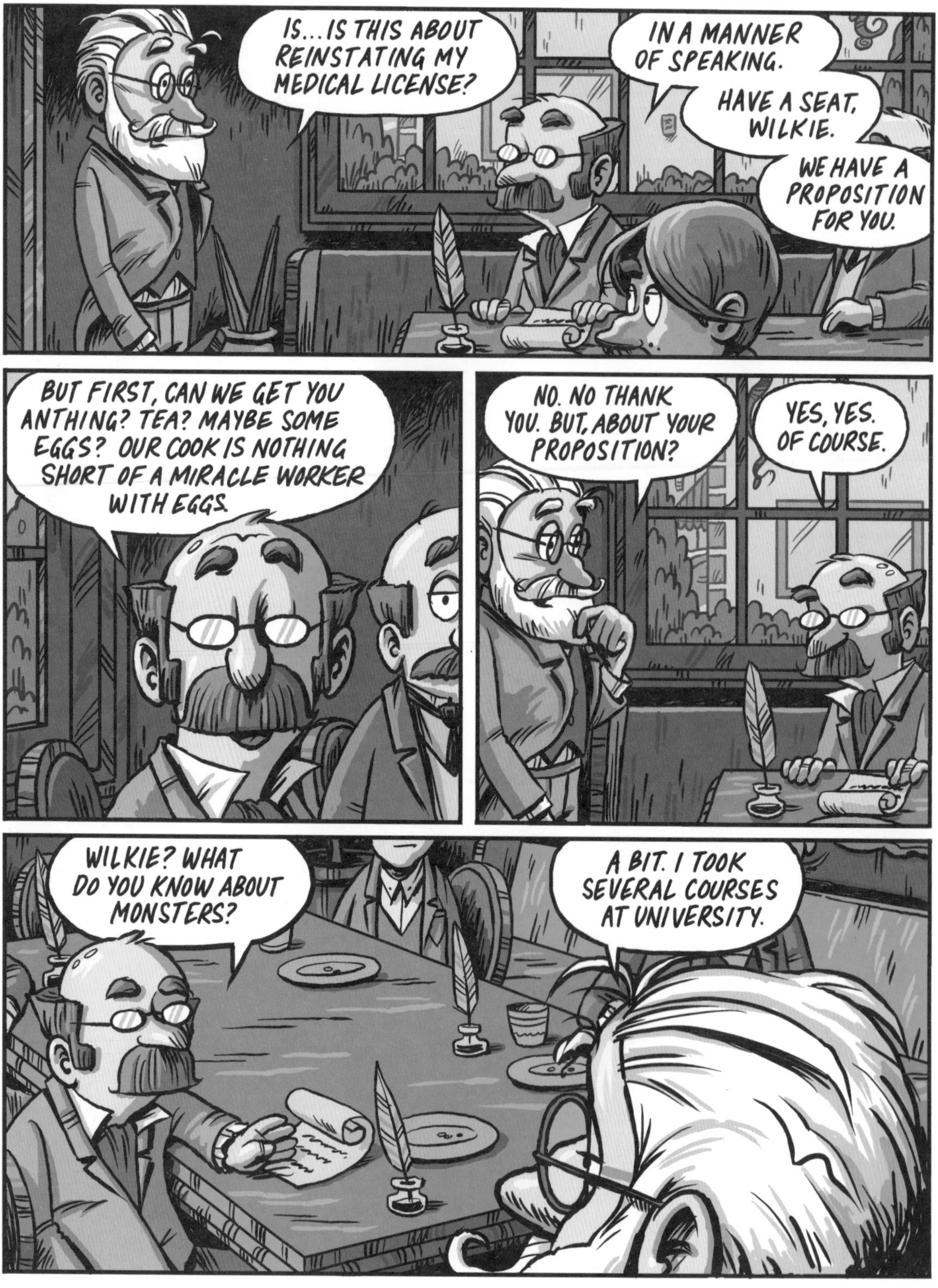
IS... IS THIS ABOUT REINSTATING MY MEDICAL LICENSE?
IN A MANNER OF SPEAKING.
HAVE A SEAT, WILKIE.
WE HAVE A PROPOSITION FOR YOU.
BUT FIRST, CAN WE GET YOU ANTHING? TEA? MAYBE SOME EGGS? OUR COOK IS NOTHING SHORT OF A MIRACLE WORKER WITH EGGS.
NO. NO THANK YOU. BUT, ABOUT YOUR PROPOSITION?
YES, YES. OF COURSE.
WILKIE? WHAT DO YOU KNOW ABOUT MONSTERS?
A BIT. I TOOK SEVERAL COURSES AT UNIVERSITY.

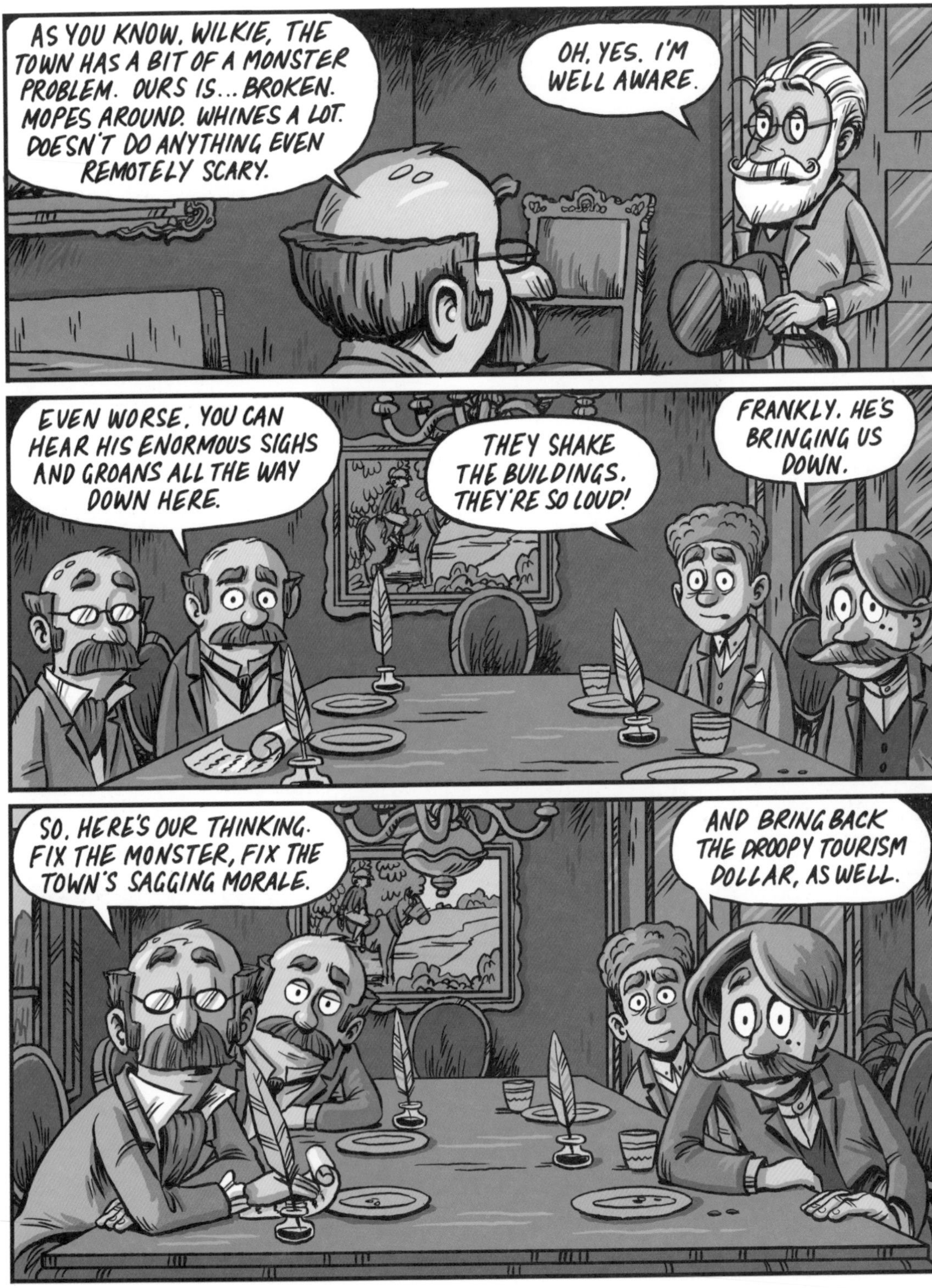
AS YOU KNOW, WILKIE, THE TOWN HAS A BIT OF A MONSTER PROBLEM. OURS IS... BROKEN. MOPES AROUND. WHINES A LOT. DOESN'T DO ANYTHING EVEN REMOTELY SCARY.
OH, YES. I'M WELL AWARE.
EVEN WORSE, YOU CAN HEAR HIS ENORMOUS SIGHS AND GROANS ALL THE WAY DOWN HERE.
THEY SHAKE THE BUILDINGS. THEY'RE SO LOUD!
FRANKLY, HE'S BRINGING US DOWN.
SO, HERE'S OUR THINKING. FIX THE MONSTER, FIX THE TOWN'S SAGGING MORALE.
AND BRING BACK THE DROOPY TOURISM DOLLAR, AS WELL.

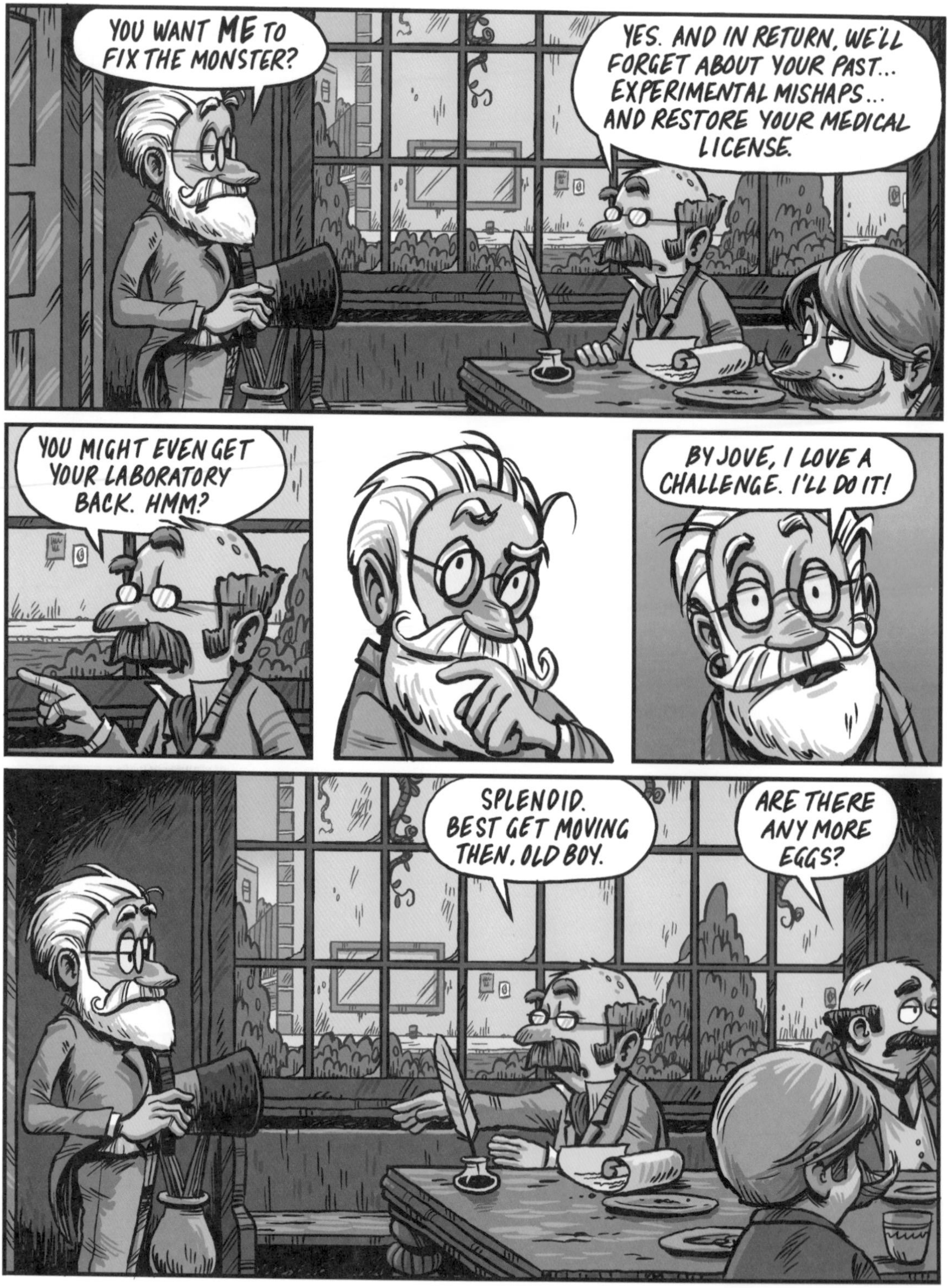
YOU WANT **ME** TO FIX THE MONSTER?
YES. AND IN RETURN, WE'LL FORGET ABOUT YOUR PAST... EXPERIMENTAL MISHAPS... AND RESTORE YOUR MEDICAL LICENSE.
YOU MIGHT EVEN GET YOUR LABORATORY BACK. HMM?
BY JOVE, I LOVE A CHALLENGE. I'LL DO IT!
SPLENDID. BEST GET MOVING THEN, OLD BOY.
ARE THERE ANY MORE EGGS?

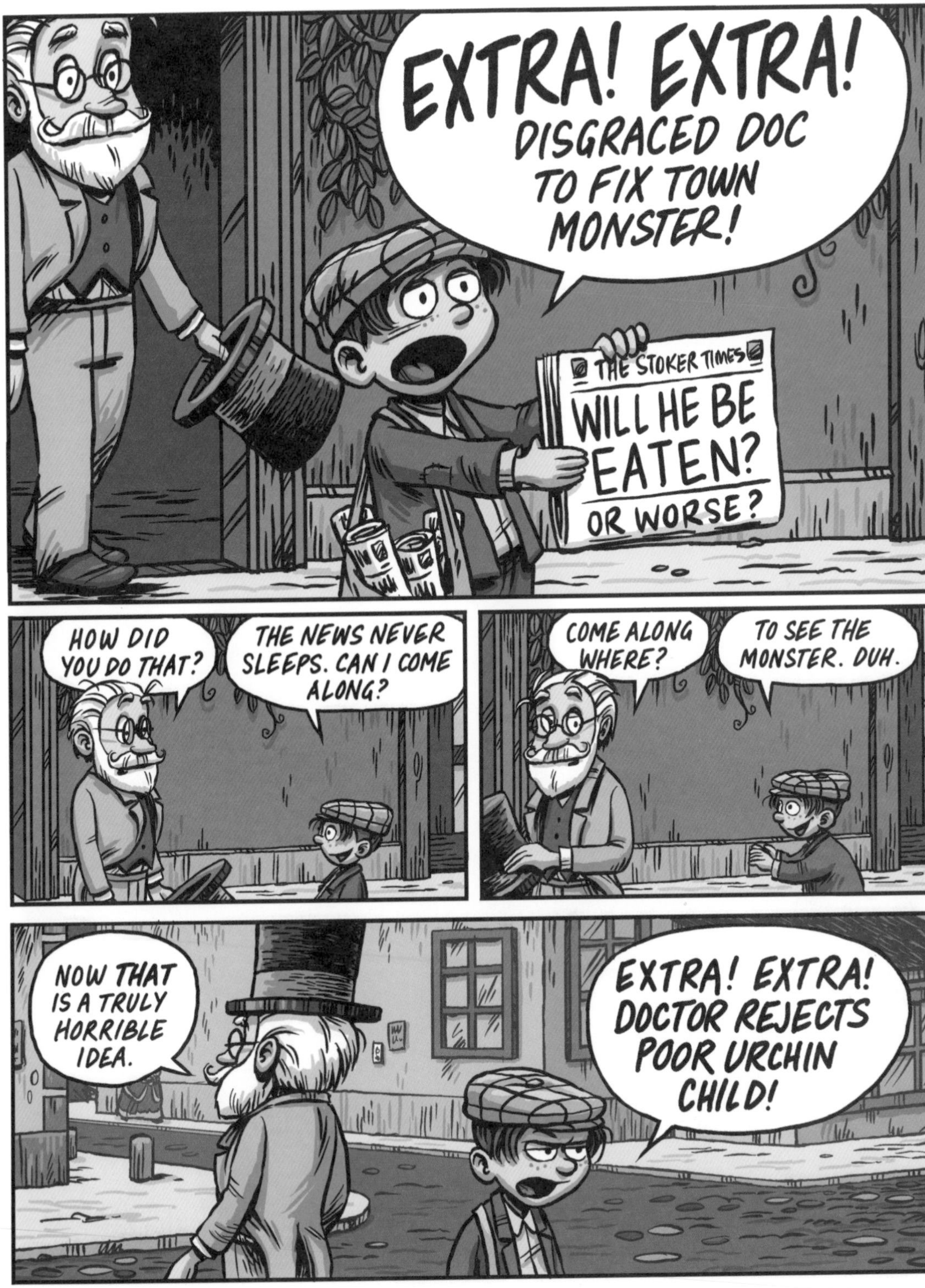
EXTRA! EXTRA! DISGRACED DOC TO FIX TOWN MONSTER!
THE STOKER TIMES
WILL HE BE EATEN? OR WORSE?
HOW DID YOU DO THAT?
THE NEWS NEVER SLEEPS. CAN I COME ALONG?
COME ALONG WHERE?
TO SEE THE MONSTER. DUH.
NOW THAT IS A TRULY HORRIBLE IDEA.
EXTRA! EXTRA! DOCTOR REJECTS POOR URCHIN CHILD!

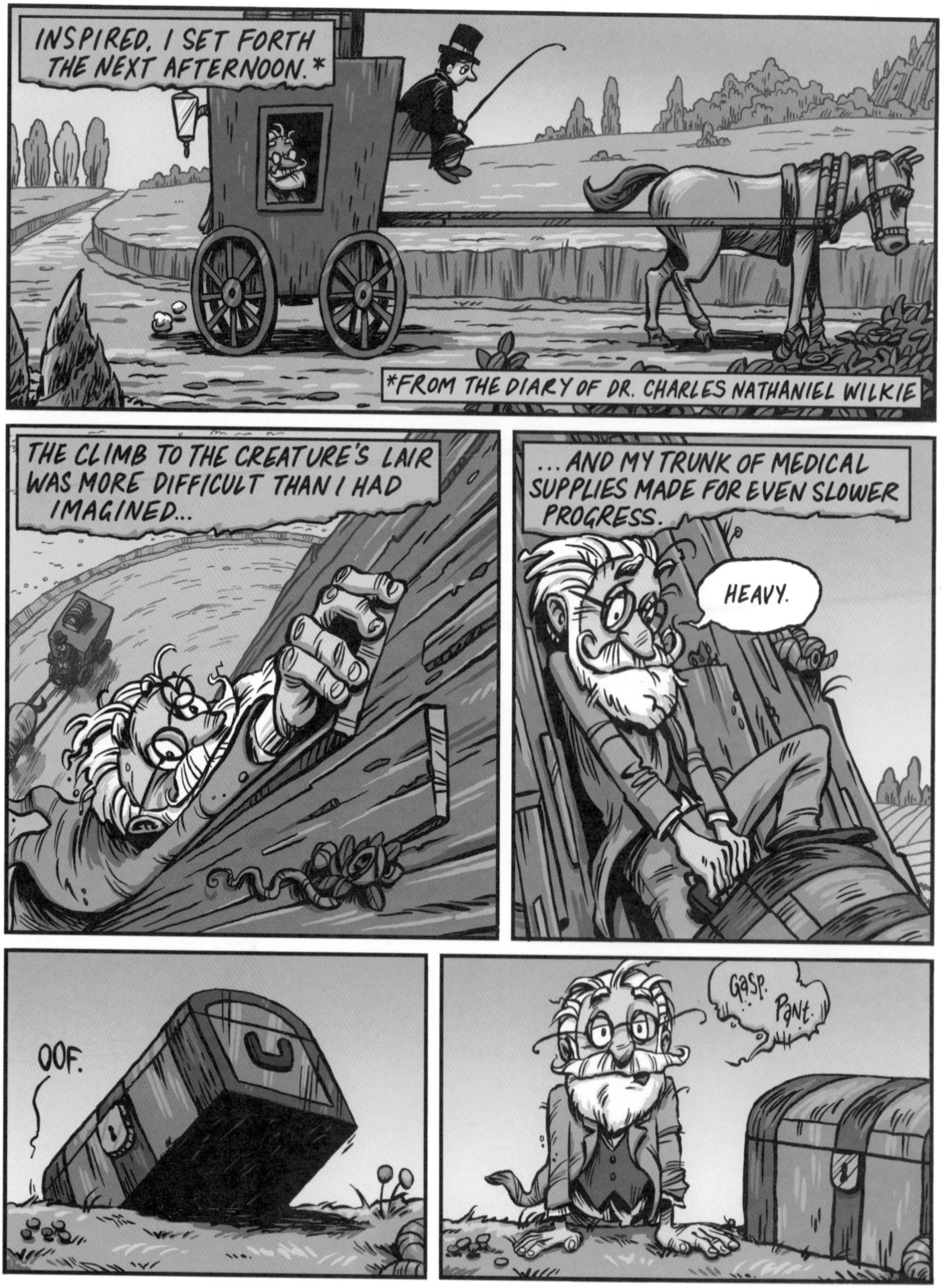
INSPIRED, I SET FORTH THE NEXT AFTERNOON.*
*FROM THE DIARY OF DR. CHARLES NATHANIEL WILKIE
THE CLIMB TO THE CREATURE'S LAIR WAS MORE DIFFICULT THAN I HAD IMAGINED...
...AND MY TRUNK OF MEDICAL SUPPLIES MADE FOR EVEN SLOWER PROGRESS.
HEAVY.
OOF.
GASP. PANT.

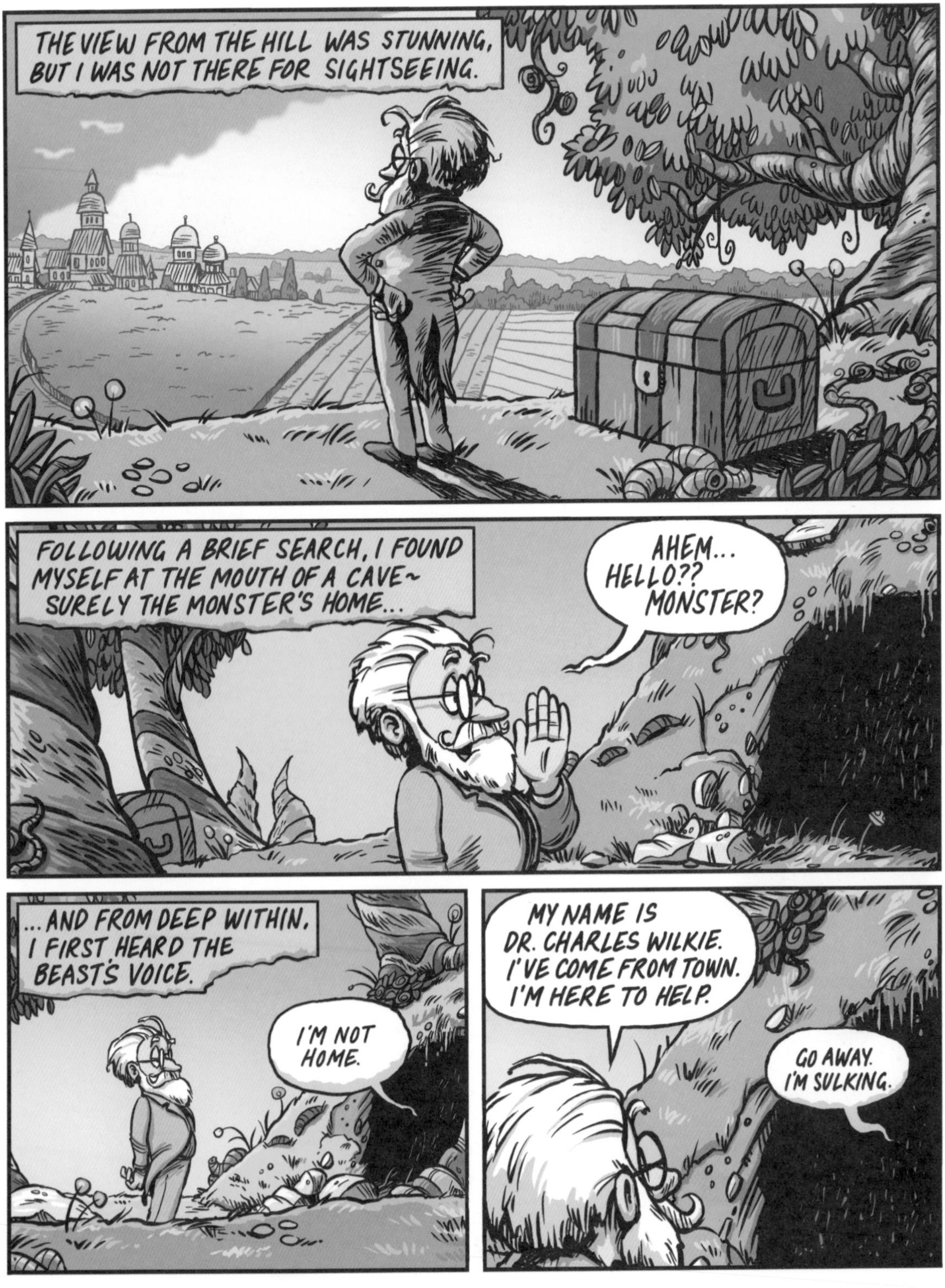
THE VIEW FROM THE HILL WAS STUNNING, BUT I WAS NOT THERE FOR SIGHTSEEING.
FOLLOWING A BRIEF SEARCH, I FOUND MYSELF AT THE MOUTH OF A CAVE~ SURELY THE MONSTER'S HOME...
AHEM... HELLO?? MONSTER?
...AND FROM DEEP WITHIN, I FIRST HEARD THE BEAST'S VOICE.
I'M NOT HOME.
MY NAME IS DR. CHARLES WILKIE. I'VE COME FROM TOWN. I'M HERE TO HELP.
GO AWAY. I'M SULKING.

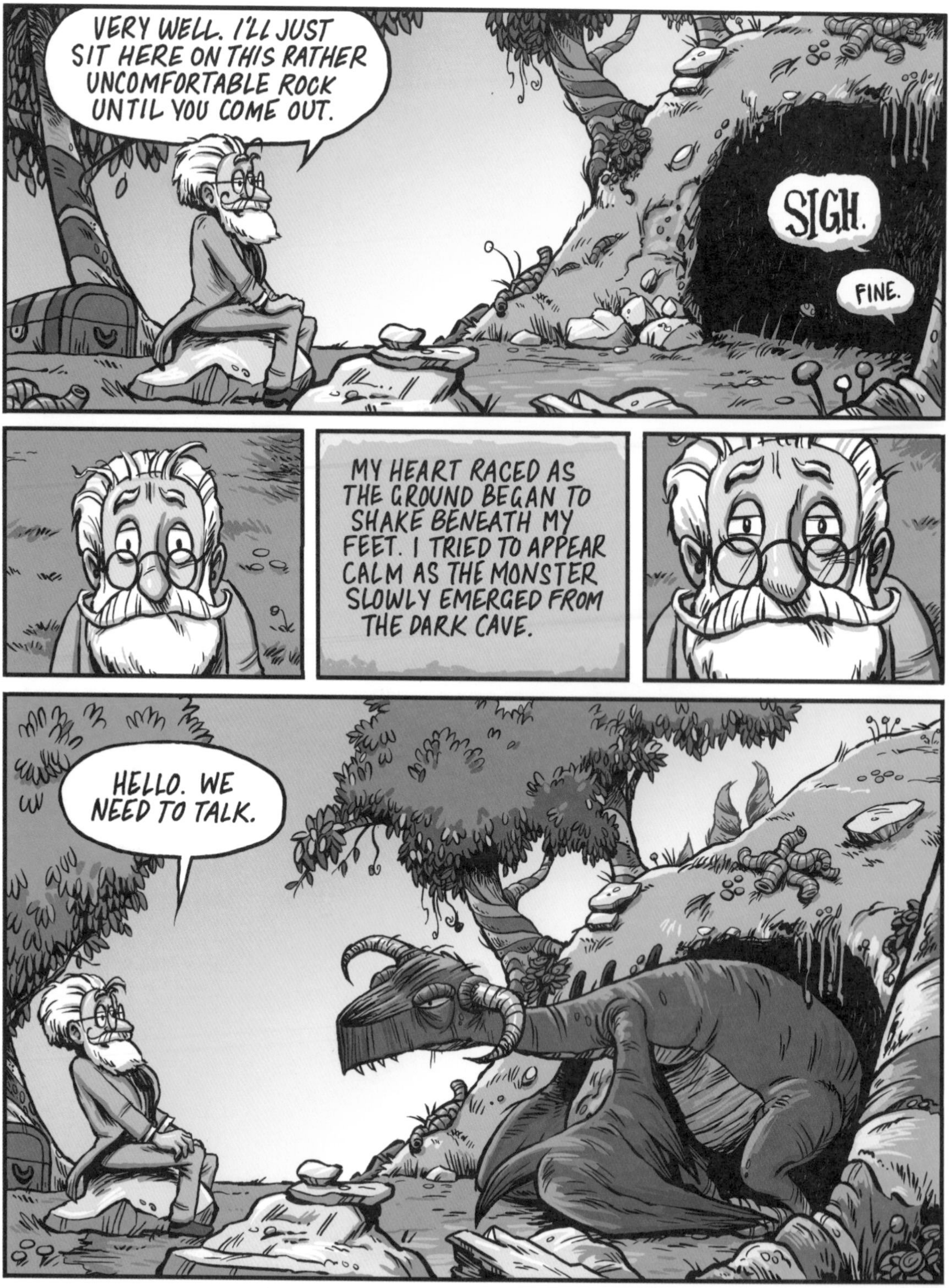
VERY WELL. I'LL JUST SIT HERE ON THIS RATHER UNCOMFORTABLE ROCK UNTIL YOU COME OUT.
SIGH.
FINE.
MY HEART RACED AS THE GROUND BEGAN TO SHAKE BENEATH MY FEET. I TRIED TO APPEAR CALM AS THE MONSTER SLOWLY EMERGED FROM THE DARK CAVE.
HELLO. WE NEED TO TALK.

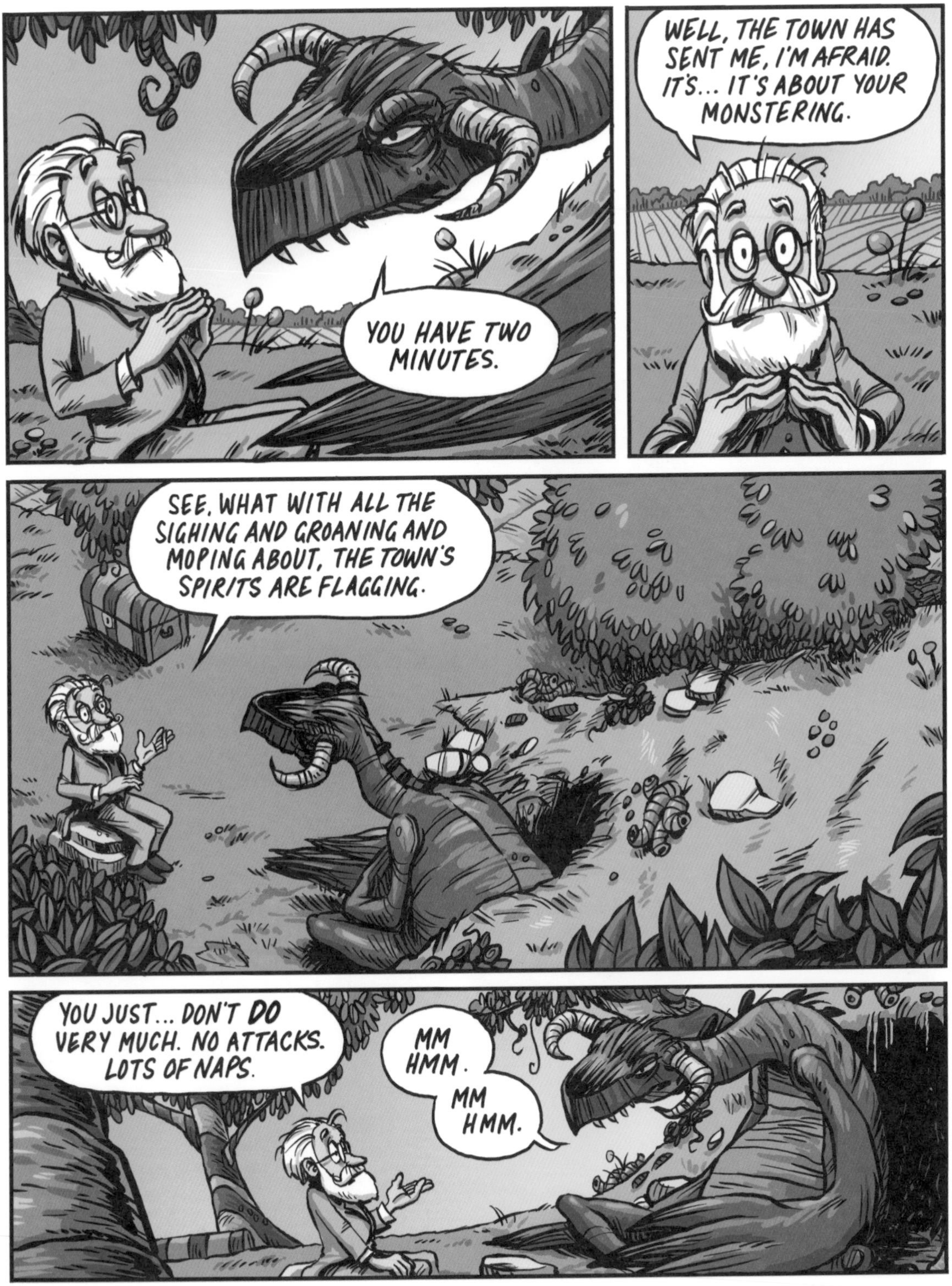
WELL, THE TOWN HAS SENT ME, I'M AFRAID. IT'S... IT'S ABOUT YOUR MONSTERING.
YOU HAVE TWO MINUTES.
SEE, WHAT WITH ALL THE SIGHING AND GROANING AND MOPING ABOUT, THE TOWN'S SPIRITS ARE FLAGGING.
YOU JUST... DON'T DO VERY MUCH. NO ATTACKS. LOTS OF NAPS.
MM HMM.
MM HMM.

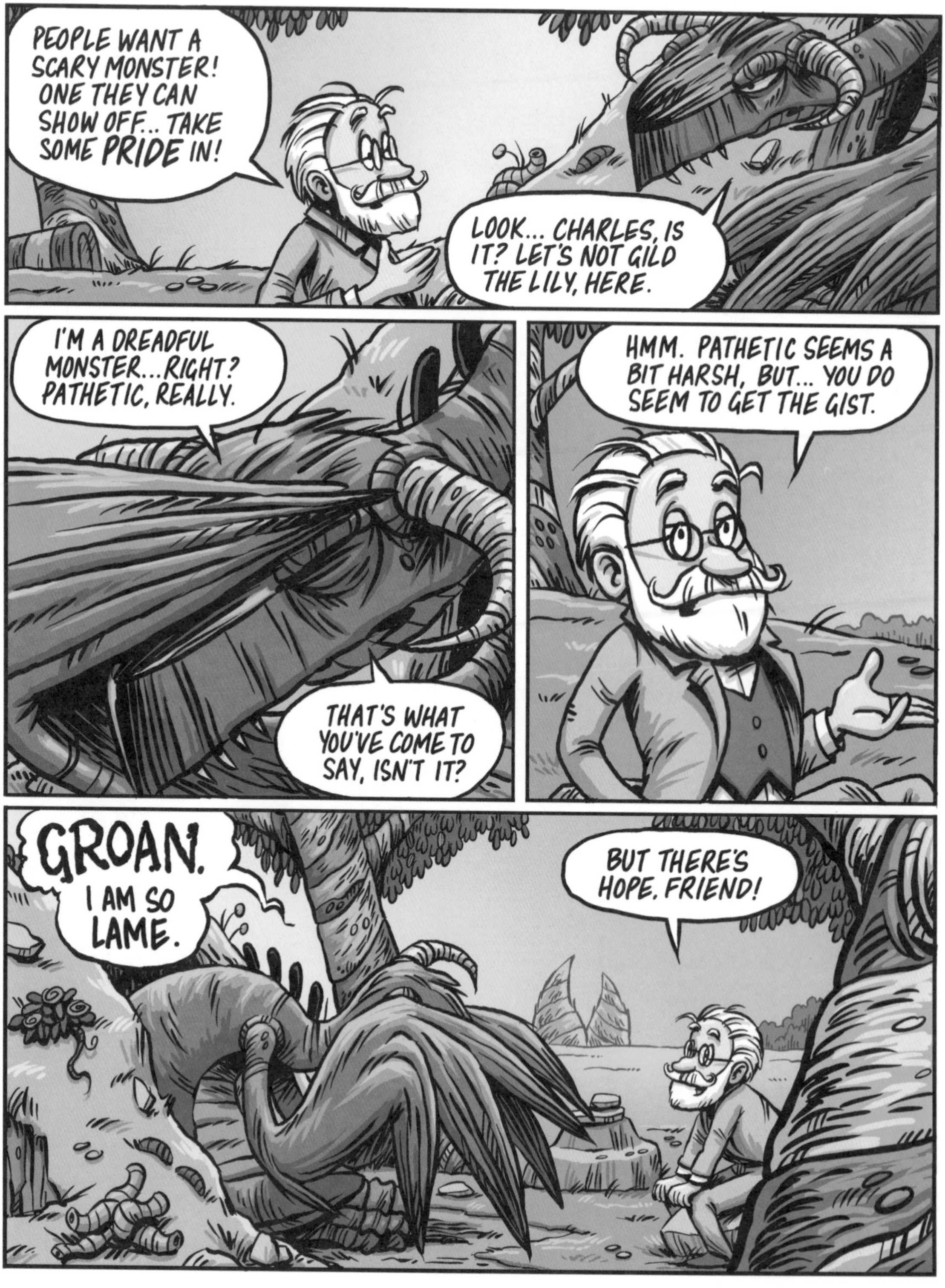
PEOPLE WANT A SCARY MONSTER! ONE THEY CAN SHOW OFF... TAKE SOME PRIDE IN!
LOOK... CHARLES, IS IT? LET'S NOT GILD THE LILY, HERE.
I'M A DREADFUL MONSTER... RIGHT? PATHETIC, REALLY.
THAT'S WHAT YOU'VE COME TO SAY, ISN'T IT?
HMM. PATHETIC SEEMS A BIT HARSH, BUT... YOU DO SEEM TO GET THE GIST.
GROAN. I AM SO LAME.
BUT THERE'S HOPE, FRIEND!

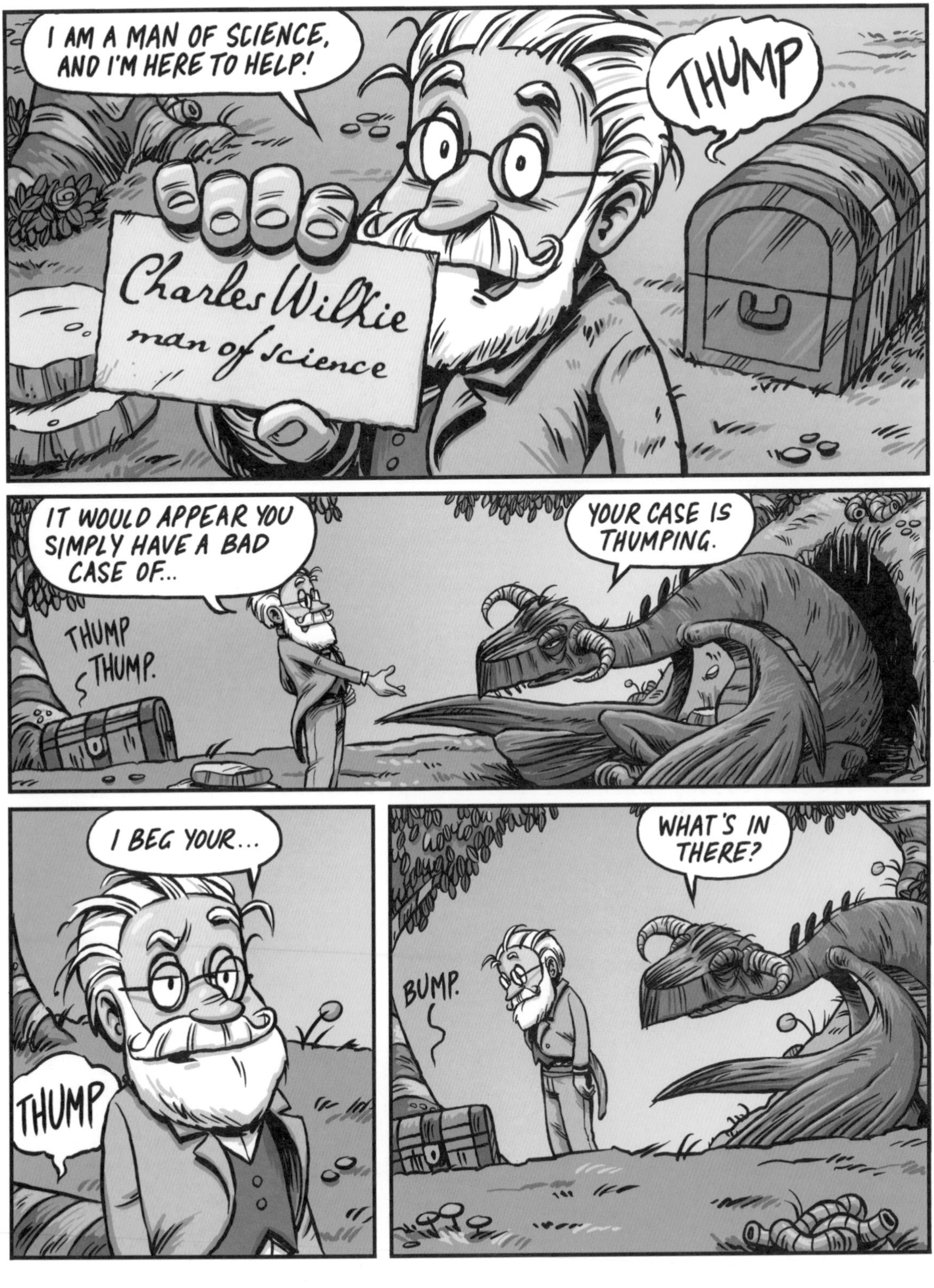
I AM A MAN OF SCIENCE, AND I'M HERE TO HELP!
THUMP
Charles Wilkie
man of science
IT WOULD APPEAR YOU SIMPLY HAVE A BAD CASE OF...
YOUR CASE IS THUMPING.
THUMP THUMP.
I BEG YOUR...
THUMP
WHAT'S IN THERE?
BUMP.

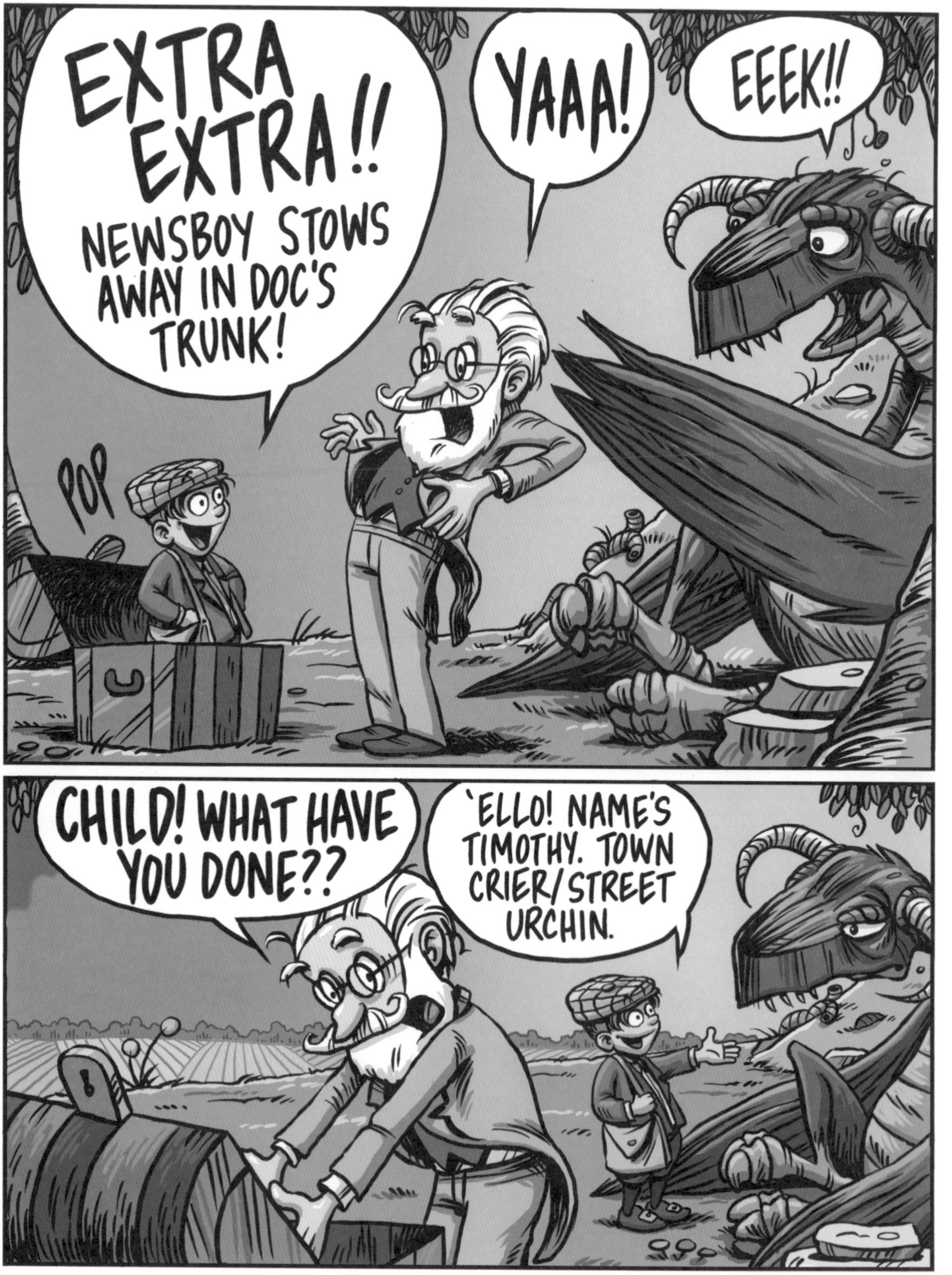
EXTRA EXTRA!! NEWSBOY STOWS AWAY IN DOC'S TRUNK!
YAAA!
EEEK!!
POP
CHILD! WHAT HAVE YOU DONE??
`ELLO! NAME'S TIMOTHY. TOWN CRIER/STREET URCHIN.

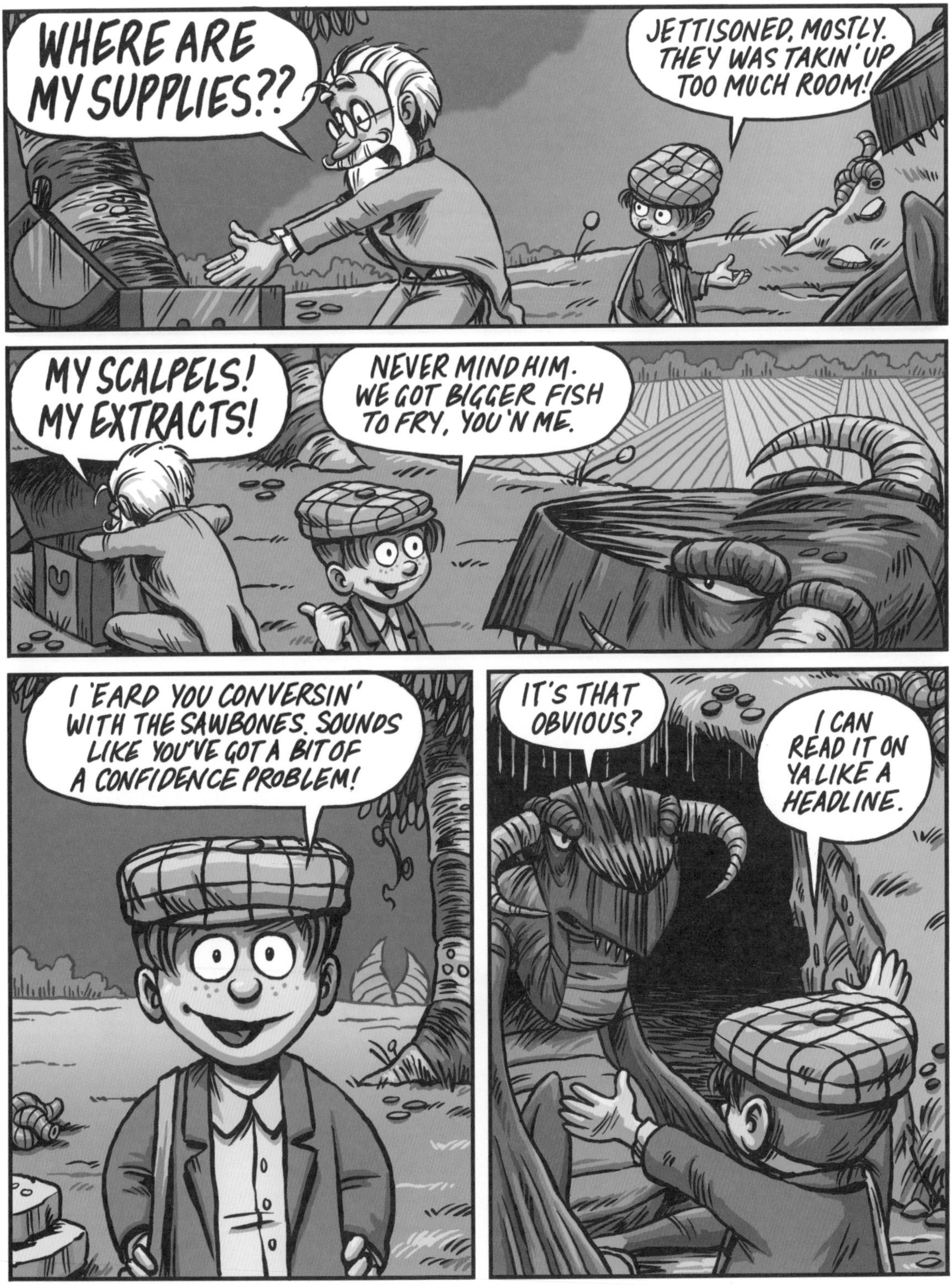
WHERE ARE MY SUPPLIES??
JETTISONED, MOSTLY. THEY WAS TAKIN' UP TOO MUCH ROOM!
MY SCALPELS! MY EXTRACTS!
NEVER MIND HIM. WE GOT BIGGER FISH TO FRY, YOU'N ME.
I 'EARD YOU CONVERSIN' WITH THE SAWBONES. SOUNDS LIKE YOU'VE GOT A BIT OF A CONFIDENCE PROBLEM!
IT'S THAT OBVIOUS?
I CAN READ IT ON YA LIKE A HEADLINE.

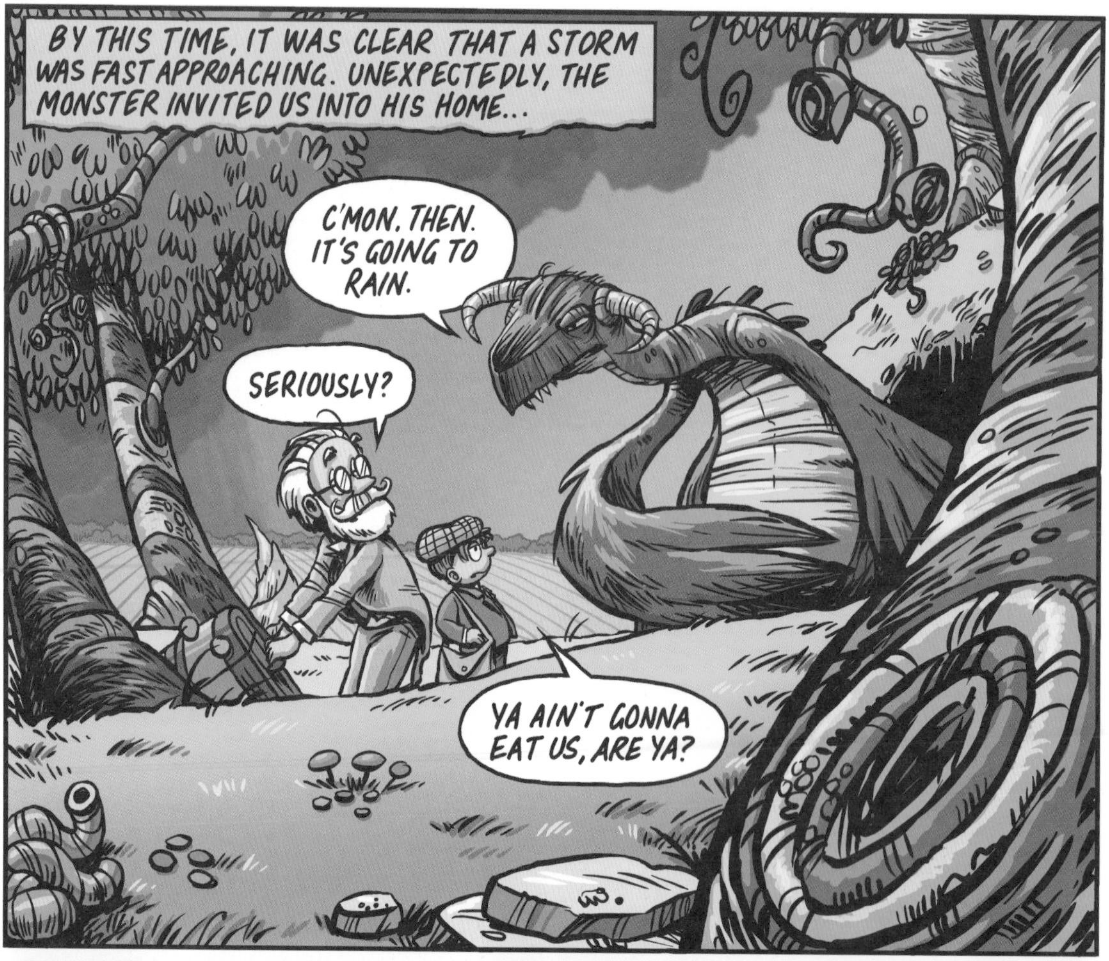
BY THIS TIME, IT WAS CLEAR THAT A STORM WAS FAST APPROACHING. UNEXPECTEDLY, THE MONSTER INVITED US INTO HIS HOME...
C'MON, THEN. IT'S GOING TO RAIN.
SERIOUSLY?
YA AIN'T GONNA EAT US, ARE YA?

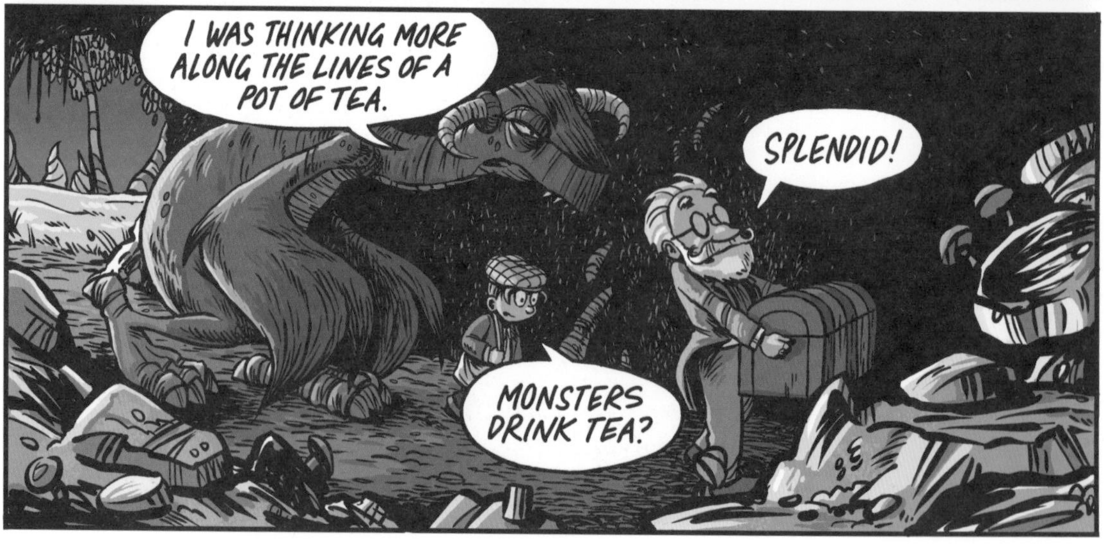
I WAS THINKING MORE ALONG THE LINES OF A POT OF TEA.
SPLENDID!
MONSTERS DRINK TEA?

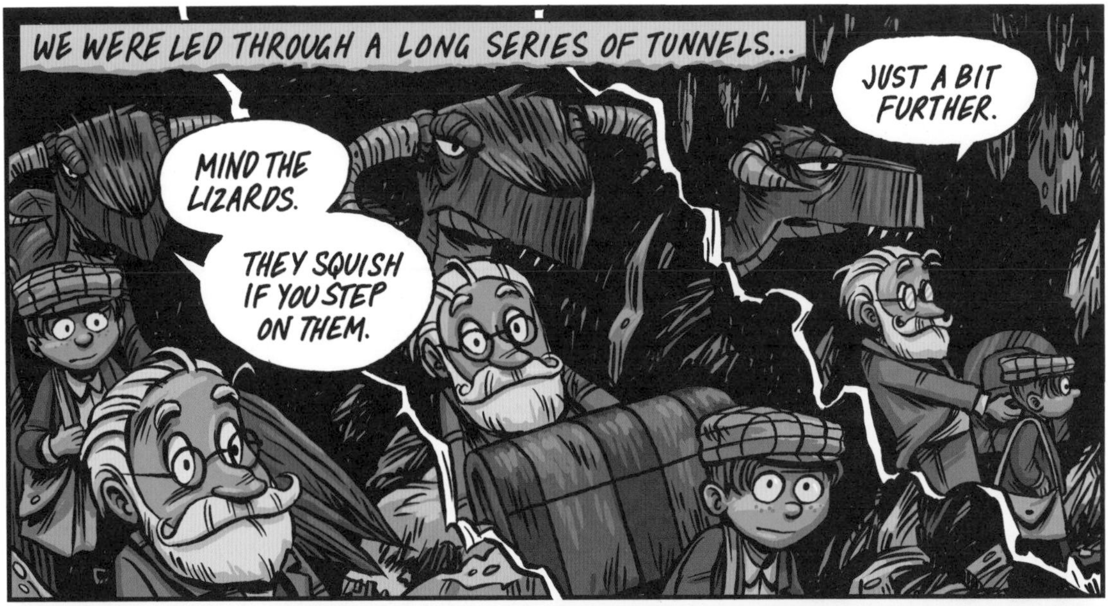
WE WERE LED THROUGH A LONG SERIES OF TUNNELS...
MIND THE LIZARDS.
THEY SQUISH IF YOU STEP ON THEM.
JUST A BIT FURTHER.

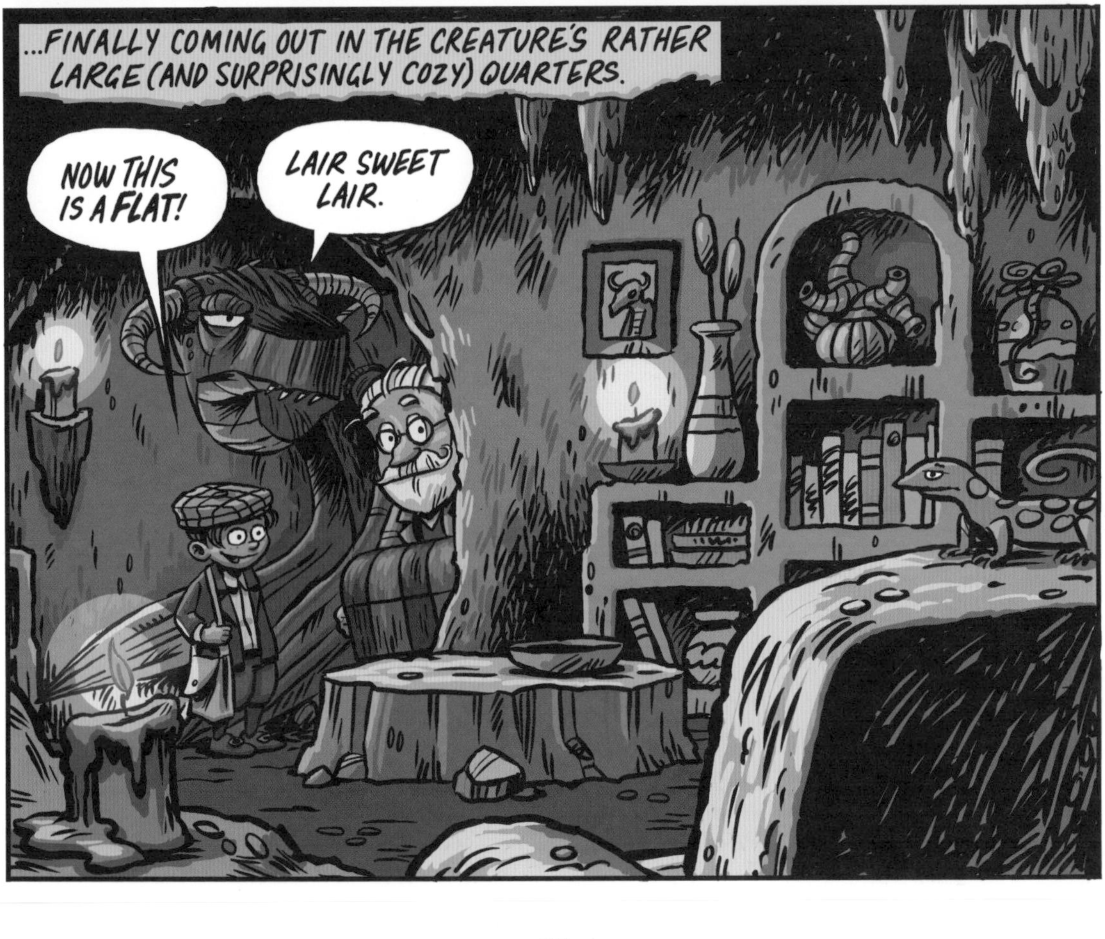
...FINALLY COMING OUT IN THE CREATURE'S RATHER LARGE (AND SURPRISINGLY COZY) QUARTERS.
NOW THIS IS A FLAT!
LAIR SWEET LAIR.

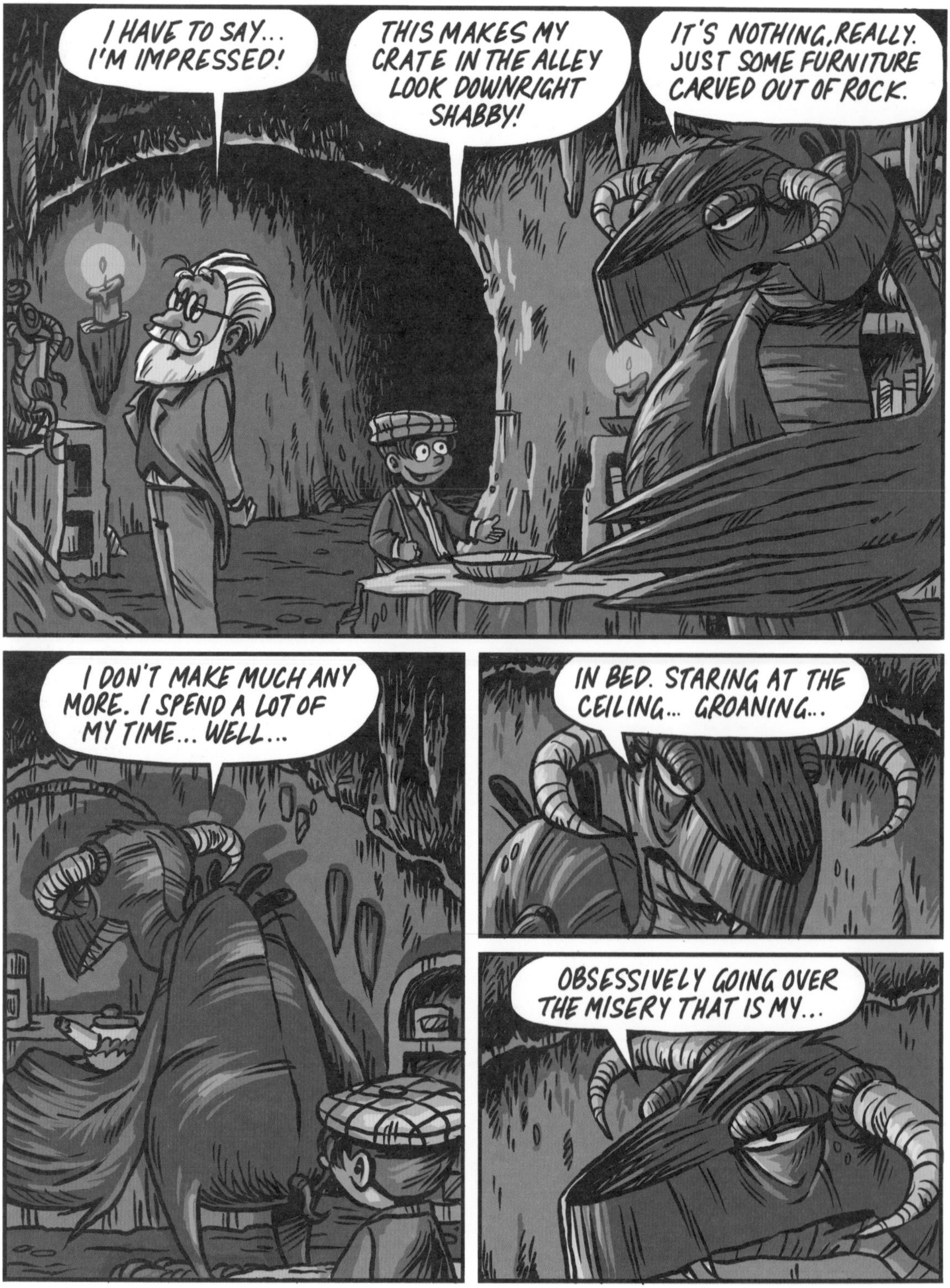
I HAVE TO SAY... I'M IMPRESSED!
THIS MAKES MY CRATE IN THE ALLEY LOOK DOWNRIGHT SHABBY!
IT'S NOTHING, REALLY. JUST SOME FURNITURE CARVED OUT OF ROCK.
I DON'T MAKE MUCH ANY MORE. I SPEND A LOT OF MY TIME... WELL...
IN BED. STARING AT THE CEILING... GROANING...
OBSESSIVELY GOING OVER THE MISERY THAT IS MY...

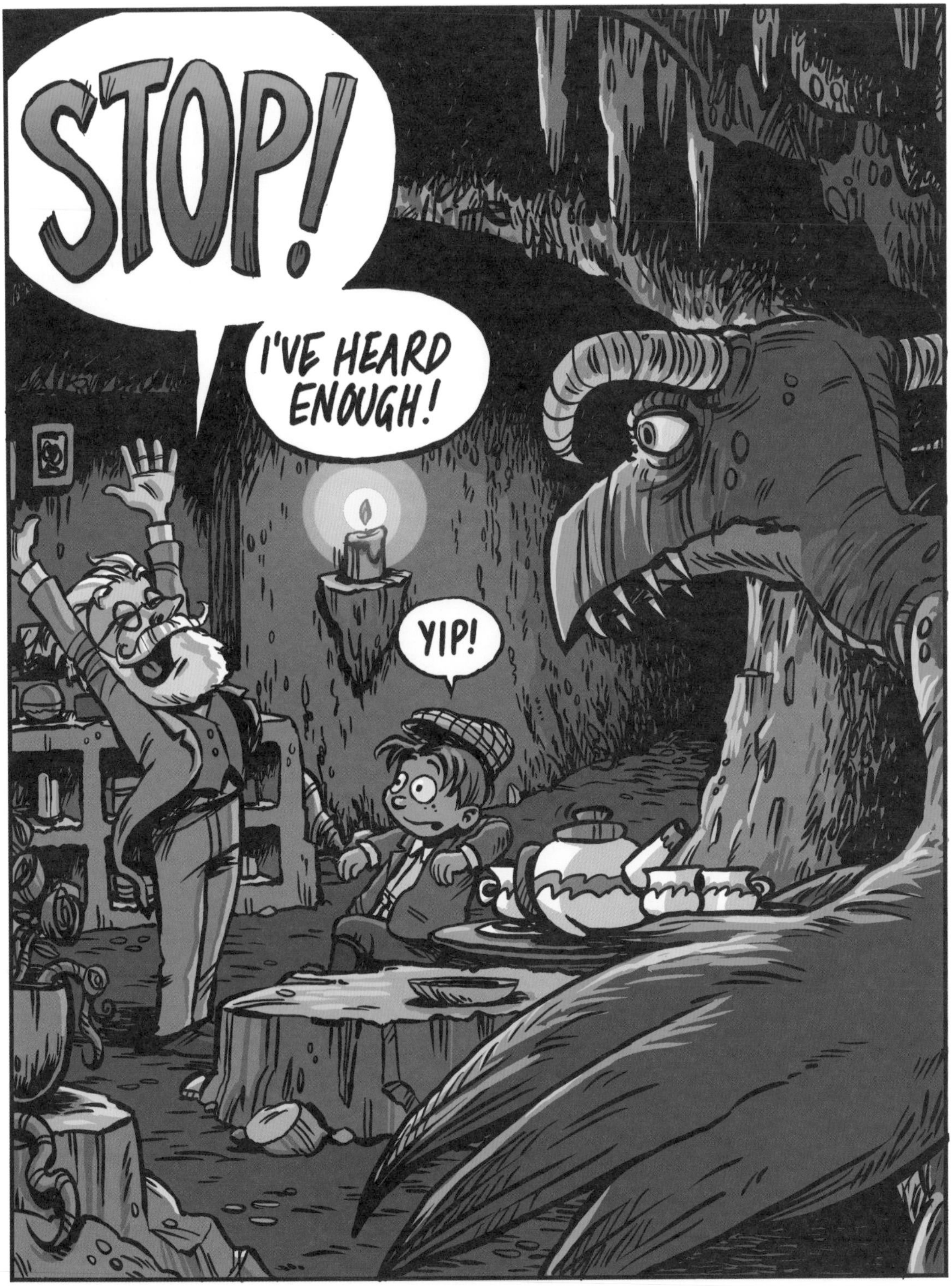
STOP!
I'VE HEARD ENOUGH!
YIP!

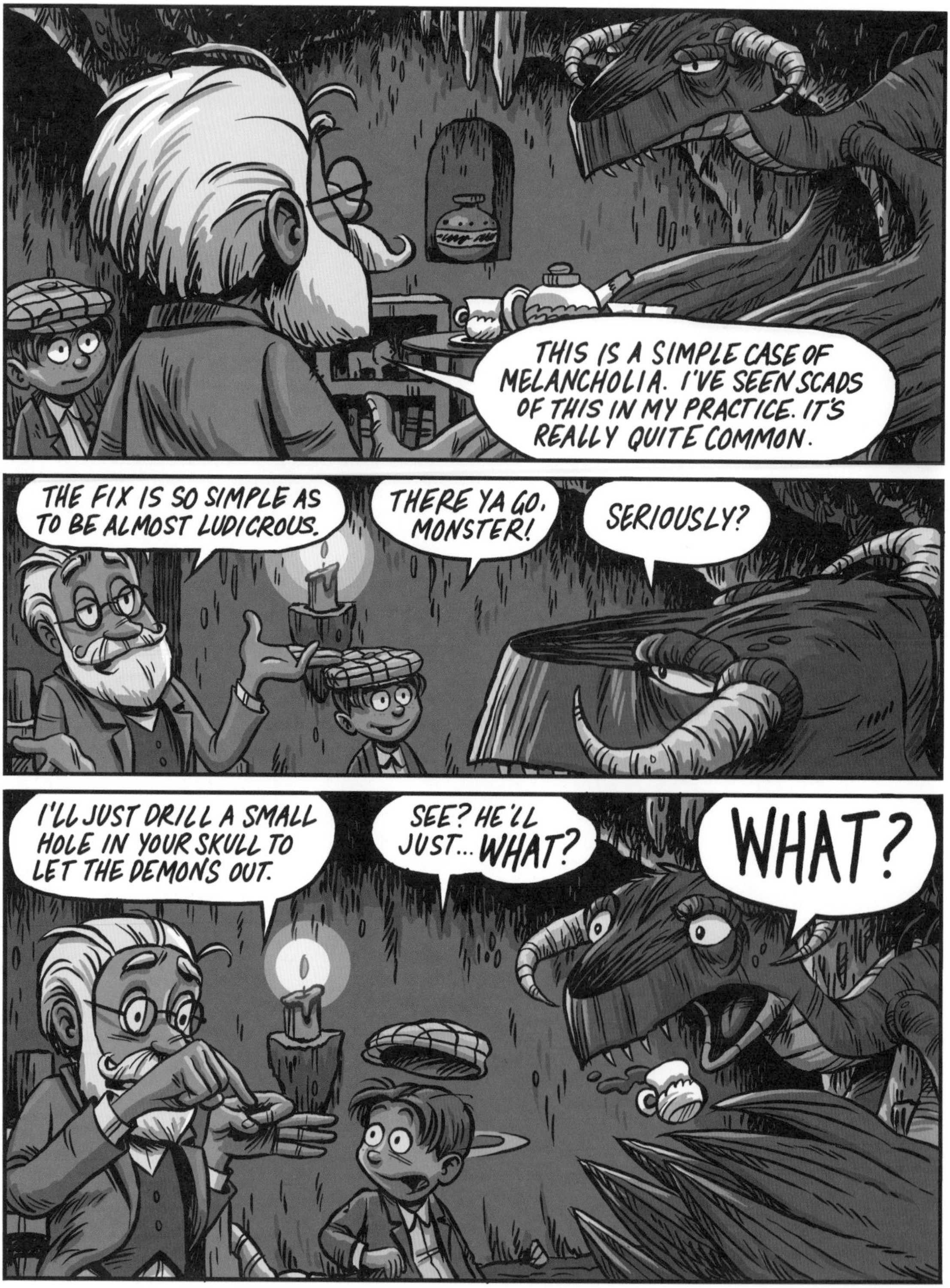
THIS IS A SIMPLE CASE OF MELANCHOLIA. I'VE SEEN SCADS OF THIS IN MY PRACTICE. IT'S REALLY QUITE COMMON.
THE FIX IS SO SIMPLE AS TO BE ALMOST LUDICROUS.
THERE YA GO, MONSTER!
SERIOUSLY?
I'LL JUST DRILL A SMALL HOLE IN YOUR SKULL TO LET THE DEMONS OUT.
SEE? HE'LL JUST... WHAT?
WHAT?

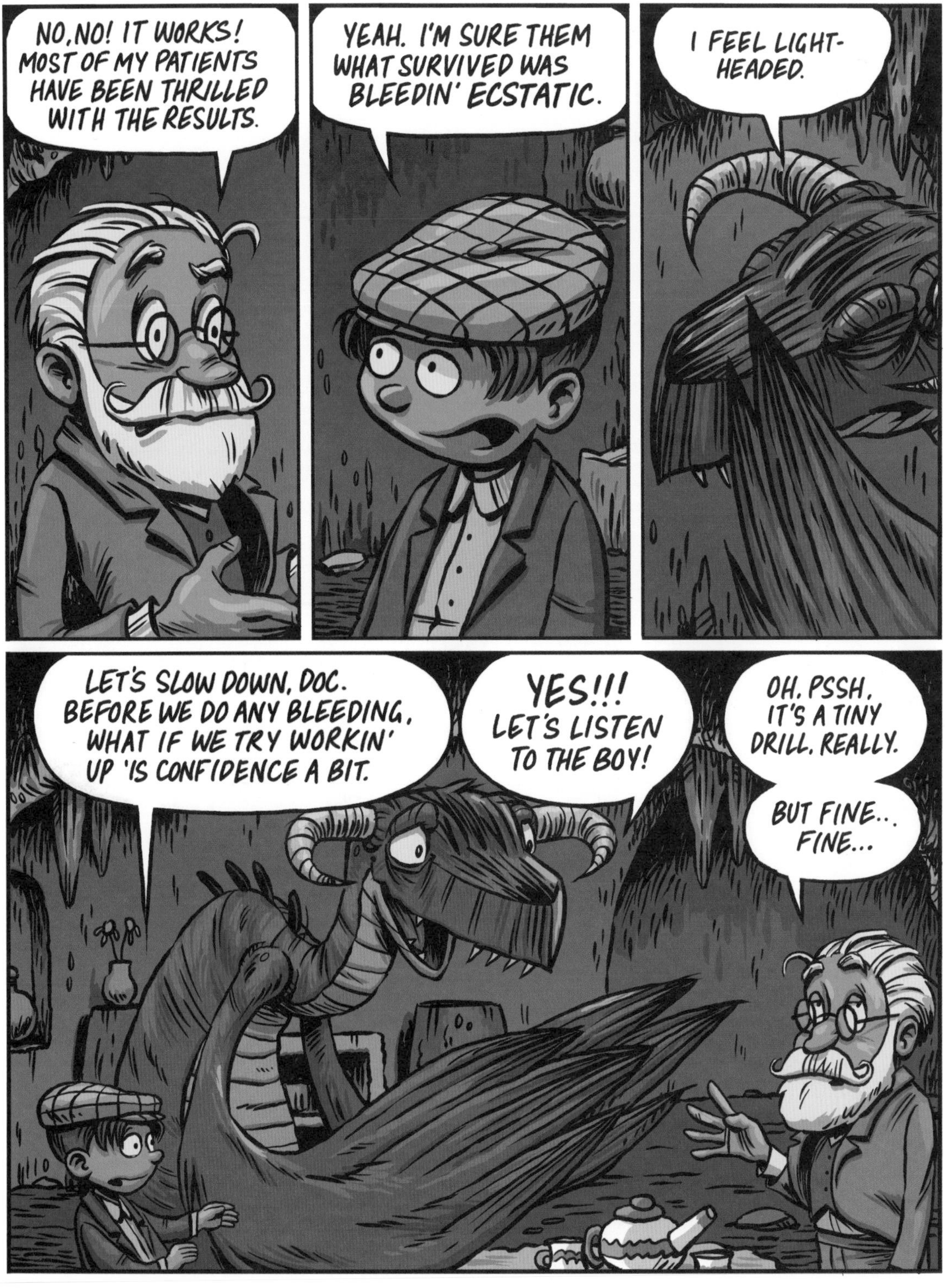
NO, NO! IT WORKS! MOST OF MY PATIENTS HAVE BEEN THRILLED WITH THE RESULTS.
YEAH. I'M SURE THEM WHAT SURVIVED WAS BLEEDIN' ECSTATIC.
I FEEL LIGHT-HEADED.
LET'S SLOW DOWN, DOC. BEFORE WE DO ANY BLEEDING, WHAT IF WE TRY WORKIN' UP 'IS CONFIDENCE A BIT.
YES!!! LET'S LISTEN TO THE BOY!
OH, PSSH, IT'S A TINY DRILL, REALLY.
BUT FINE... FINE...

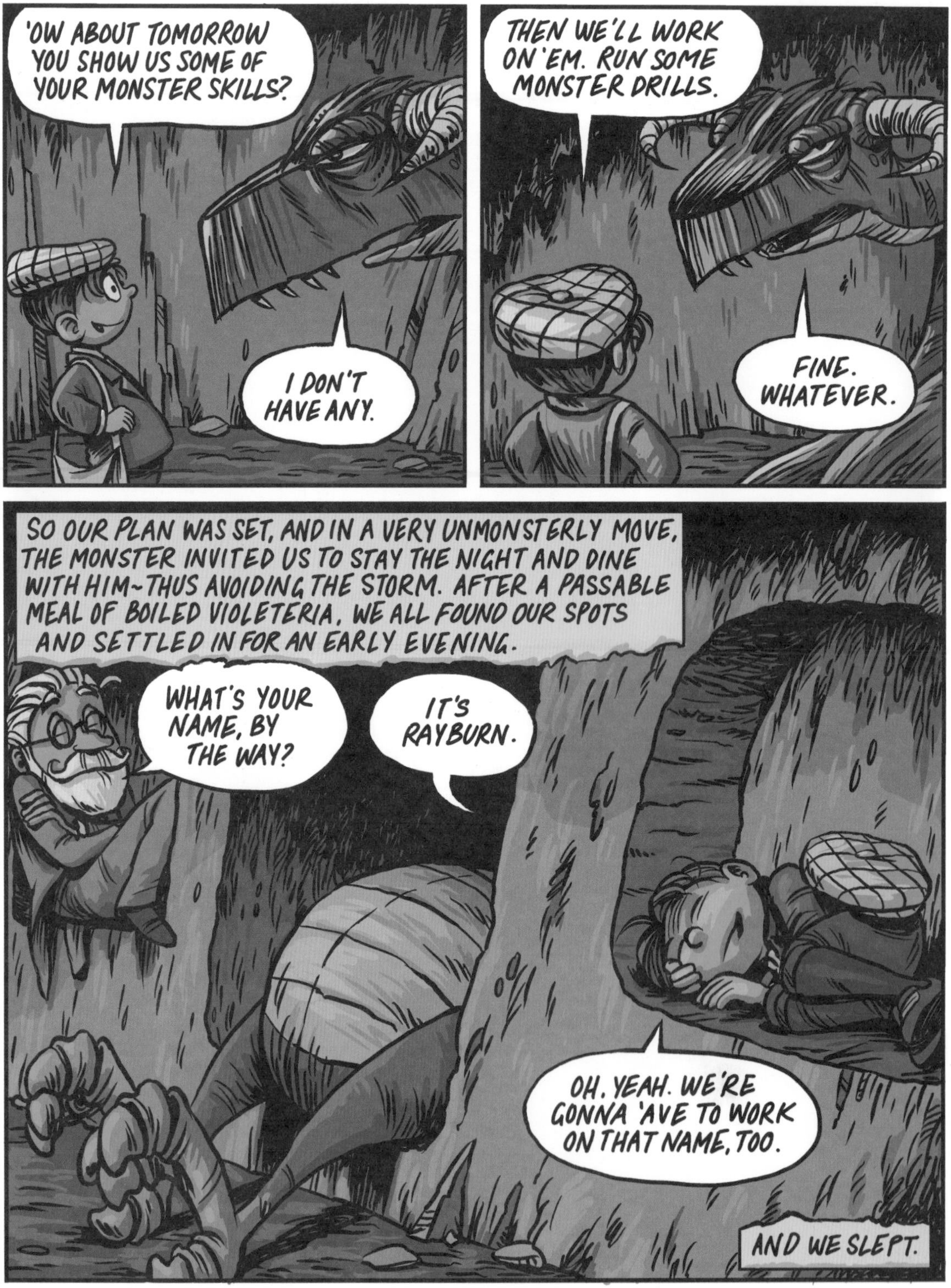
'OW ABOUT TOMORROW YOU SHOW US SOME OF YOUR MONSTER SKILLS?
I DON'T HAVE ANY.
THEN WE'LL WORK ON 'EM. RUN SOME MONSTER DRILLS.
FINE. WHATEVER.
SO OUR PLAN WAS SET, AND IN A VERY UNMONSTERLY MOVE, THE MONSTER INVITED US TO STAY THE NIGHT AND DINE WITH HIM~THUS AVOIDING THE STORM. AFTER A PASSABLE MEAL OF BOILED VIOLETERIA, WE ALL FOUND OUR SPOTS AND SETTLED IN FOR AN EARLY EVENING.
WHAT'S YOUR NAME, BY THE WAY?
IT'S RAYBURN.
OH. YEAH. WE'RE GONNA 'AVE TO WORK ON THAT NAME, TOO.
AND WE SLEPT.

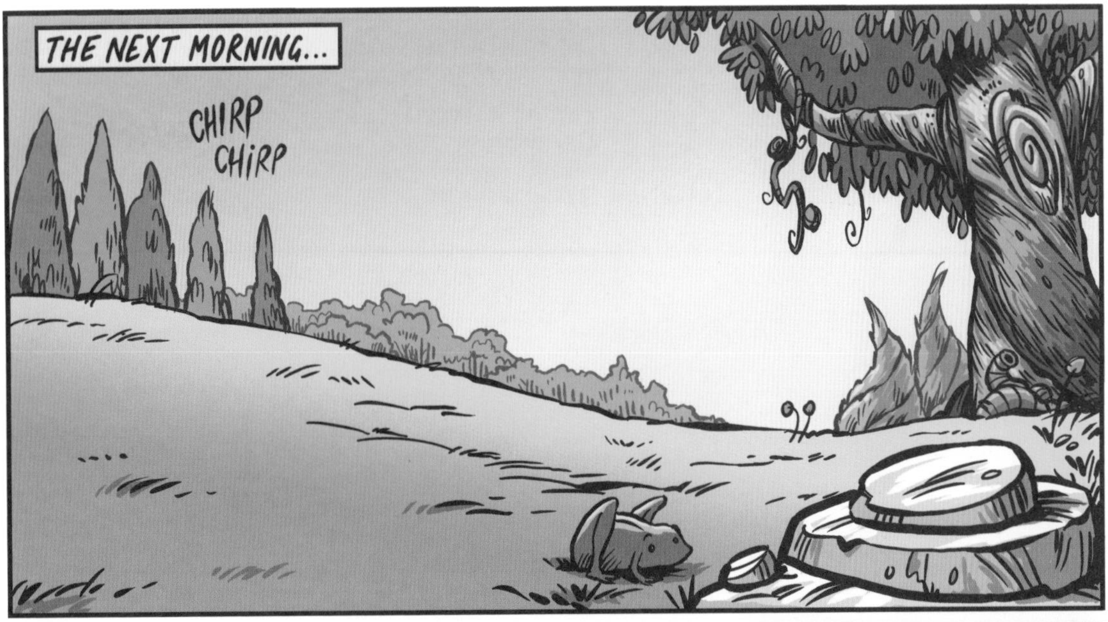
THE NEXT MORNING...
CHIRP CHIRP

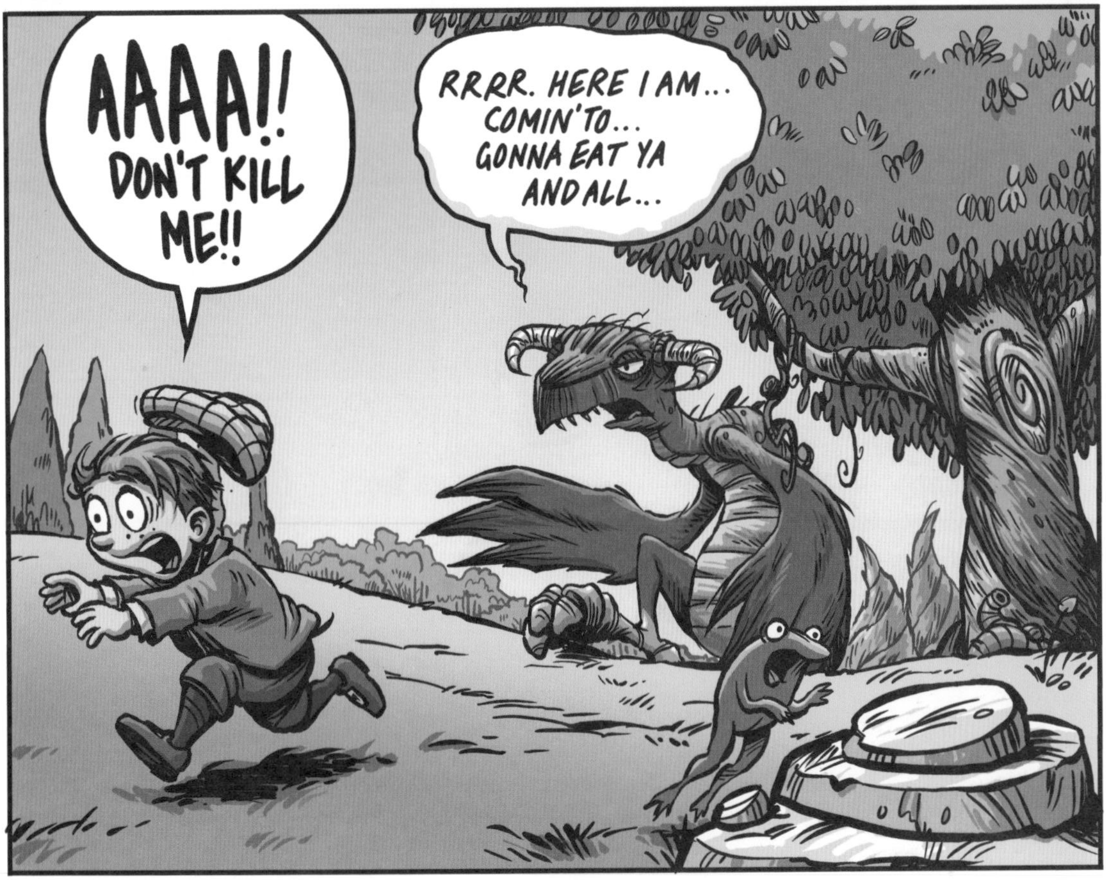
AAAA!! DON'T KILL ME!!
RRRR. HERE I AM... COMIN'TO... GONNA EAT YA AND ALL...

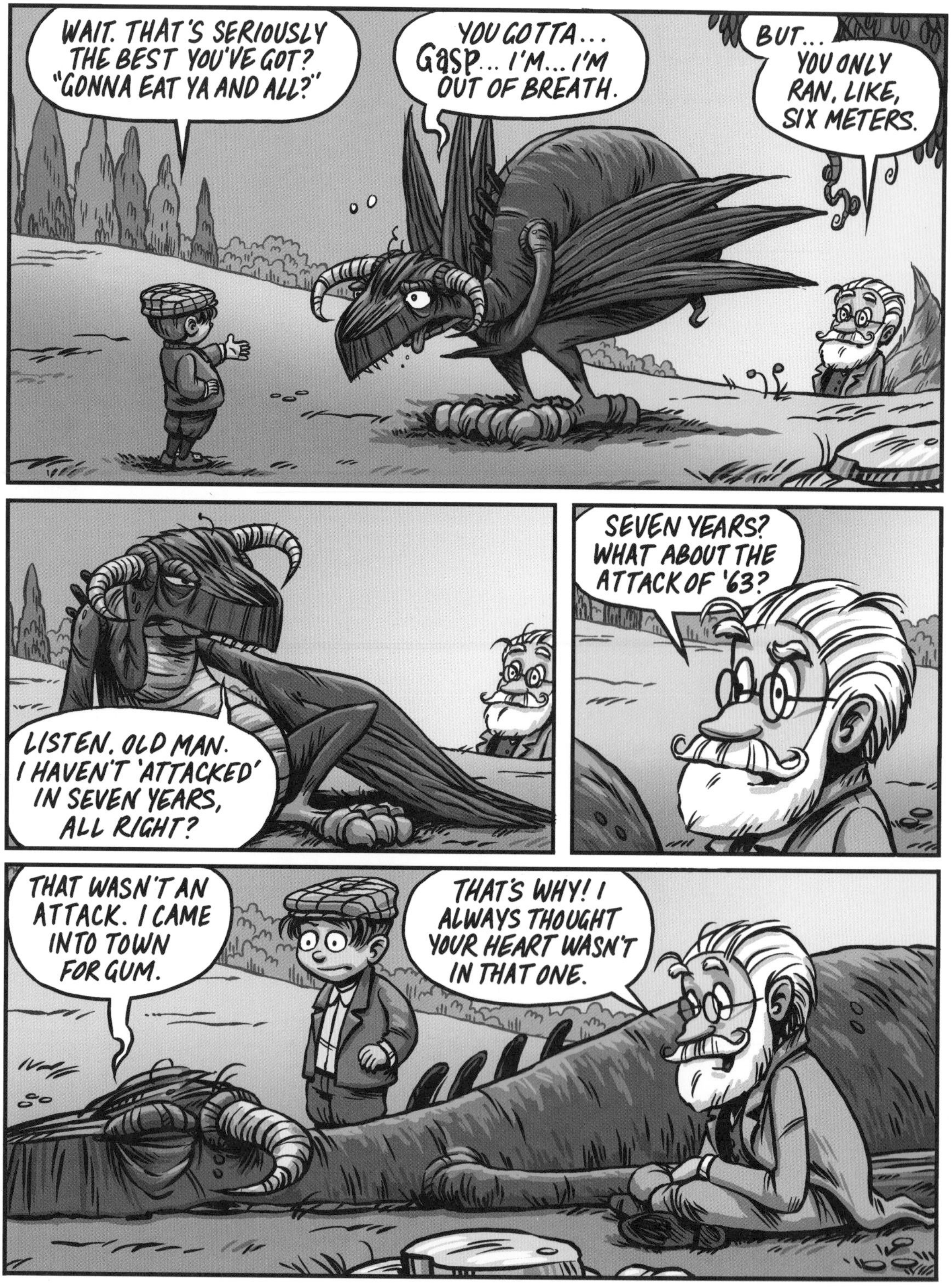
WAIT. THAT'S SERIOUSLY THE BEST YOU'VE GOT? "GONNA EAT YA AND ALL?"
YOU GOTTA... Gasp... I'M... I'M OUT OF BREATH.
BUT... YOU ONLY RAN, LIKE, SIX METERS.
LISTEN, OLD MAN. I HAVEN'T 'ATTACKED' IN SEVEN YEARS, ALL RIGHT?
SEVEN YEARS? WHAT ABOUT THE ATTACK OF '63?
THAT WASN'T AN ATTACK. I CAME INTO TOWN FOR GUM.
THAT'S WHY! I ALWAYS THOUGHT YOUR HEART WASN'T IN THAT ONE.

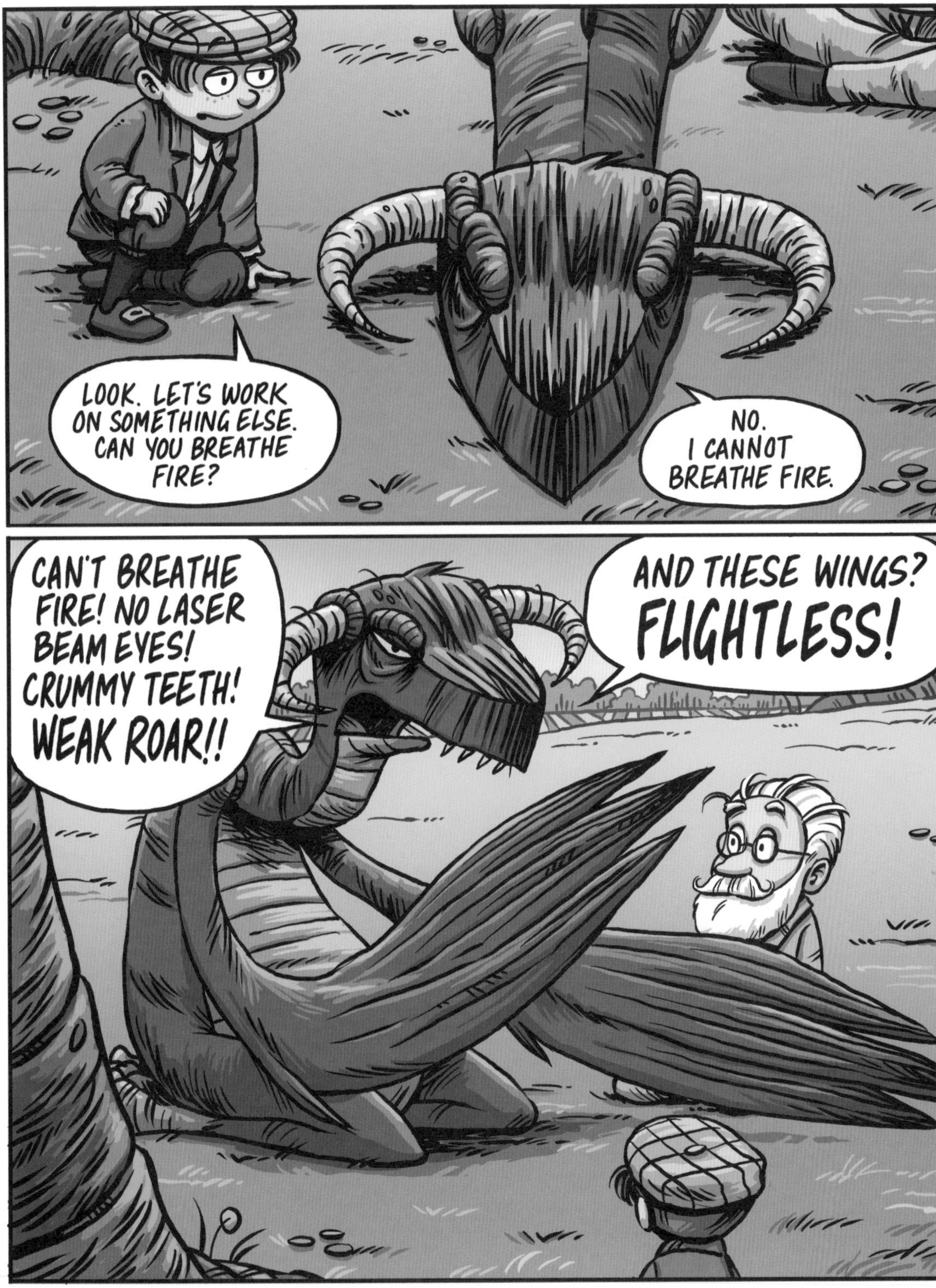
LOOK. LET'S WORK ON SOMETHING ELSE. CAN YOU BREATHE FIRE?
NO. I CANNOT BREATHE FIRE.
CAN'T BREATHE FIRE! NO LASER BEAM EYES! CRUMMY TEETH! WEAK ROAR!!
AND THESE WINGS? FLIGHTLESS!

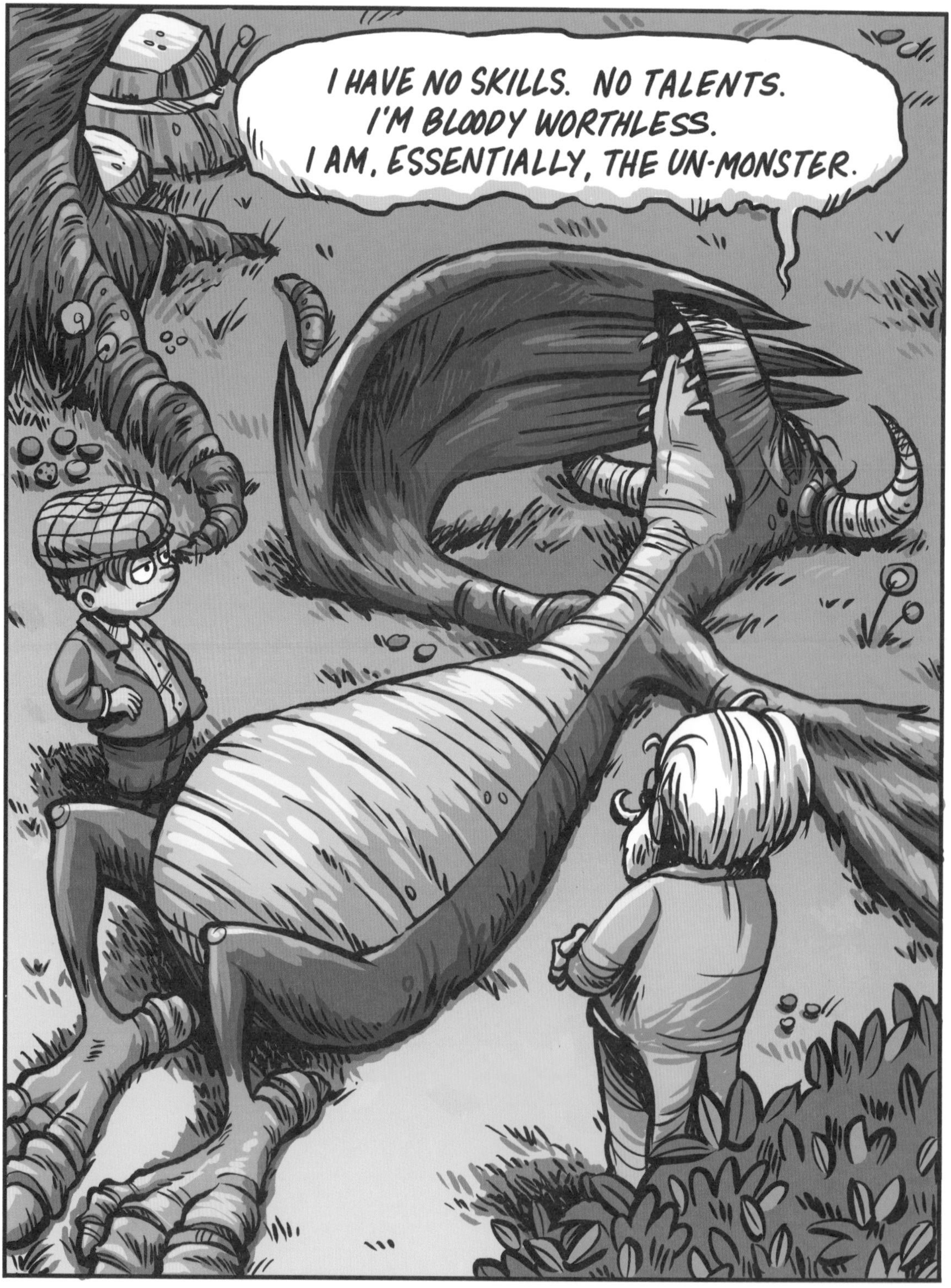
I HAVE NO SKILLS. NO TALENTS. I'M BLOODY WORTHLESS. I AM, ESSENTIALLY, THE UN-MONSTER.

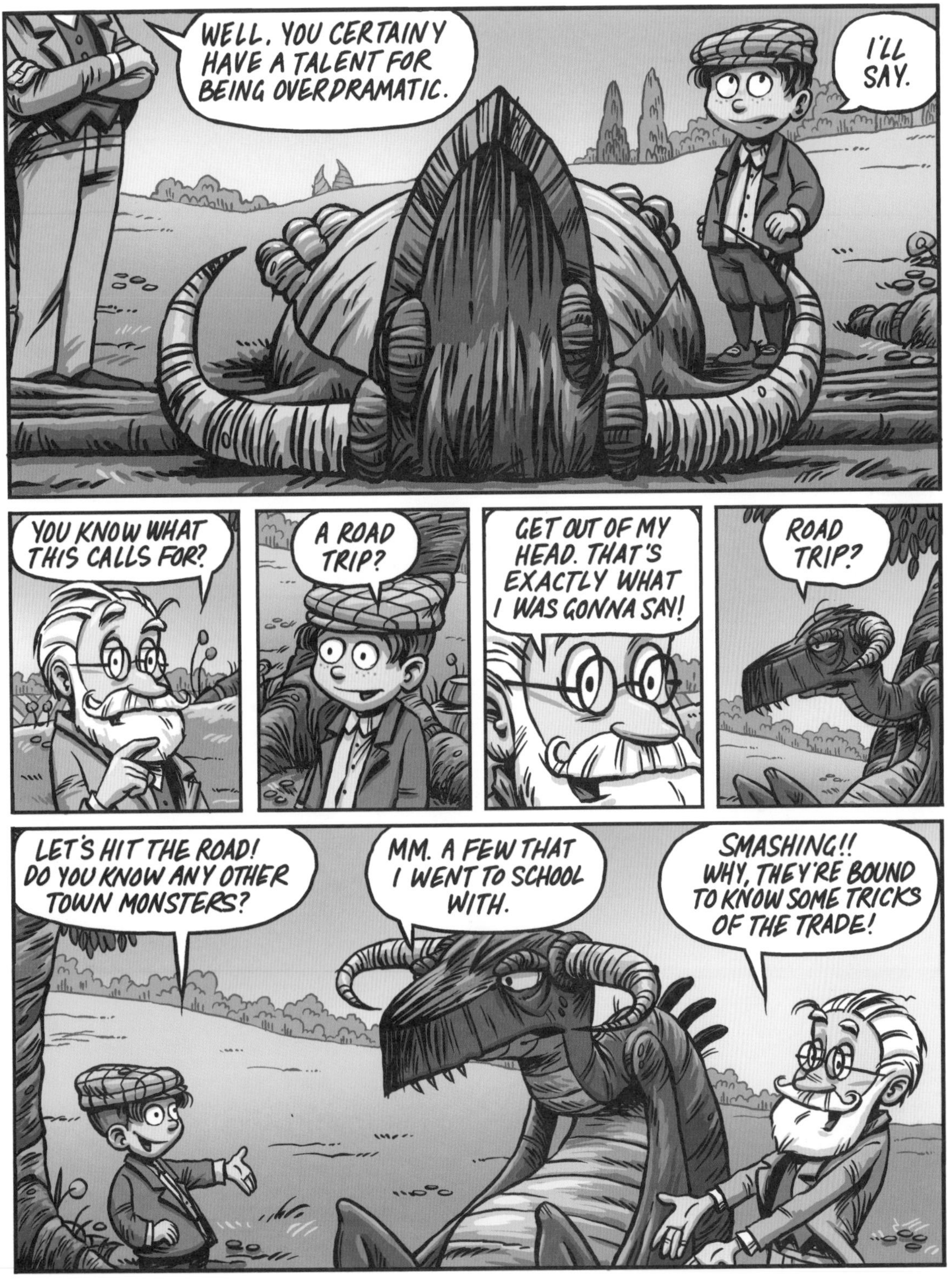
WELL. YOU CERTAINY HAVE A TALENT FOR BEING OVERDRAMATIC.
I'LL SAY.
YOU KNOW WHAT THIS CALLS FOR?
A ROAD TRIP?
GET OUT OF MY HEAD. THAT'S EXACTLY WHAT I WAS GONNA SAY!
ROAD TRIP?
LET'S HIT THE ROAD! DO YOU KNOW ANY OTHER TOWN MONSTERS?
MM. A FEW THAT I WENT TO SCHOOL WITH.
SMASHING!! WHY, THEY'RE BOUND TO KNOW SOME TRICKS OF THE TRADE!

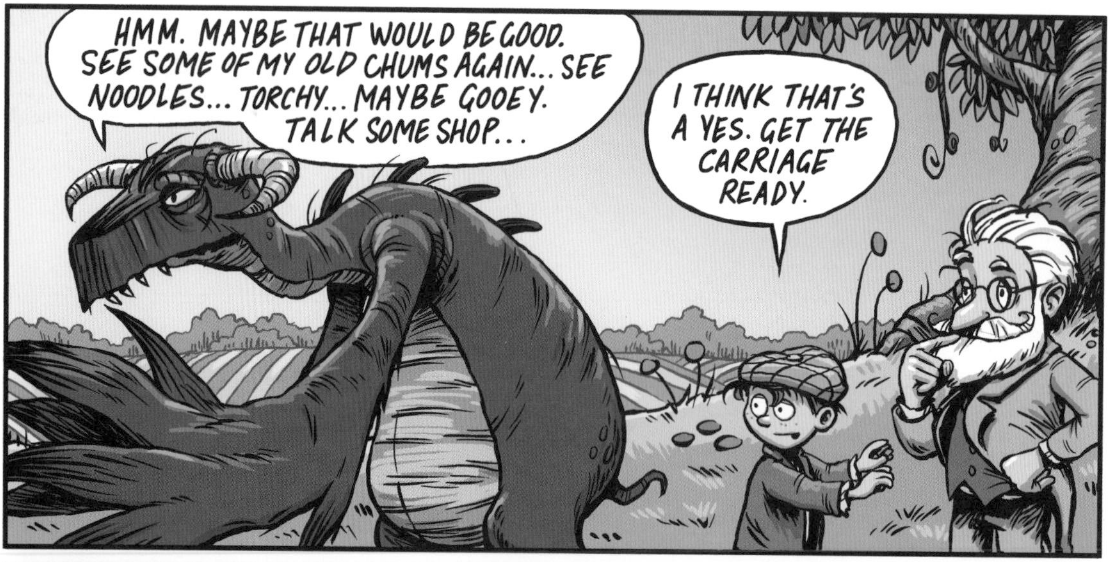
HMM. MAYBE THAT WOULD BE GOOD. SEE SOME OF MY OLD CHUMS AGAIN... SEE NOODLES... TORCHY... MAYBE GOOEY. TALK SOME SHOP...
I THINK THAT'S A YES. GET THE CARRIAGE READY.

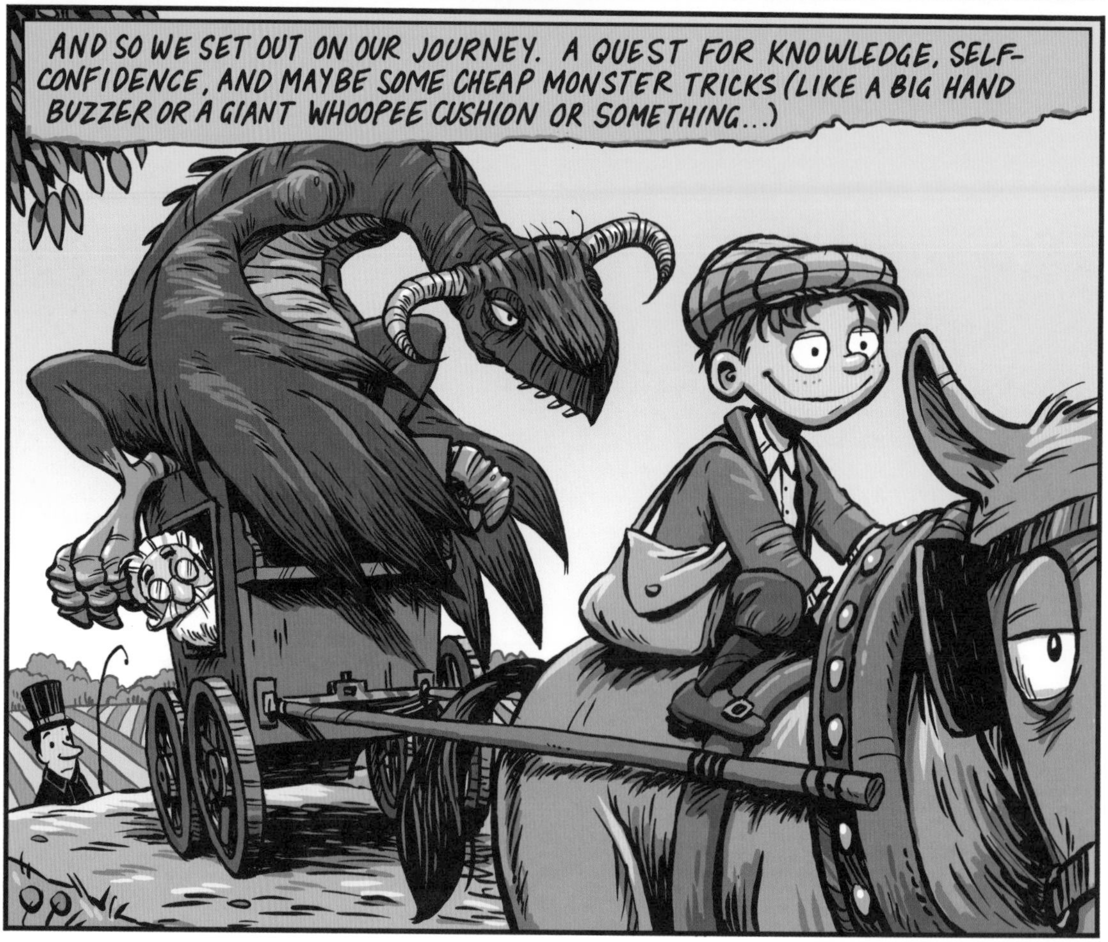
AND SO WE SET OUT ON OUR JOURNEY. A QUEST FOR KNOWLEDGE, SELF-CONFIDENCE, AND MAYBE SOME CHEAP MONSTER TRICKS (LIKE A BIG HAND BUZZER OR A GIANT WHOOPEE CUSHION OR SOMETHING...)

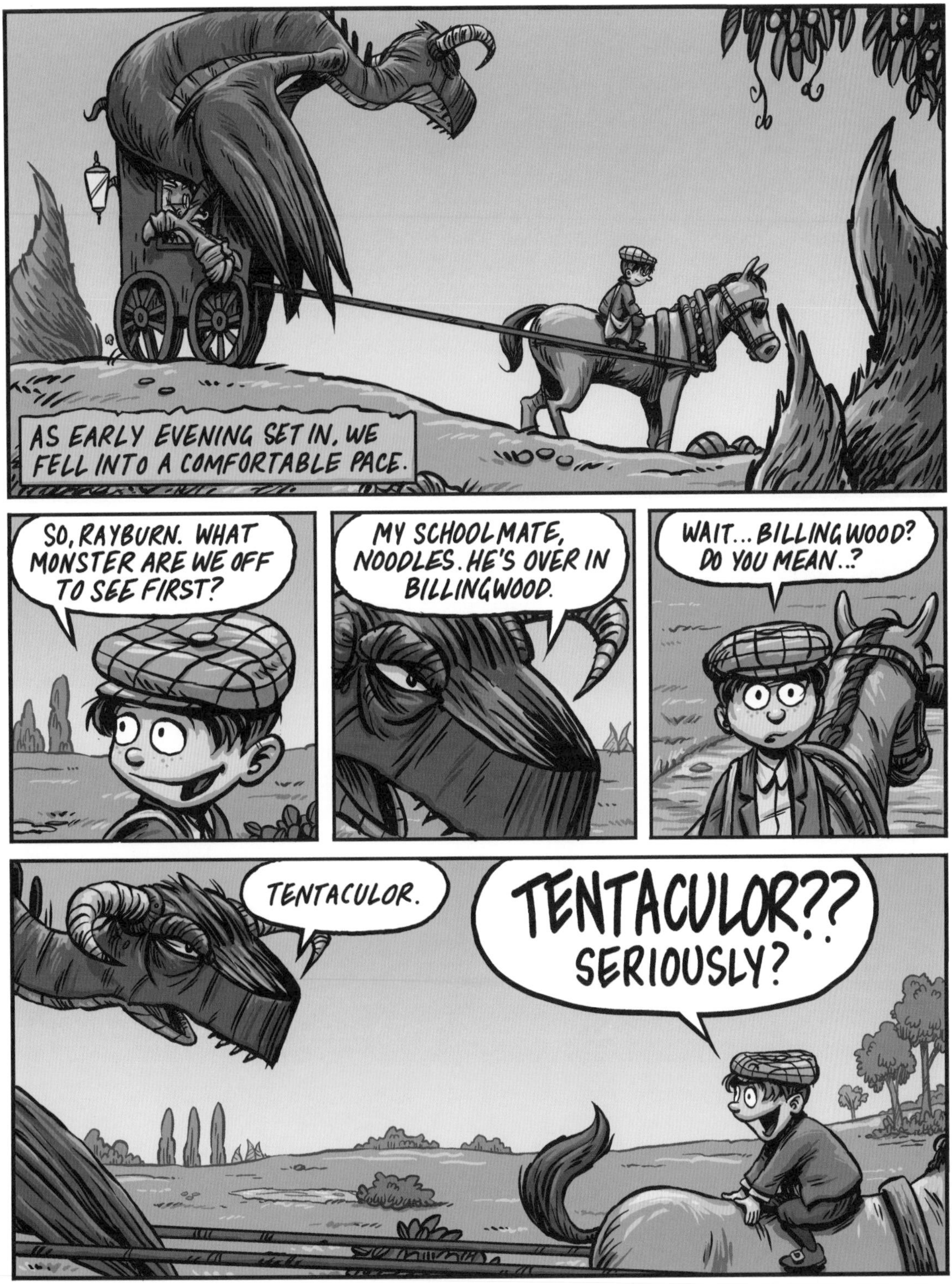
AS EARLY EVENING SET IN, WE FELL INTO A COMFORTABLE PACE.
SO, RAYBURN. WHAT MONSTER ARE WE OFF TO SEE FIRST?
MY SCHOOLMATE, NOODLES. HE'S OVER IN BILLINGWOOD.
WAIT... BILLINGWOOD? DO YOU MEAN..?
TENTACULOR.
TENTACULOR?? SERIOUSLY?

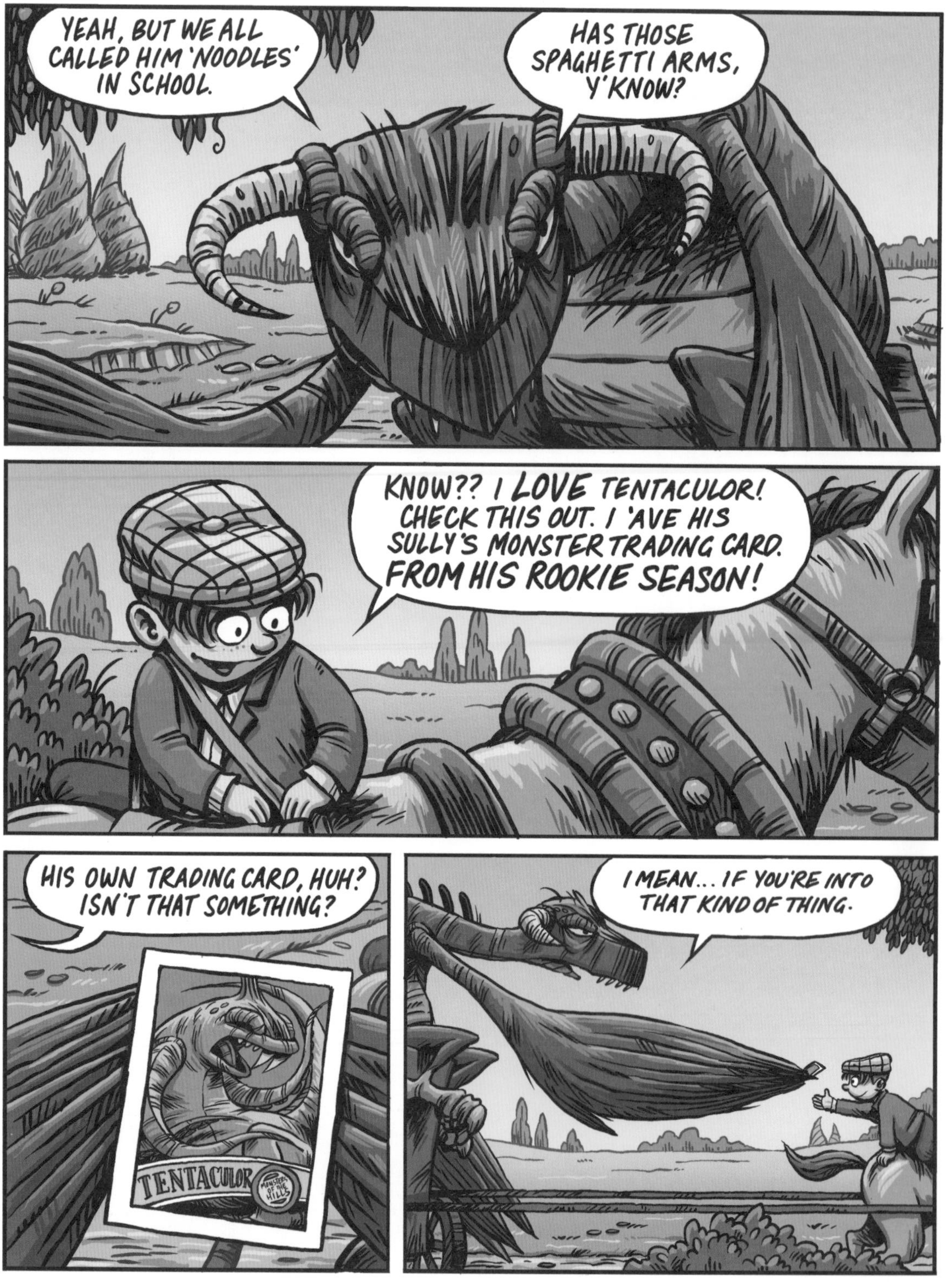
YEAH, BUT WE ALL CALLED HIM 'NOODLES' IN SCHOOL.
HAS THOSE SPAGHETTI ARMS, Y'KNOW?
KNOW?? I LOVE TENTACULOR! CHECK THIS OUT. I 'AVE HIS SULLY'S MONSTER TRADING CARD. FROM HIS ROOKIE SEASON!
HIS OWN TRADING CARD, HUH? ISN'T THAT SOMETHING?
TENTACULOR
MONSTERS OF THE HILLS
I MEAN... IF YOU'RE INTO THAT KIND OF THING.

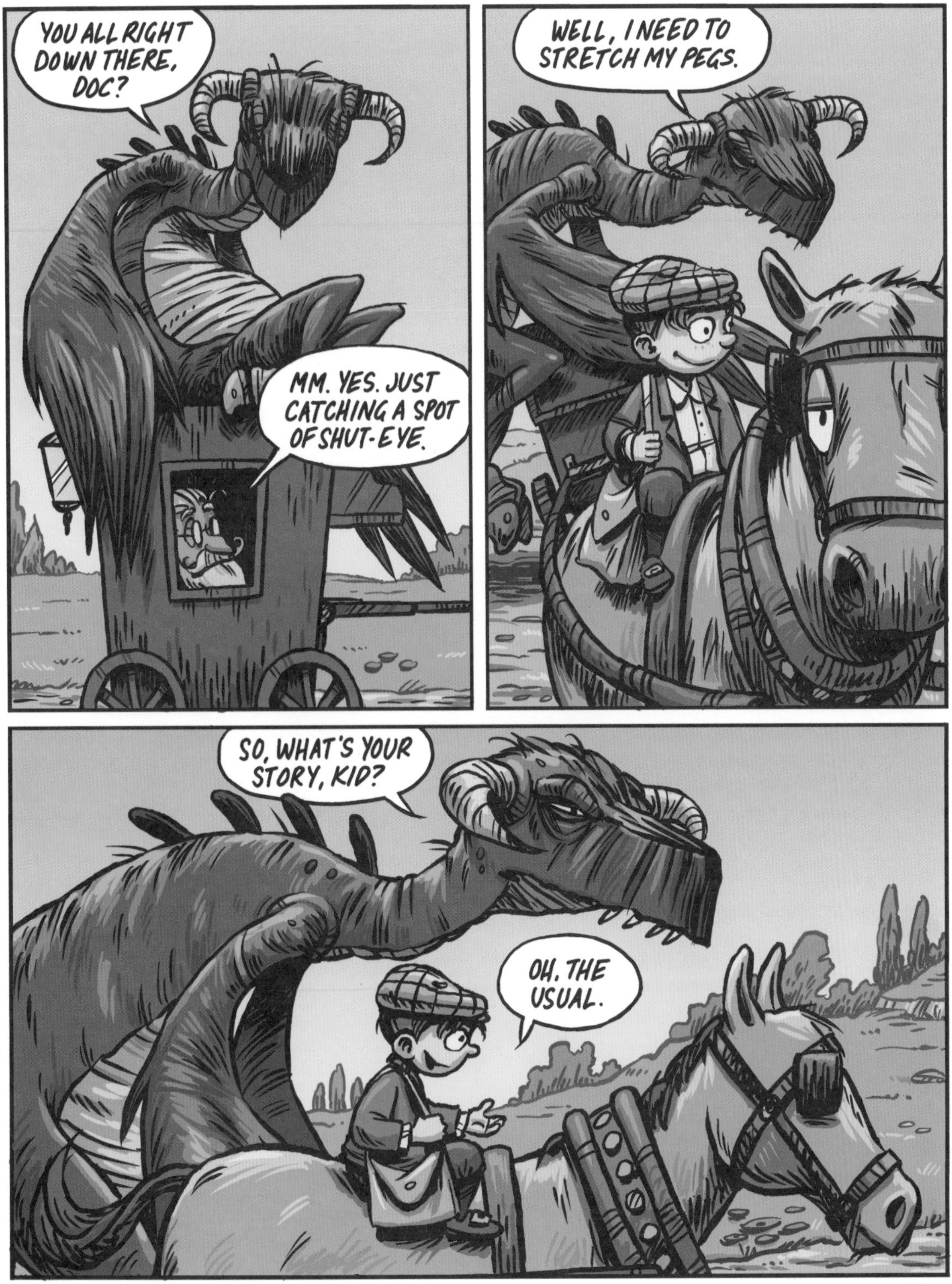
YOU ALL RIGHT DOWN THERE, DOC?
MM. YES. JUST CATCHING A SPOT OF SHUT-EYE.
WELL, I NEED TO STRETCH MY PEGS.
SO, WHAT'S YOUR STORY, KID?
OH, THE USUAL.

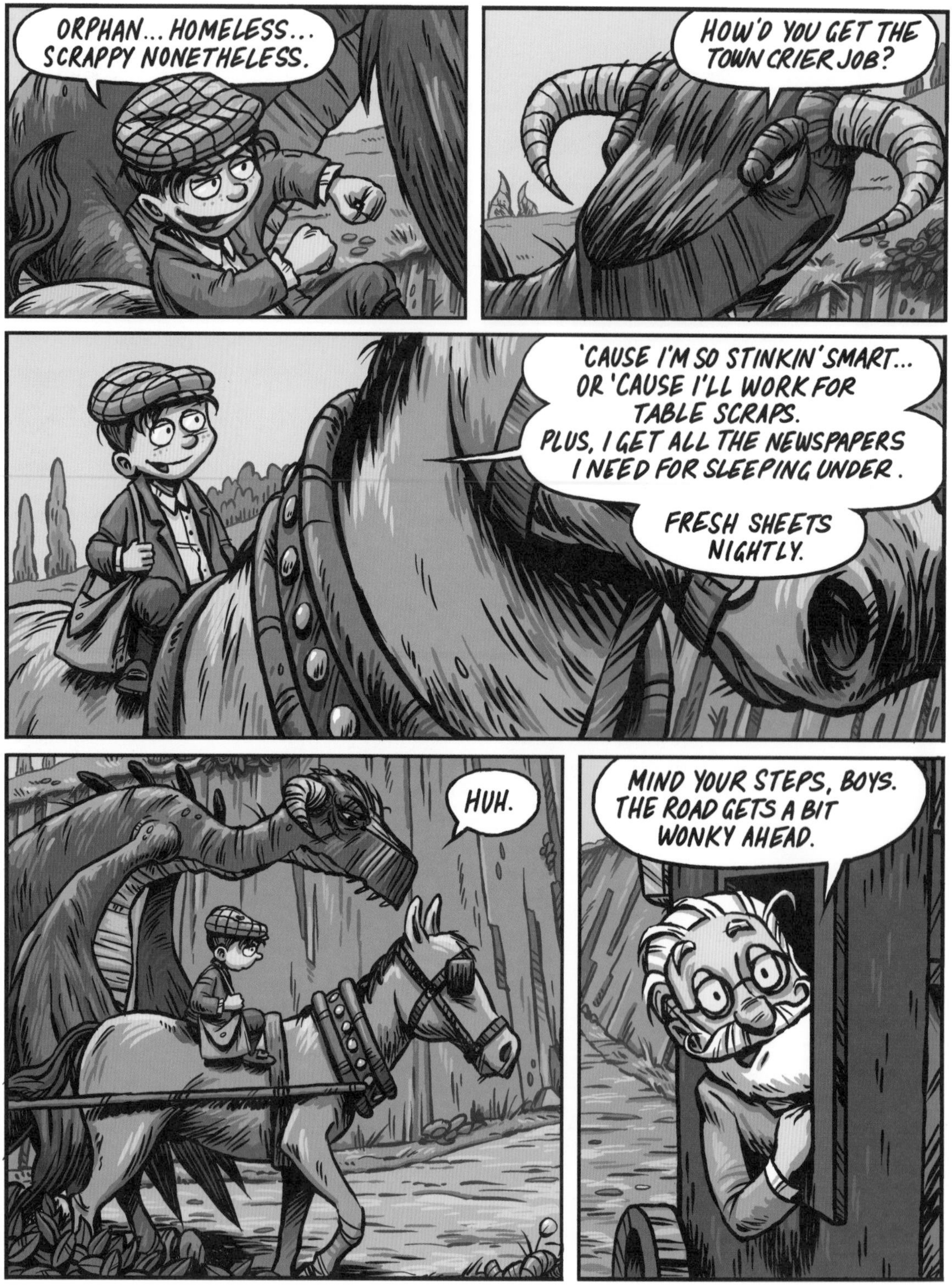
ORPHAN... HOMELESS... SCRAPPY NONETHELESS.
HOW'D YOU GET THE TOWN CRIER JOB?
'CAUSE I'M SO STINKIN' SMART... OR 'CAUSE I'LL WORK FOR TABLE SCRAPS. PLUS, I GET ALL THE NEWSPAPERS I NEED FOR SLEEPING UNDER.
FRESH SHEETS NIGHTLY.
HUH.
MIND YOUR STEPS, BOYS. THE ROAD GETS A BIT WONKY AHEAD.

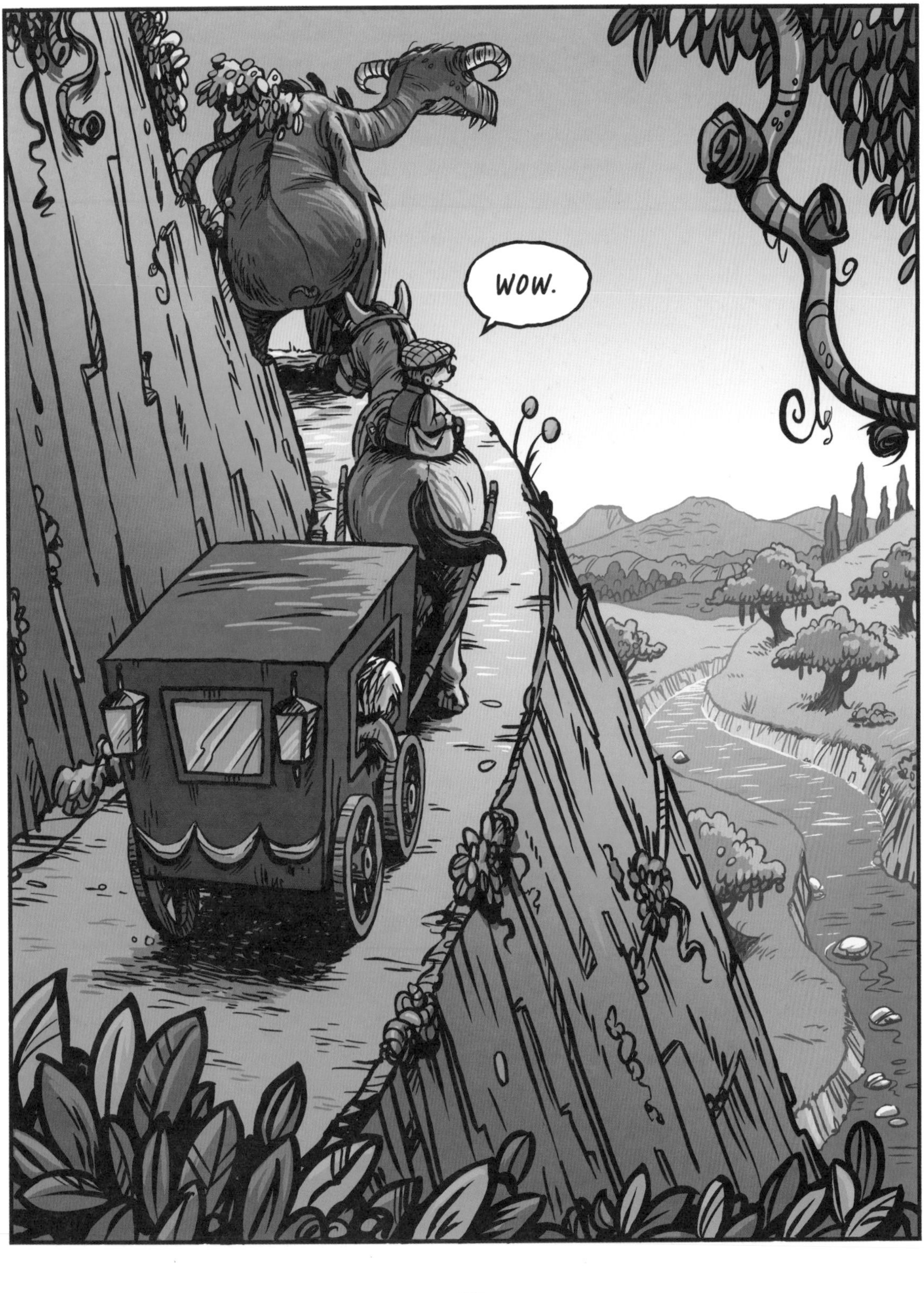
WOW.

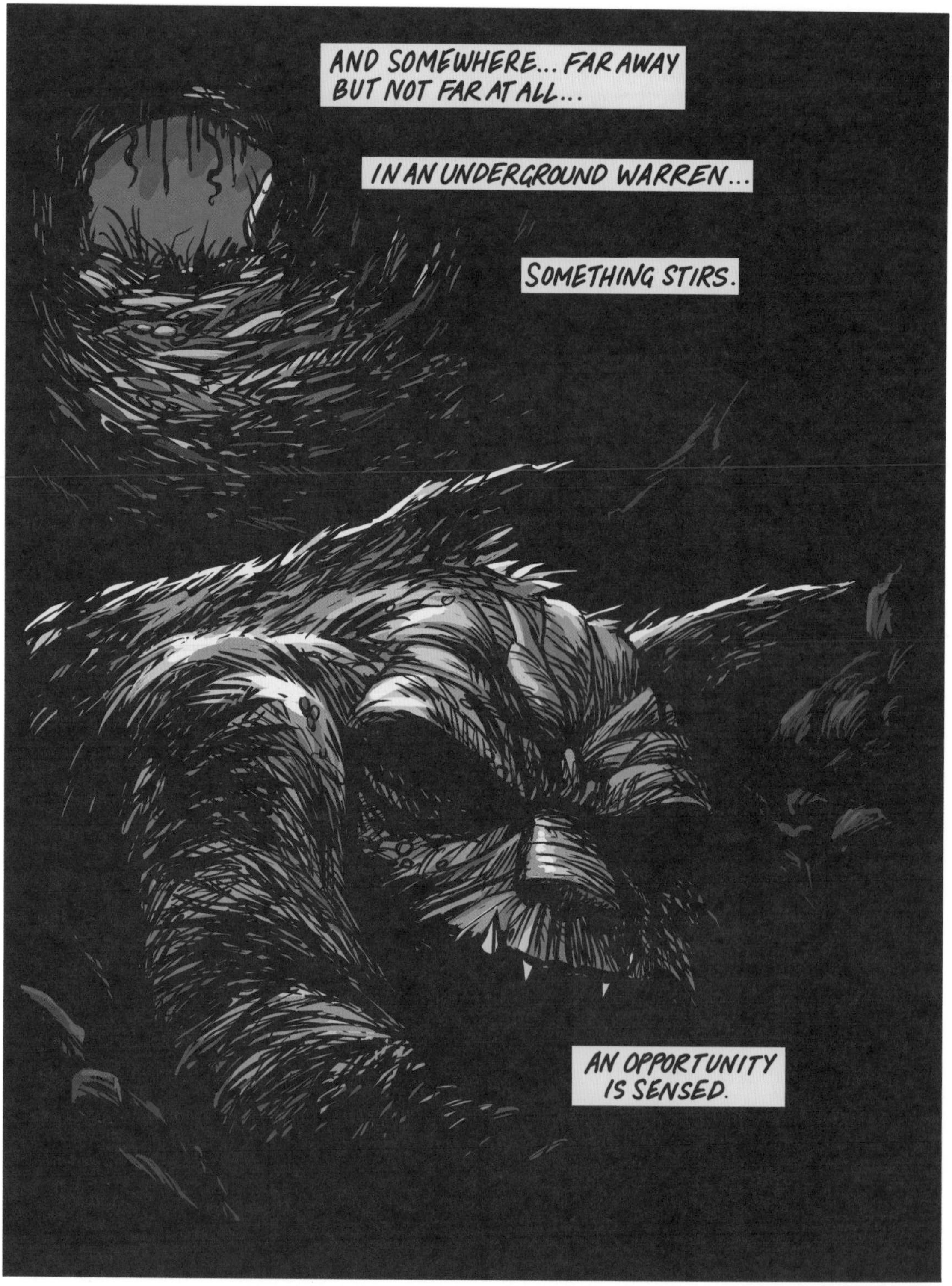
AND SOMEWHERE... FAR AWAY BUT NOT FAR AT ALL...
IN AN UNDERGROUND WARREN...
SOMETHING STIRS.
AN OPPORTUNITY IS SENSED.

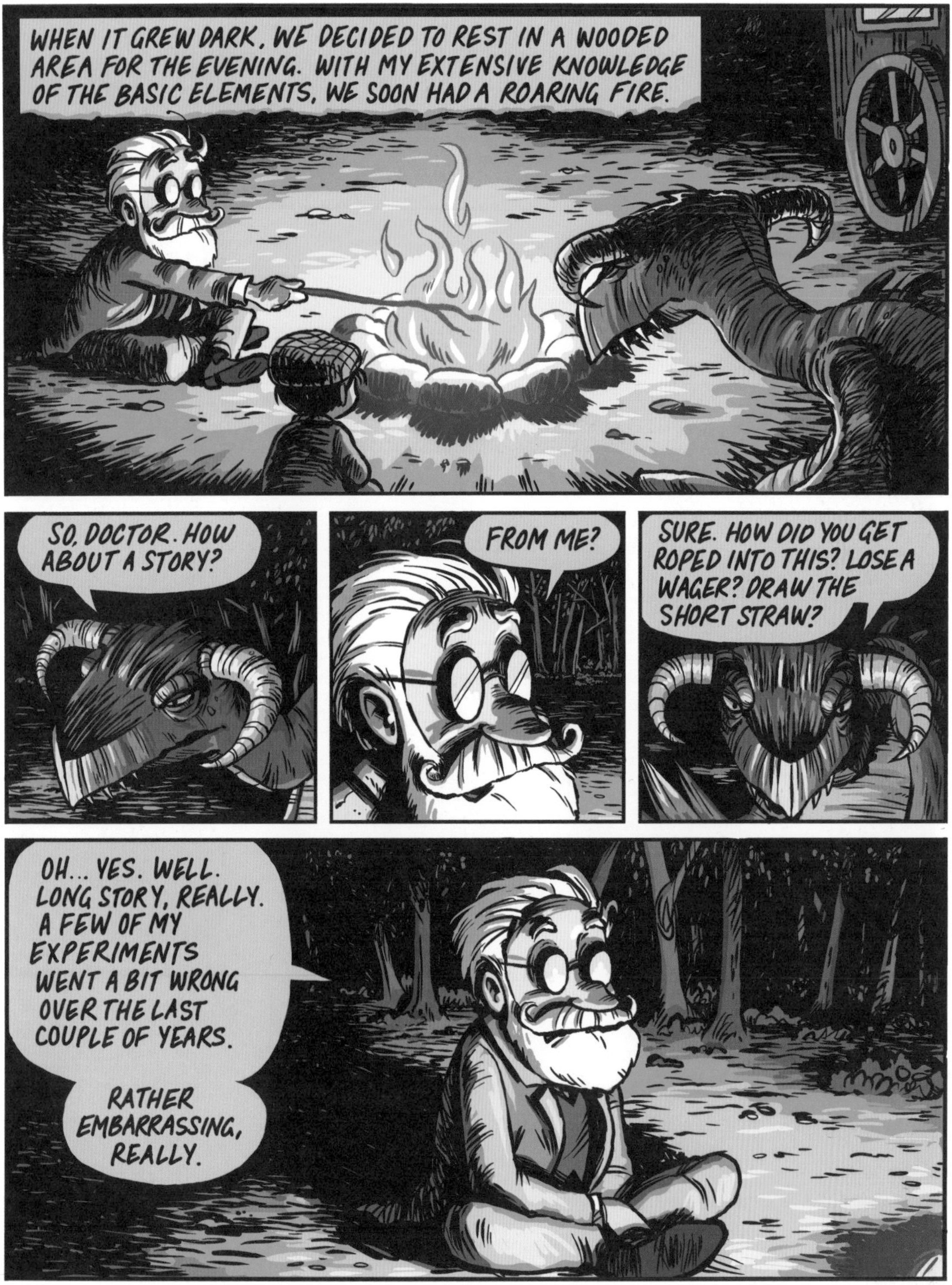
WHEN IT GREW DARK, WE DECIDED TO REST IN A WOODED AREA FOR THE EVENING. WITH MY EXTENSIVE KNOWLEDGE OF THE BASIC ELEMENTS, WE SOON HAD A ROARING FIRE.
SO, DOCTOR. HOW ABOUT A STORY?
FROM ME?
SURE. HOW DID YOU GET ROPED INTO THIS? LOSE A WAGER? DRAW THE SHORT STRAW?
OH... YES. WELL. LONG STORY, REALLY. A FEW OF MY EXPERIMENTS WENT A BIT WRONG OVER THE LAST COUPLE OF YEARS.
RATHER EMBARRASSING, REALLY.

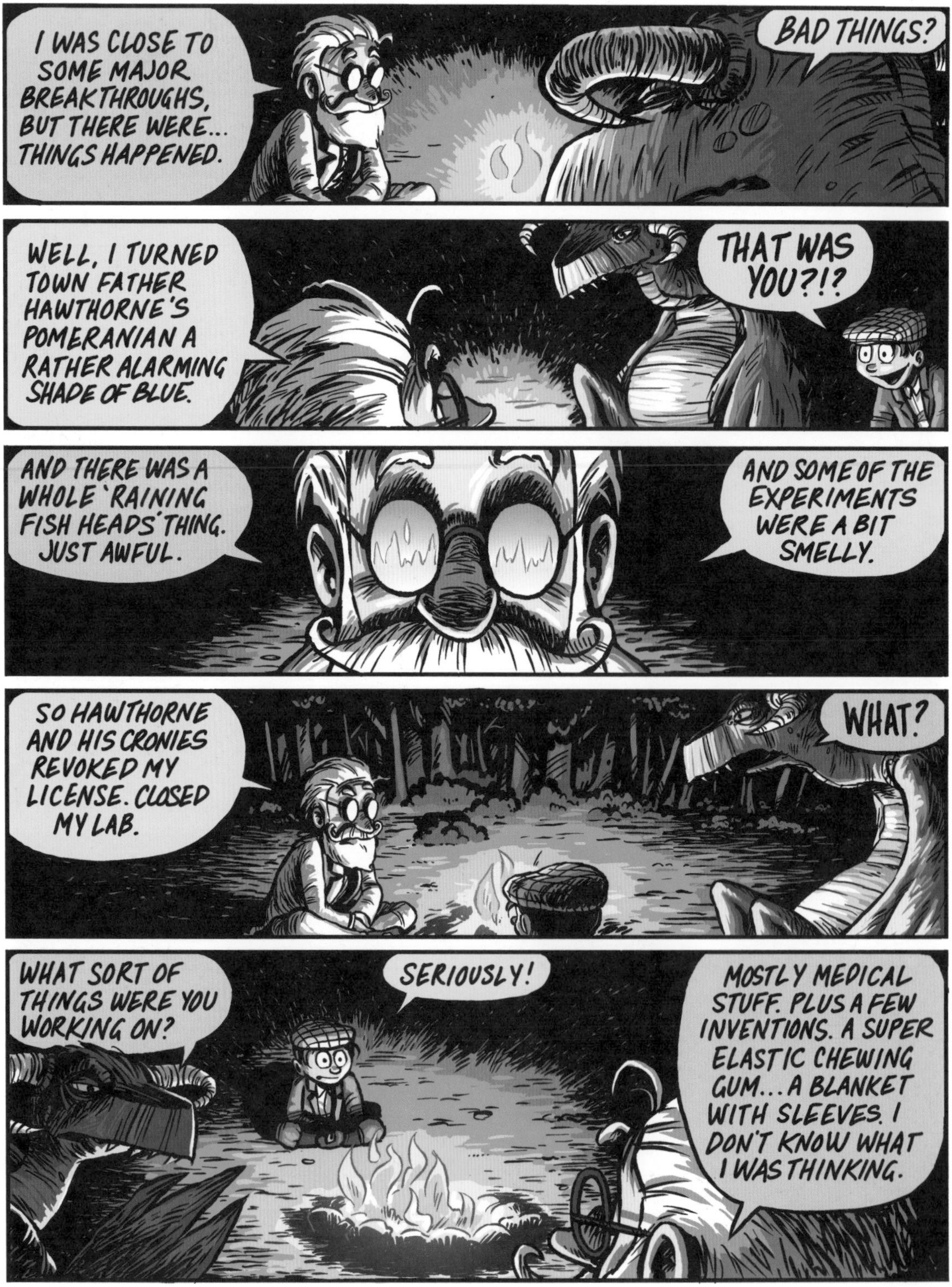
I WAS CLOSE TO SOME MAJOR BREAKTHROUGHS, BUT THERE WERE... THINGS HAPPENED.
BAD THINGS?
WELL, I TURNED TOWN FATHER HAWTHORNE'S POMERANIAN A RATHER ALARMING SHADE OF BLUE.
THAT WAS YOU?!?
AND THERE WAS A WHOLE 'RAINING FISH HEADS' THING. JUST AWFUL.
AND SOME OF THE EXPERIMENTS WERE A BIT SMELLY.
SO HAWTHORNE AND HIS CRONIES REVOKED MY LICENSE. CLOSED MY LAB.
WHAT?
WHAT SORT OF THINGS WERE YOU WORKING ON?
SERIOUSLY!
MOSTLY MEDICAL STUFF. PLUS A FEW INVENTIONS. A SUPER ELASTIC CHEWING GUM... A BLANKET WITH SLEEVES. I DON'T KNOW WHAT I WAS THINKING.

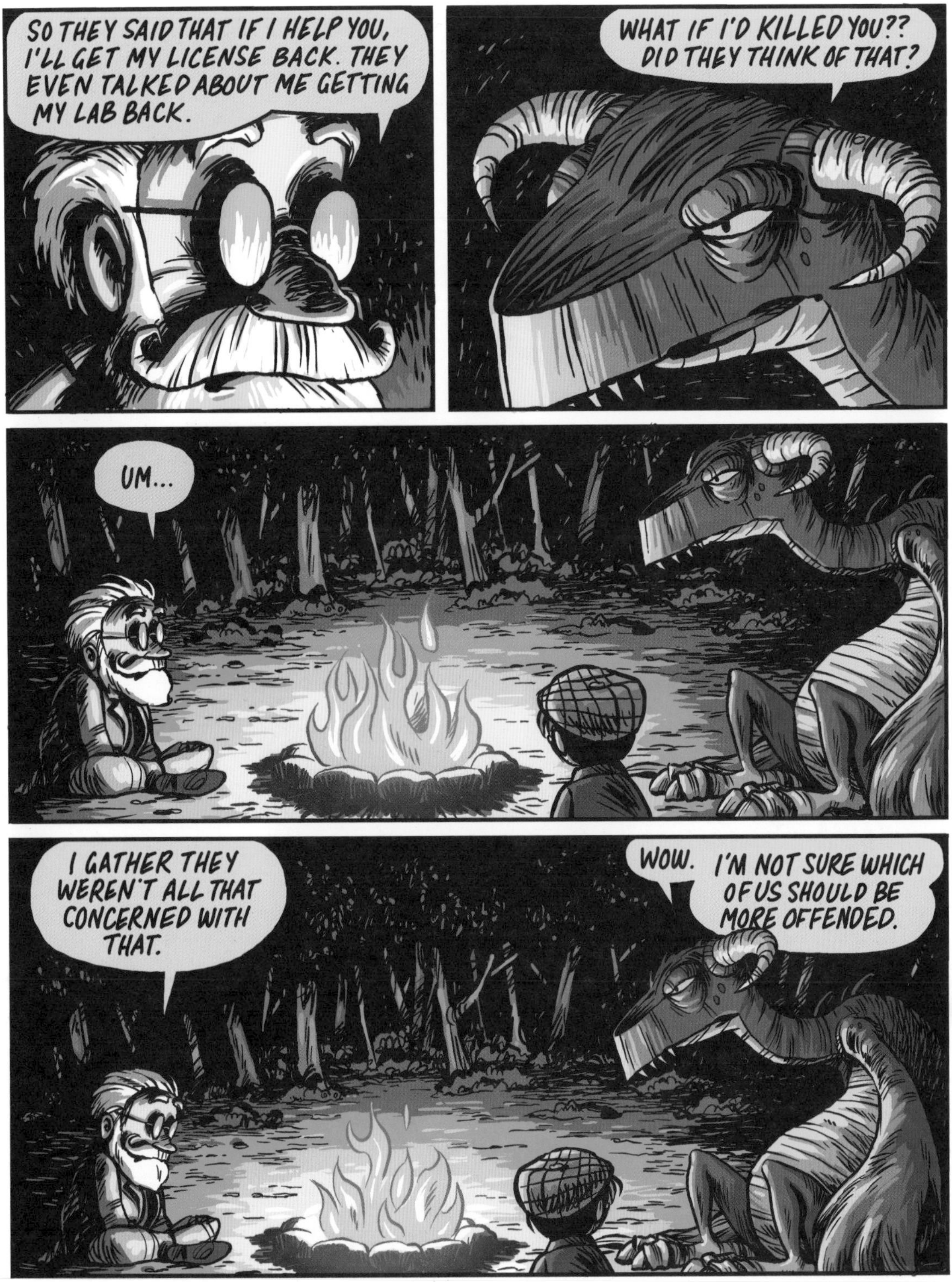
SO THEY SAID THAT IF I HELP YOU, I'LL GET MY LICENSE BACK. THEY EVEN TALKED ABOUT ME GETTING MY LAB BACK.
WHAT IF I'D KILLED YOU?? DID THEY THINK OF THAT?
UM...
I GATHER THEY WEREN'T ALL THAT CONCERNED WITH THAT.
WOW.
I'M NOT SURE WHICH OF US SHOULD BE MORE OFFENDED.

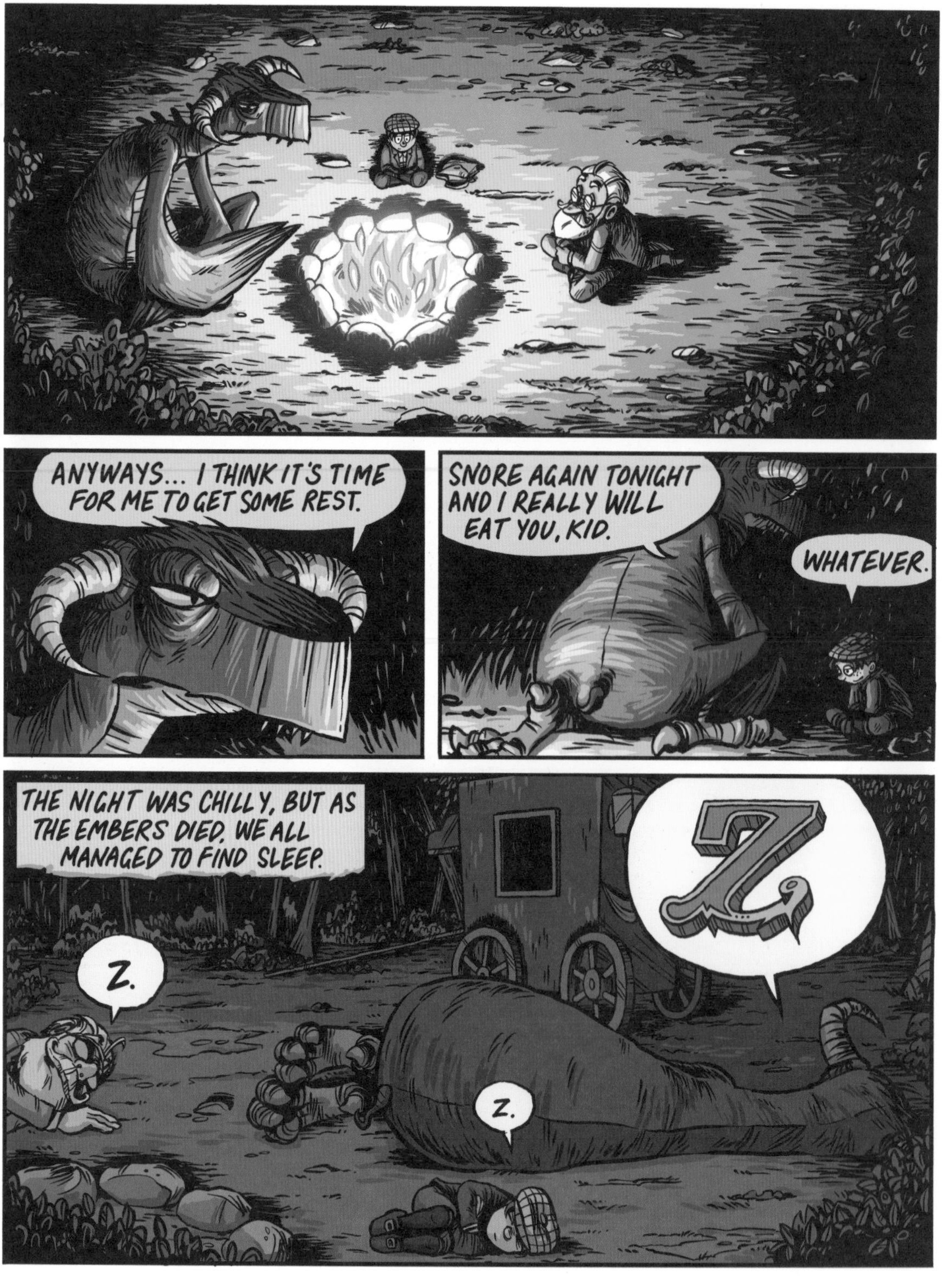

ANYWAYS... I THINK IT'S TIME FOR ME TO GET SOME REST.
SNORE AGAIN TONIGHT AND I REALLY WILL EAT YOU, KID.
WHATEVER.
THE NIGHT WAS CHILLY, BUT AS THE EMBERS DIED, WE ALL MANAGED TO FIND SLEEP.
Z
Z.
Z.

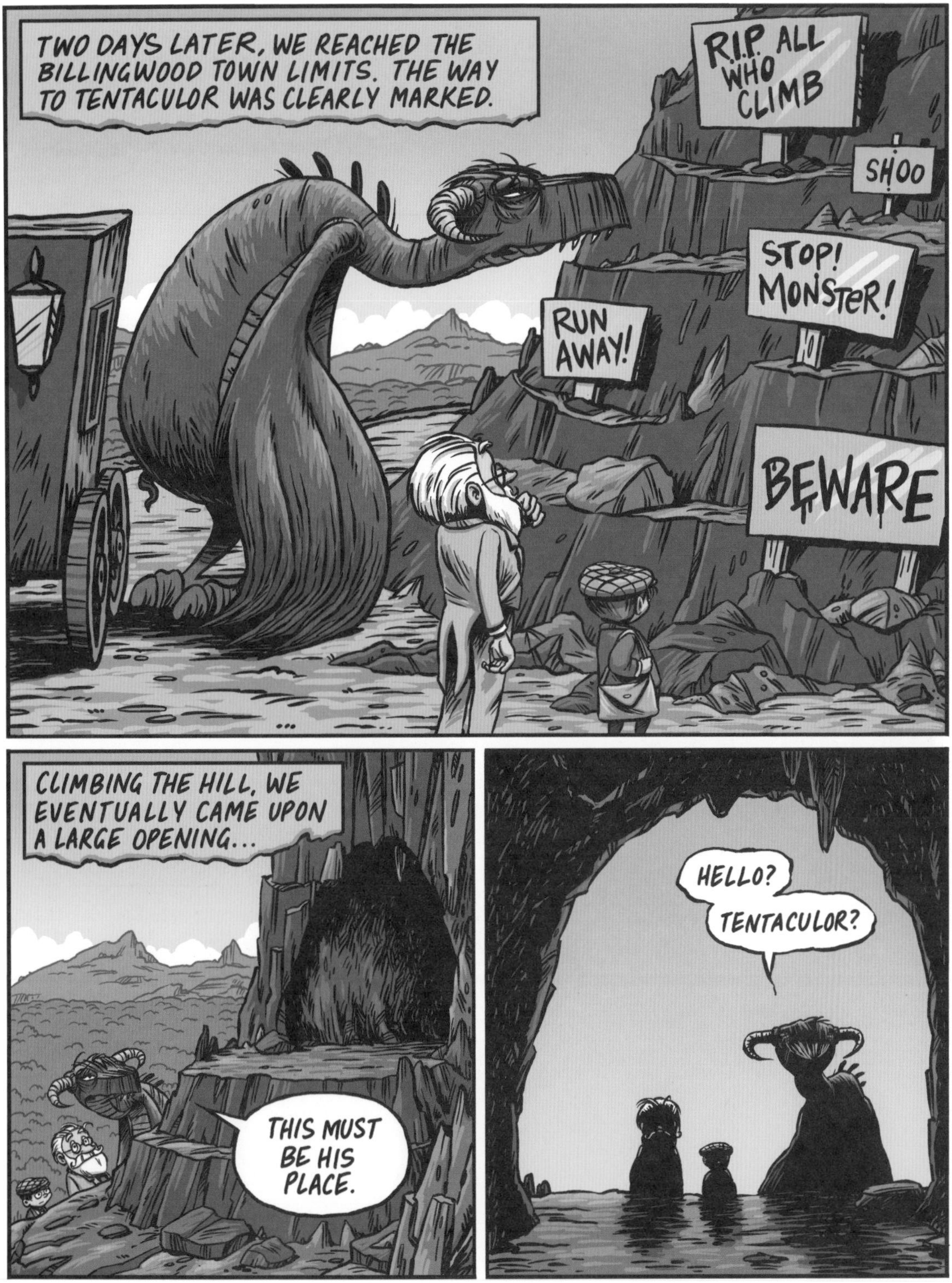
TWO DAYS LATER, WE REACHED THE BILLINGWOOD TOWN LIMITS. THE WAY TO TENTACULOR WAS CLEARLY MARKED.
R.I.P. ALL WHO CLIMB
SHOO
STOP! MONSTER!
RUN AWAY!
BEWARE
CLIMBING THE HILL, WE EVENTUALLY CAME UPON A LARGE OPENING...
THIS MUST BE HIS PLACE.
HELLO?
TENTACULOR?

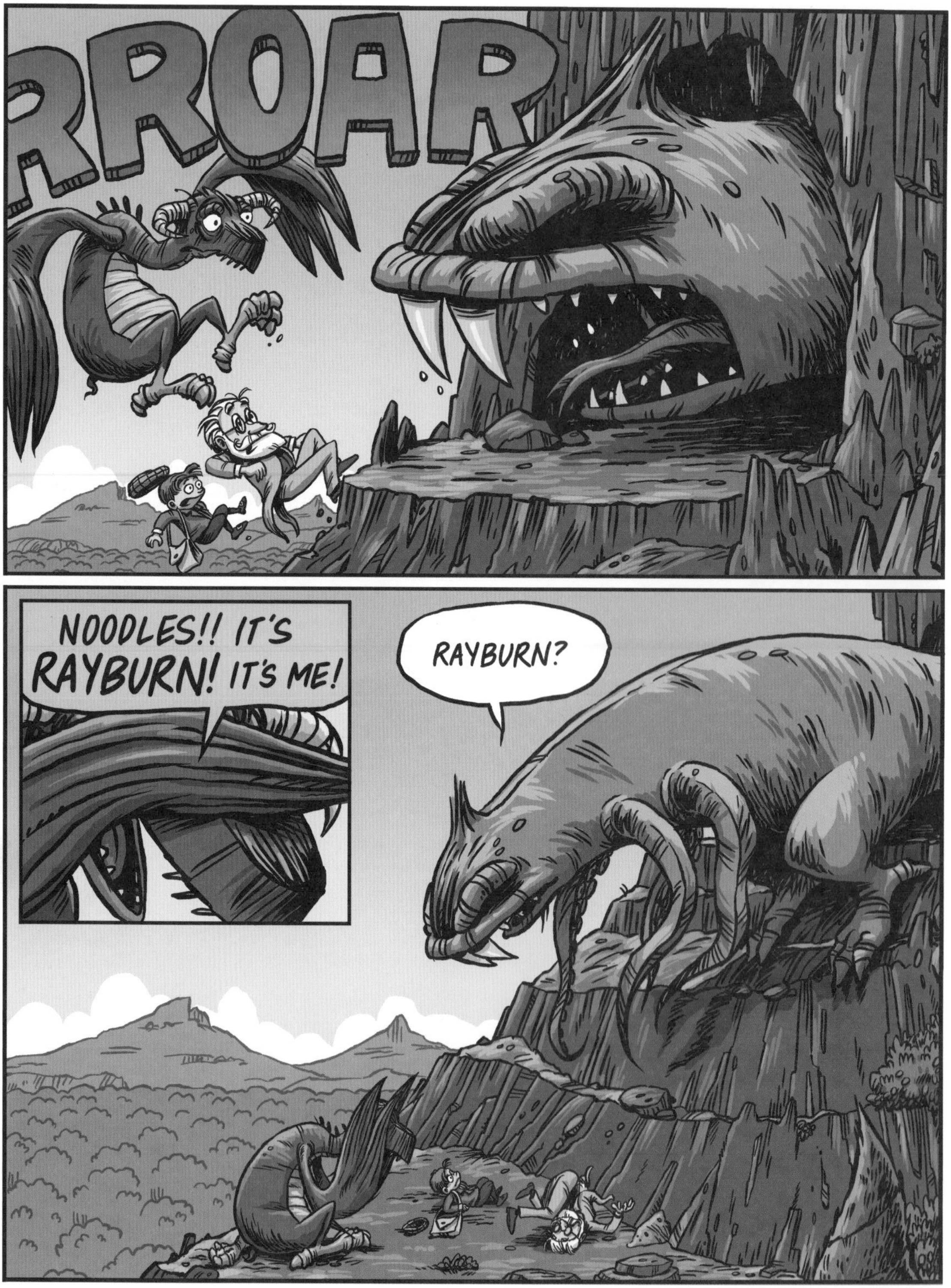
RROAR
NOODLES!! IT'S RAYBURN! IT'S ME!
RAYBURN?

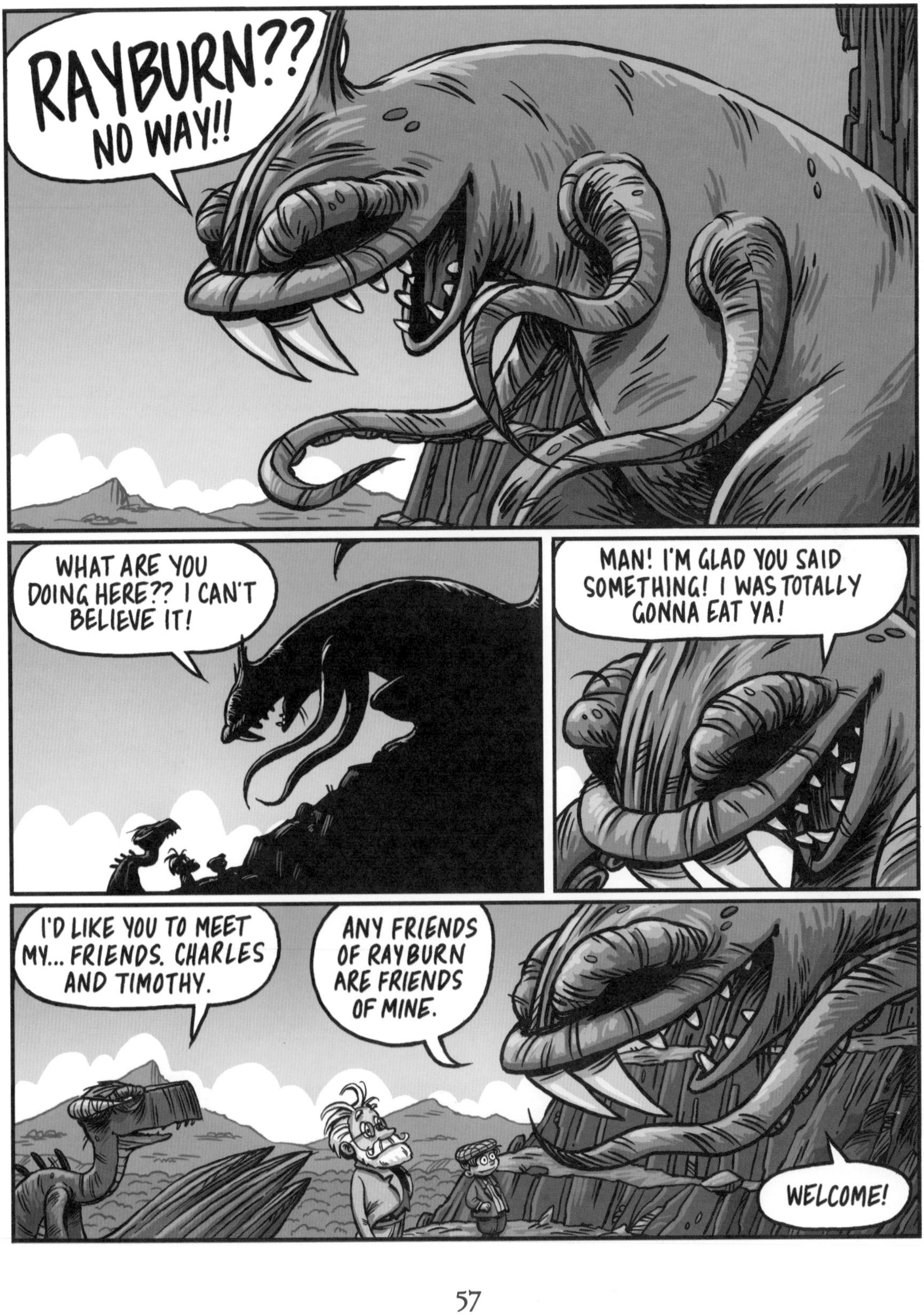
RAYBURN?? NO WAY!!
WHAT ARE YOU DOING HERE?? I CAN'T BELIEVE IT!
MAN! I'M GLAD YOU SAID SOMETHING! I WAS TOTALLY GONNA EAT YA!
I'D LIKE YOU TO MEET MY... FRIENDS. CHARLES AND TIMOTHY.
ANY FRIENDS OF RAYBURN ARE FRIENDS OF MINE.
WELCOME!

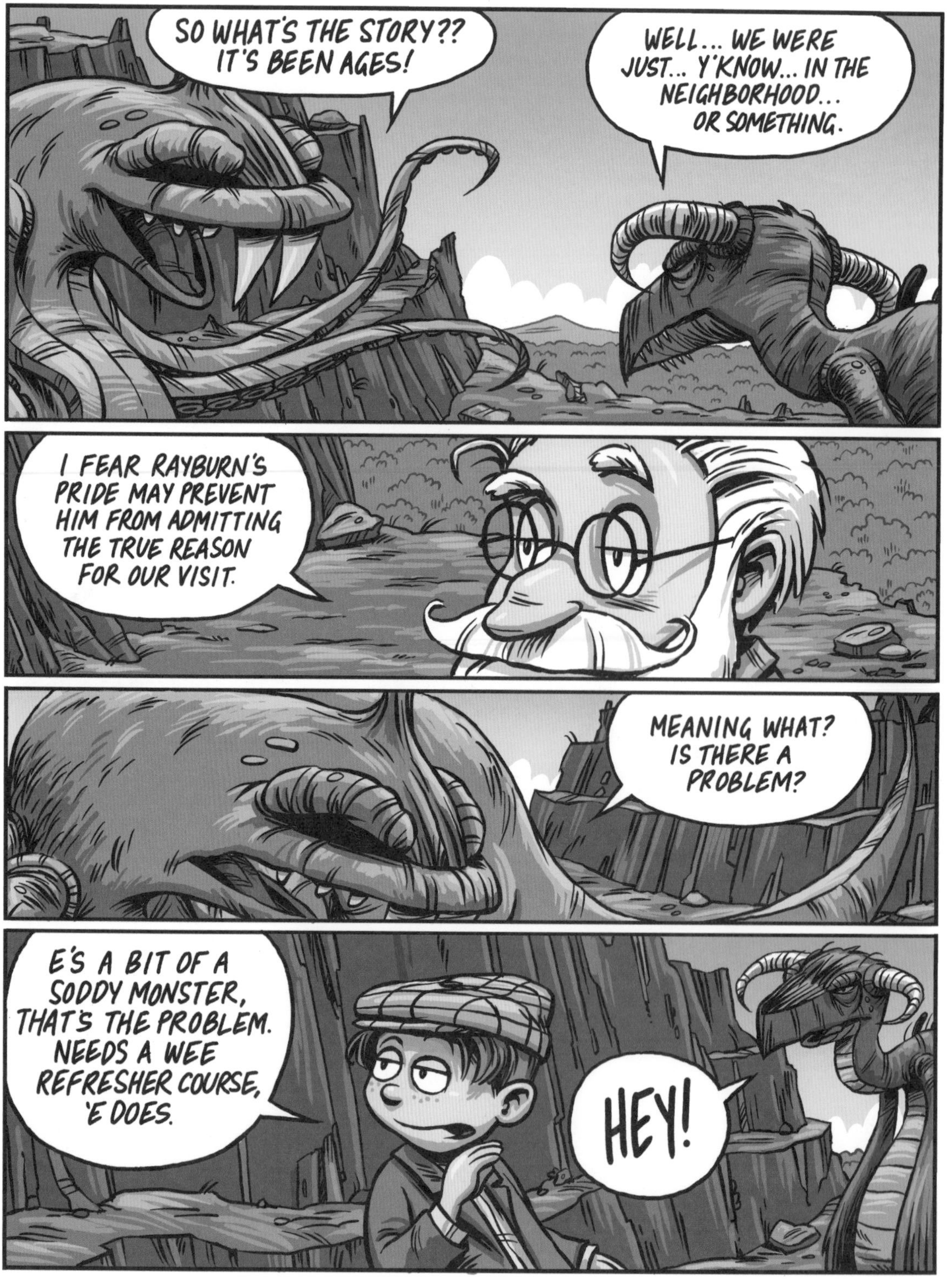
SO WHAT'S THE STORY?? IT'S BEEN AGES!
WELL... WE WERE JUST... Y'KNOW... IN THE NEIGHBORHOOD... OR SOMETHING.
I FEAR RAYBURN'S PRIDE MAY PREVENT HIM FROM ADMITTING THE TRUE REASON FOR OUR VISIT.
MEANING WHAT? IS THERE A PROBLEM?
E'S A BIT OF A SODDY MONSTER, THAT'S THE PROBLEM. NEEDS A WEE REFRESHER COURSE, 'E DOES.
HEY!

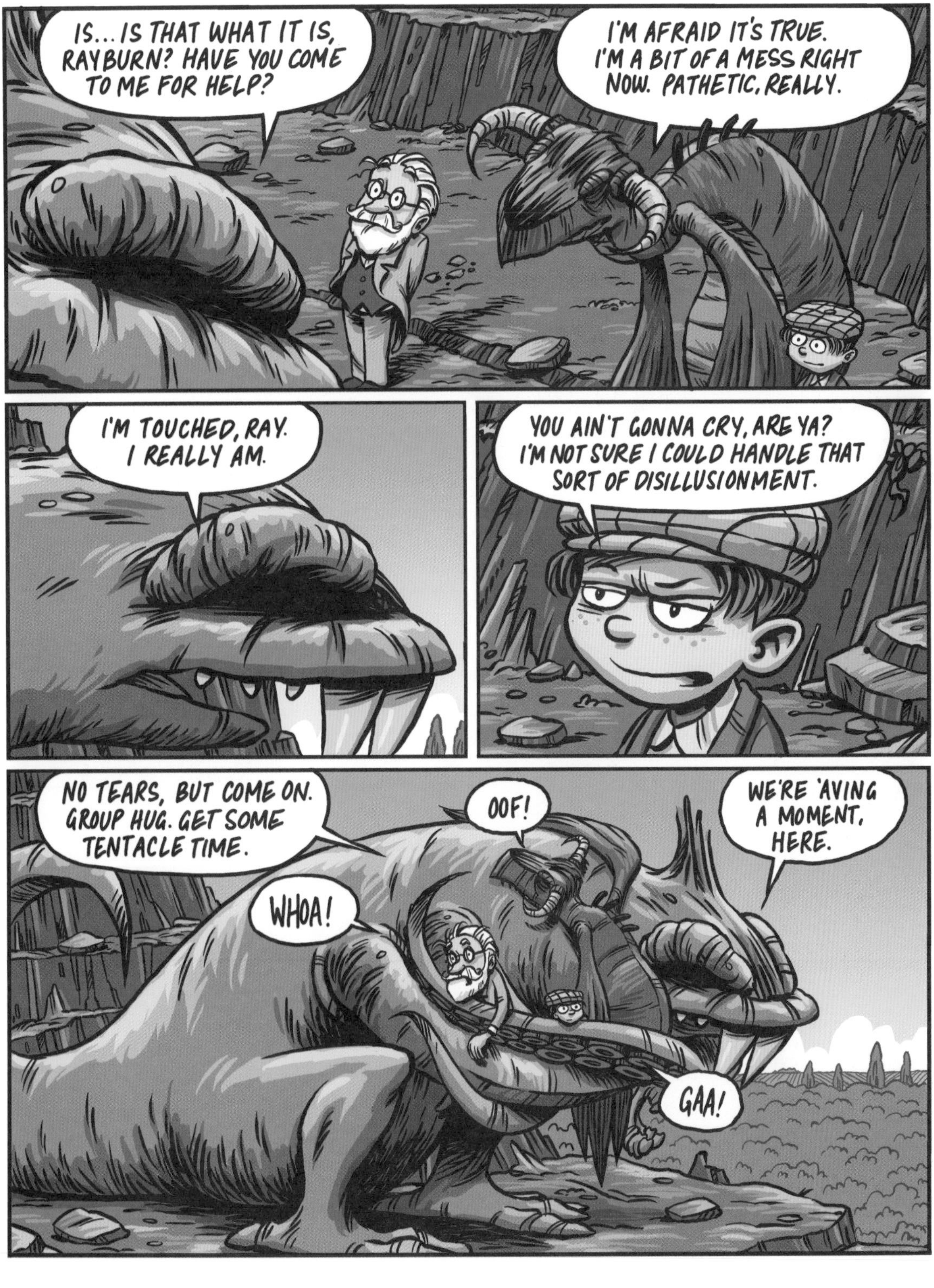
IS... IS THAT WHAT IT IS, RAYBURN? HAVE YOU COME TO ME FOR HELP?
I'M AFRAID IT'S TRUE. I'M A BIT OF A MESS RIGHT NOW. PATHETIC, REALLY.
I'M TOUCHED, RAY. I REALLY AM.
YOU AIN'T GONNA CRY, ARE YA? I'M NOT SURE I COULD HANDLE THAT SORT OF DISILLUSIONMENT.
NO TEARS, BUT COME ON. GROUP HUG. GET SOME TENTACLE TIME.
OOF!
WE'RE 'AVING A MOMENT, HERE.
WHOA!
GAA!

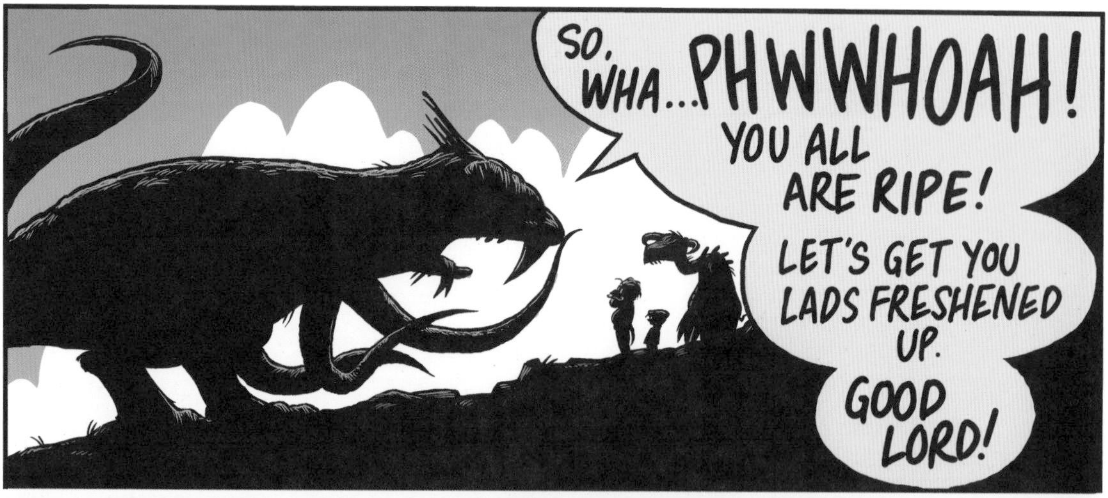
SO, WHA...PHWWHOAH! YOU ALL ARE RIPE! LET'S GET YOU LADS FRESHENED UP. GOOD LORD!

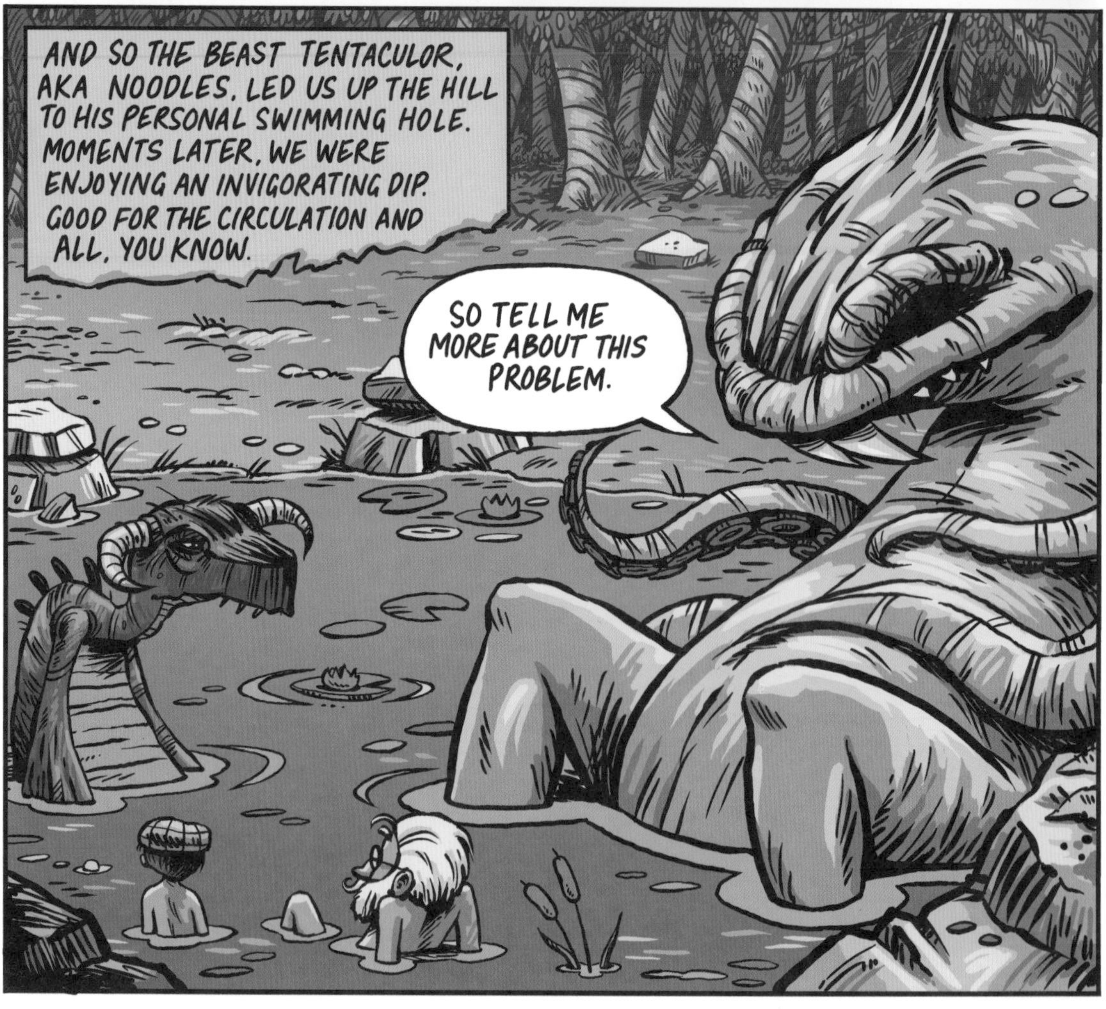
AND SO THE BEAST TENTACULOR, AKA NOODLES, LED US UP THE HILL TO HIS PERSONAL SWIMMING HOLE. MOMENTS LATER, WE WERE ENJOYING AN INVIGORATING DIP. GOOD FOR THE CIRCULATION AND ALL, YOU KNOW.
SO TELL ME MORE ABOUT THIS PROBLEM.

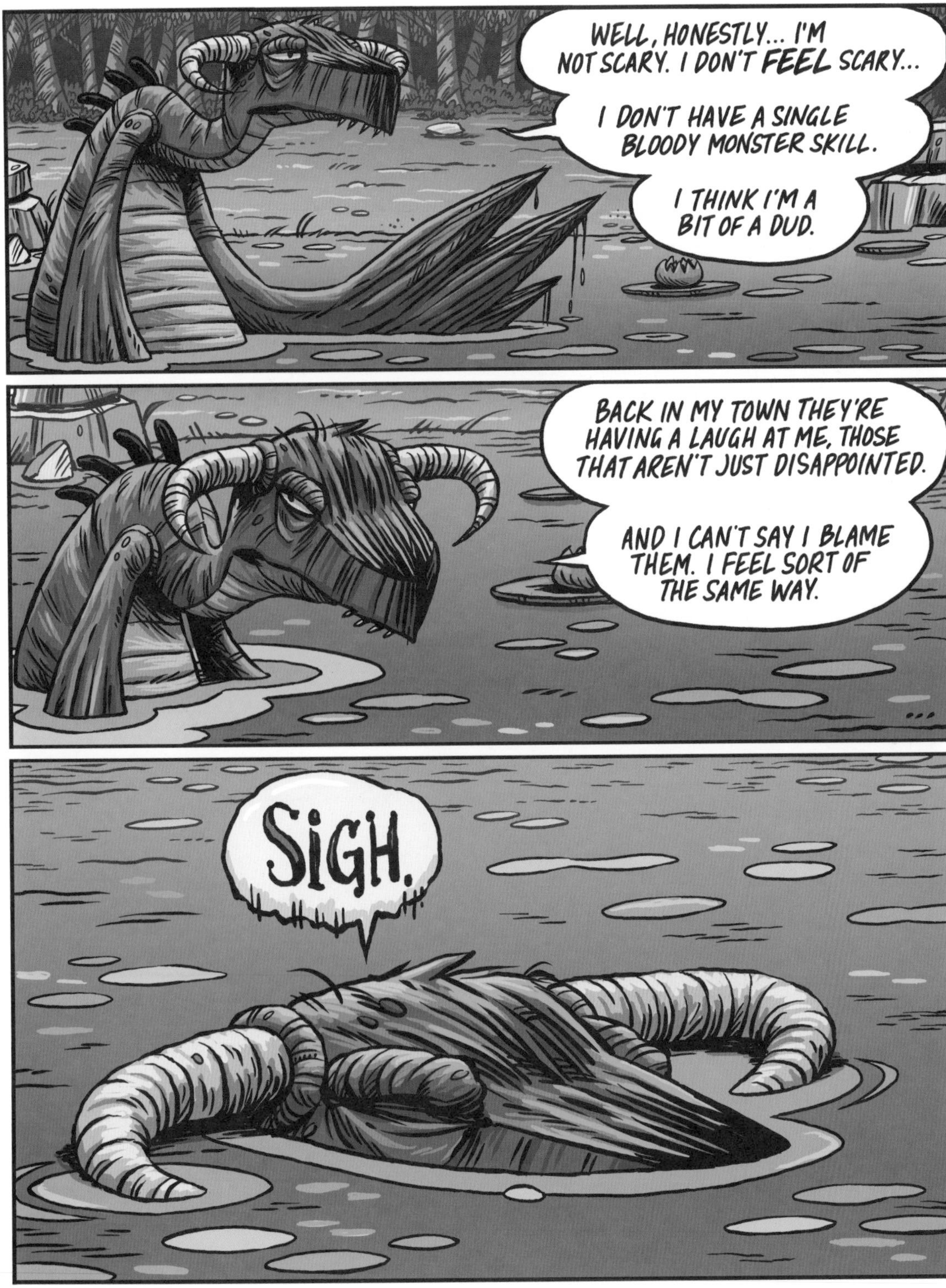
WELL, HONESTLY... I'M NOT SCARY. I DON'T FEEL SCARY...
I DON'T HAVE A SINGLE BLOODY MONSTER SKILL.
I THINK I'M A BIT OF A DUD.
BACK IN MY TOWN THEY'RE HAVING A LAUGH AT ME, THOSE THAT AREN'T JUST DISAPPOINTED.
AND I CAN'T SAY I BLAME THEM. I FEEL SORT OF THE SAME WAY.
SIGH.

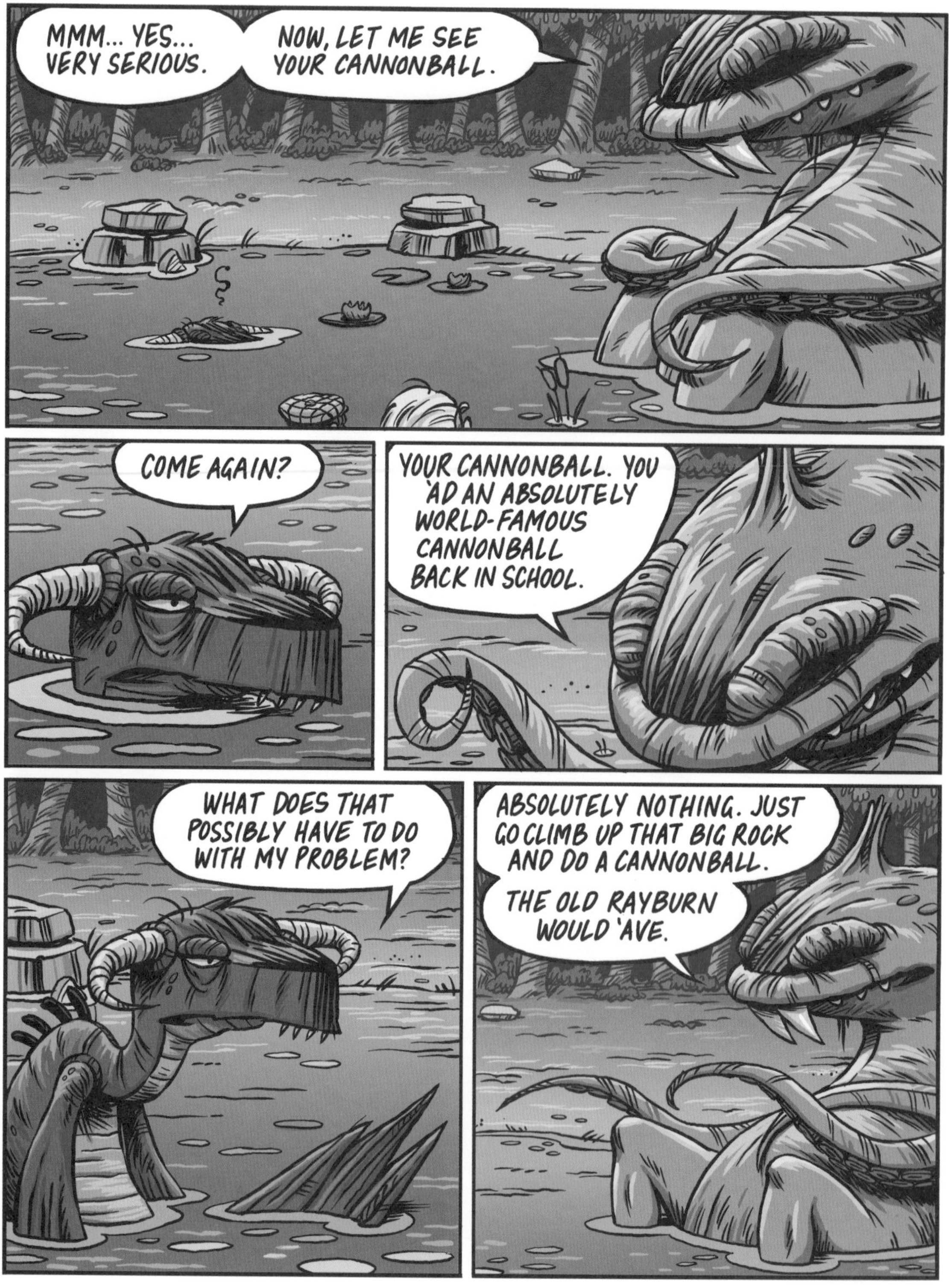
MMM... YES... VERY SERIOUS.
NOW, LET ME SEE YOUR CANNONBALL.
COME AGAIN?
YOUR CANNONBALL. YOU 'AD AN ABSOLUTELY WORLD-FAMOUS CANNONBALL BACK IN SCHOOL.
WHAT DOES THAT POSSIBLY HAVE TO DO WITH MY PROBLEM?
ABSOLUTELY NOTHING. JUST GO CLIMB UP THAT BIG ROCK AND DO A CANNONBALL.
THE OLD RAYBURN WOULD 'AVE.

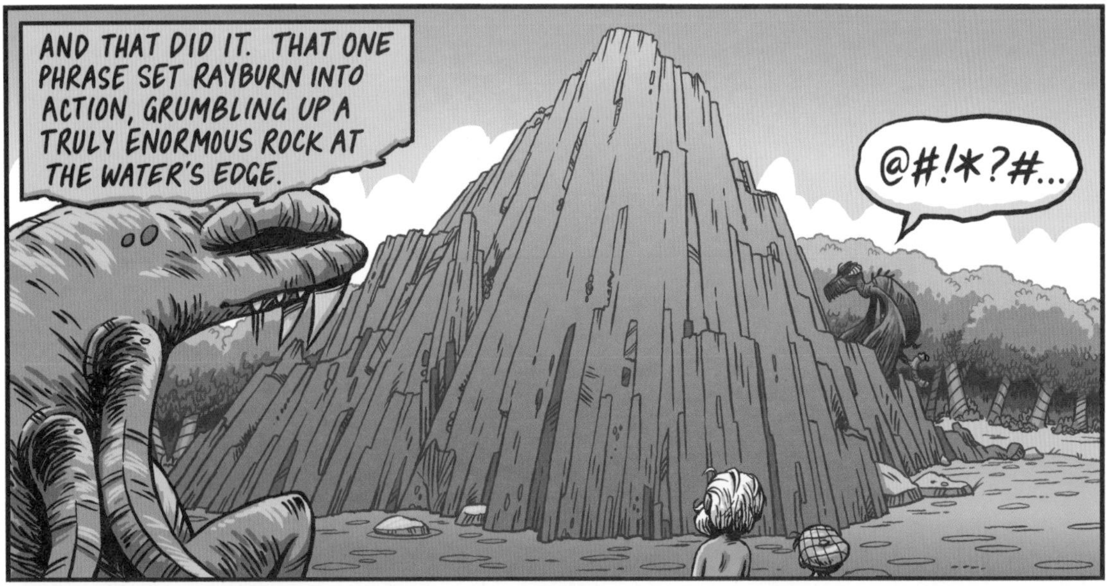
AND THAT DID IT. THAT ONE PHRASE SET RAYBURN INTO ACTION, GRUMBLING UP A TRULY ENORMOUS ROCK AT THE WATER'S EDGE.
@#!*?#...

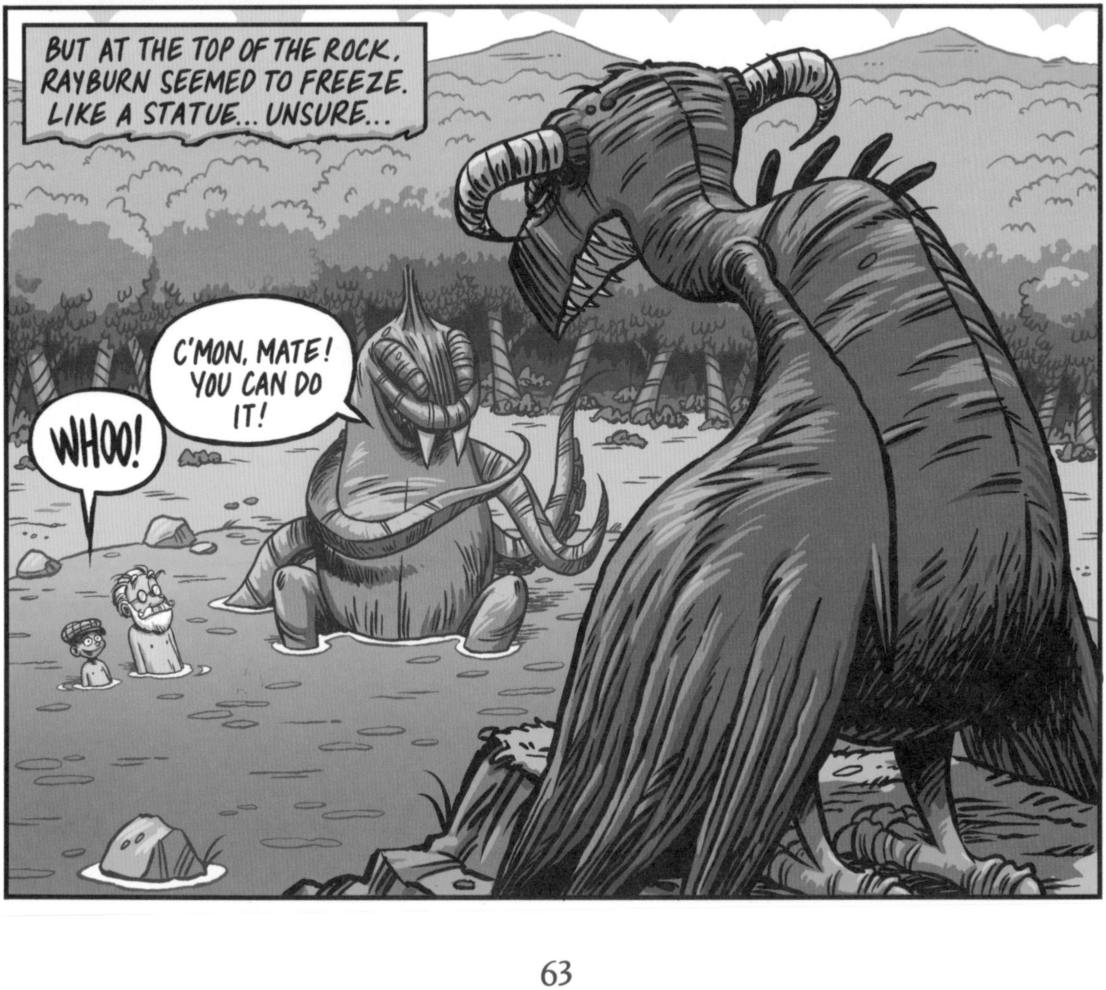
BUT AT THE TOP OF THE ROCK, RAYBURN SEEMED TO FREEZE. LIKE A STATUE... UNSURE...
C'MON, MATE! YOU CAN DO IT!
WHOO!

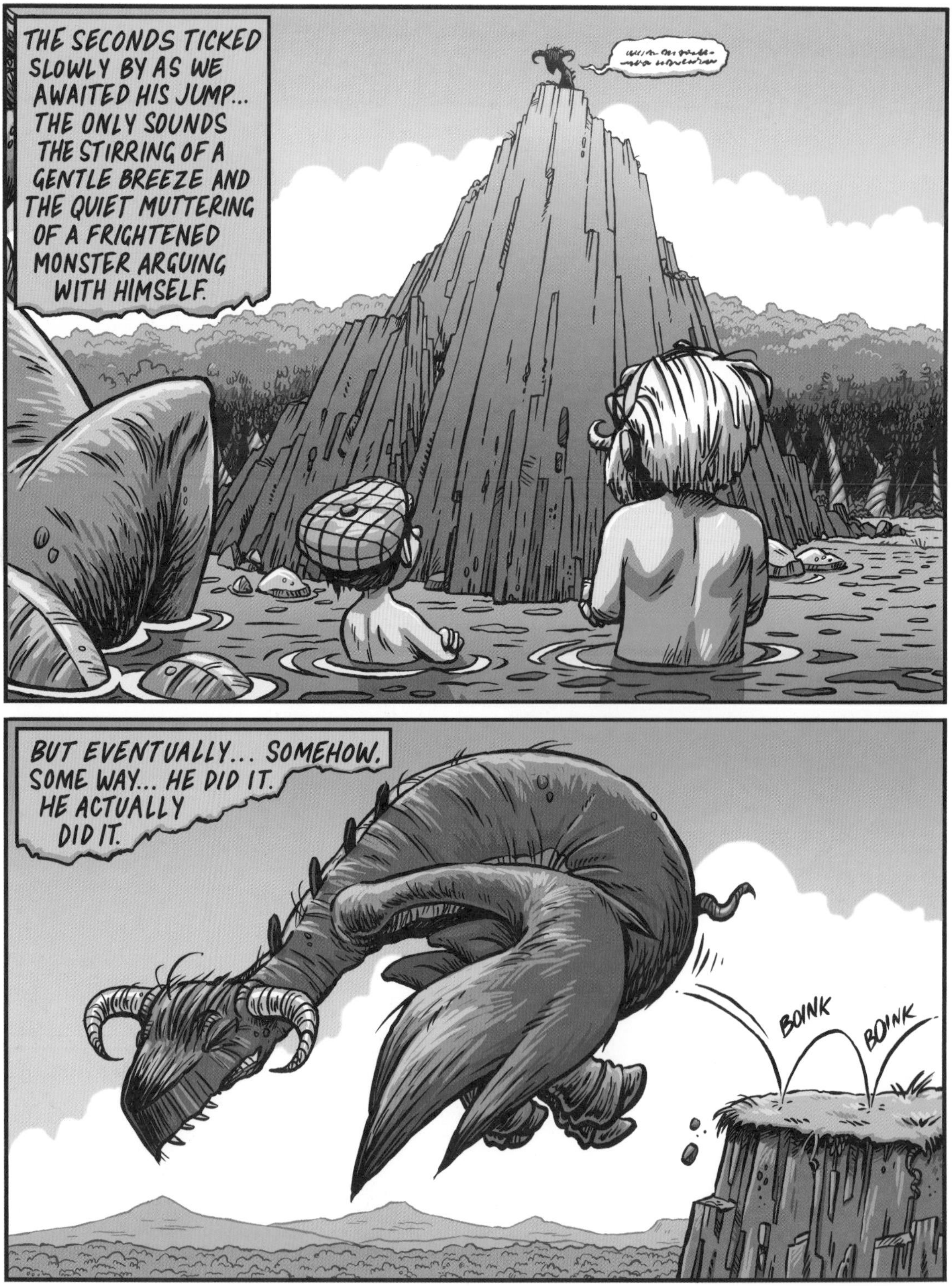

THE SECONDS TICKED SLOWLY BY AS WE AWAITED HIS JUMP... THE ONLY SOUNDS THE STIRRING OF A GENTLE BREEZE AND THE QUIET MUTTERING OF A FRIGHTENED MONSTER ARGUING WITH HIMSELF.
BUT EVENTUALLY... SOMEHOW. SOME WAY... HE DID IT. HE ACTUALLY DID IT.
BOINK
BOINK

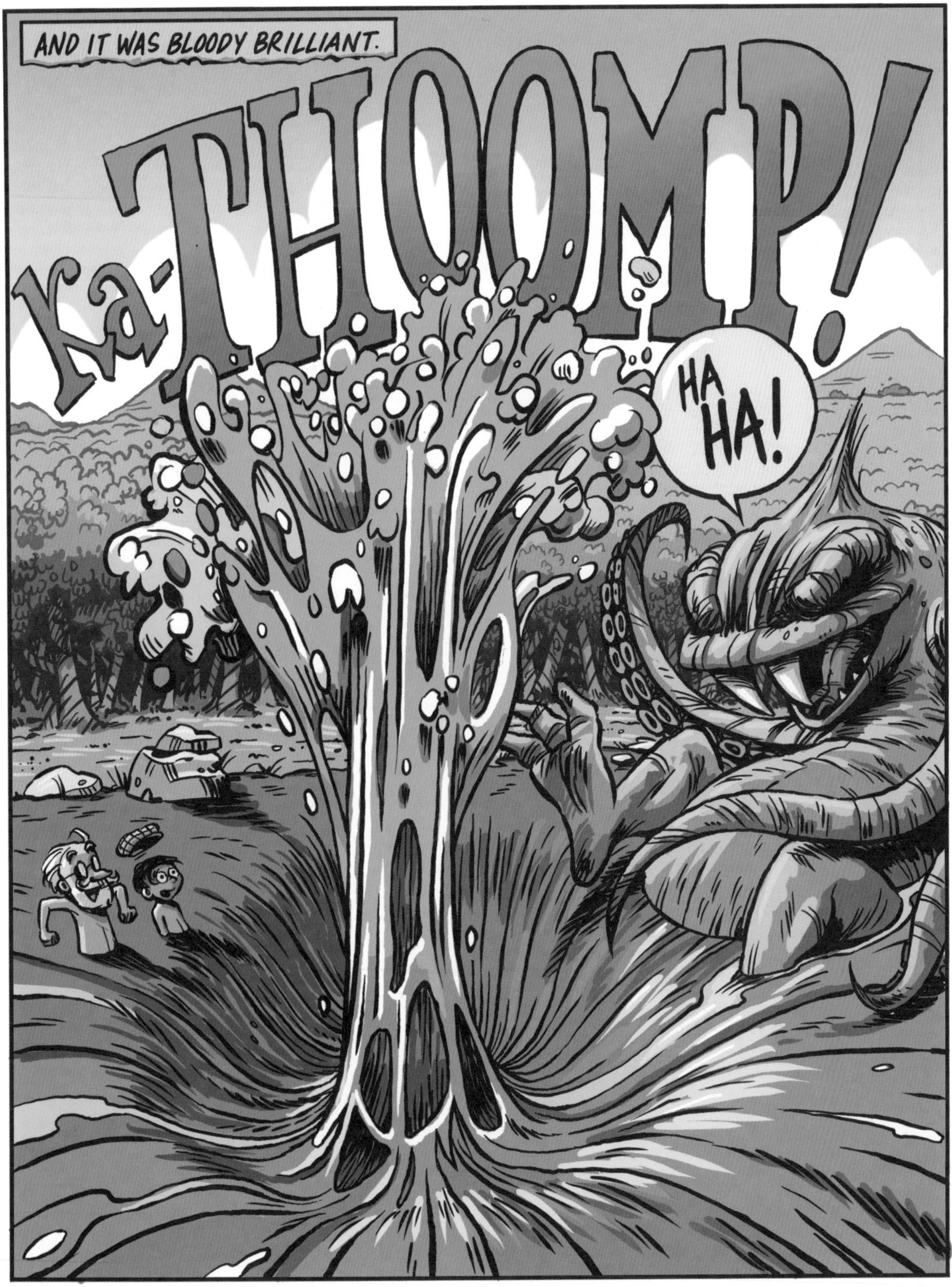
AND IT WAS BLOODY BRILLIANT.
KA-THOOMP!
HA HA!

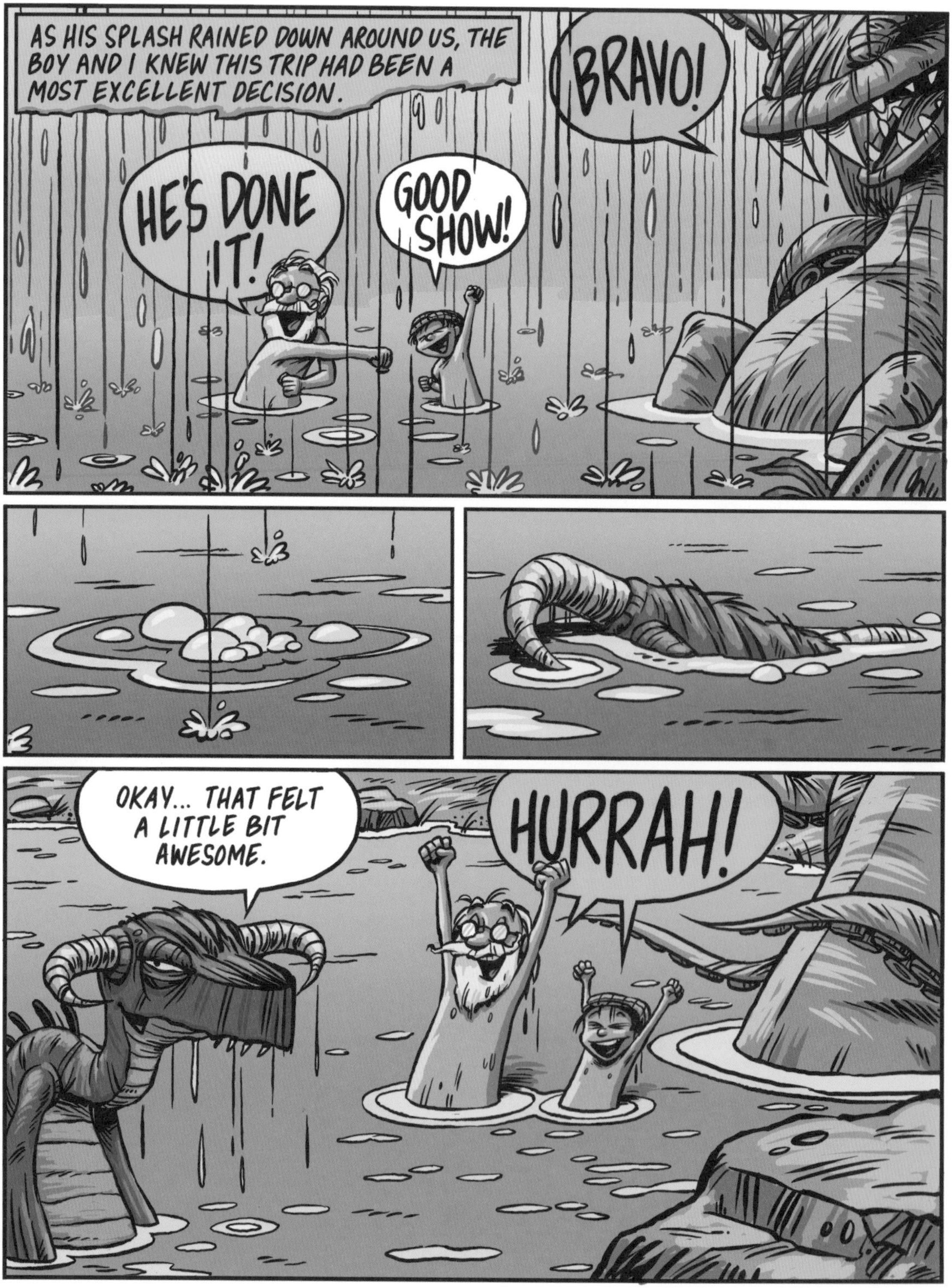
AS HIS SPLASH RAINED DOWN AROUND US, THE BOY AND I KNEW THIS TRIP HAD BEEN A MOST EXCELLENT DECISION.
BRAVO!
HE'S DONE IT!
GOOD SHOW!
OKAY... THAT FELT A LITTLE BIT AWESOME.
HURRAH!

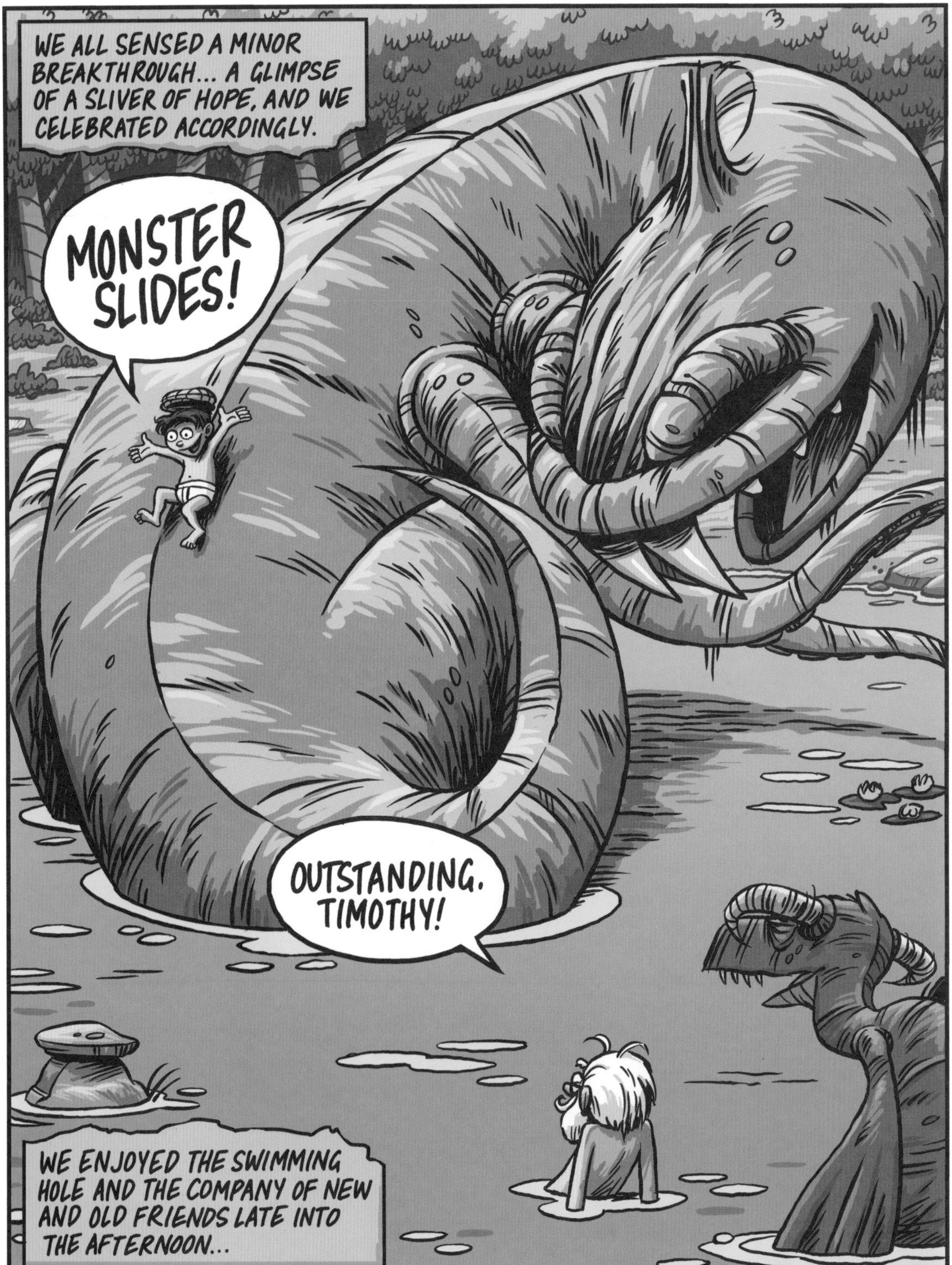
WE ALL SENSED A MINOR BREAKTHROUGH... A GLIMPSE OF A SLIVER OF HOPE, AND WE CELEBRATED ACCORDINGLY.
MONSTER SLIDES!
OUTSTANDING, TIMOTHY!
WE ENJOYED THE SWIMMING HOLE AND THE COMPANY OF NEW AND OLD FRIENDS LATE INTO THE AFTERNOON...

SO... HOW DO YOU DO IT, NOODLES?
DO WHAT?
ATTACK YOUR TOWN! SCARE YOUR PEOPLE! YOU MAKE IT LOOK EASY.
WELL, IN A WAY, IT IS. LIKE LEAPING FROM THAT ROCK TODAY. YOU JUST... GO... RUN... JUMP... STOMP... SMASH... ROAR.
AND DON'T FORGET. YOUR TOWN IS PULLING FOR YA. THEY WANT YOU TO BE FRIGHTENING.
YEAH. I'VE ALWAYS HAD TROUBLE WITH THAT CONCEPT.

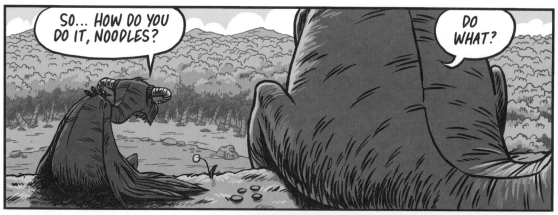

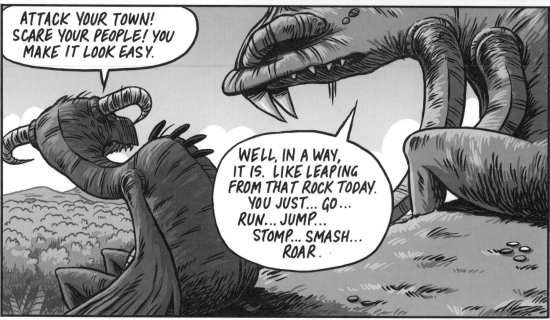

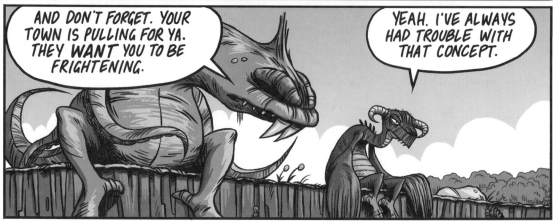

THAT'S REALLY ALL THEY WANT, YOU KNOW? JUST FRIGHTEN THE STUFFING OUT OF THEM NOW AND AGAIN.

PLUS IT 'ELPS THEM SLEEP AT NIGHT, KNOWING YOU COULD PROTECT THEM IF THE MURK WERE TO COME CALLING.

(SHUDDER) I TRY DESPERATELY NOT TO THINK ABOUT THAT.

YEAH, BUT YOU KIND OF 'AVE TO, A BIT. THE MURK DON'T PLAY BY THE RULES, 'E DON'T.

I 'EAR 'E'S NOT ACTUALLY A MONSTER AT ALL. 'E'S SOMETHING FAR WORSE.

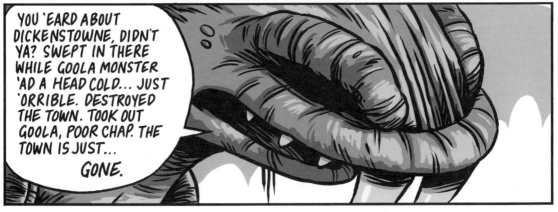

YOU 'EARD ABOUT DICKENSTOWNE, DIDN'T YA? SWEPT IN THERE WHILE GOOLA MONSTER 'AD A HEAD COLD... JUST 'ORRIBLE. DESTROYED THE TOWN. TOOK OUT GOOLA, POOR CHAP. THE TOWN IS JUST...

GONE.

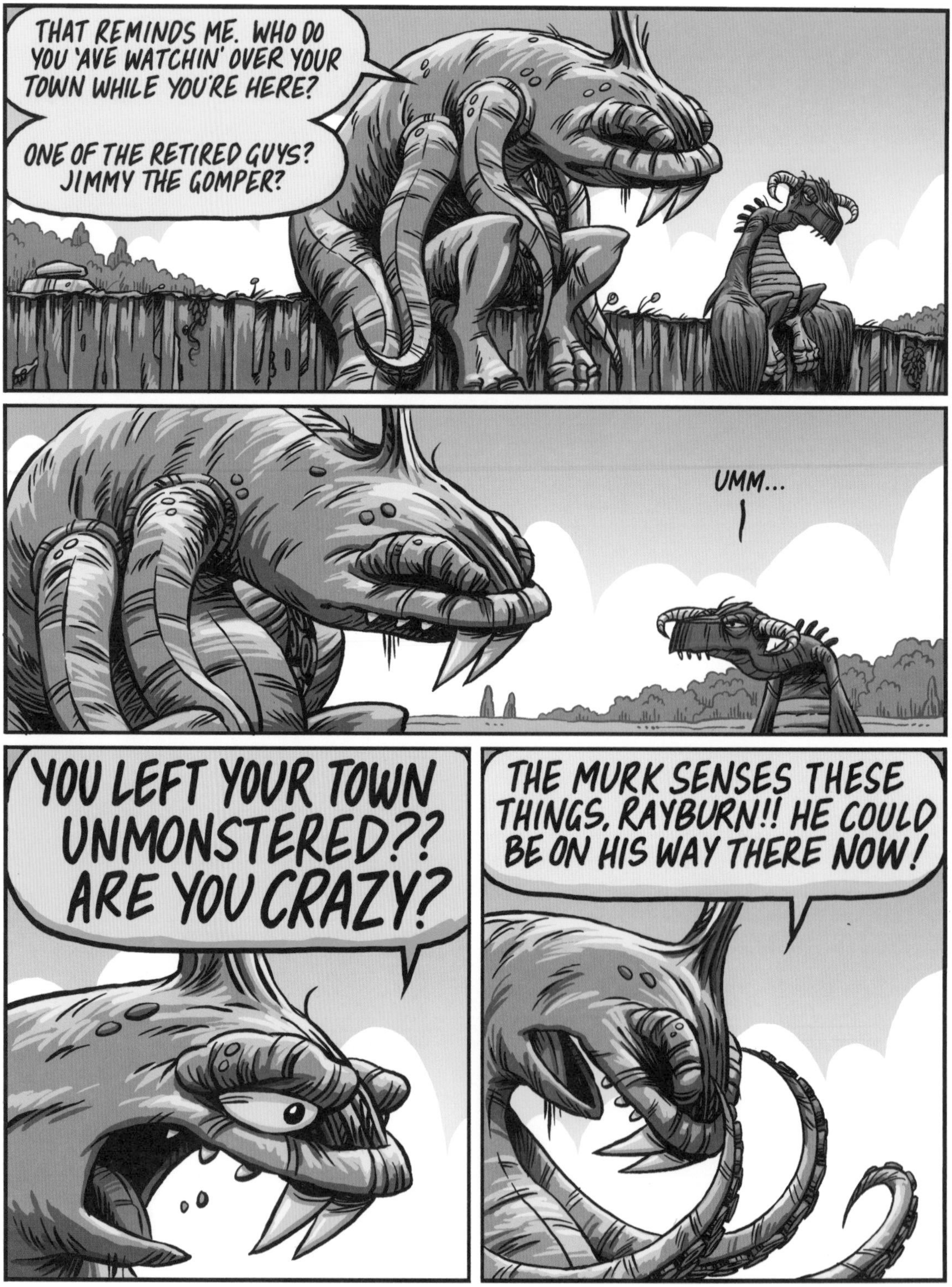
THAT REMINDS ME. WHO DO YOU 'AVE WATCHIN' OVER YOUR TOWN WHILE YOU'RE HERE?
ONE OF THE RETIRED GUYS? JIMMY THE GOMPER?
UMM...
YOU LEFT YOUR TOWN UNMONSTERED?? ARE YOU CRAZY?
THE MURK SENSES THESE THINGS, RAYBURN!! HE COULD BE ON HIS WAY THERE NOW!

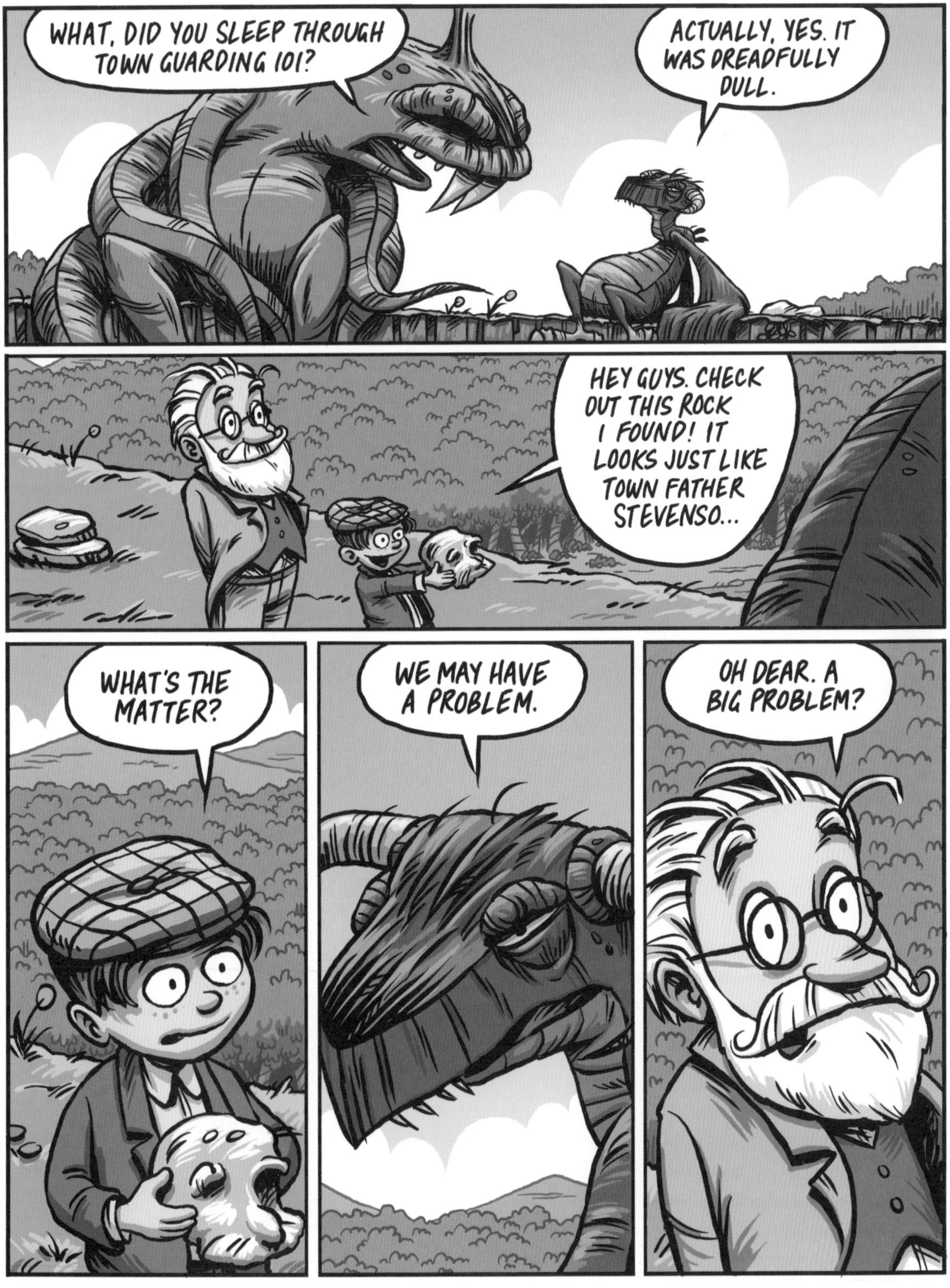

WHAT, DID YOU SLEEP THROUGH TOWN GUARDING 101?
ACTUALLY, YES. IT WAS DREADFULLY DULL.
HEY GUYS. CHECK OUT THIS ROCK I FOUND! IT LOOKS JUST LIKE TOWN FATHER STEVENSO...
WHAT'S THE MATTER?
WE MAY HAVE A PROBLEM.
OH DEAR. A BIG PROBLEM?

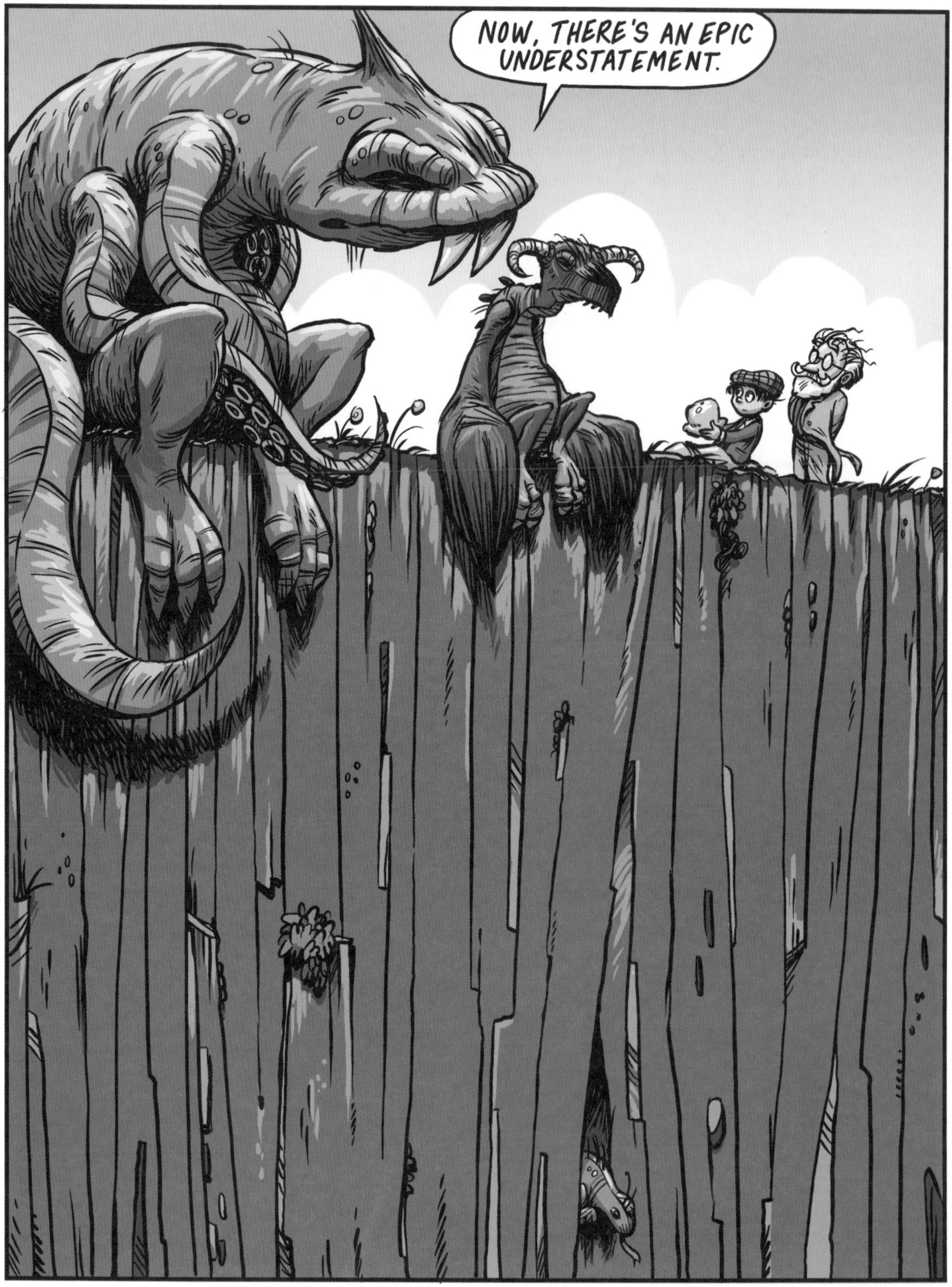
NOW, THERE'S AN EPIC UNDERSTATEMENT.

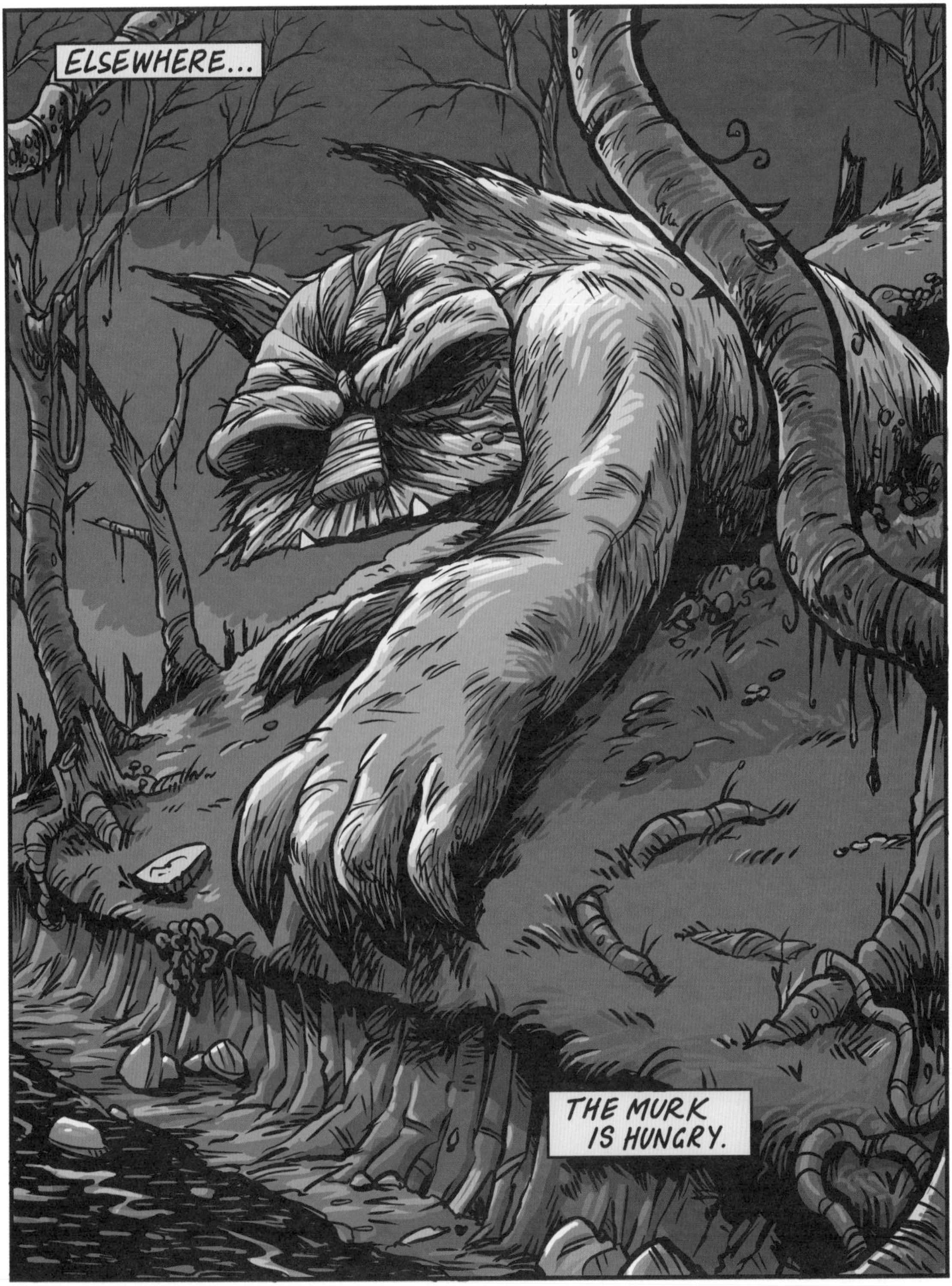
ELSEWHERE...
THE MURK IS HUNGRY.

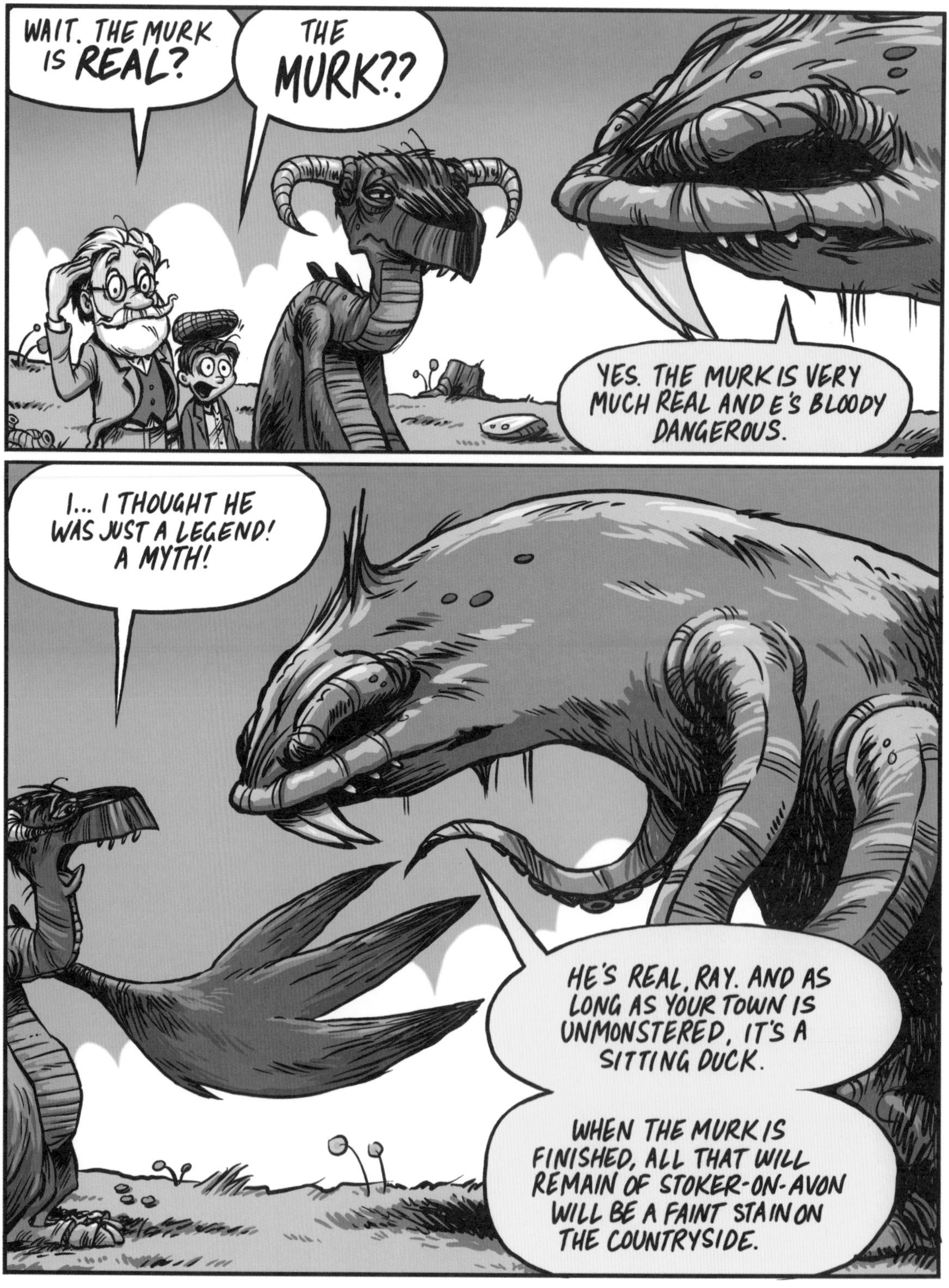
WAIT. THE MURK IS REAL?
THE MURK??
YES. THE MURK IS VERY MUCH REAL AND E'S BLOODY DANGEROUS.
I... I THOUGHT HE WAS JUST A LEGEND! A MYTH!
HE'S REAL, RAY. AND AS LONG AS YOUR TOWN IS UNMONSTERED, IT'S A SITTING DUCK.
WHEN THE MURK IS FINISHED, ALL THAT WILL REMAIN OF STOKER-ON-AVON WILL BE A FAINT STAIN ON THE COUNTRYSIDE.

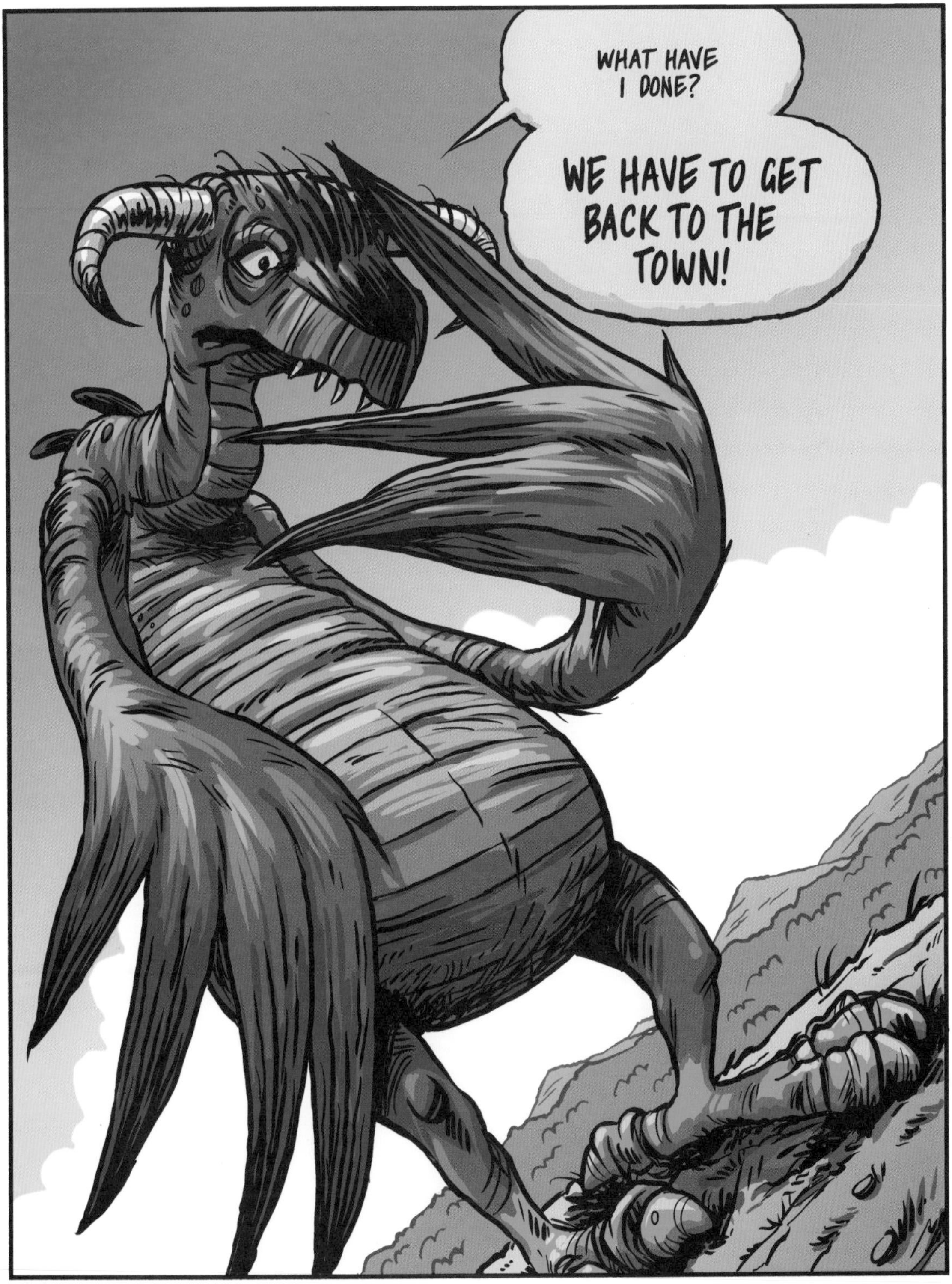
WHAT HAVE I DONE?
WE HAVE TO GET BACK TO THE TOWN!

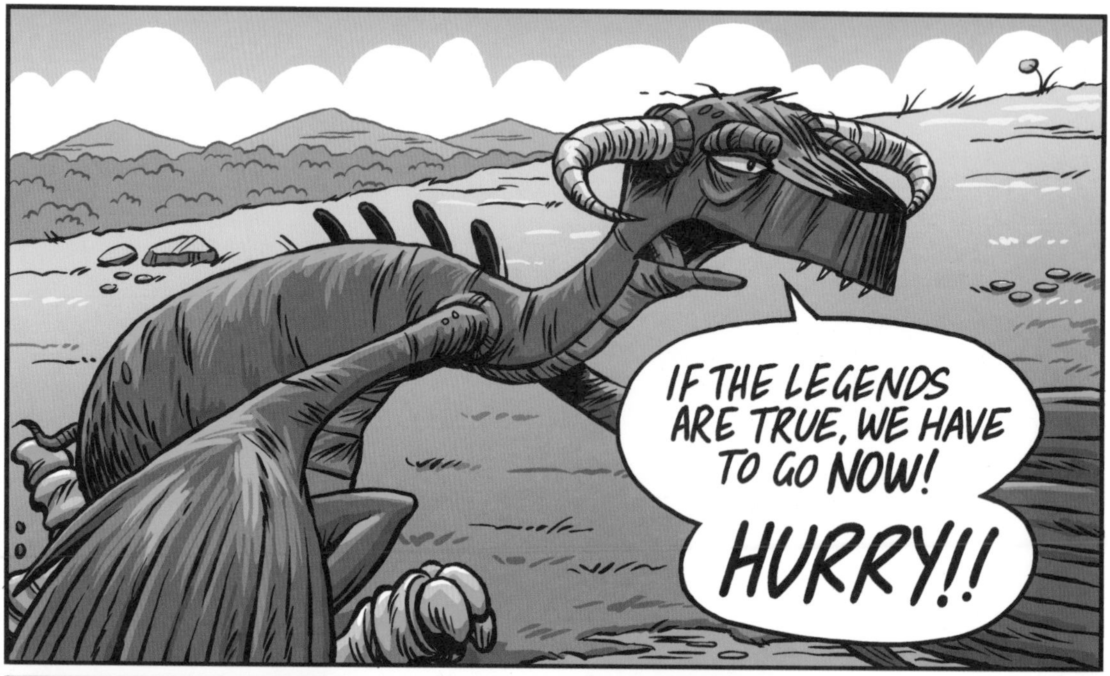
IF THE LEGENDS ARE TRUE, WE HAVE TO GO NOW!
HURRY!!

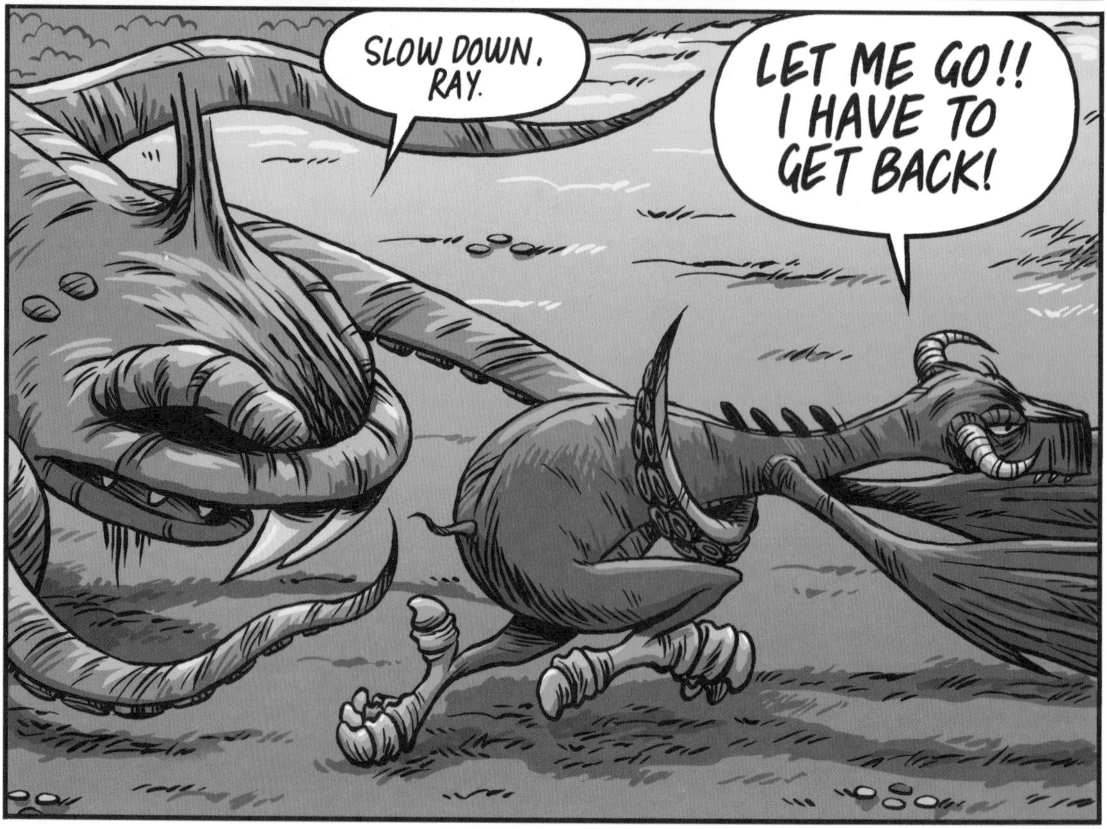
SLOW DOWN, RAY.
LET ME GO!! I HAVE TO GET BACK!

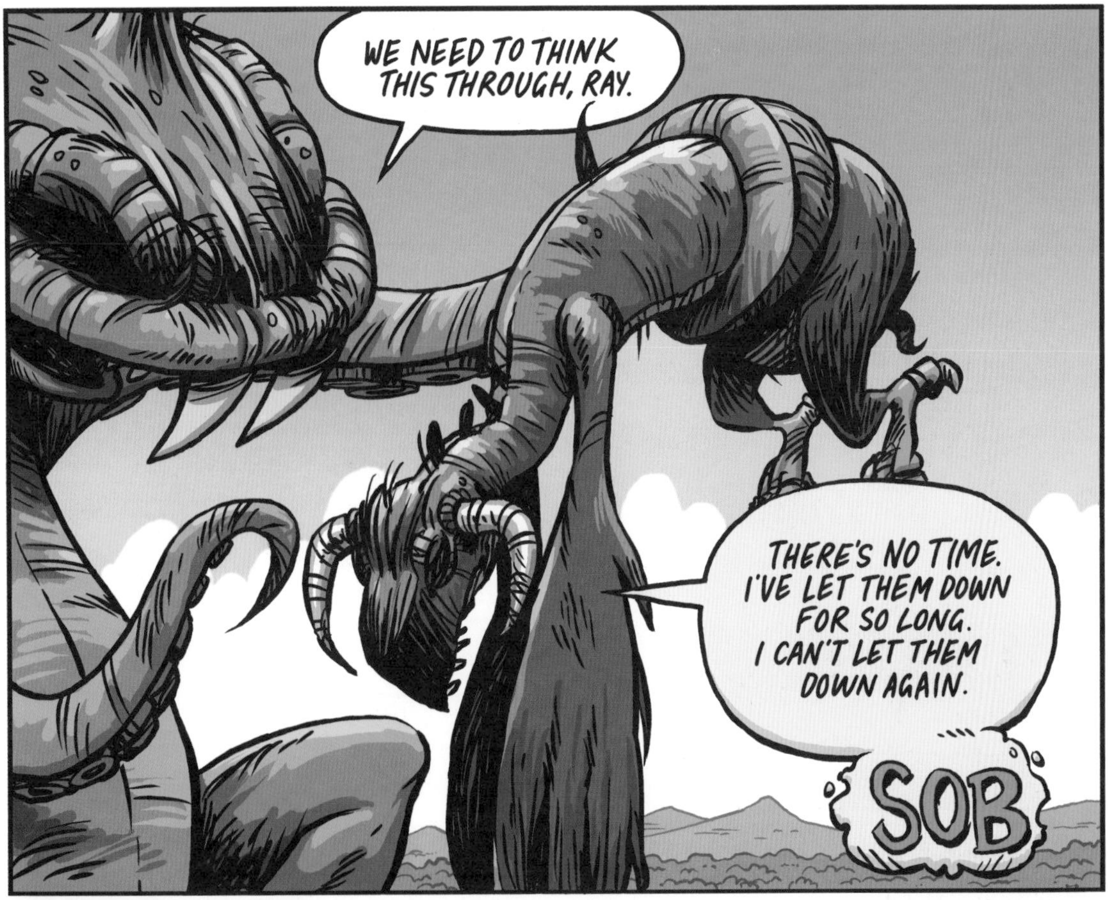
WE NEED TO THINK THIS THROUGH, RAY.
THERE'S NO TIME. I'VE LET THEM DOWN FOR SO LONG. I CAN'T LET THEM DOWN AGAIN.
SOB

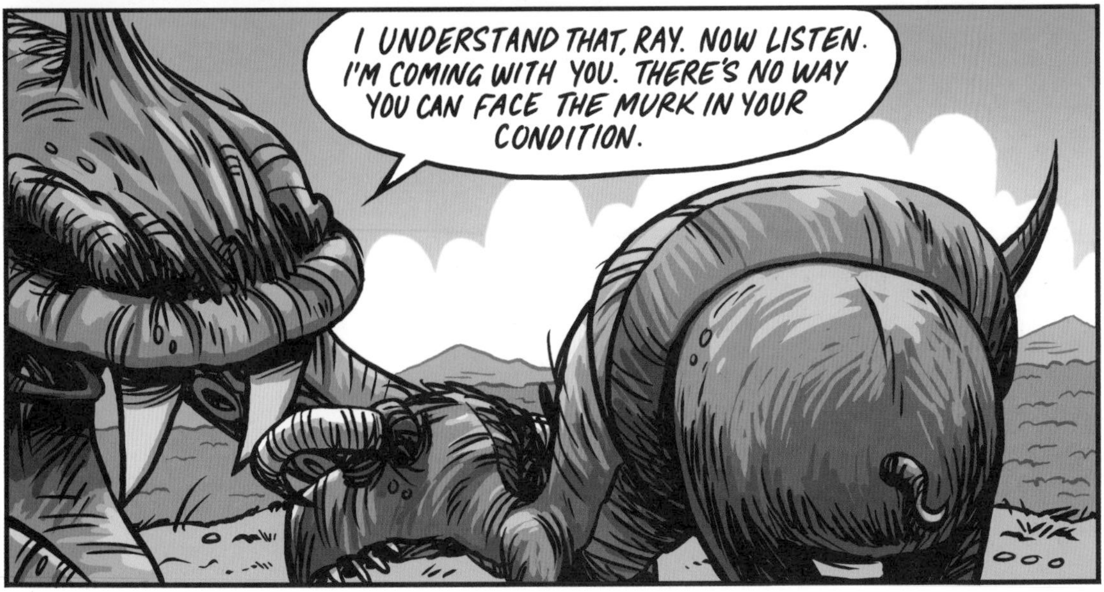
I UNDERSTAND THAT, RAY. NOW LISTEN. I'M COMING WITH YOU. THERE'S NO WAY YOU CAN FACE THE MURK IN YOUR CONDITION.

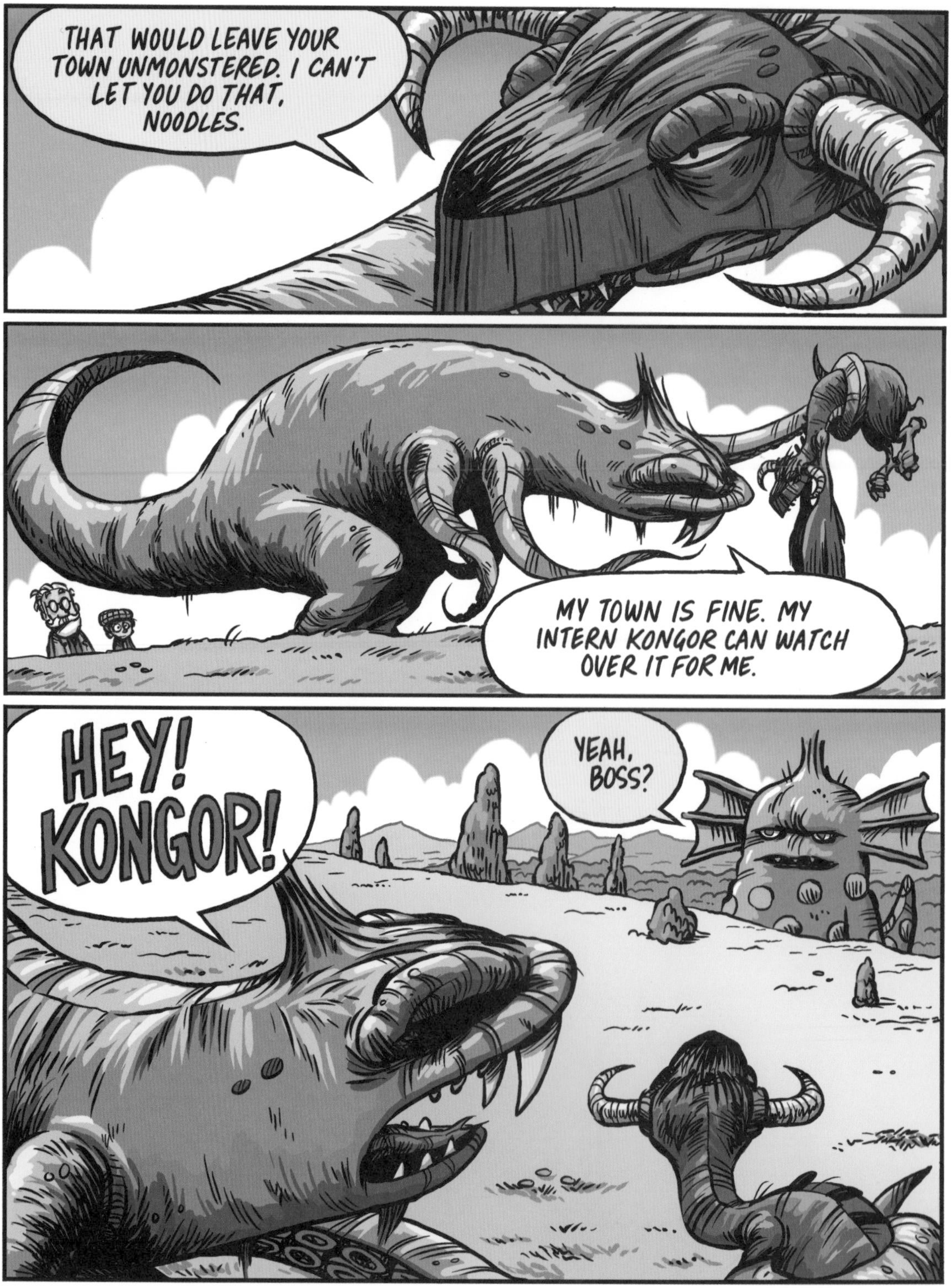
THAT WOULD LEAVE YOUR TOWN UNMONSTERED. I CAN'T LET YOU DO THAT, NOODLES.
MY TOWN IS FINE. MY INTERN KONGOR CAN WATCH OVER IT FOR ME.
HEY! KONGOR!
YEAH, BOSS?

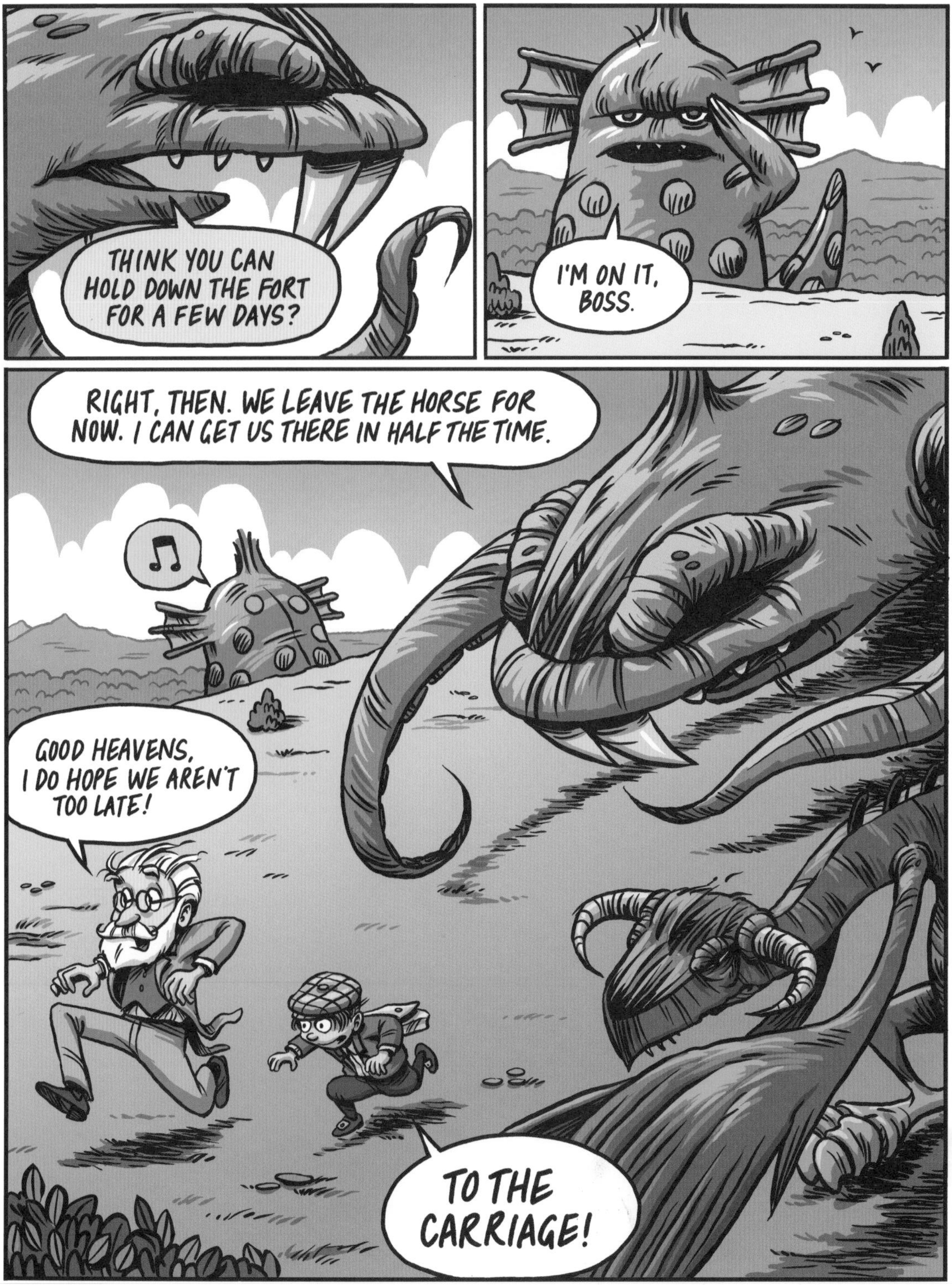
THINK YOU CAN HOLD DOWN THE FORT FOR A FEW DAYS?
I'M ON IT, BOSS.
RIGHT, THEN. WE LEAVE THE HORSE FOR NOW. I CAN GET US THERE IN HALF THE TIME.
GOOD HEAVENS, I DO HOPE WE AREN'T TOO LATE!
TO THE CARRIAGE!

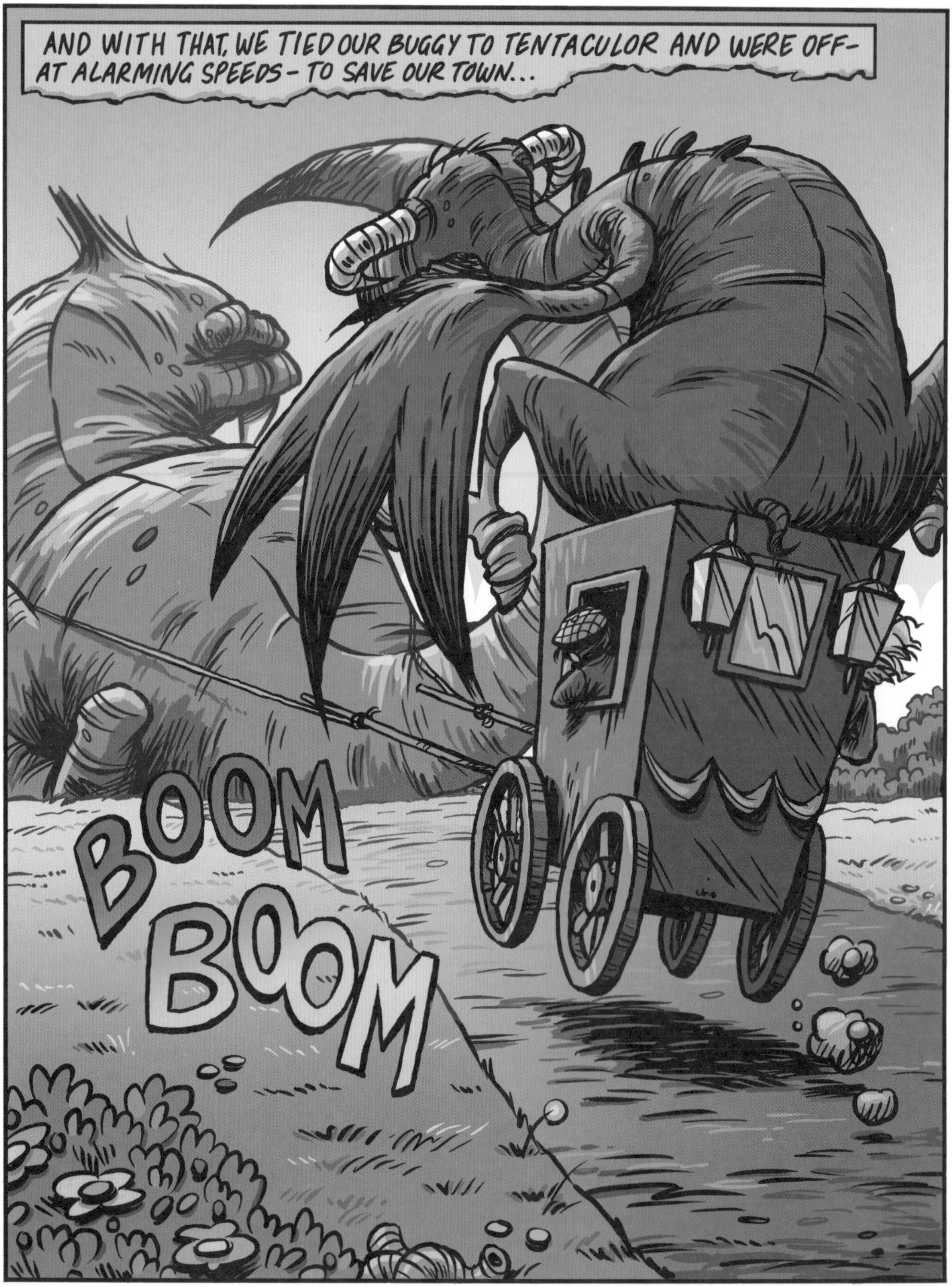
AND WITH THAT, WE TIED OUR BUGGY TO TENTACULOR AND WERE OFF-
AT ALARMING SPEEDS - TO SAVE OUR TOWN...
BOOM
BOOM

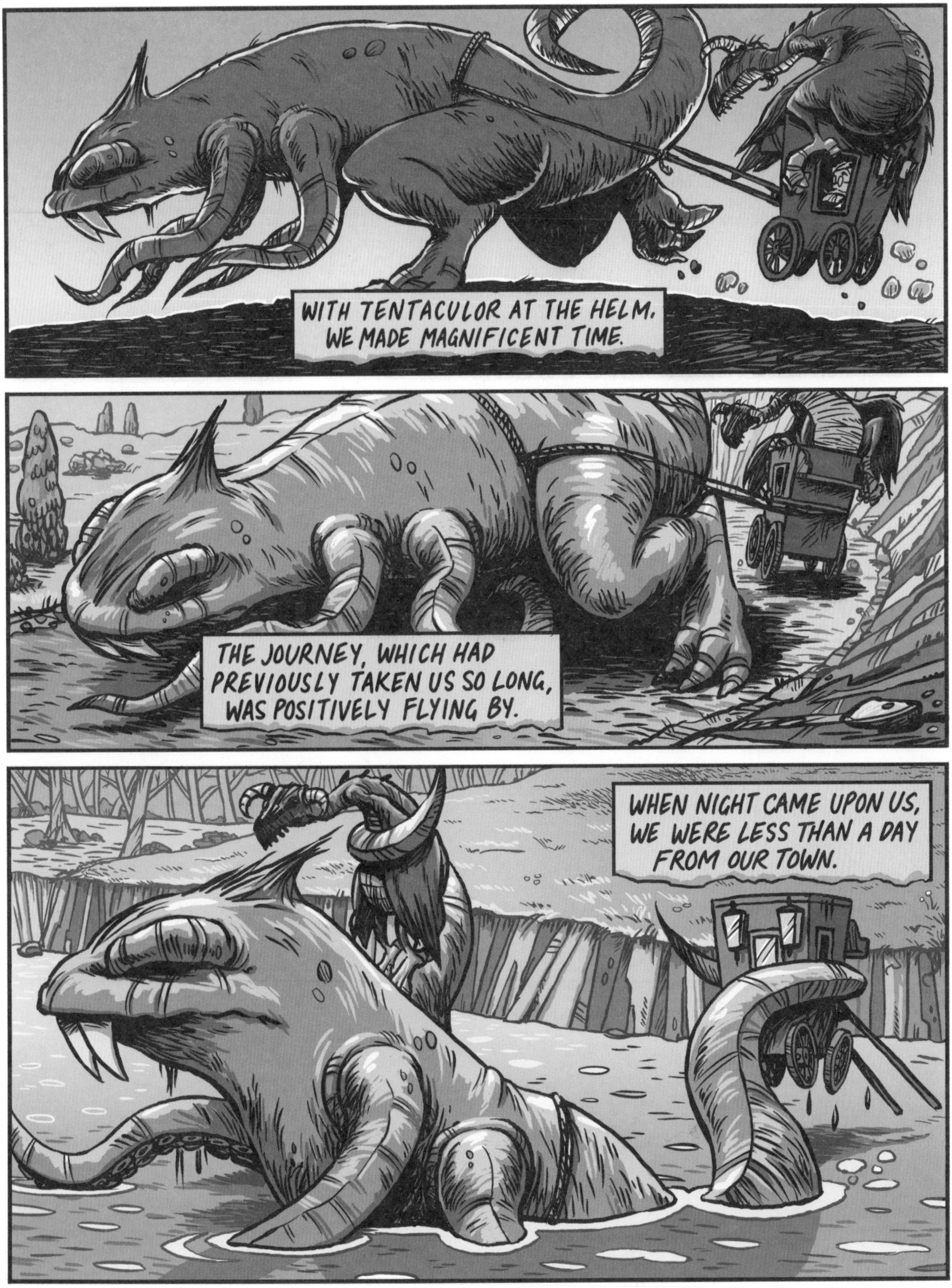
WITH TENTACULOR AT THE HELM, WE MADE MAGNIFICENT TIME.
THE JOURNEY, WHICH HAD PREVIOUSLY TAKEN US SO LONG, WAS POSITIVELY FLYING BY.
WHEN NIGHT CAME UPON US, WE WERE LESS THAN A DAY FROM OUR TOWN.

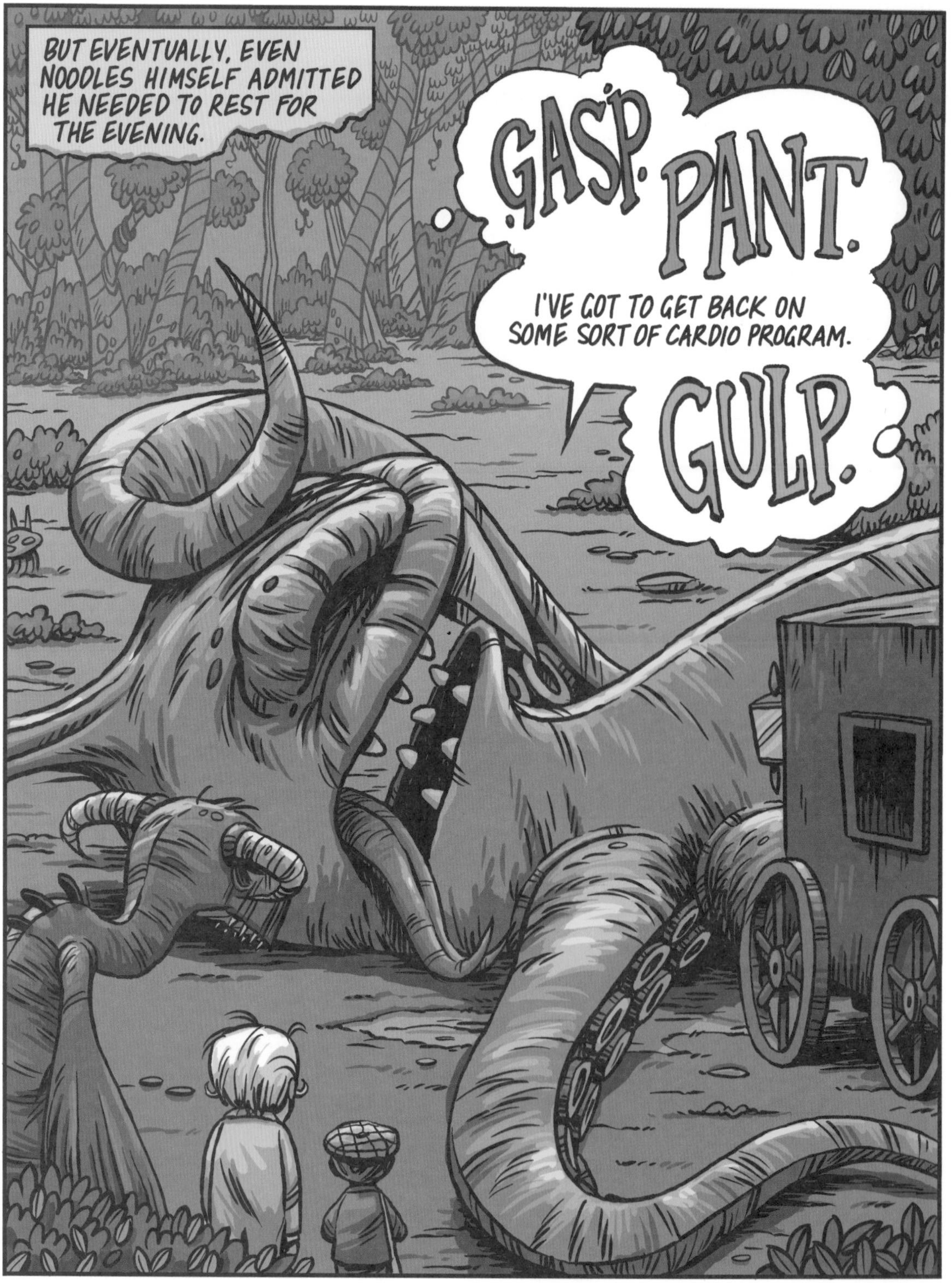
BUT EVENTUALLY, EVEN NOODLES HIMSELF ADMITTED HE NEEDED TO REST FOR THE EVENING.
GASP. PANT.
I'VE GOT TO GET BACK ON SOME SORT OF CARDIO PROGRAM.
GULP.

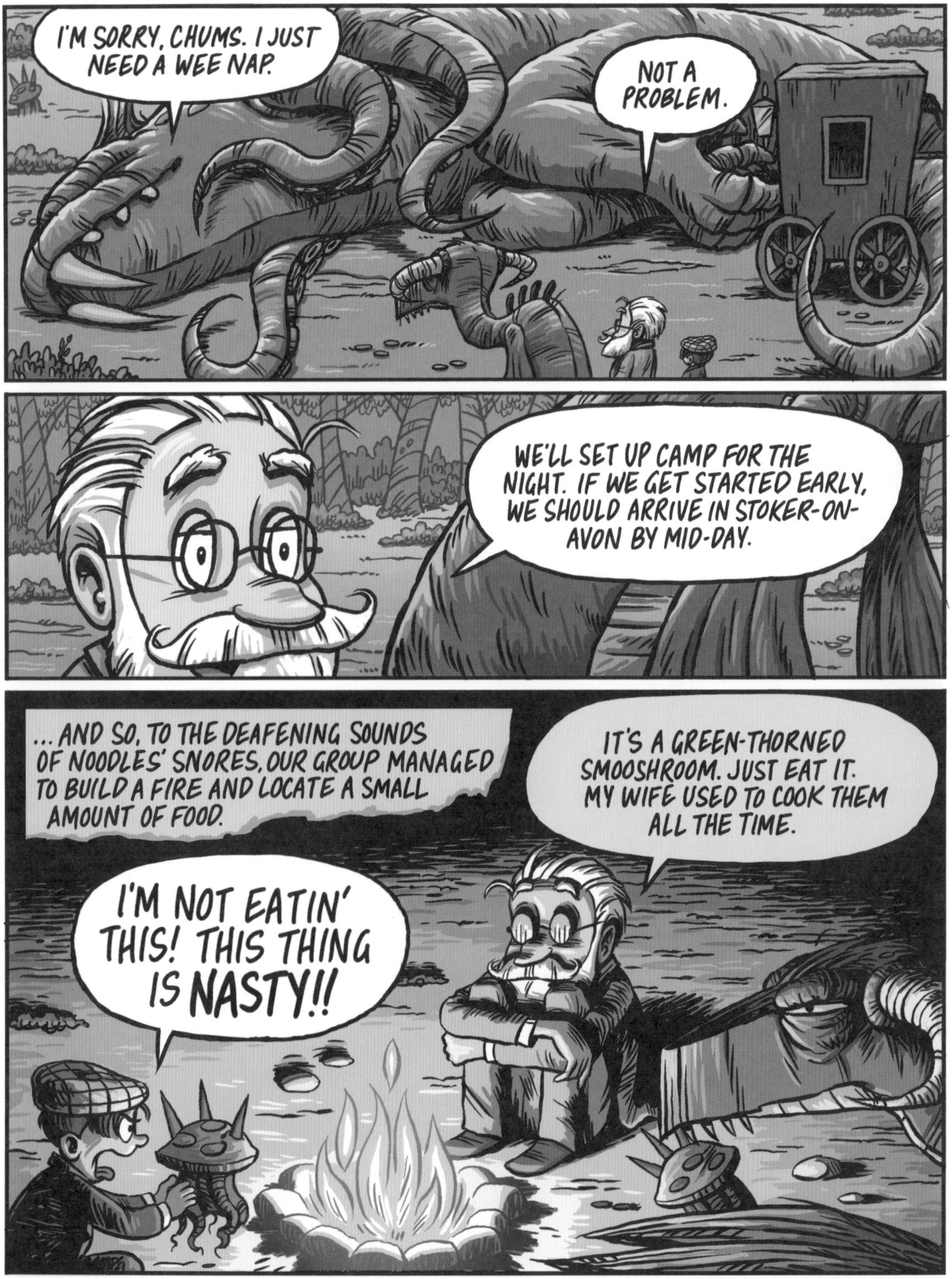
I'M SORRY, CHUMS. I JUST NEED A WEE NAP.
NOT A PROBLEM.
WE'LL SET UP CAMP FOR THE NIGHT. IF WE GET STARTED EARLY, WE SHOULD ARRIVE IN STOKER-ON-AVON BY MID-DAY.
...AND SO, TO THE DEAFENING SOUNDS OF NOODLES' SNORES, OUR GROUP MANAGED TO BUILD A FIRE AND LOCATE A SMALL AMOUNT OF FOOD.
IT'S A GREEN-THORNED SMOOSHROOM. JUST EAT IT. MY WIFE USED TO COOK THEM ALL THE TIME.
I'M NOT EATIN' THIS! THIS THING IS NASTY!!

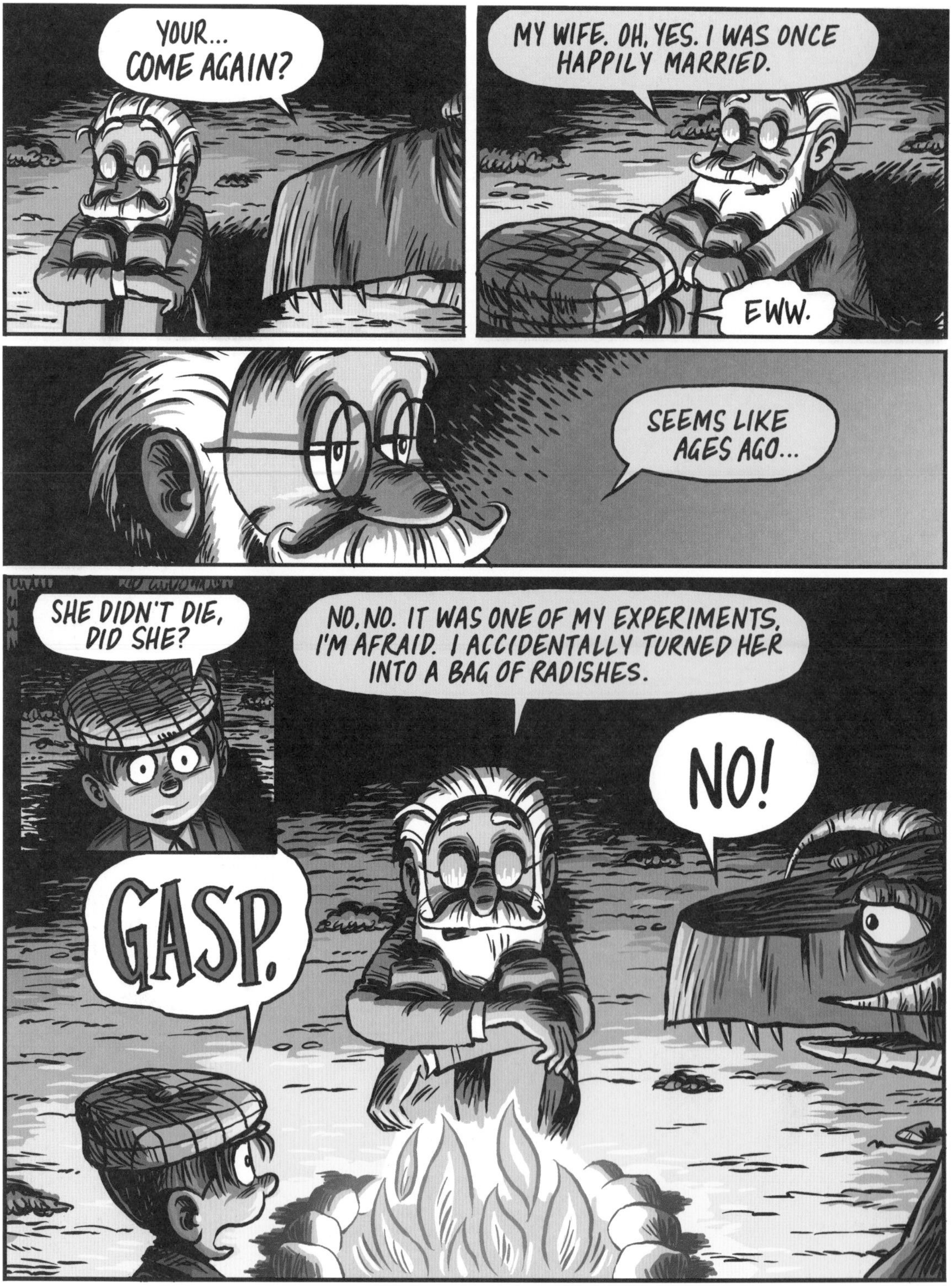
YOUR...
COME AGAIN?
MY WIFE. OH, YES. I WAS ONCE HAPPILY MARRIED.
EWW.
SEEMS LIKE AGES AGO...
SHE DIDN'T DIE, DID SHE?
NO, NO. IT WAS ONE OF MY EXPERIMENTS, I'M AFRAID. I ACCIDENTALLY TURNED HER INTO A BAG OF RADISHES.
NO!
GASP.

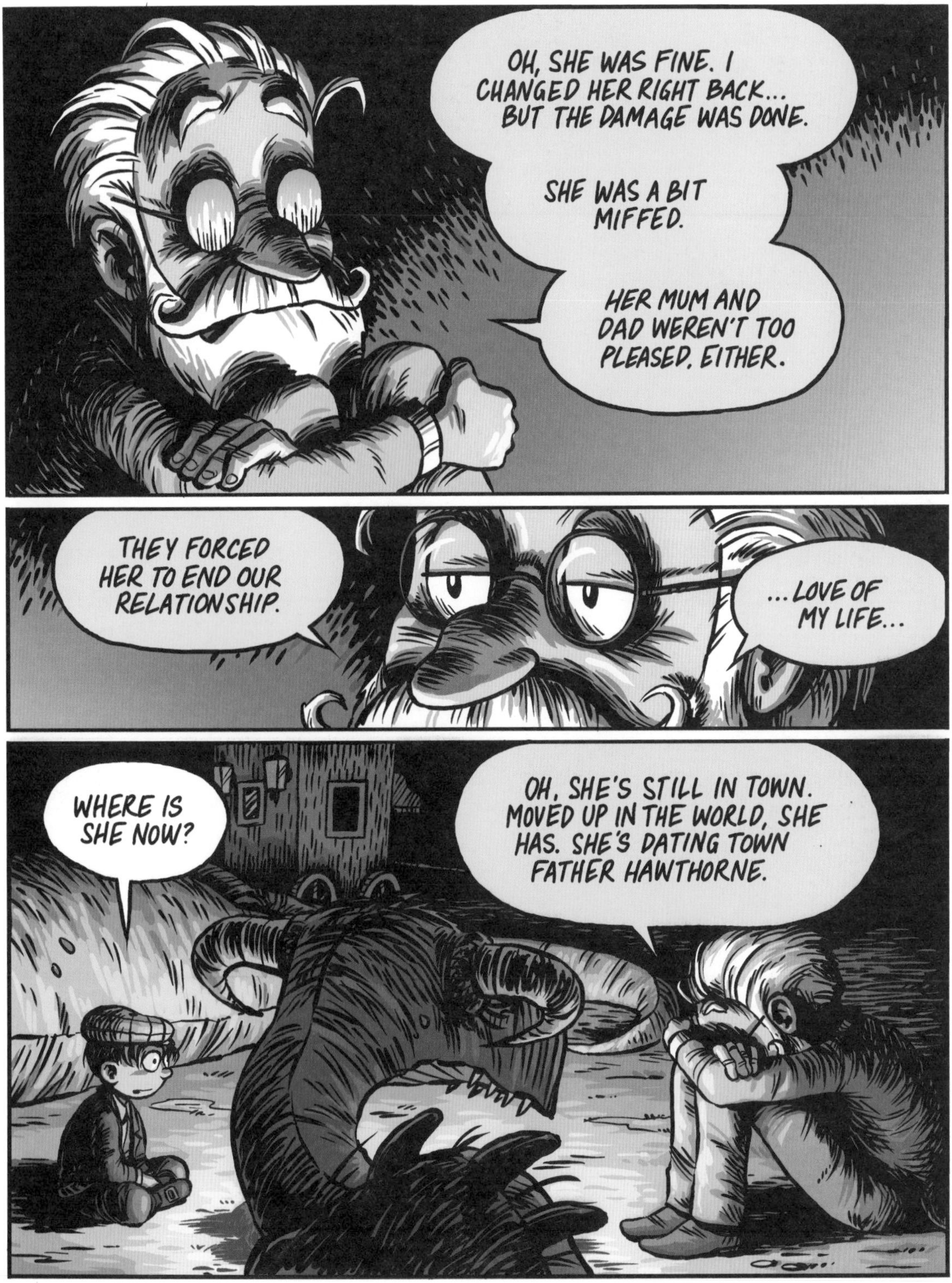
OH, SHE WAS FINE. I CHANGED HER RIGHT BACK... BUT THE DAMAGE WAS DONE.
SHE WAS A BIT MIFFED.
HER MUM AND DAD WEREN'T TOO PLEASED, EITHER.
THEY FORCED HER TO END OUR RELATIONSHIP.
...LOVE OF MY LIFE...
WHERE IS SHE NOW?
OH, SHE'S STILL IN TOWN. MOVED UP IN THE WORLD, SHE HAS. SHE'S DATING TOWN FATHER HAWTHORNE.

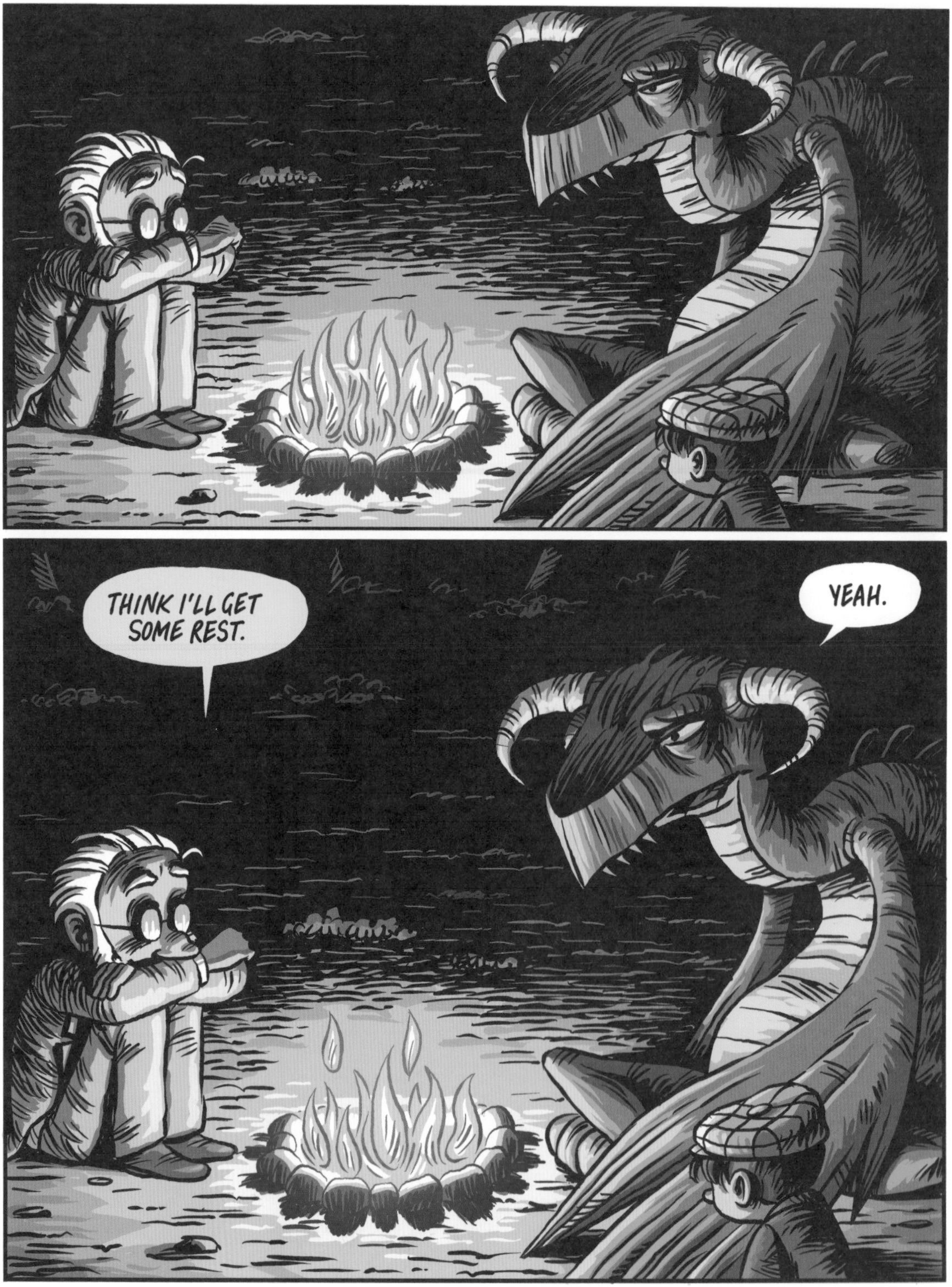
THINK I'LL GET SOME REST.
YEAH.

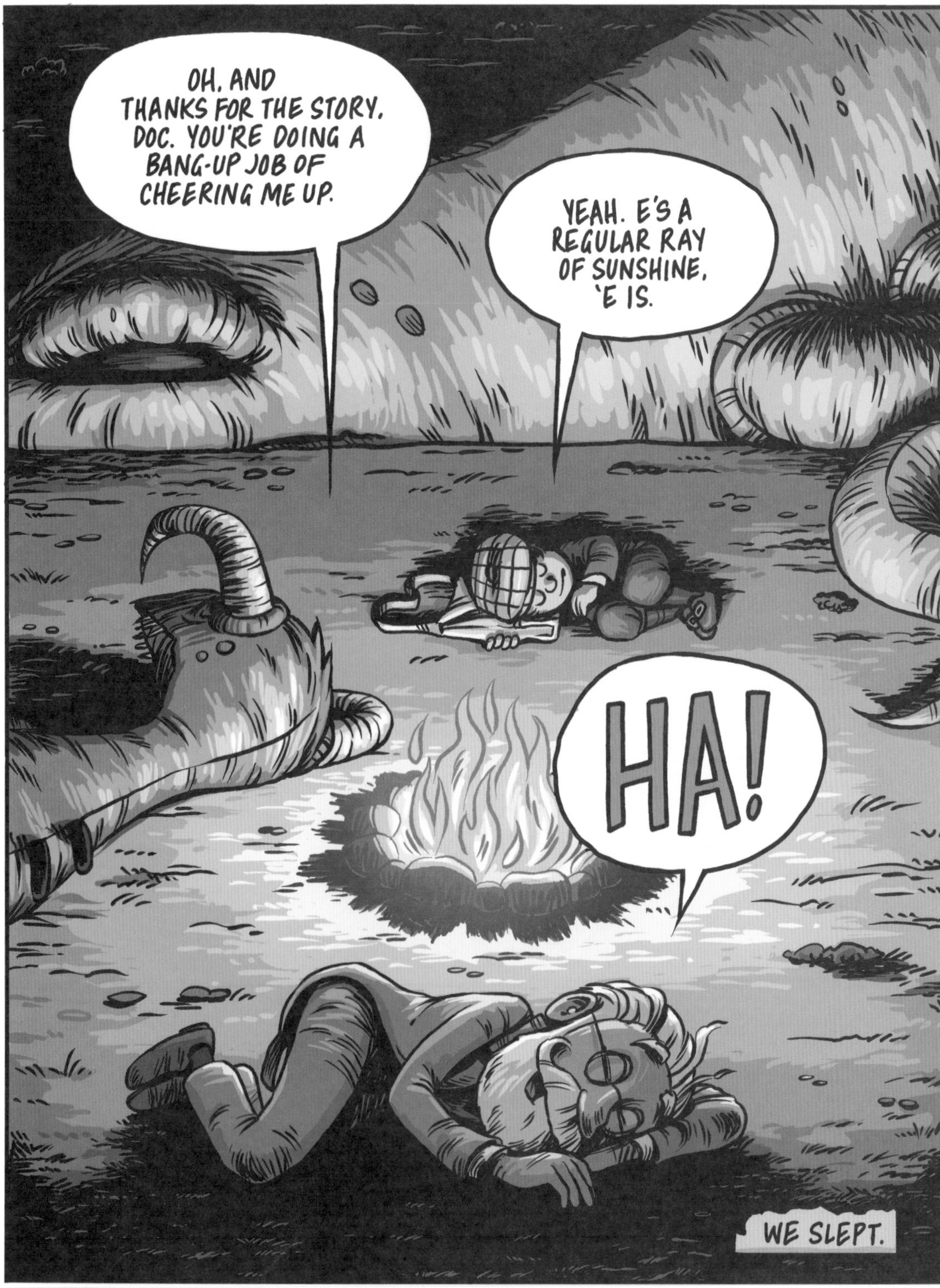
OH, AND THANKS FOR THE STORY, DOC. YOU'RE DOING A BANG-UP JOB OF CHEERING ME UP.
YEAH. E'S A REGULAR RAY OF SUNSHINE, 'E IS.
HA!
WE SLEPT.

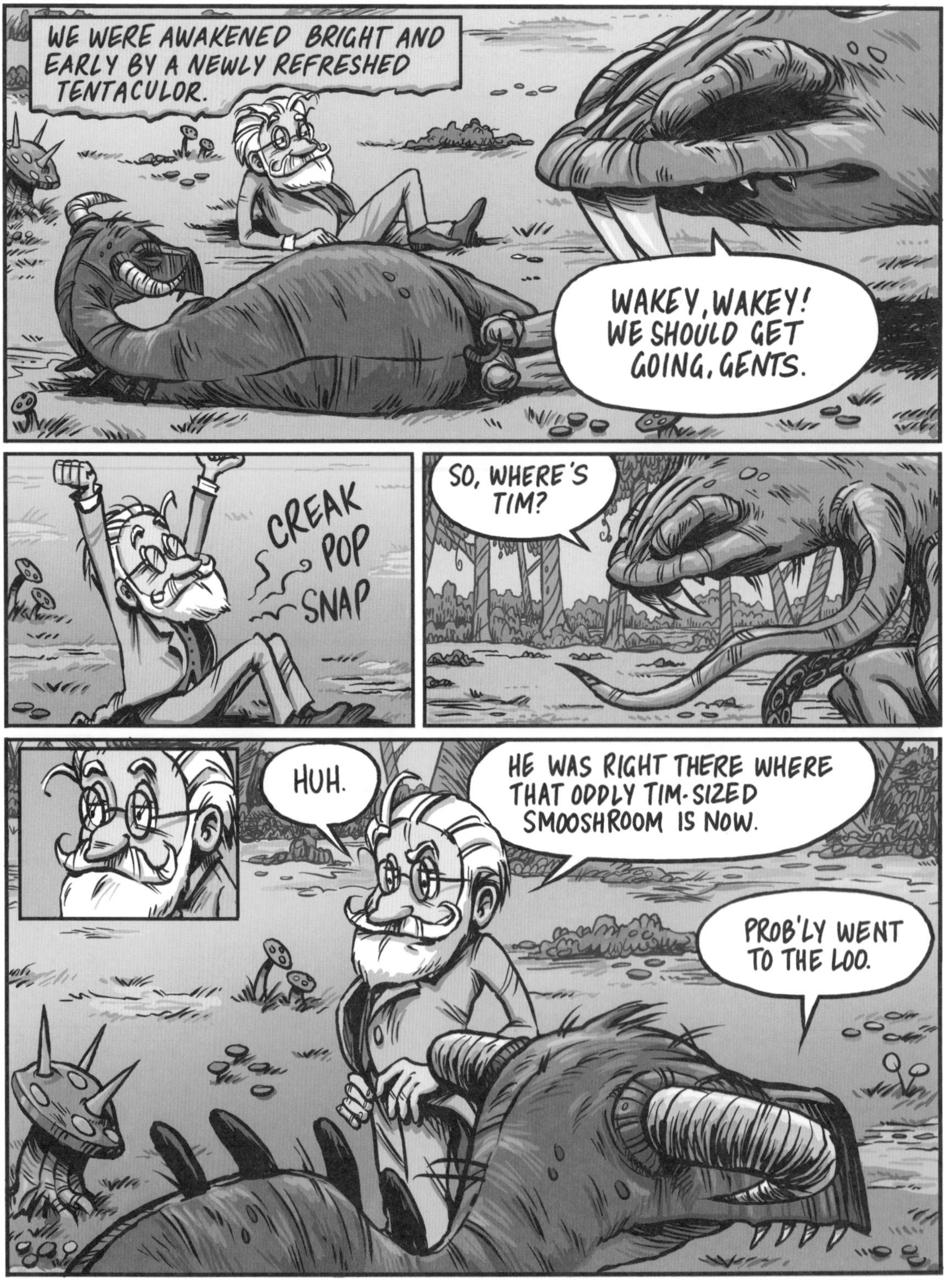

WE WERE AWAKENED BRIGHT AND EARLY BY A NEWLY REFRESHED TENTACULOR.
WAKEY, WAKEY! WE SHOULD GET GOING, GENTS.
CREAK
POP
SNAP
SO, WHERE'S TIM?
HUH.
HE WAS RIGHT THERE WHERE THAT ODDLY TIM-SIZED SMOOSHROOM IS NOW.
PROB'LY WENT TO THE LOO.

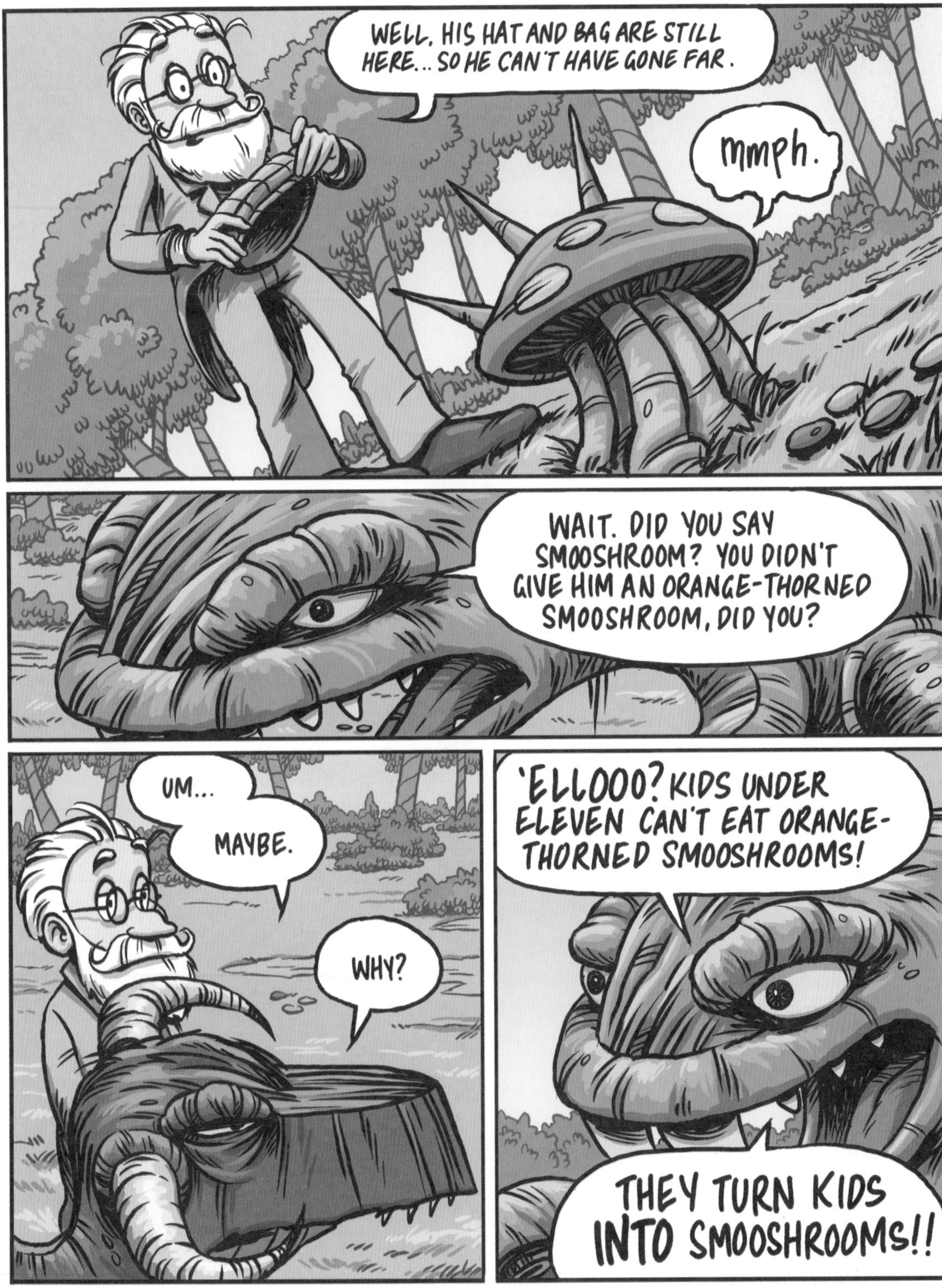
WELL, HIS HAT AND BAG ARE STILL HERE... SO HE CAN'T HAVE GONE FAR.
mmph.
WAIT. DID YOU SAY SMOOSHROOM? YOU DIDN'T GIVE HIM AN ORANGE-THORNED SMOOSHROOM, DID YOU?
UM...
MAYBE.
WHY?
'ELLOOO? KIDS UNDER ELEVEN CAN'T EAT ORANGE-THORNED SMOOSHROOMS!
THEY TURN KIDS INTO SMOOSHROOMS!!

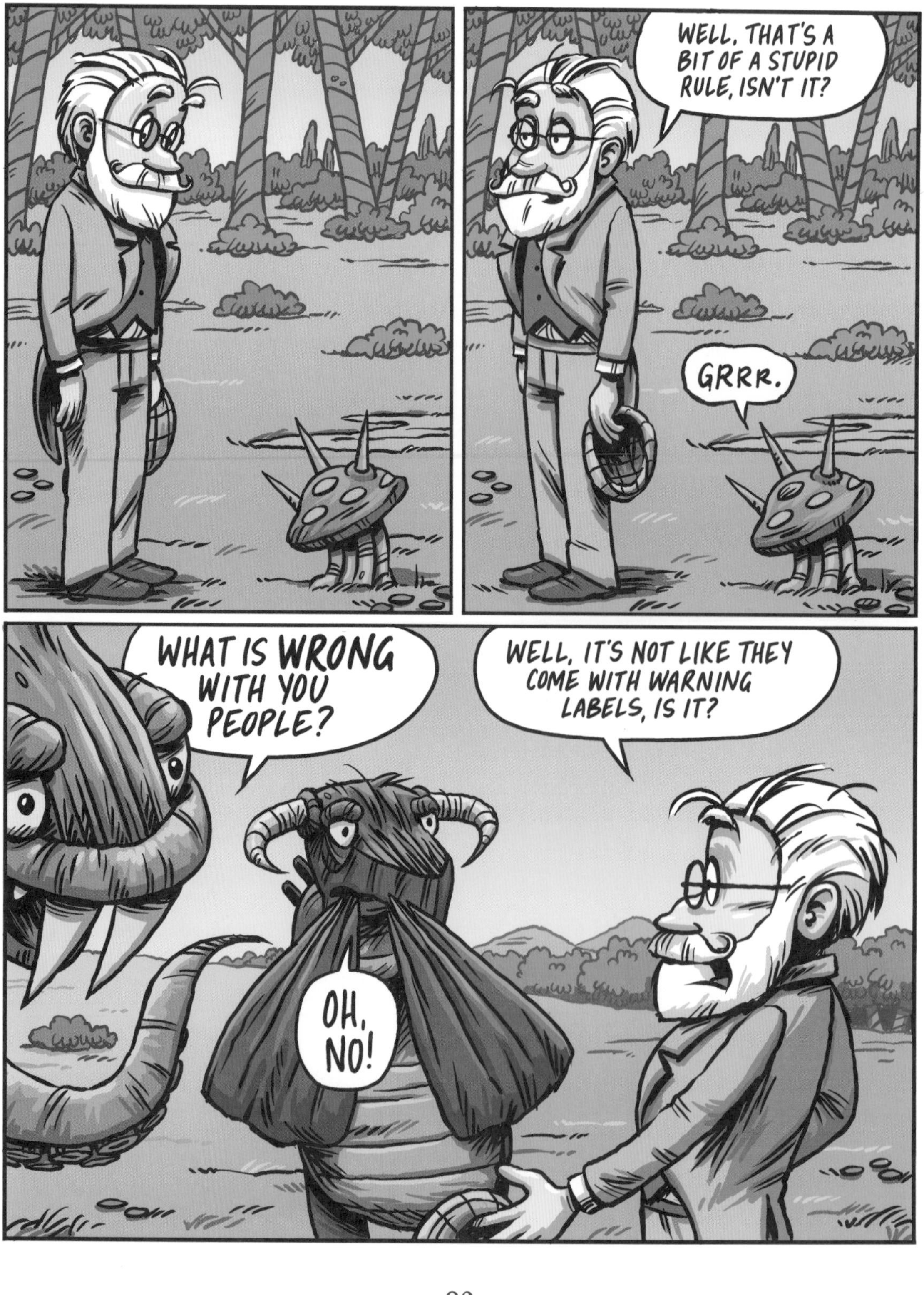
WELL, THAT'S A BIT OF A STUPID RULE, ISN'T IT?
GRRR.
WHAT IS WRONG WITH YOU PEOPLE?
WELL, IT'S NOT LIKE THEY COME WITH WARNING LABELS, IS IT?
OH, NO!

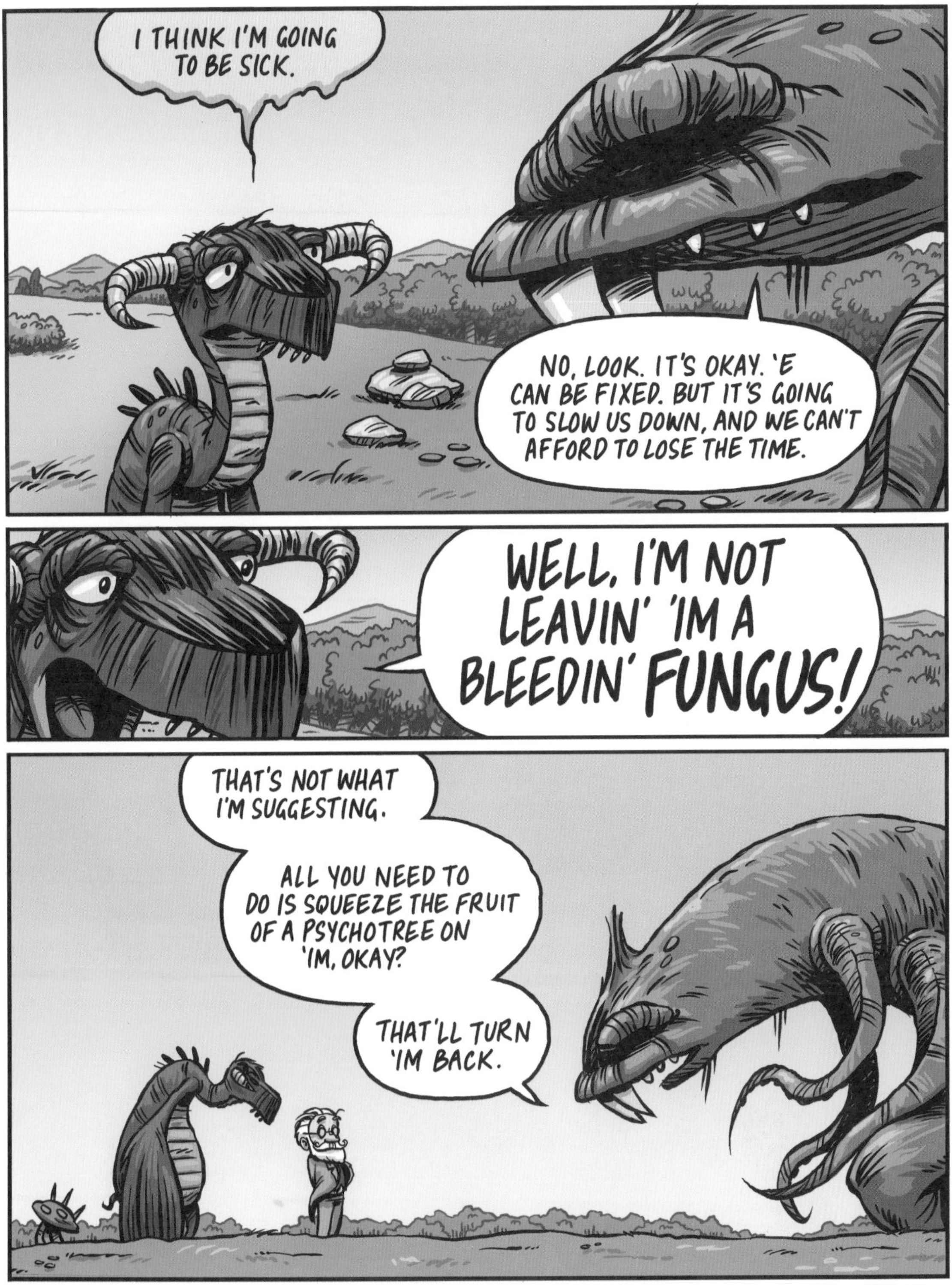
I THINK I'M GOING TO BE SICK.
NO, LOOK. IT'S OKAY. 'E CAN BE FIXED. BUT IT'S GOING TO SLOW US DOWN, AND WE CAN'T AFFORD TO LOSE THE TIME.
WELL, I'M NOT LEAVIN' 'IM A BLEEDIN' FUNGUS!
THAT'S NOT WHAT I'M SUGGESTING.
ALL YOU NEED TO DO IS SQUEEZE THE FRUIT OF A PSYCHOTREE ON 'IM, OKAY?
THAT'LL TURN 'IM BACK.

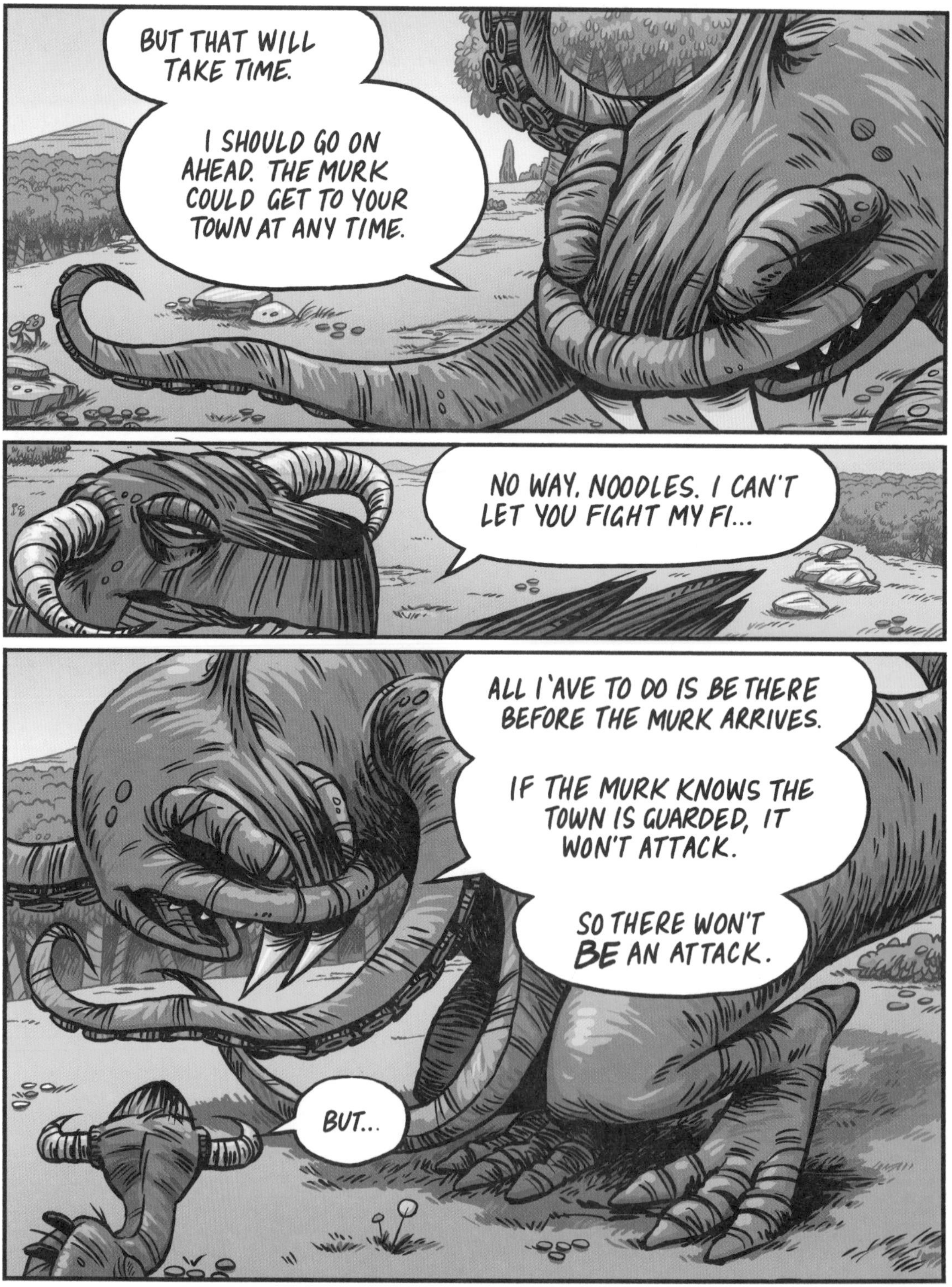
BUT THAT WILL TAKE TIME.
I SHOULD GO ON AHEAD. THE MURK COULD GET TO YOUR TOWN AT ANY TIME.
NO WAY, NOODLES. I CAN'T LET YOU FIGHT MY FI...
ALL I'AVE TO DO IS BE THERE BEFORE THE MURK ARRIVES.
IF THE MURK KNOWS THE TOWN IS GUARDED, IT WON'T ATTACK.
SO THERE WON'T **BE** AN ATTACK.
BUT...

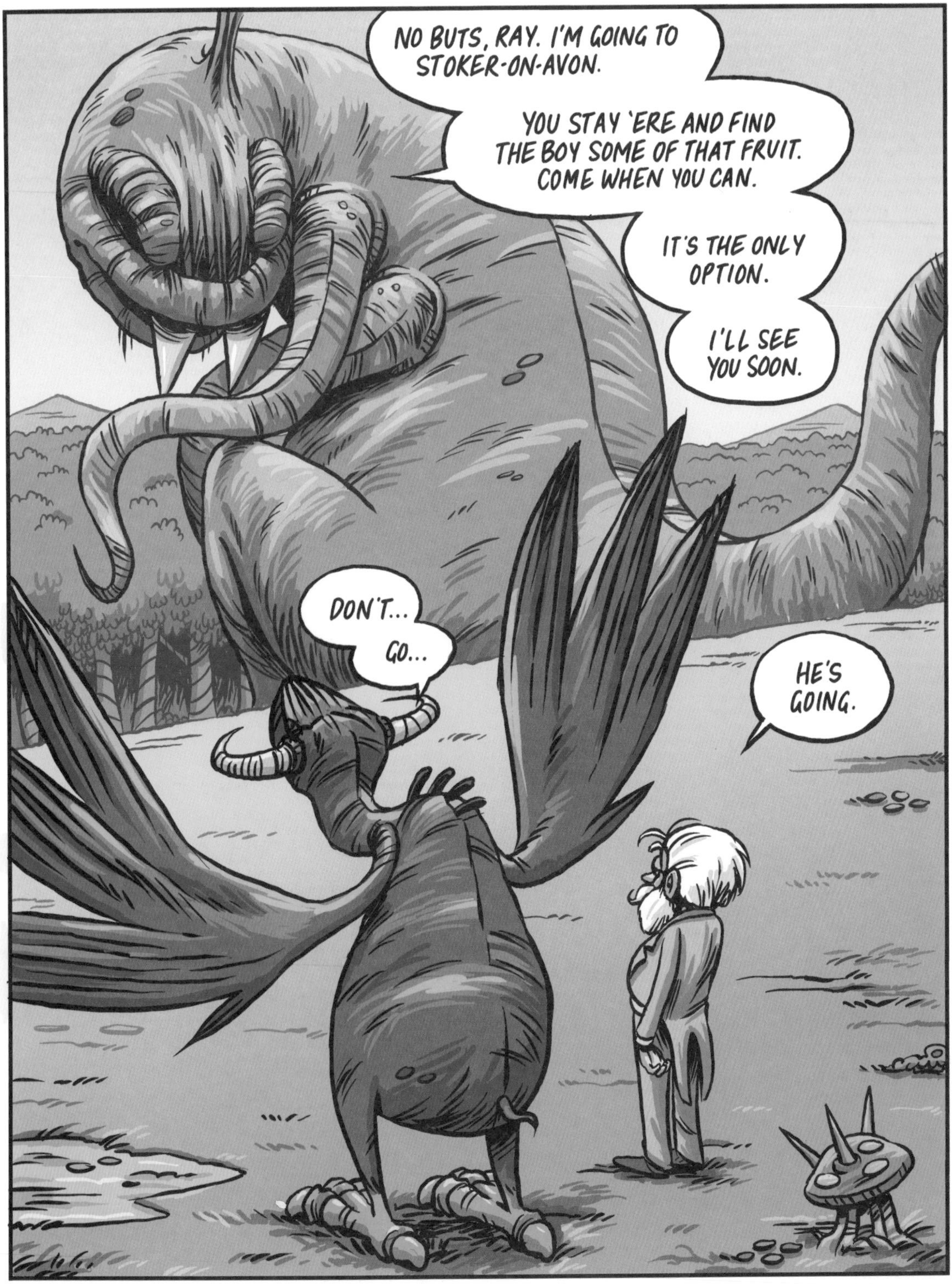
NO BUTS, RAY. I'M GOING TO STOKER-ON-AVON.
YOU STAY 'ERE AND FIND THE BOY SOME OF THAT FRUIT. COME WHEN YOU CAN.
IT'S THE ONLY OPTION.
I'LL SEE YOU SOON.
DON'T...
GO...
HE'S GOING.

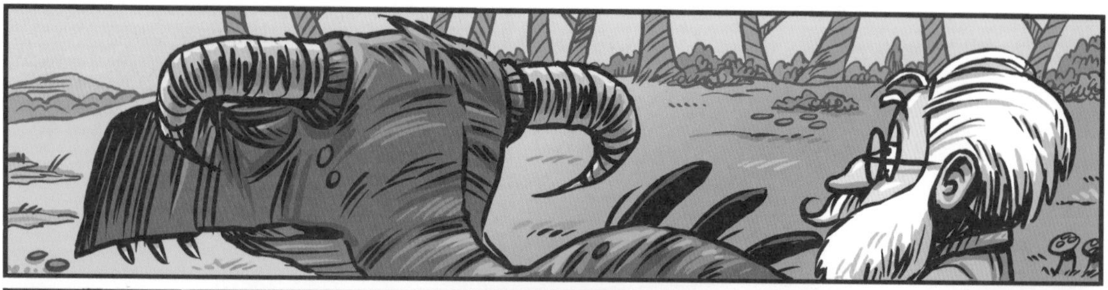

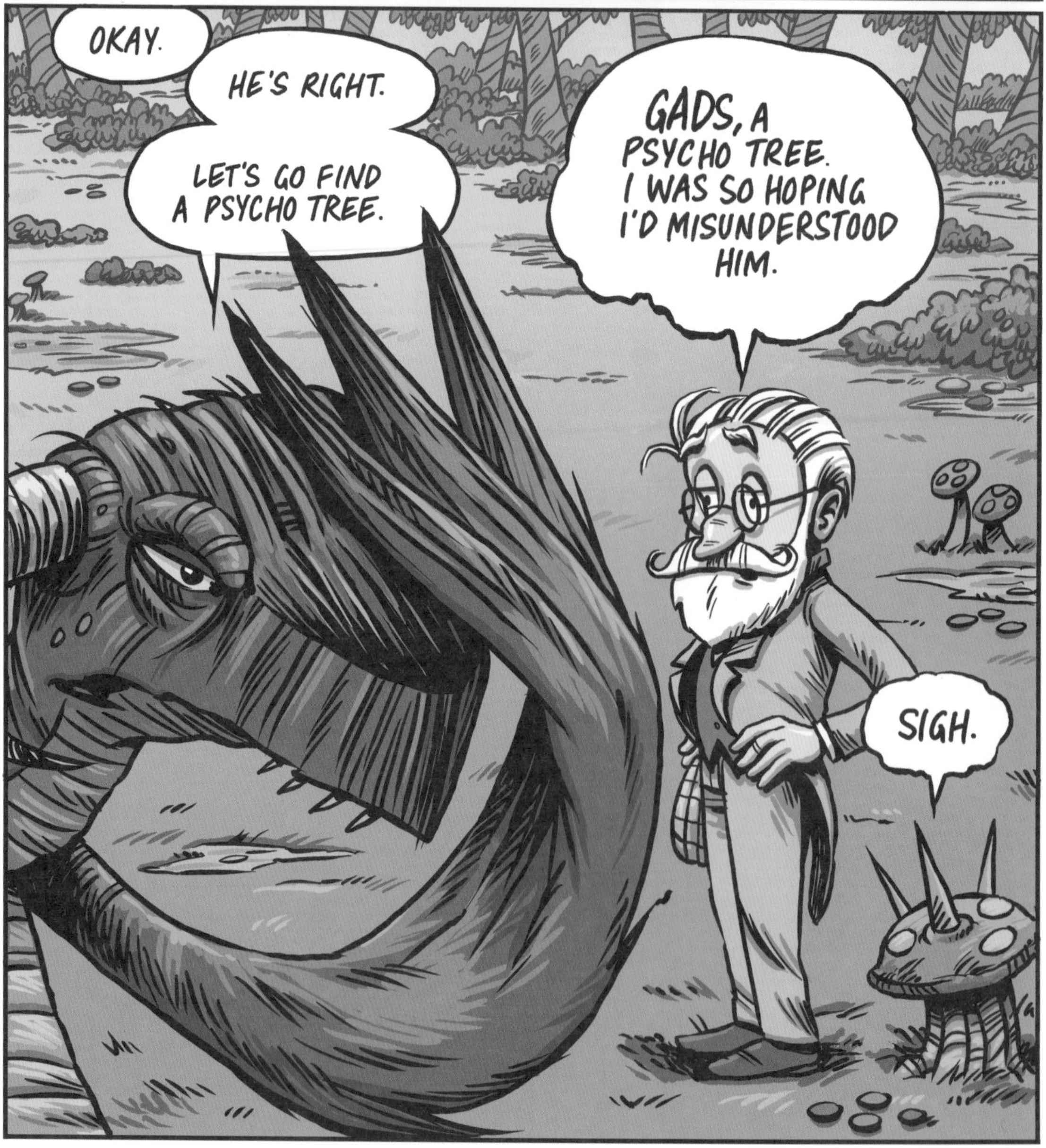
OKAY.
HE'S RIGHT.
LET'S GO FIND A PSYCHO TREE.
GADS, A PSYCHO TREE. I WAS SO HOPING I'D MISUNDERSTOOD HIM.
SIGH.

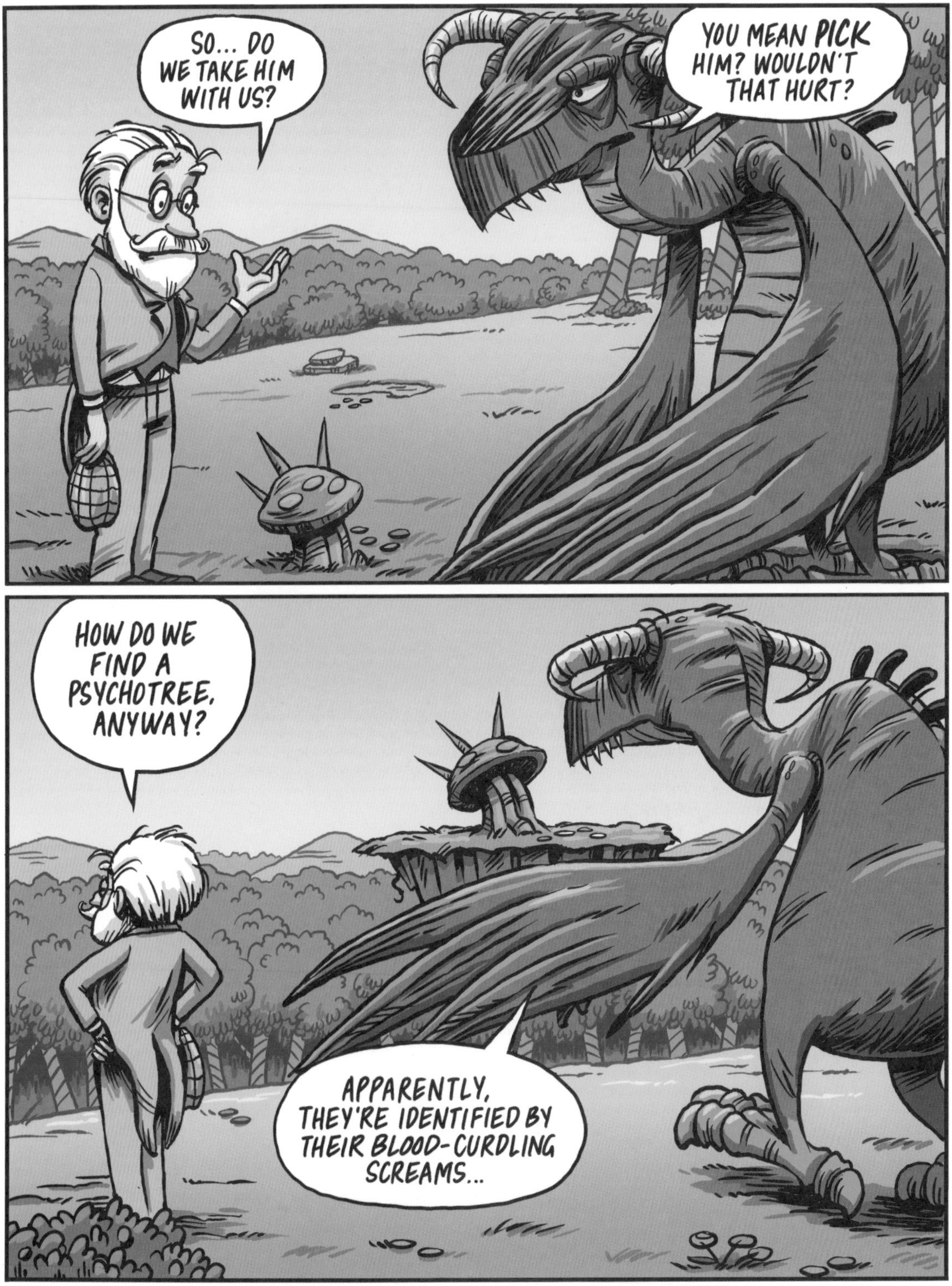
SO... DO WE TAKE HIM WITH US?
YOU MEAN PICK HIM? WOULDN'T THAT HURT?
HOW DO WE FIND A PSYCHOTREE, ANYWAY?
APPARENTLY, THEY'RE IDENTIFIED BY THEIR BLOOD-CURDLING SCREAMS...

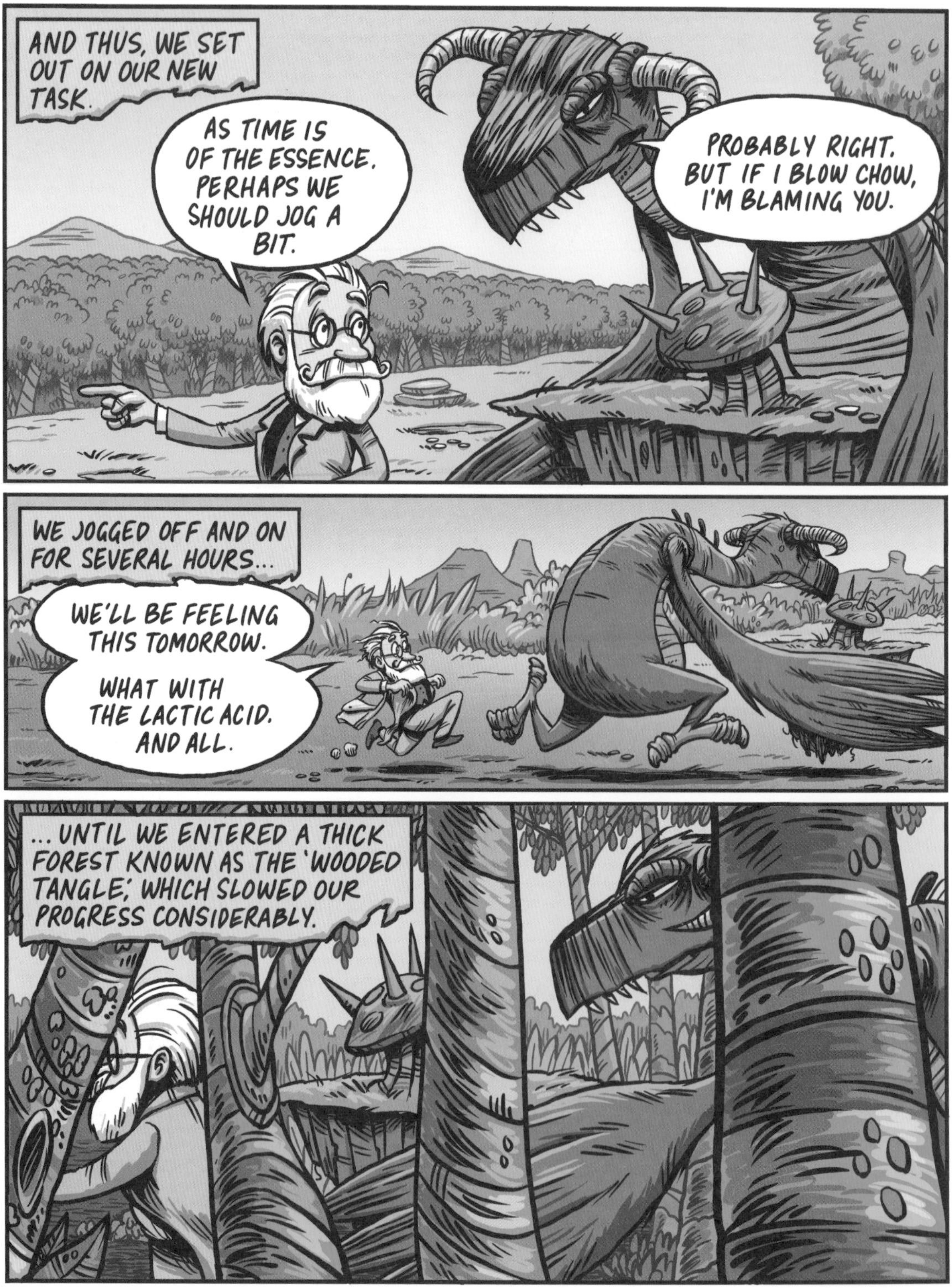

AND THUS, WE SET OUT ON OUR NEW TASK.
AS TIME IS OF THE ESSENCE. PERHAPS WE SHOULD JOG A BIT.
PROBABLY RIGHT. BUT IF I BLOW CHOW, I'M BLAMING YOU.
WE JOGGED OFF AND ON FOR SEVERAL HOURS...
WE'LL BE FEELING THIS TOMORROW.
WHAT WITH THE LACTIC ACID. AND ALL.
...UNTIL WE ENTERED A THICK FOREST KNOWN AS THE 'WOODED TANGLE,' WHICH SLOWED OUR PROGRESS CONSIDERABLY.

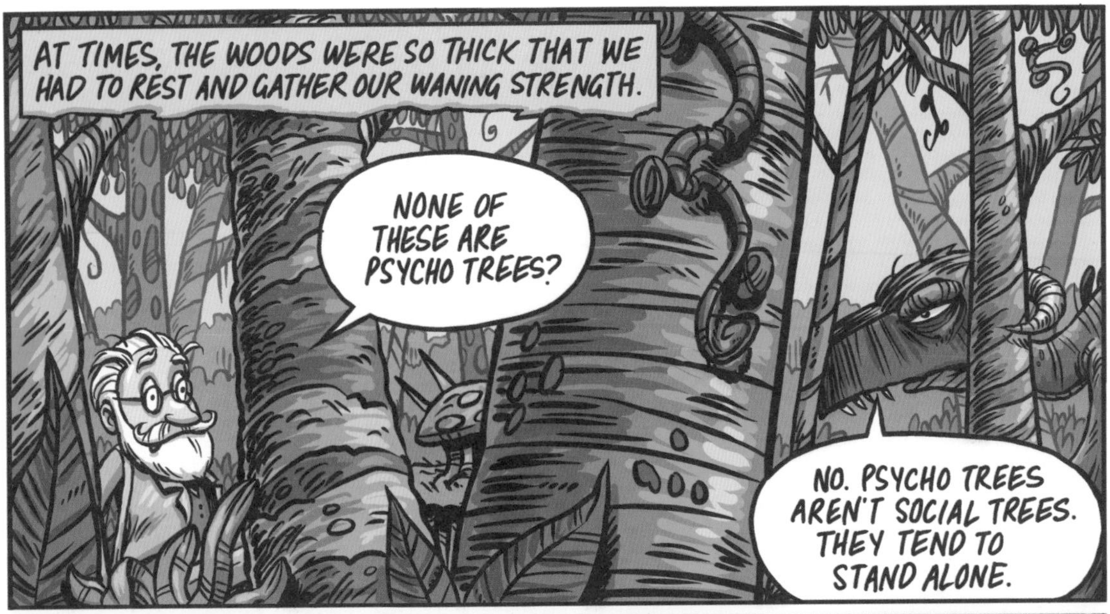
AT TIMES, THE WOODS WERE SO THICK THAT WE HAD TO REST AND GATHER OUR WANING STRENGTH.
NONE OF THESE ARE PSYCHO TREES?
NO. PSYCHO TREES AREN'T SOCIAL TREES. THEY TEND TO STAND ALONE.

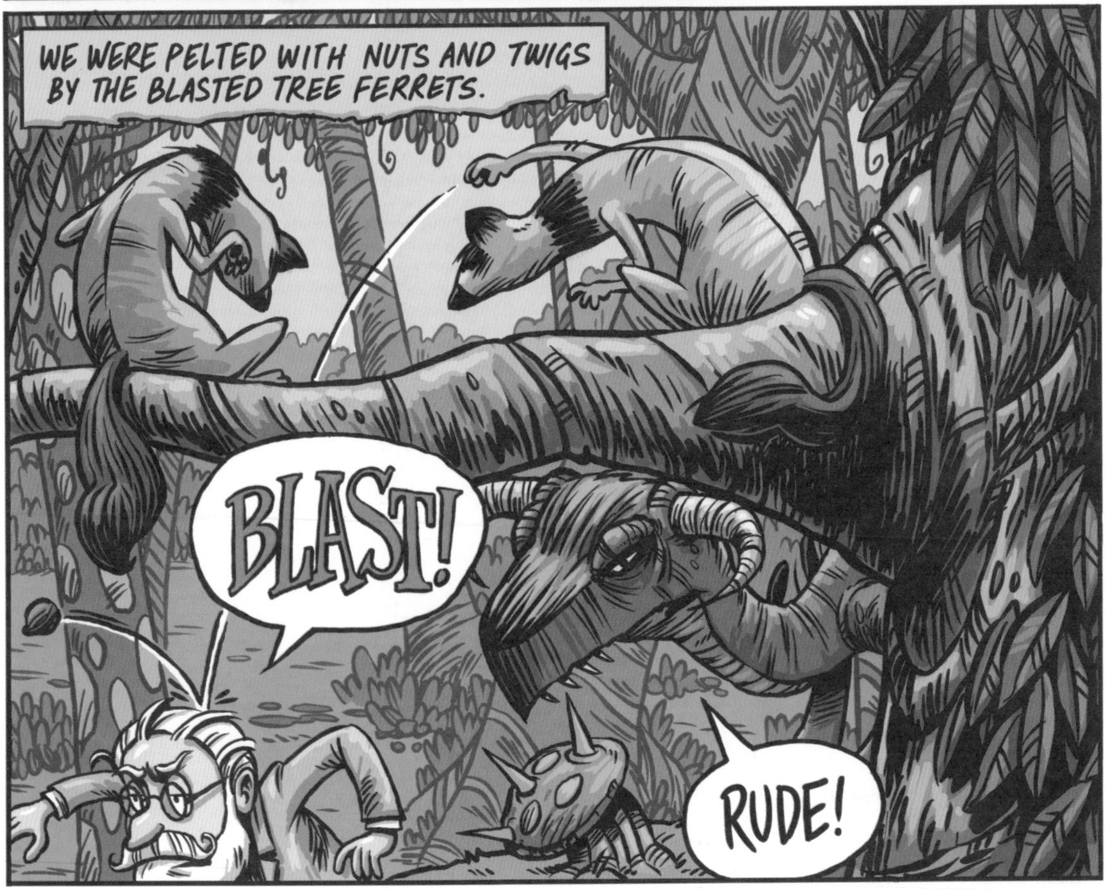
WE WERE PELTED WITH NUTS AND TWIGS BY THE BLASTED TREE FERRETS.
BLAST!
RUDE!

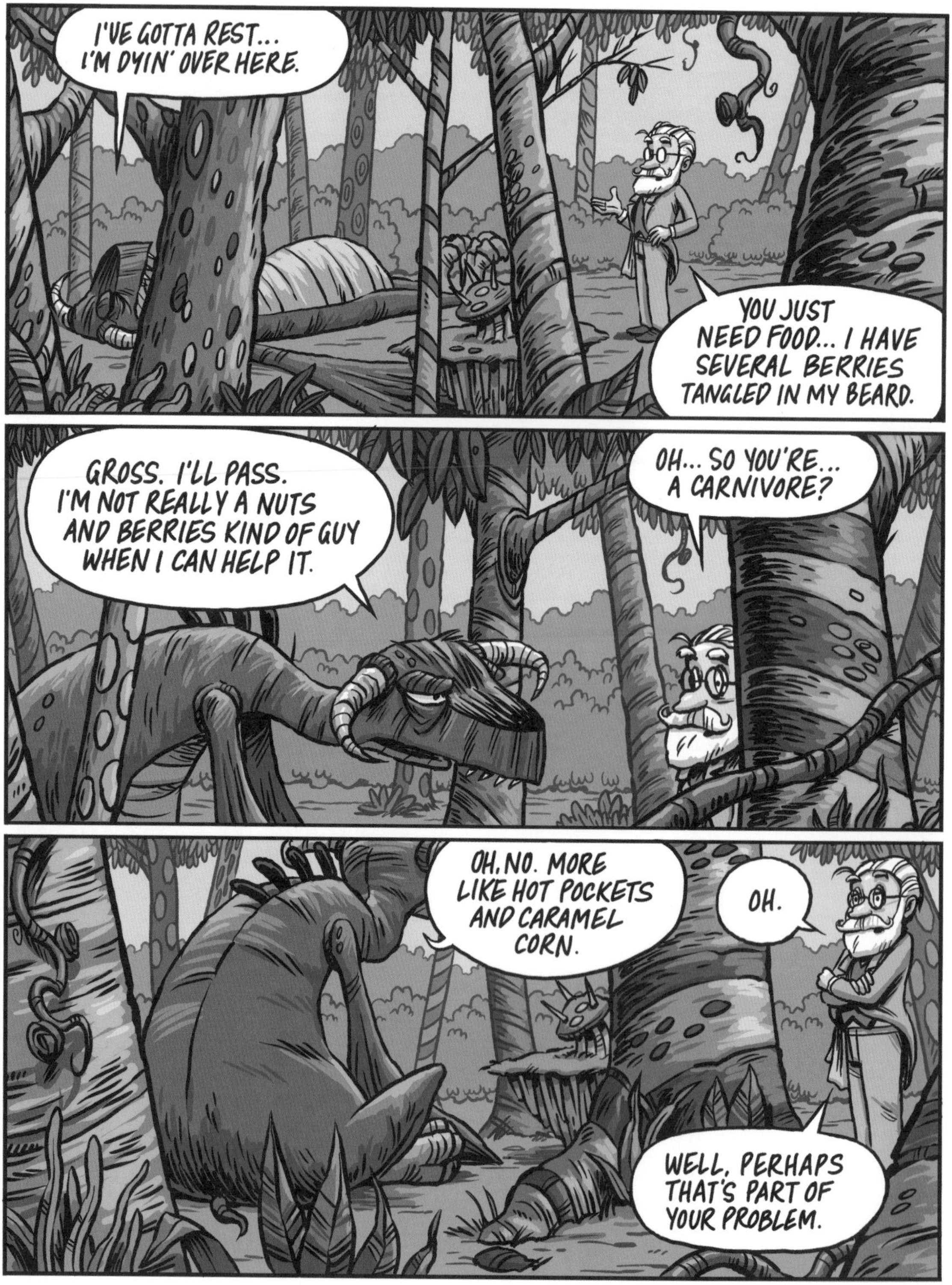
I'VE GOTTA REST... I'M DYIN' OVER HERE.
YOU JUST NEED FOOD... I HAVE SEVERAL BERRIES TANGLED IN MY BEARD.
GROSS. I'LL PASS. I'M NOT REALLY A NUTS AND BERRIES KIND OF GUY WHEN I CAN HELP IT.
OH... SO YOU'RE... A CARNIVORE?
OH, NO. MORE LIKE HOT POCKETS AND CARAMEL CORN.
OH.
WELL, PERHAPS THAT'S PART OF YOUR PROBLEM.

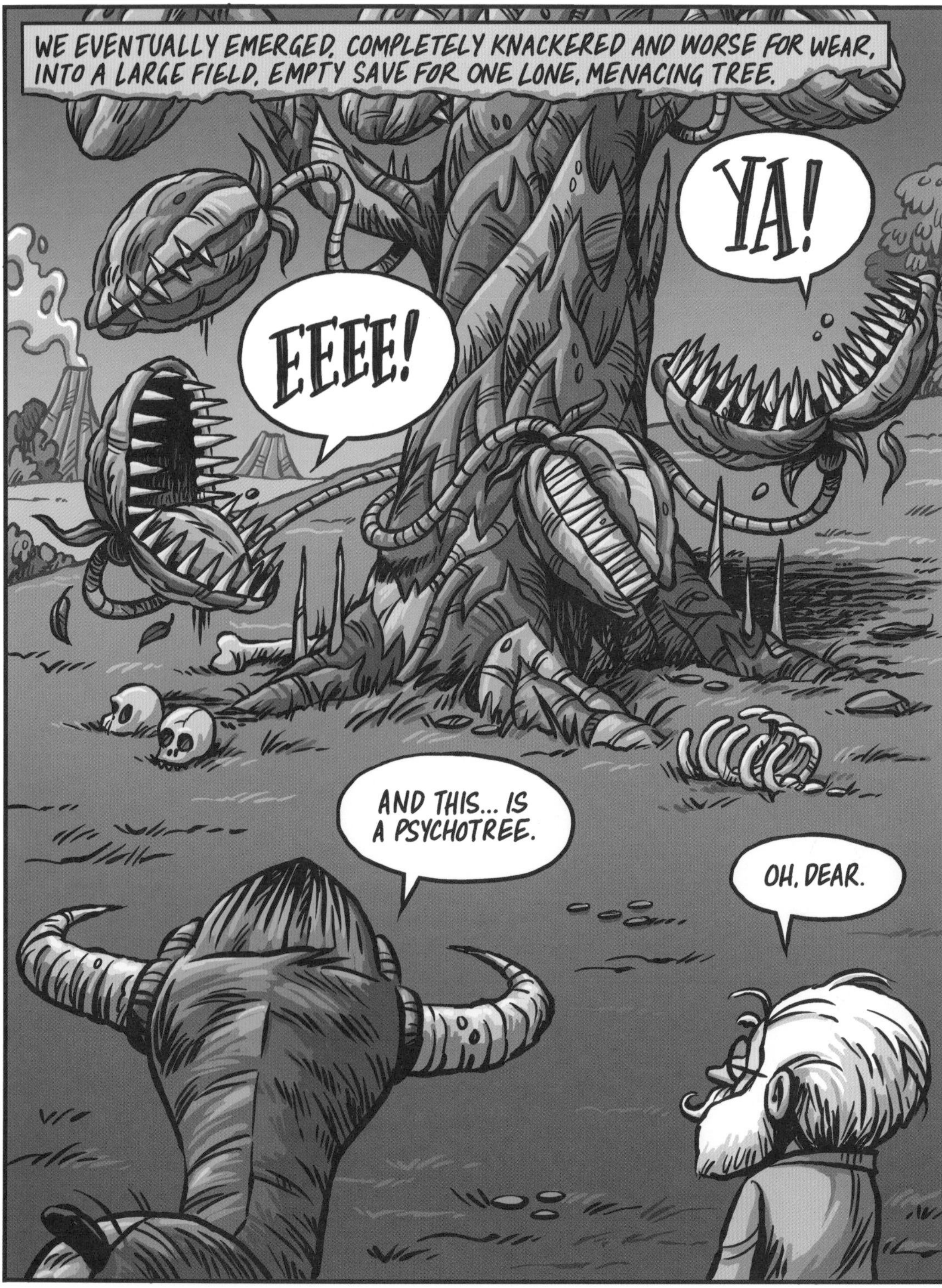
WE EVENTUALLY EMERGED, COMPLETELY KNACKERED AND WORSE FOR WEAR, INTO A LARGE FIELD, EMPTY SAVE FOR ONE LONE, MENACING TREE.
YA!
EEEE!
AND THIS... IS A PSYCHOTREE.
OH, DEAR.

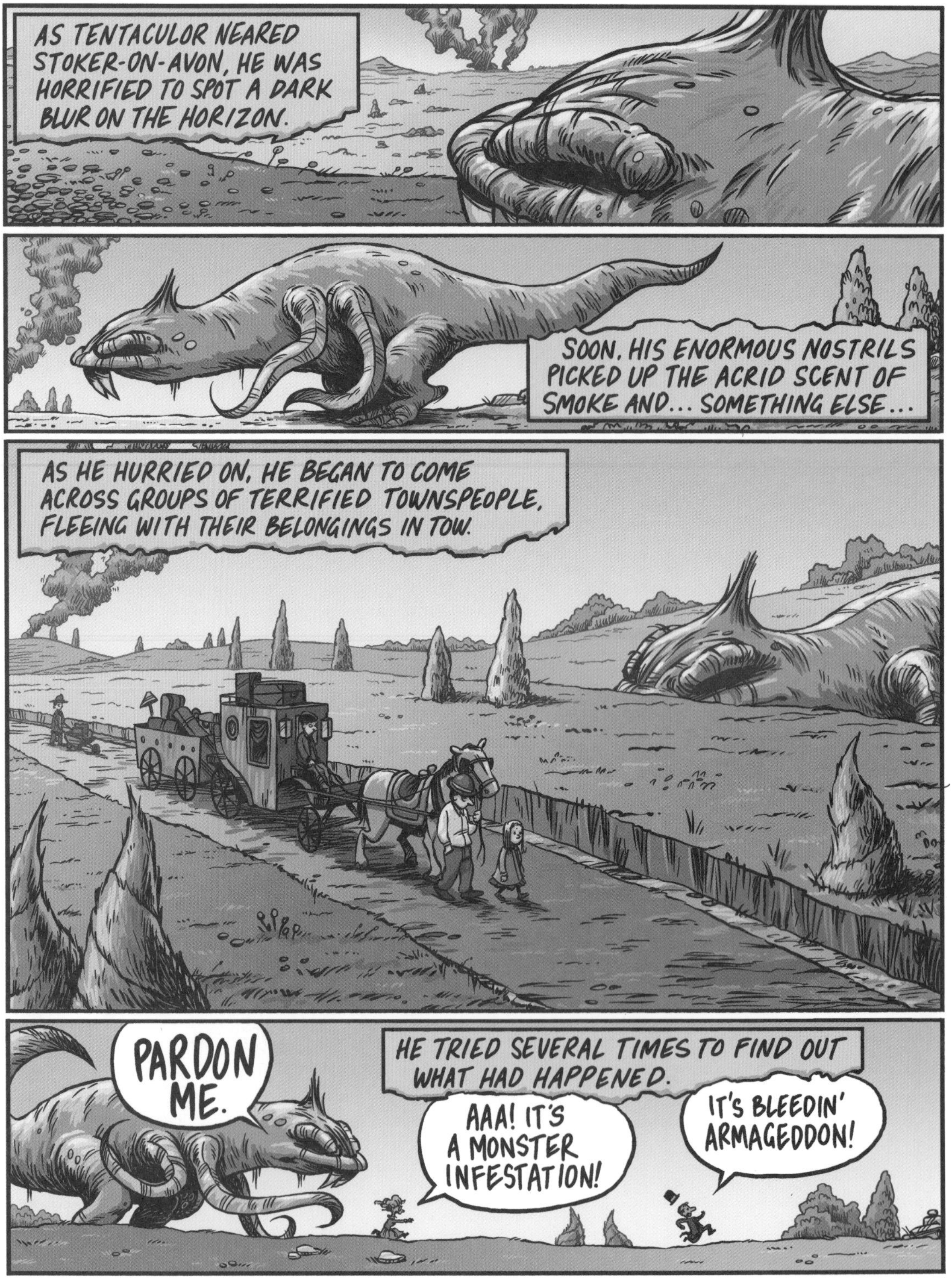
AS TENTACULOR NEARED STOKER-ON-AVON, HE WAS HORRIFIED TO SPOT A DARK BLUR ON THE HORIZON.
SOON, HIS ENORMOUS NOSTRILS PICKED UP THE ACRID SCENT OF SMOKE AND... SOMETHING ELSE...
AS HE HURRIED ON, HE BEGAN TO COME ACROSS GROUPS OF TERRIFIED TOWNSPEOPLE, FLEEING WITH THEIR BELONGINGS IN TOW.
PARDON ME.
HE TRIED SEVERAL TIMES TO FIND OUT WHAT HAD HAPPENED.
AAA! IT'S A MONSTER INFESTATION!
IT'S BLEEDIN' ARMAGEDDON!

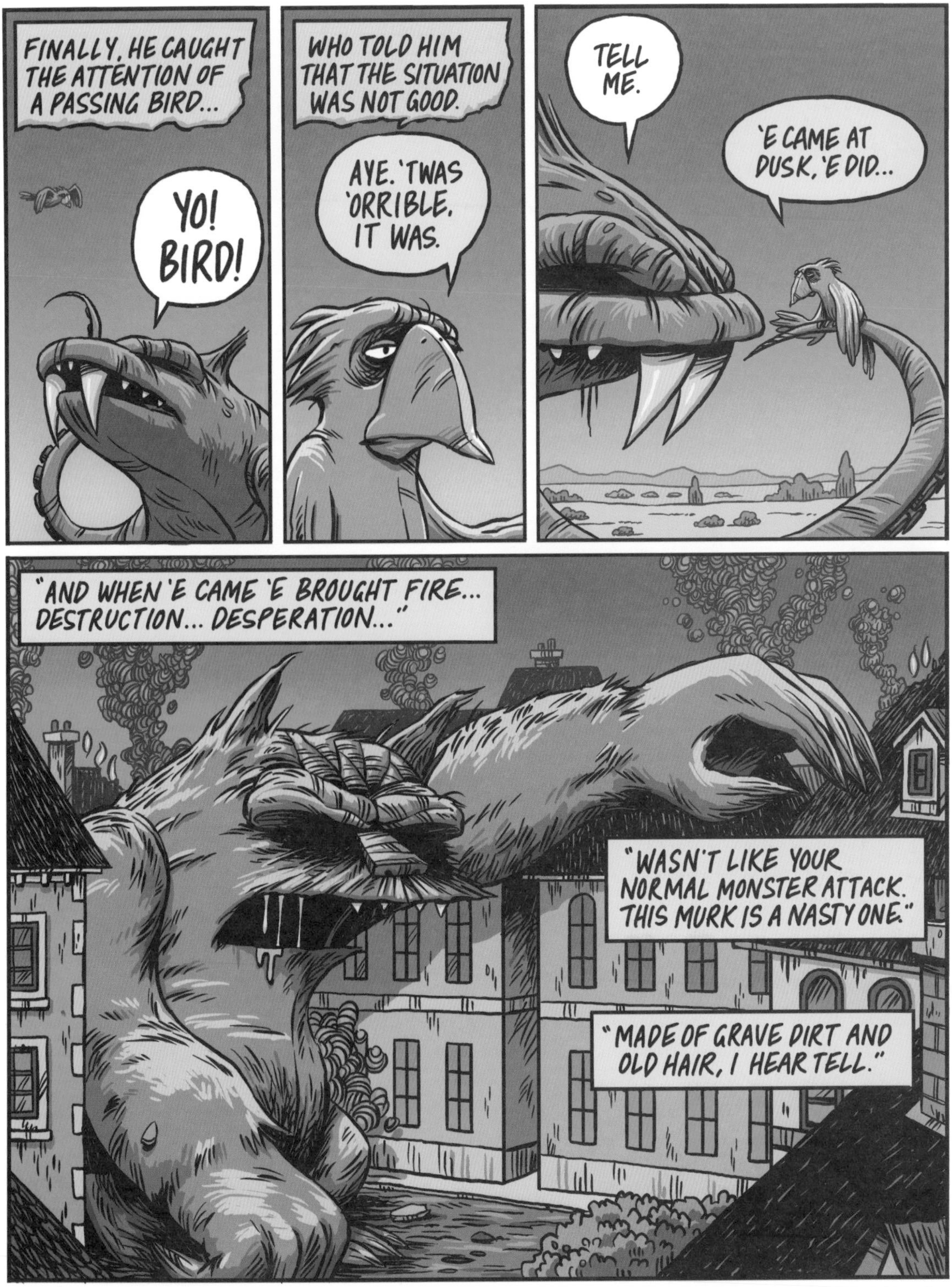
FINALLY, HE CAUGHT THE ATTENTION OF A PASSING BIRD...
YO! BIRD!
WHO TOLD HIM THAT THE SITUATION WAS NOT GOOD.
AYE. 'TWAS 'ORRIBLE, IT WAS.
TELL ME.
'E CAME AT DUSK, 'E DID...
"AND WHEN 'E CAME 'E BROUGHT FIRE... DESTRUCTION... DESPERATION..."
"WASN'T LIKE YOUR NORMAL MONSTER ATTACK. THIS MURK IS A NASTY ONE."
"MADE OF GRAVE DIRT AND OLD HAIR, I HEAR TELL."

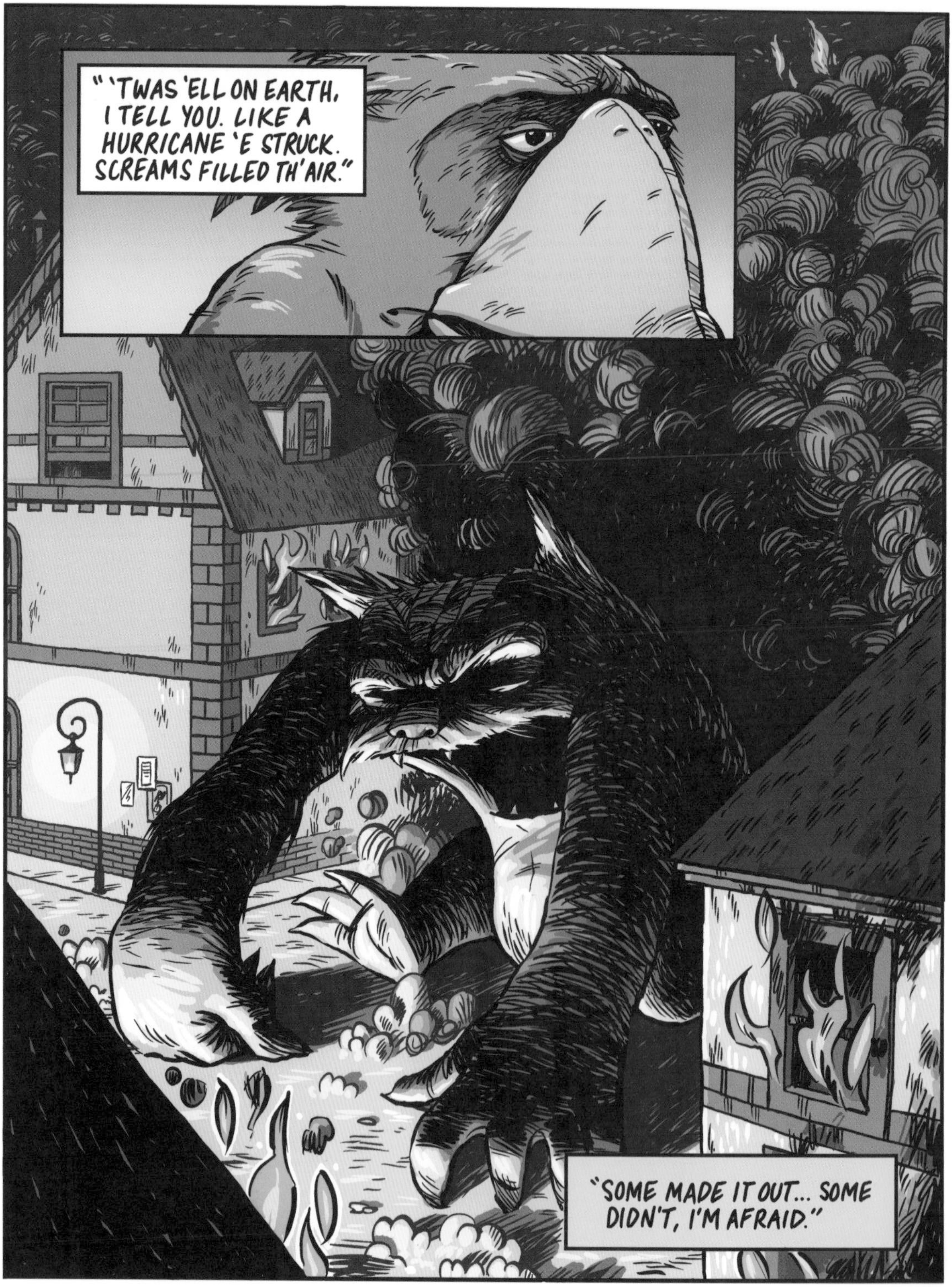
"'TWAS 'ELL ON EARTH, I TELL YOU. LIKE A HURRICANE 'E STRUCK. SCREAMS FILLED TH'AIR."
"SOME MADE IT OUT... SOME DIDN'T, I'M AFRAID."

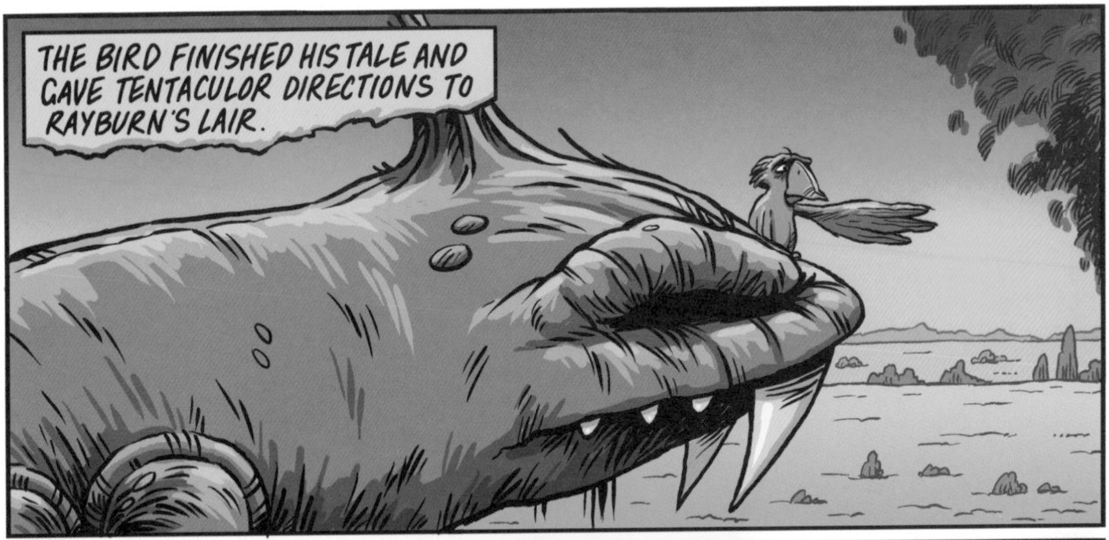
THE BIRD FINISHED HIS TALE AND GAVE TENTACULOR DIRECTIONS TO RAYBURN'S LAIR.

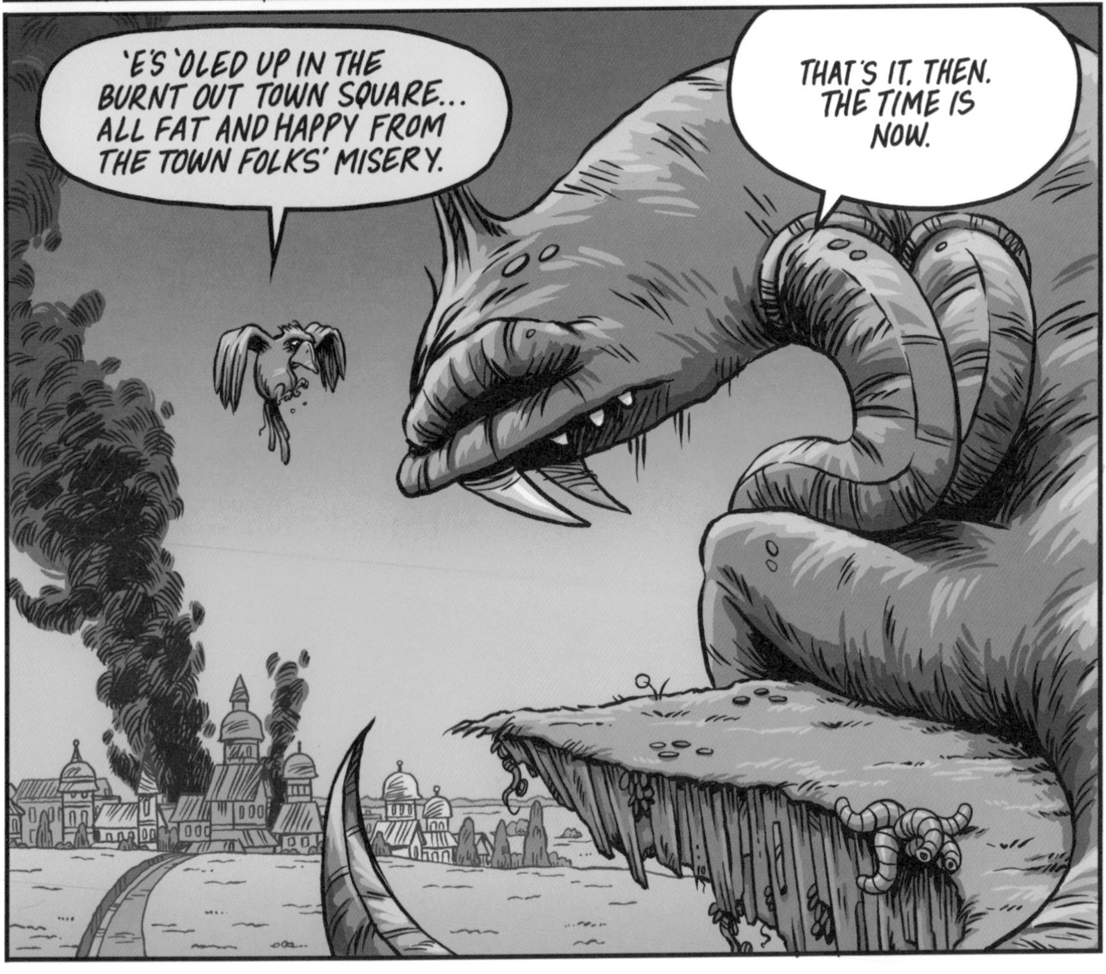
'E'S 'OLED UP IN THE BURNT OUT TOWN SQUARE... ALL FAT AND HAPPY FROM THE TOWN FOLKS' MISERY.
THAT'S IT, THEN. THE TIME IS NOW.

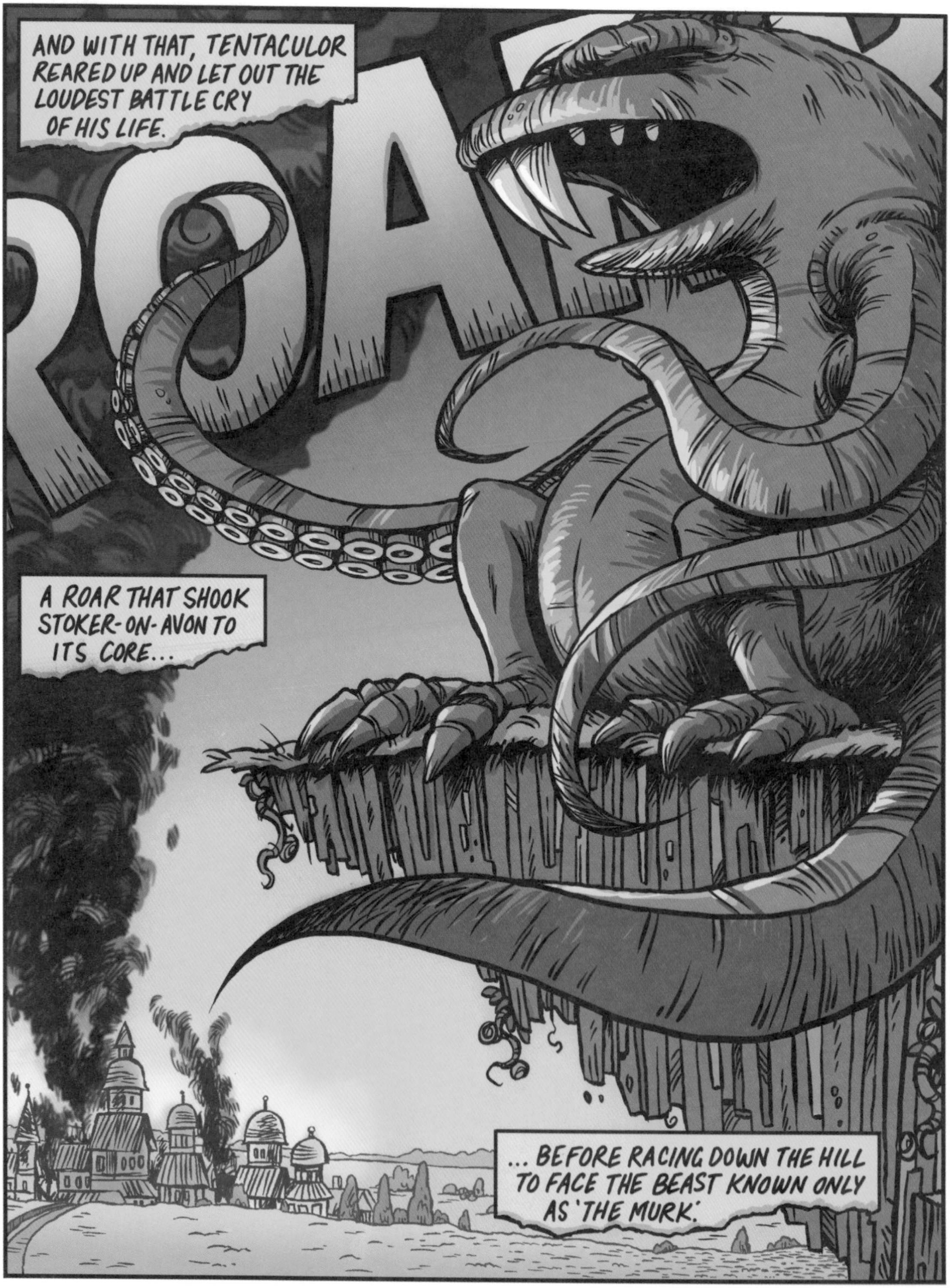
AND WITH THAT, TENTACULOR REARED UP AND LET OUT THE LOUDEST BATTLE CRY OF HIS LIFE.
ROAR
A ROAR THAT SHOOK STOKER-ON-AVON TO ITS CORE...
... BEFORE RACING DOWN THE HILL TO FACE THE BEAST KNOWN ONLY AS 'THE MURK.'

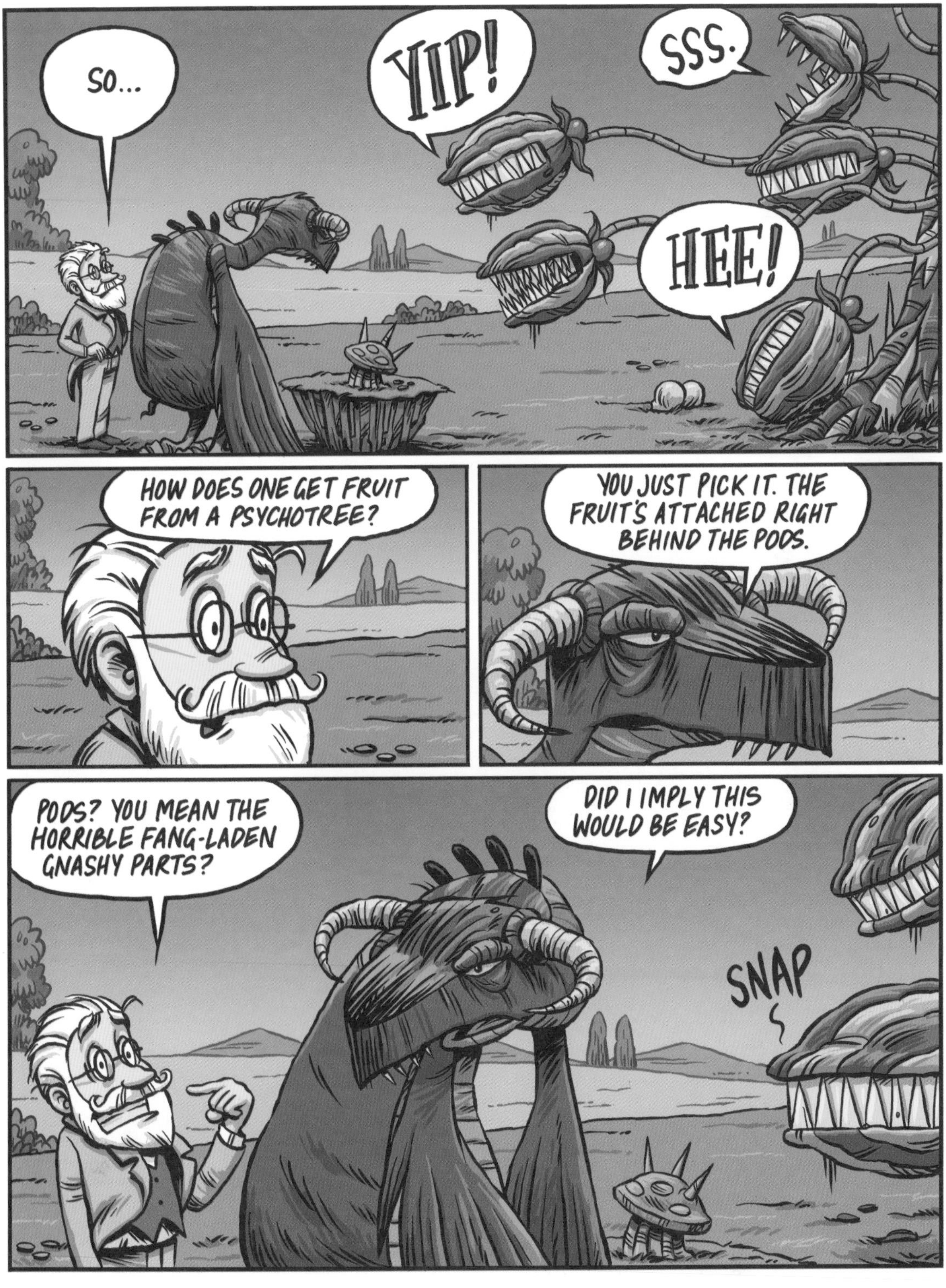

SO...
YIP!
SSS.
HEE!
HOW DOES ONE GET FRUIT FROM A PSYCHOTREE?
YOU JUST PICK IT. THE FRUIT'S ATTACHED RIGHT BEHIND THE PODS.
PODS? YOU MEAN THE HORRIBLE FANG-LADEN GNASHY PARTS?
DID I IMPLY THIS WOULD BE EASY?
SNAP

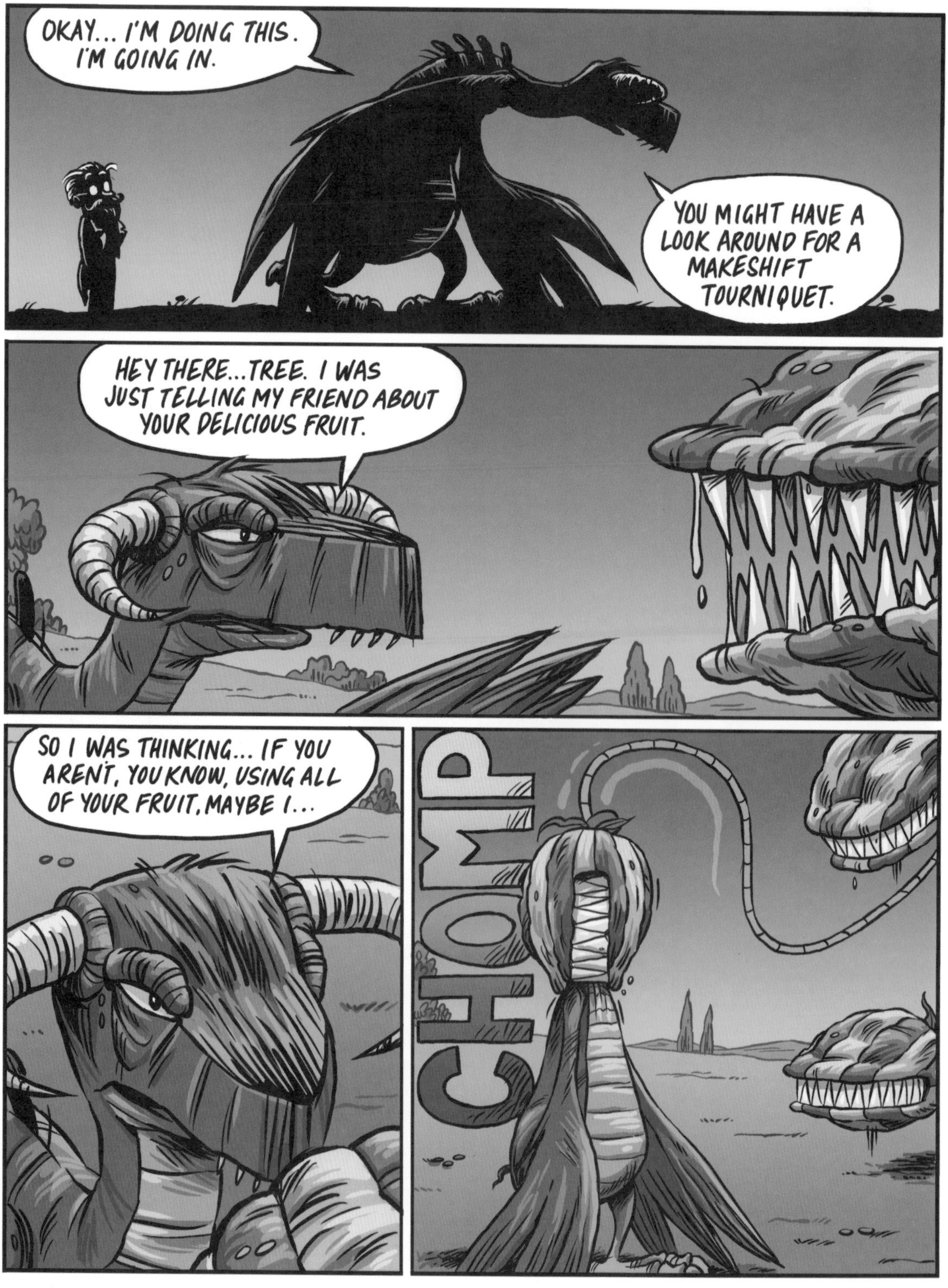
OKAY... I'M DOING THIS. I'M GOING IN.
YOU MIGHT HAVE A LOOK AROUND FOR A MAKESHIFT TOURNIQUET.
HEY THERE...TREE. I WAS JUST TELLING MY FRIEND ABOUT YOUR DELICIOUS FRUIT.
SO I WAS THINKING... IF YOU AREN'T, YOU KNOW, USING ALL OF YOUR FRUIT, MAYBE I...
CHOMP

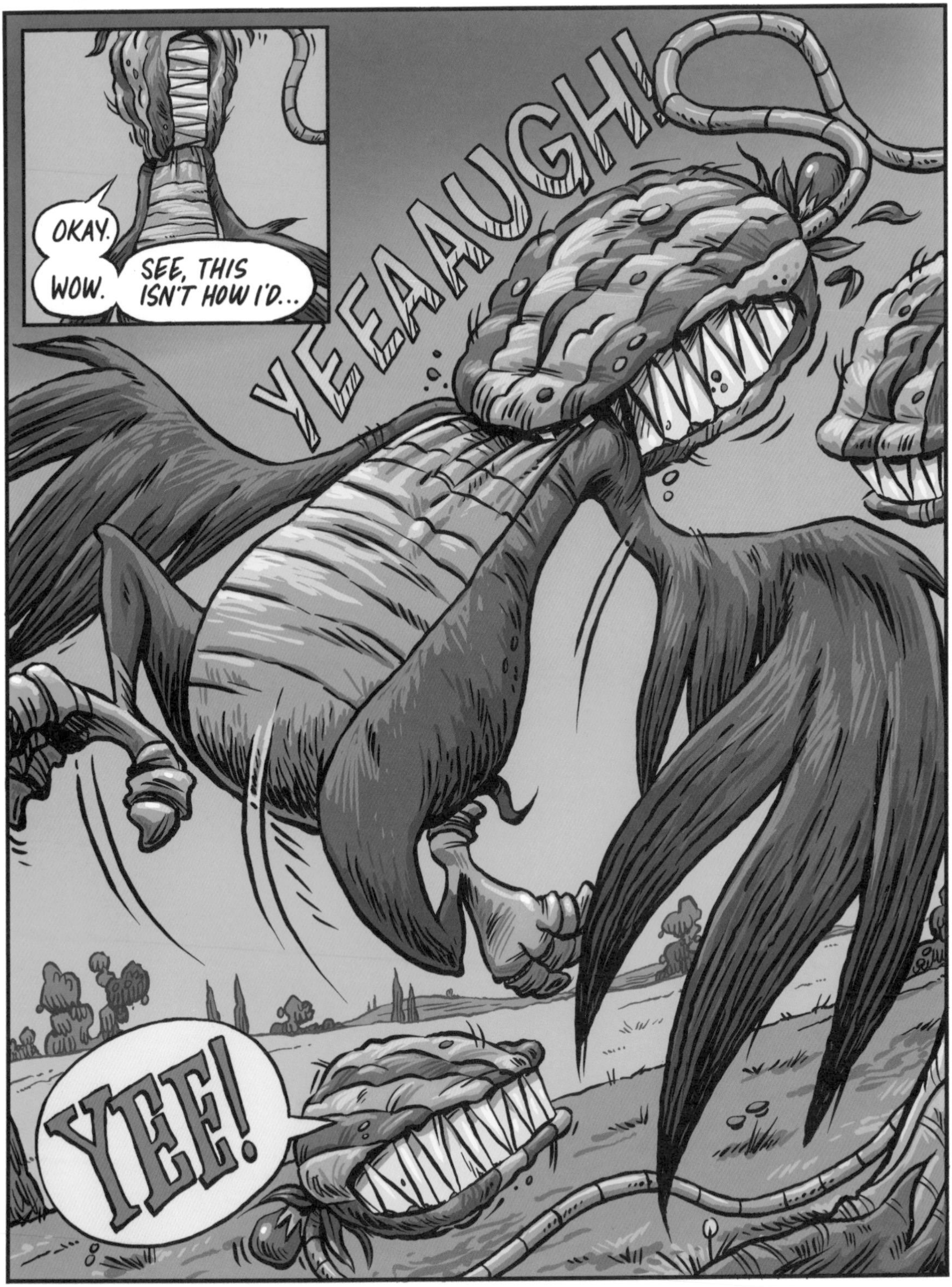
OKAY.
WOW.
SEE, THIS ISN'T HOW I'D...
YEEAAUGH!
YEE!

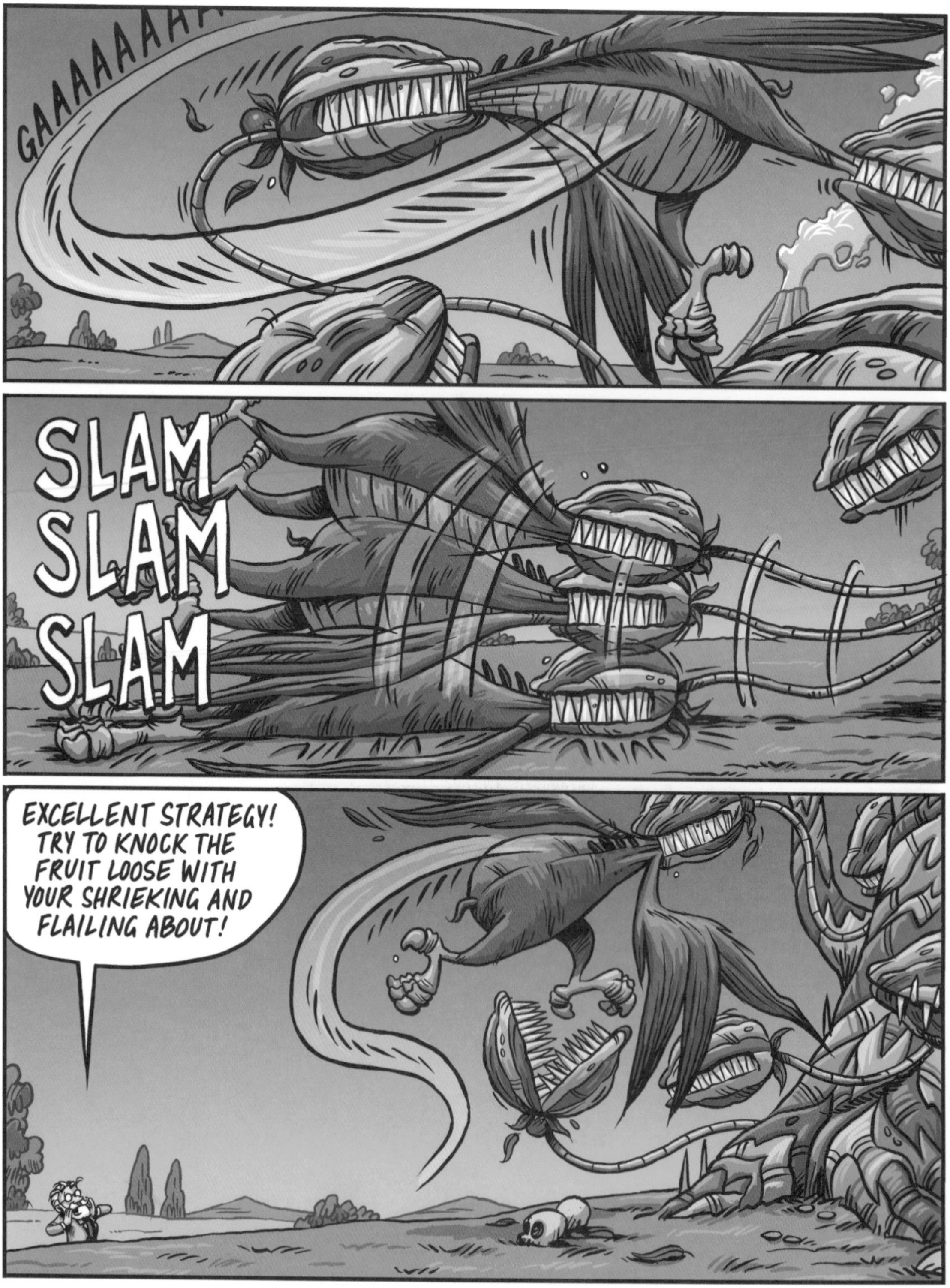
GAAAAAAAA
SLAM
SLAM
SLAM
EXCELLENT STRATEGY! TRY TO KNOCK THE FRUIT LOOSE WITH YOUR SHRIEKING AND FLAILING ABOUT!

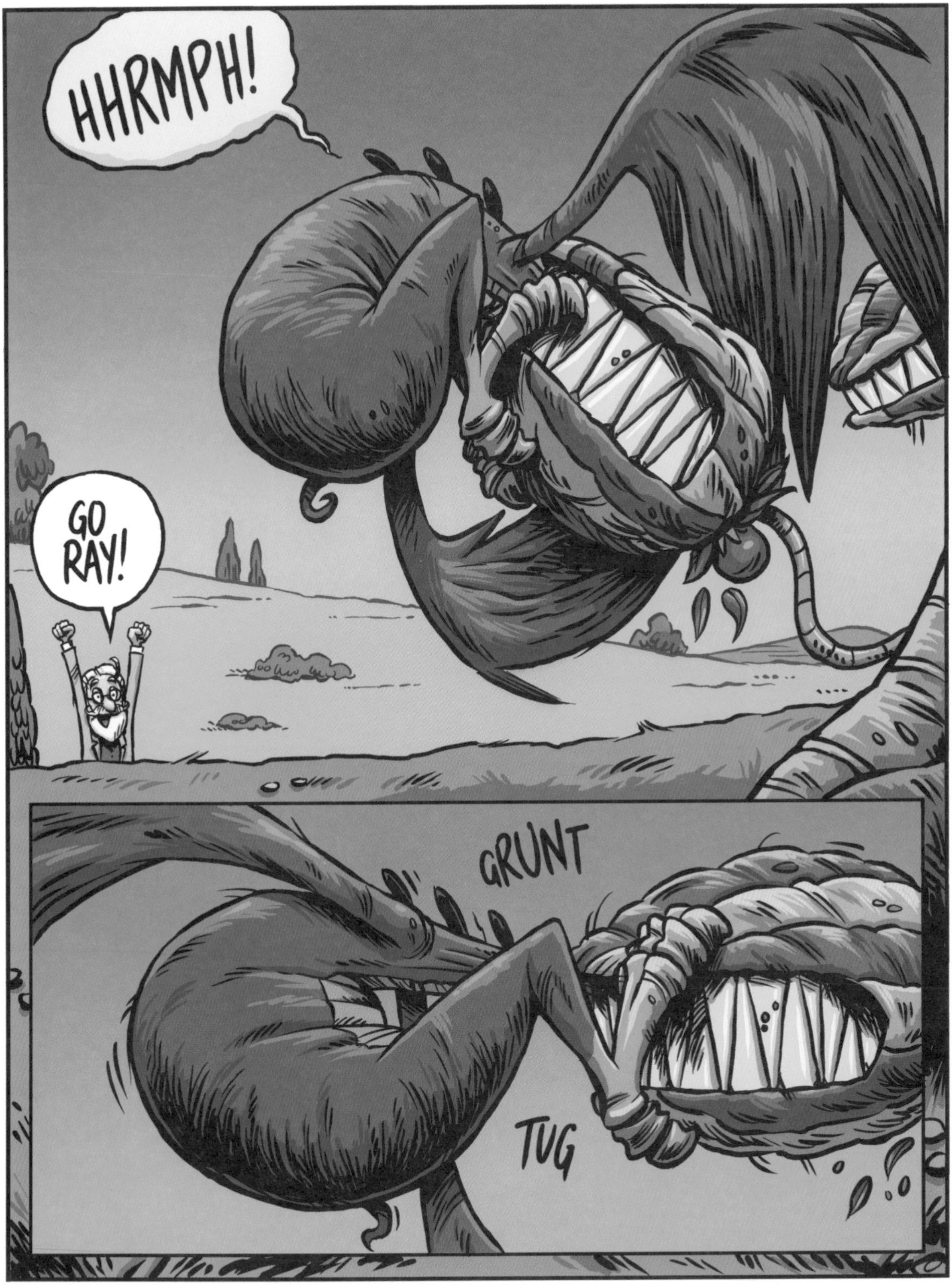
HHRMPH!
GO RAY!
GRUNT
TUG

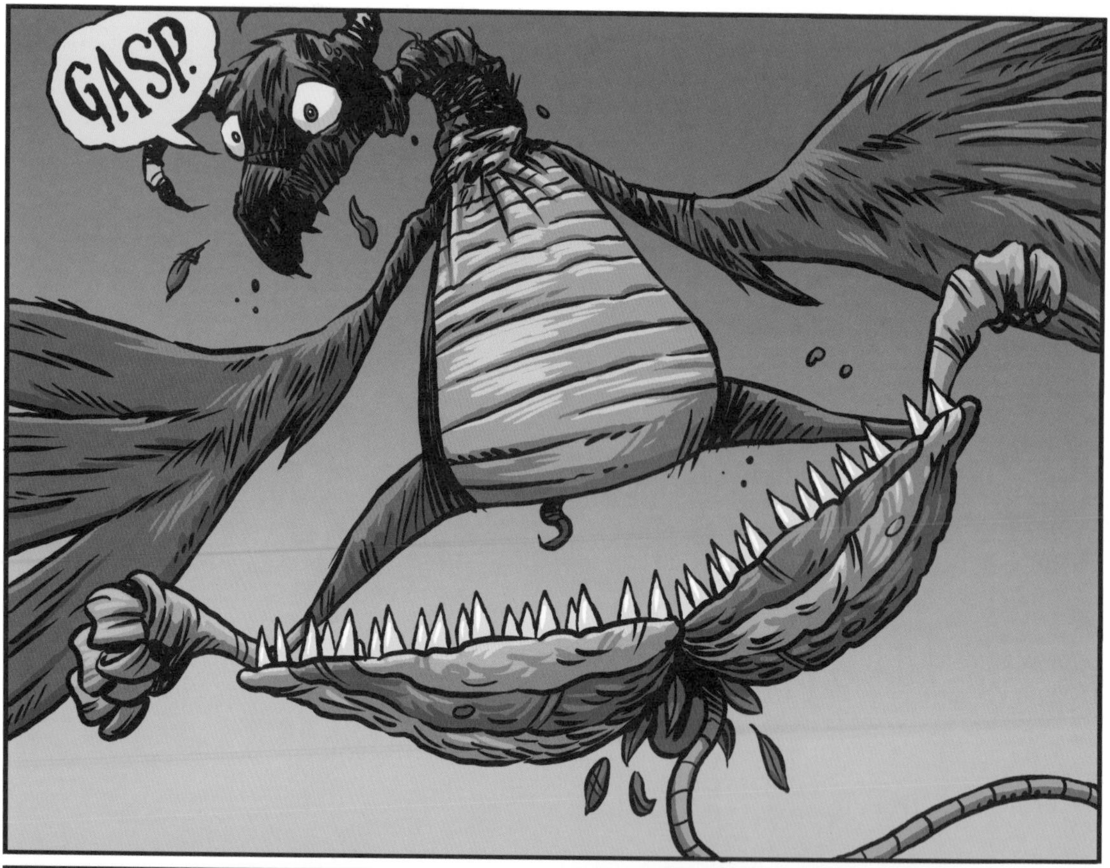
GASP.

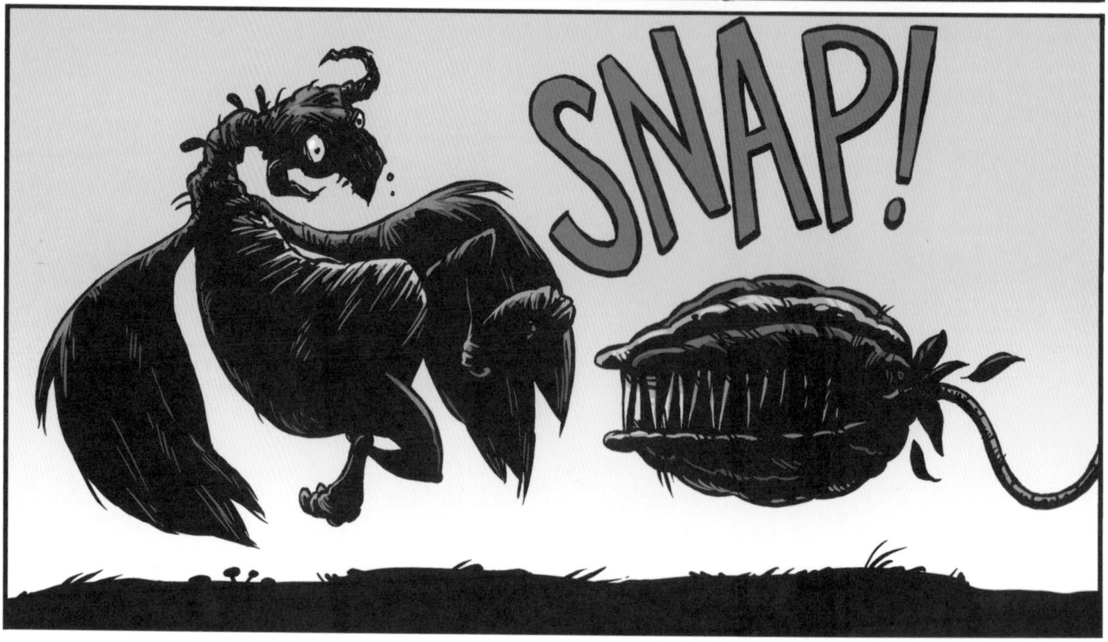
SNAP!

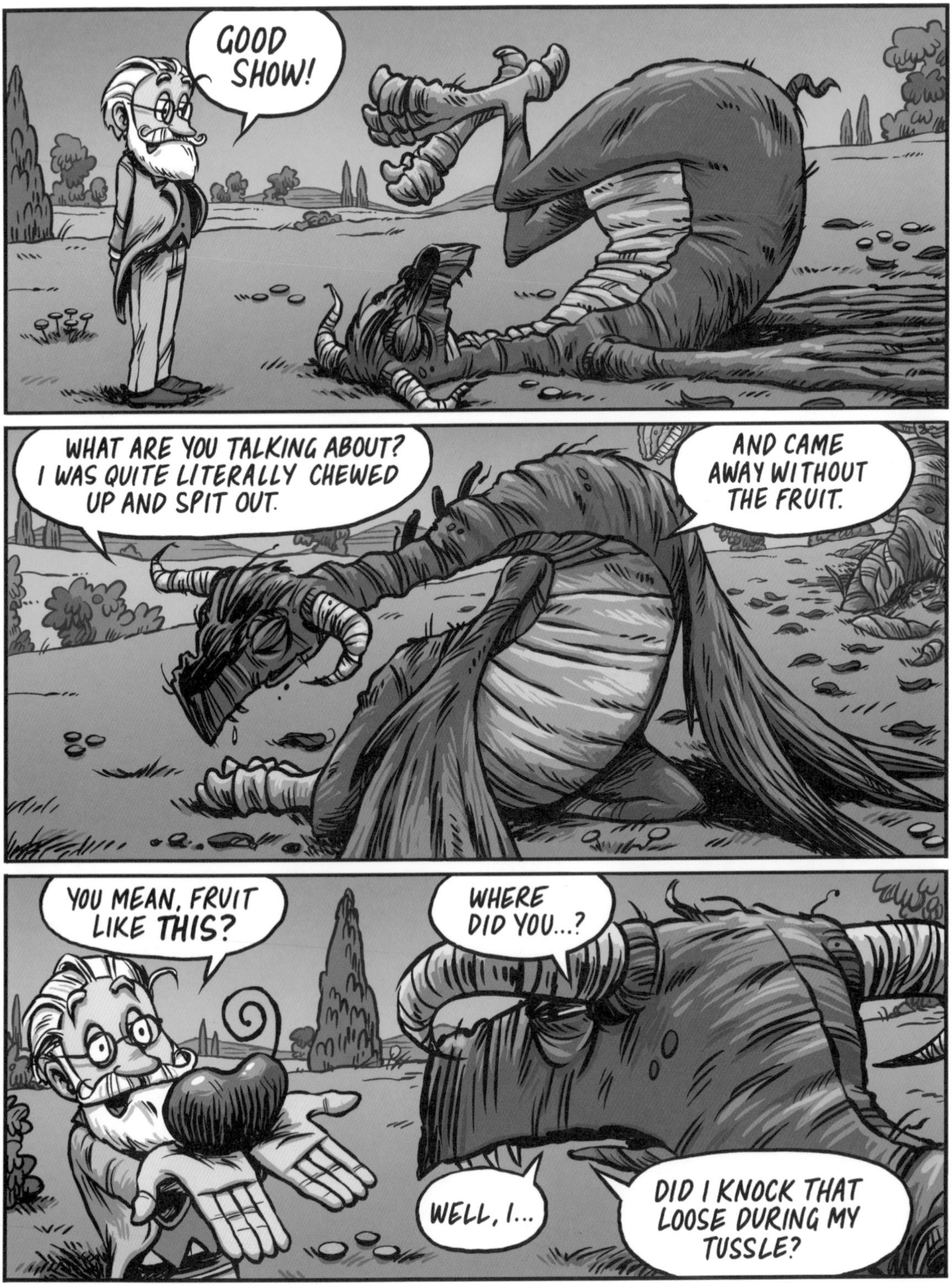
GOOD SHOW!
WHAT ARE YOU TALKING ABOUT? I WAS QUITE LITERALLY CHEWED UP AND SPIT OUT.
AND CAME AWAY WITHOUT THE FRUIT.
YOU MEAN, FRUIT LIKE THIS?
WHERE DID YOU...?
WELL, I...
DID I KNOCK THAT LOOSE DURING MY TUSSLE?

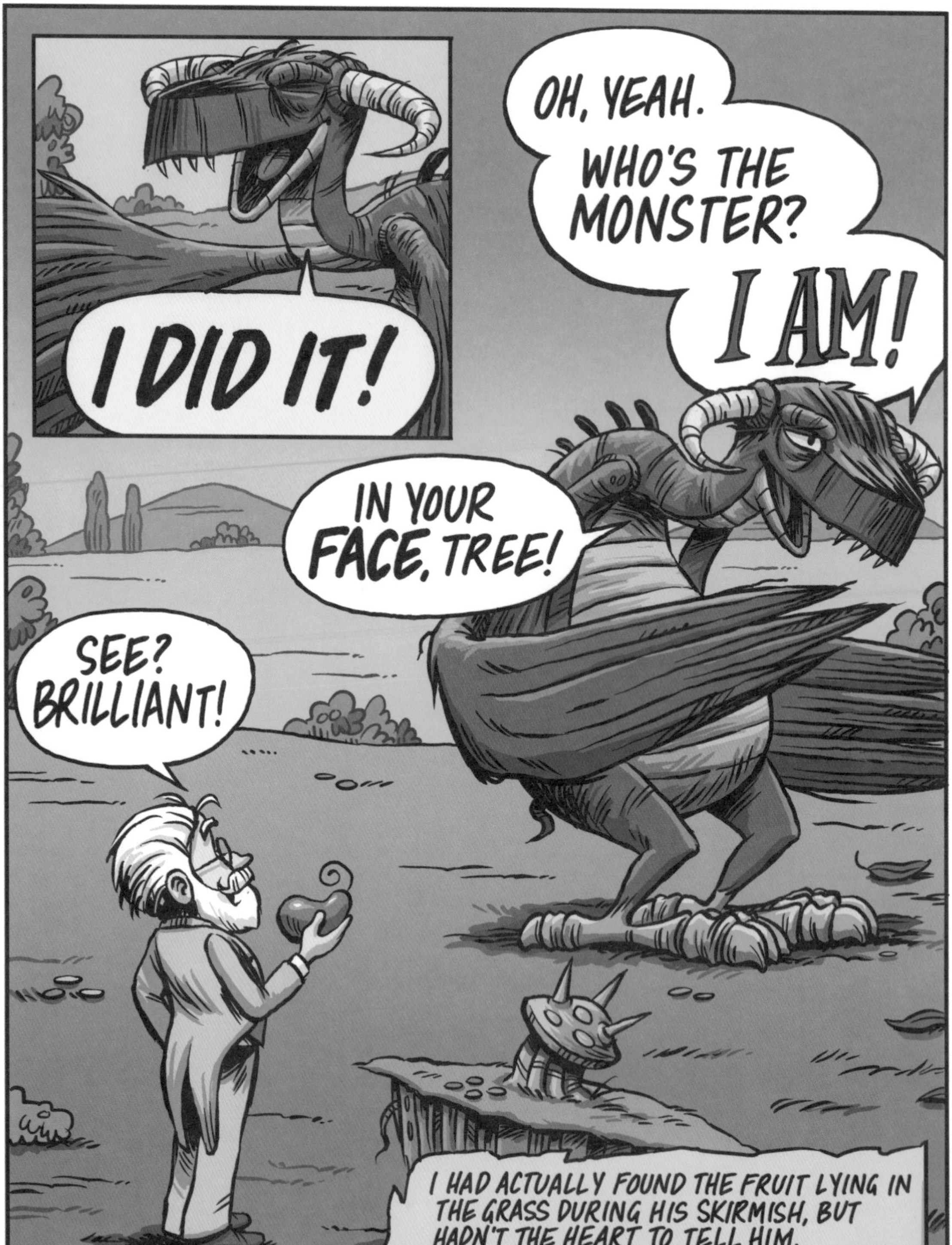
I DID IT!
OH, YEAH.
WHO'S THE MONSTER?
I AM!
IN YOUR FACE, TREE!
SEE? BRILLIANT!
I HAD ACTUALLY FOUND THE FRUIT LYING IN THE GRASS DURING HIS SKIRMISH, BUT HADN'T THE HEART TO TELL HIM.

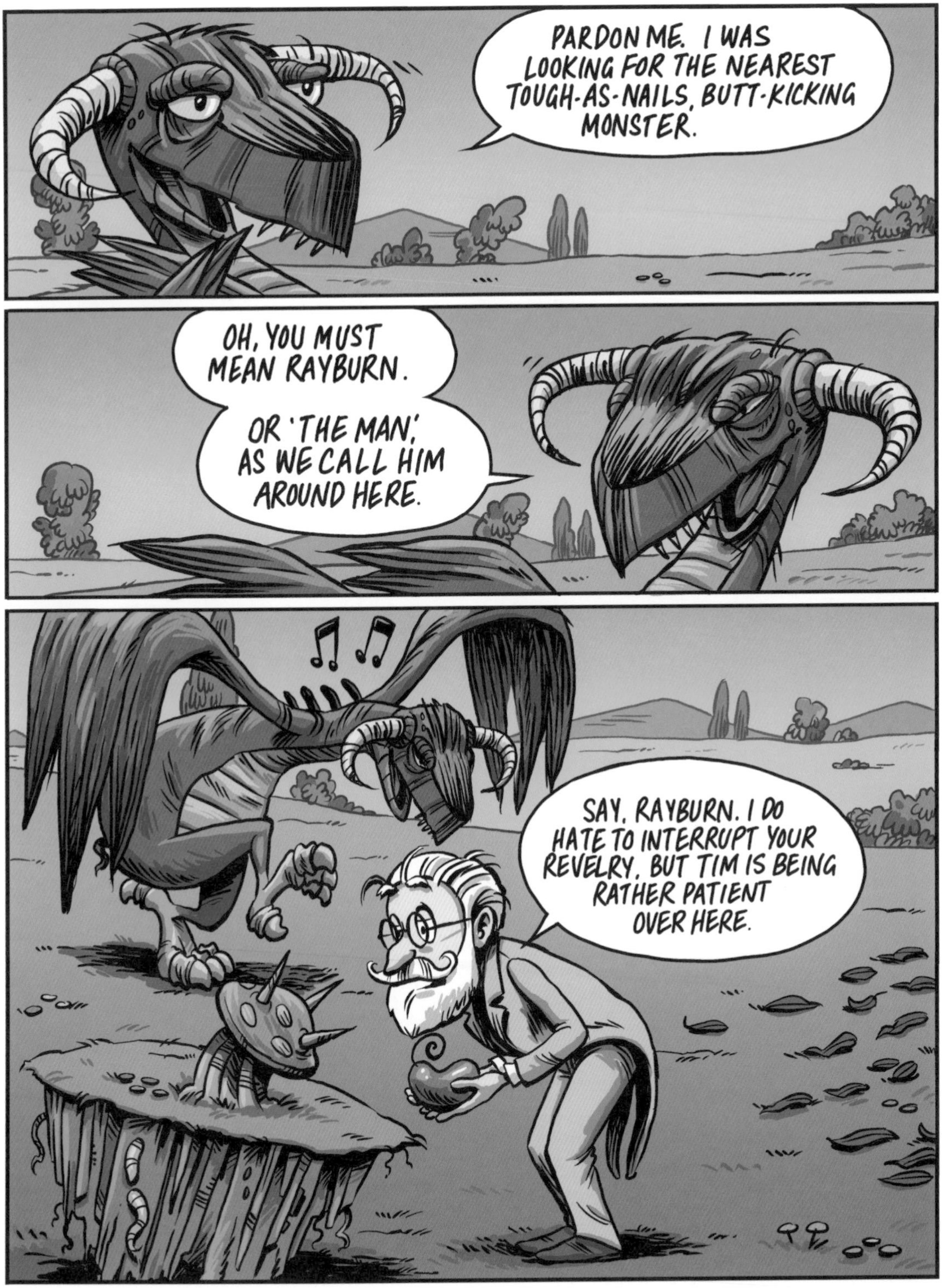
PARDON ME. I WAS LOOKING FOR THE NEAREST TOUGH-AS-NAILS, BUTT-KICKING MONSTER.
OH, YOU MUST MEAN RAYBURN.
OR 'THE MAN,' AS WE CALL HIM AROUND HERE.
SAY, RAYBURN. I DO HATE TO INTERRUPT YOUR REVELRY, BUT TIM IS BEING RATHER PATIENT OVER HERE.

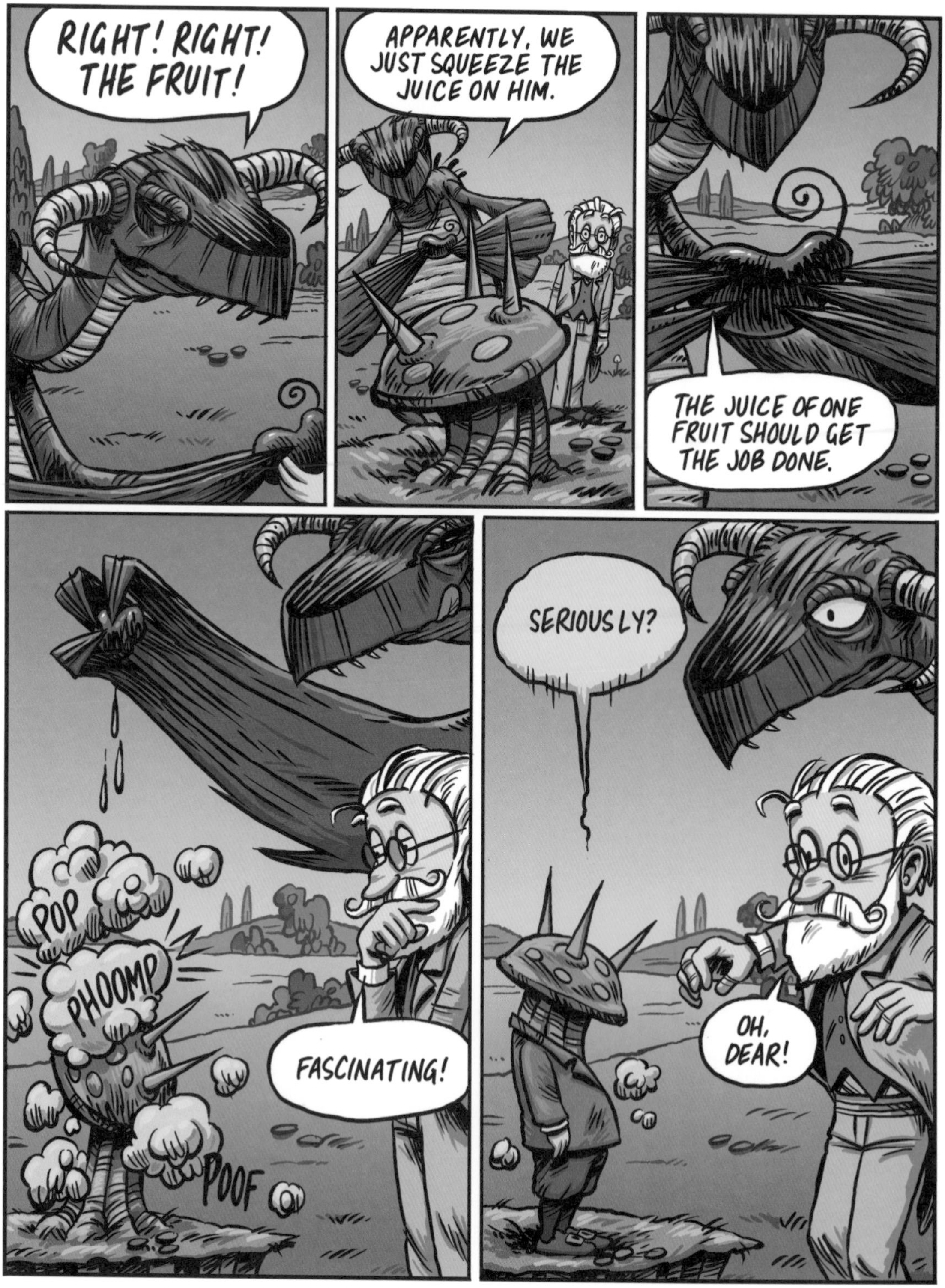
RIGHT! RIGHT! THE FRUIT!
APPARENTLY, WE JUST SQUEEZE THE JUICE ON HIM.
THE JUICE OF ONE FRUIT SHOULD GET THE JOB DONE.
POP
PHOOMP
POOF
FASCINATING!
SERIOUSLY?
OH, DEAR!

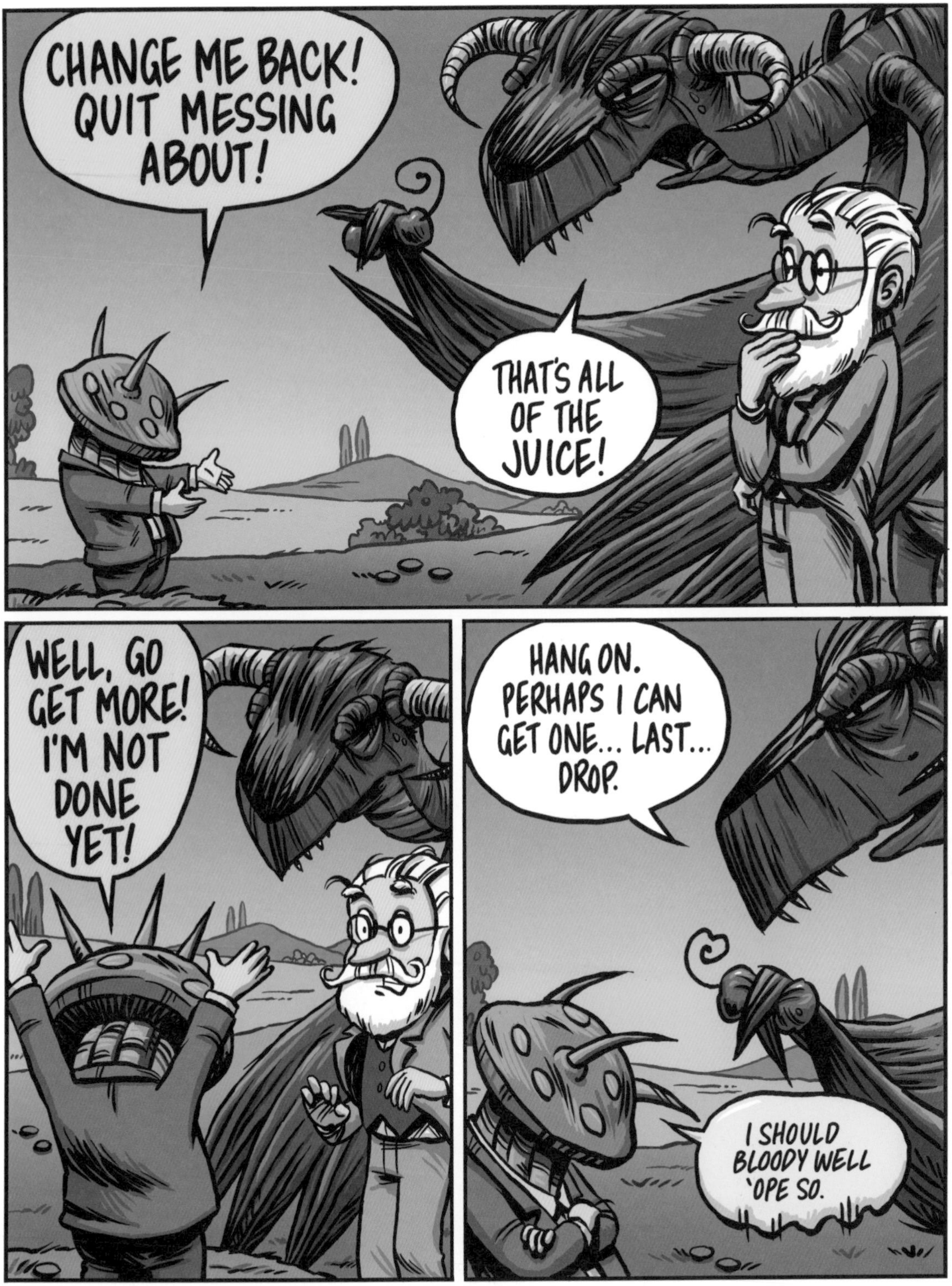
CHANGE ME BACK! QUIT MESSING ABOUT!
THAT'S ALL OF THE JUICE!
WELL, GO GET MORE! I'M NOT DONE YET!
HANG ON. PERHAPS I CAN GET ONE... LAST... DROP.
I SHOULD BLOODY WELL 'OPE SO.

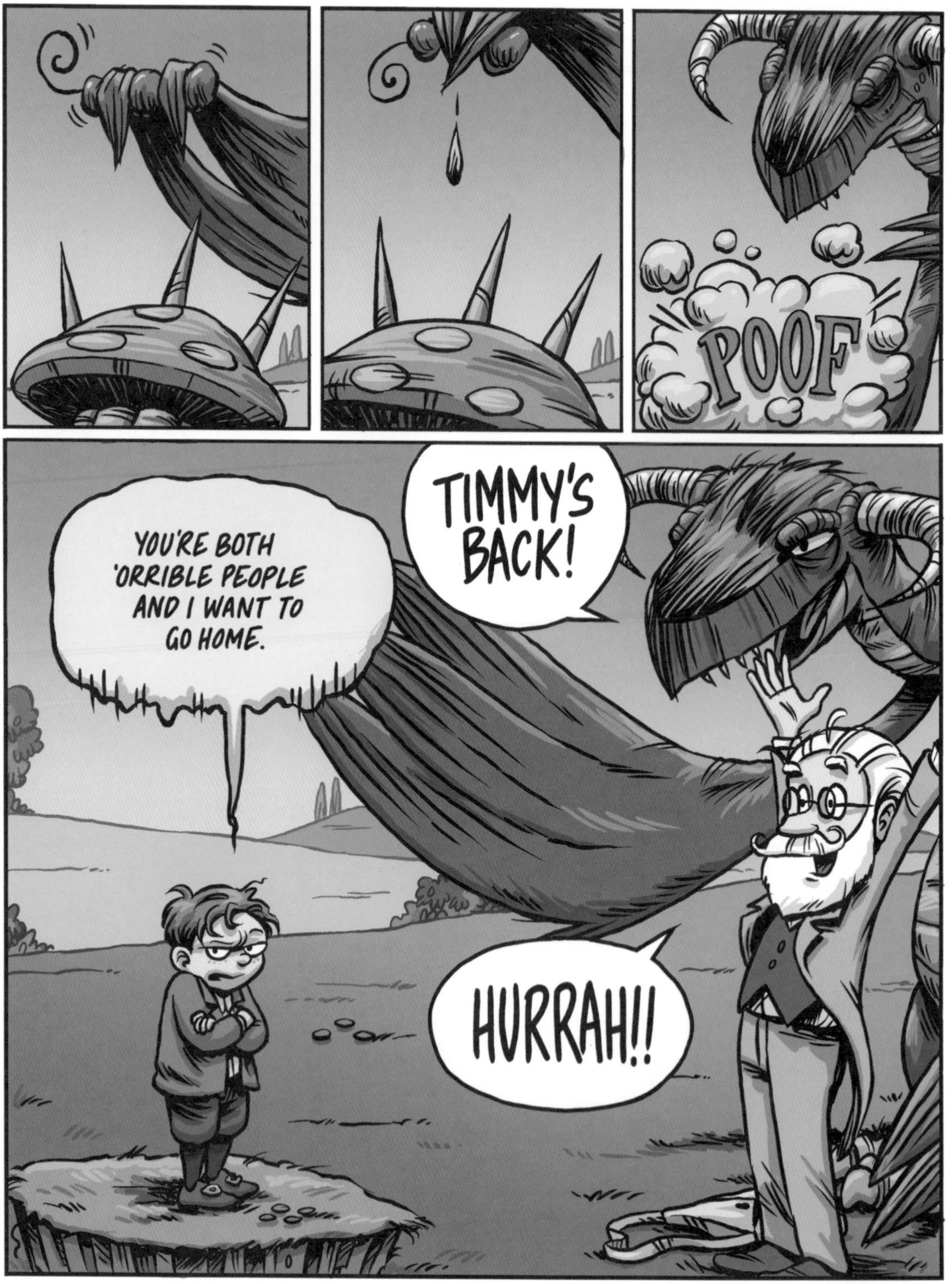
POOF
TIMMY'S BACK!
YOU'RE BOTH 'ORRIBLE PEOPLE AND I WANT TO GO HOME.
HURRAH!!

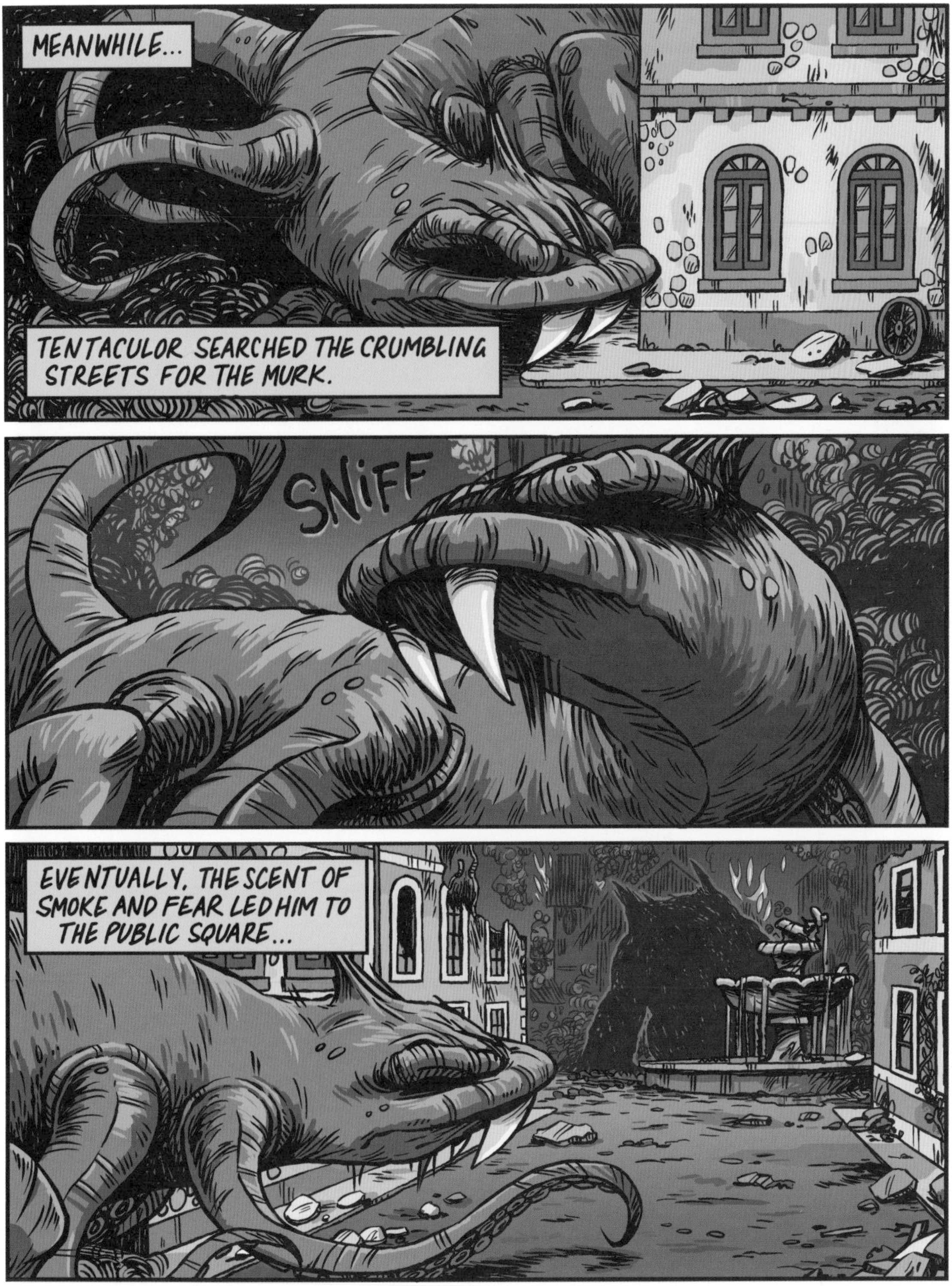
MEANWHILE...
TENTACULOR SEARCHED THE CRUMBLING STREETS FOR THE MURK.
SNIFF
EVENTUALLY, THE SCENT OF SMOKE AND FEAR LED HIM TO THE PUBLIC SQUARE...

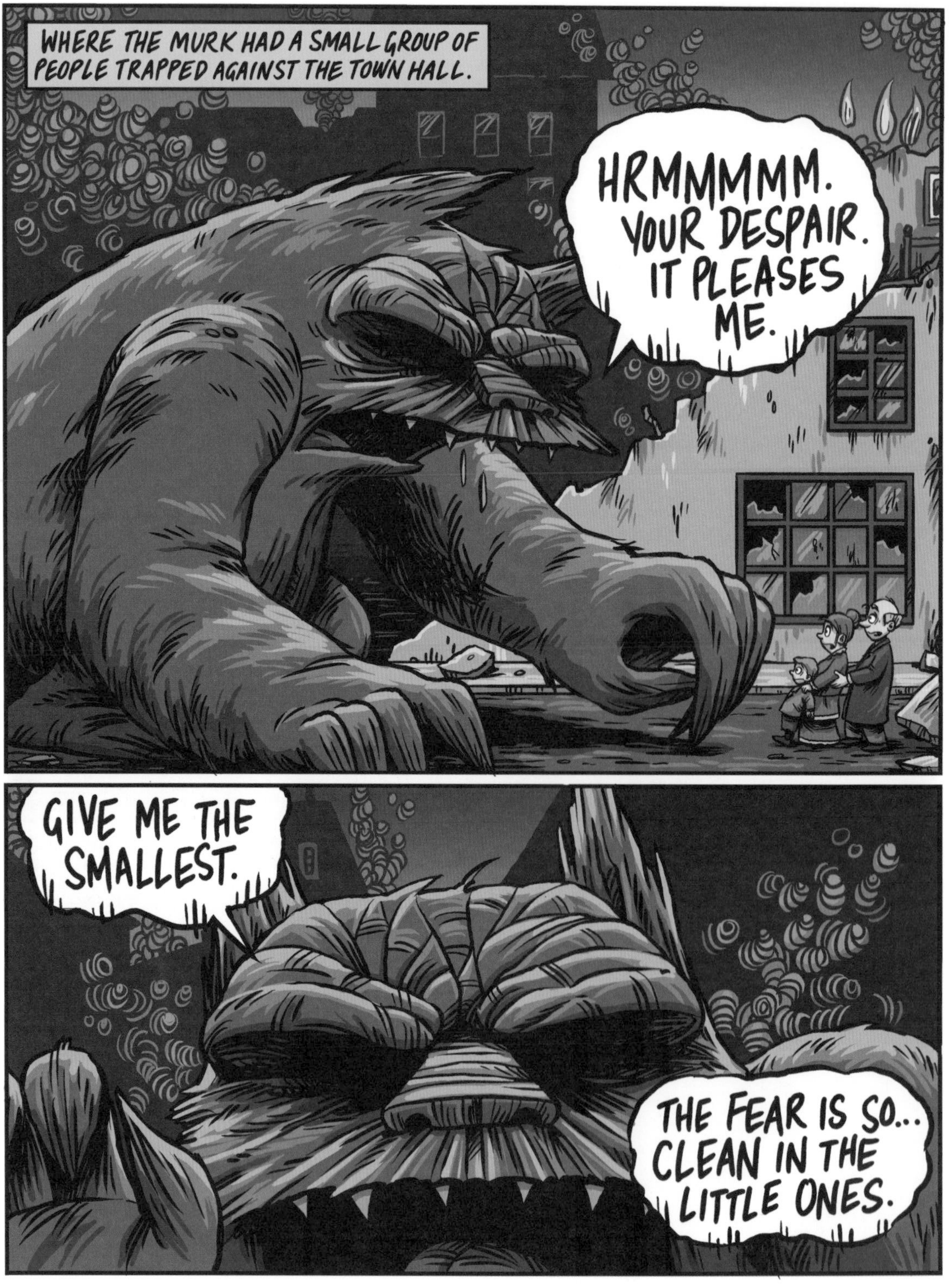
WHERE THE MURK HAD A SMALL GROUP OF PEOPLE TRAPPED AGAINST THE TOWN HALL.
HRMMMMM. YOUR DESPAIR. IT PLEASES ME.
GIVE ME THE SMALLEST.
THE FEAR IS SO... CLEAN IN THE LITTLE ONES.

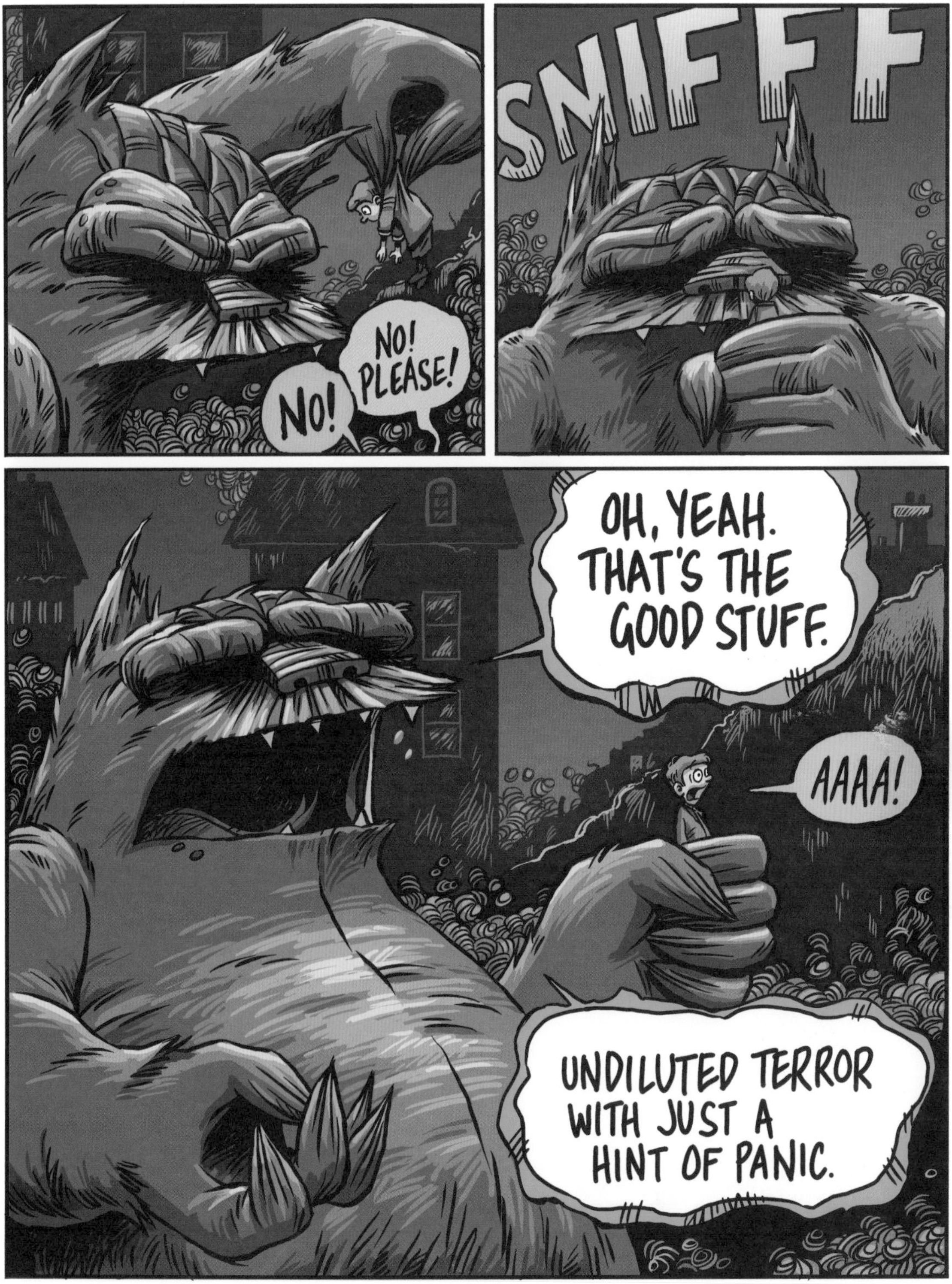
No!
No! Please!
SNIFFF
Oh, yeah. That's the good stuff.
AAAA!
Undiluted terror with just a hint of panic.

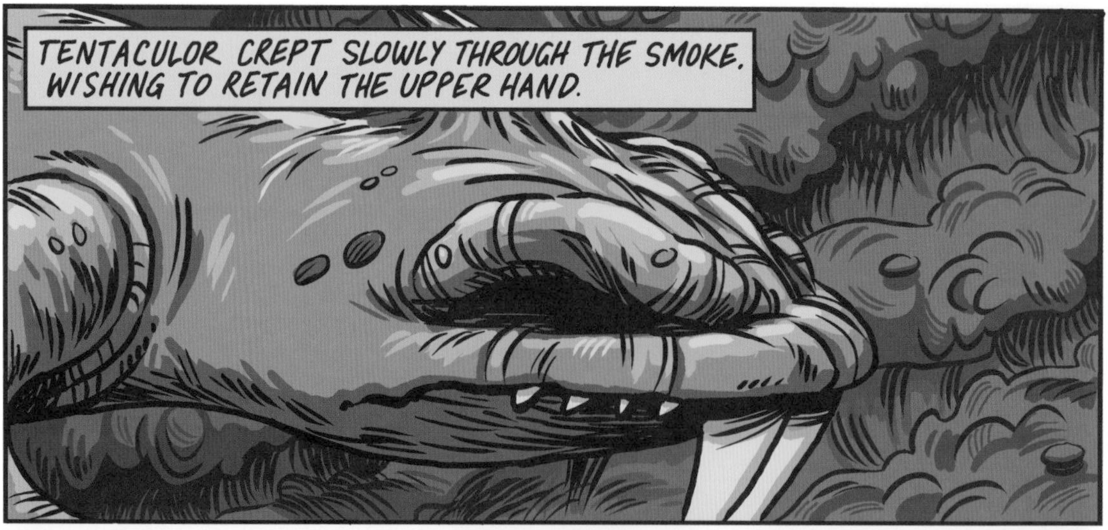
TENTACULOR CREPT SLOWLY THROUGH THE SMOKE, WISHING TO RETAIN THE UPPER HAND.

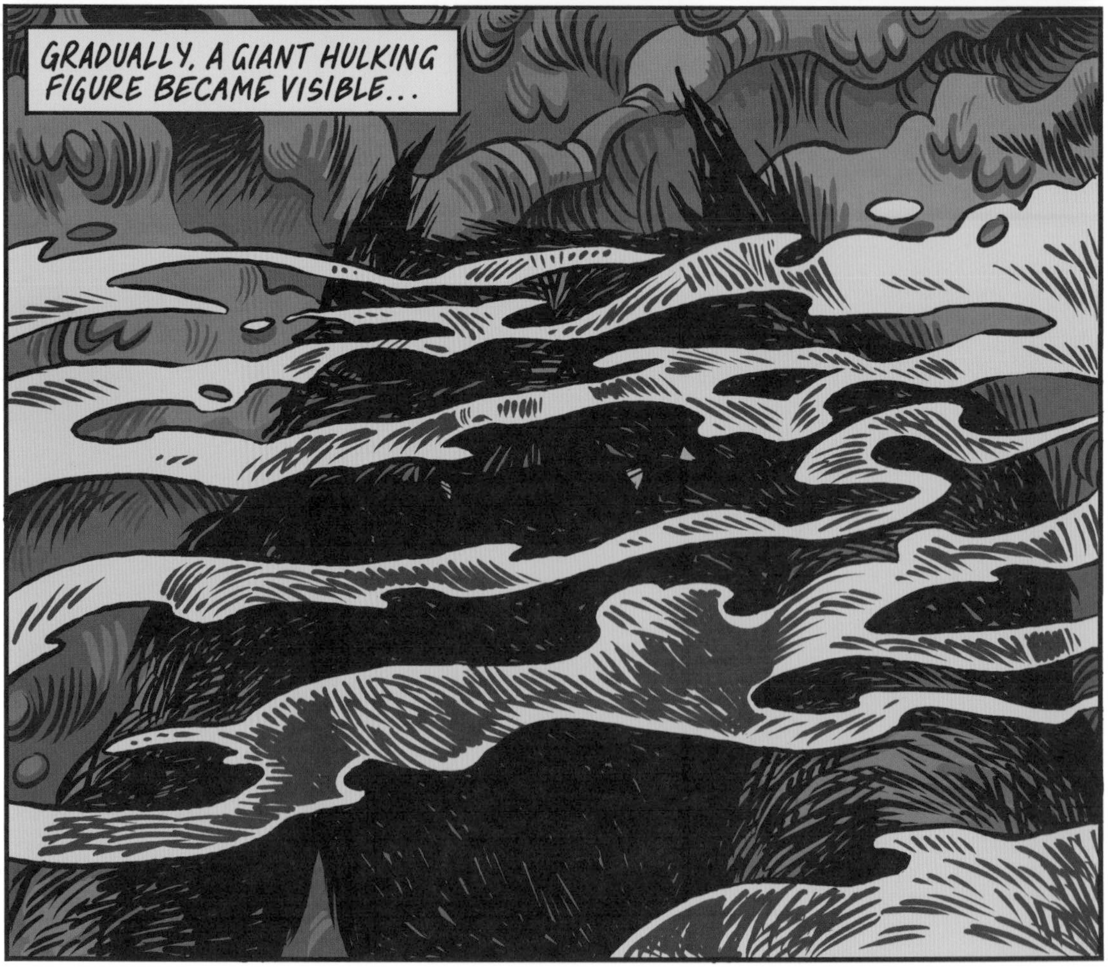
GRADUALLY, A GIANT HULKING FIGURE BECAME VISIBLE...

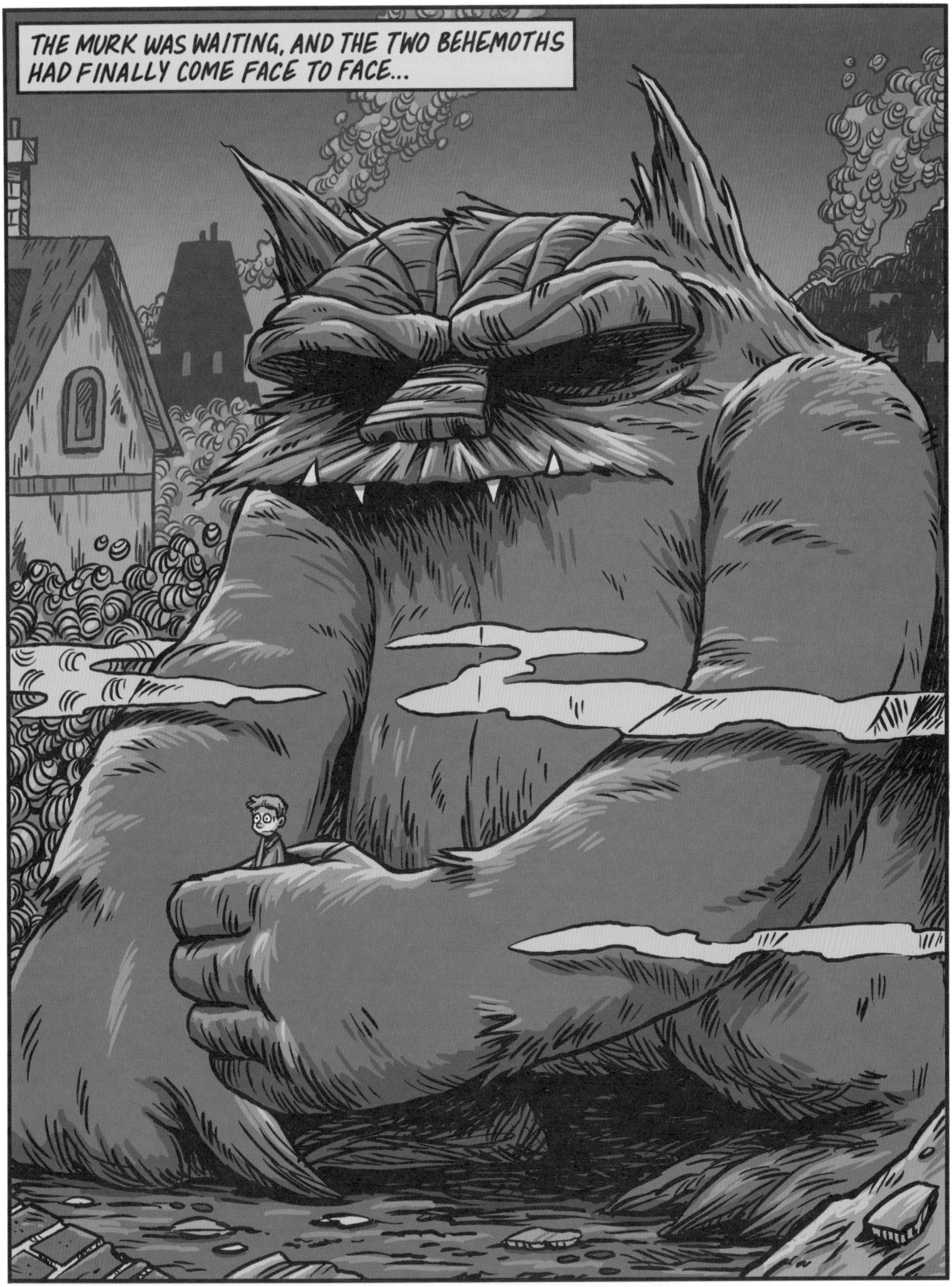
THE MURK WAS WAITING, AND THE TWO BEHEMOTHS HAD FINALLY COME FACE TO FACE...

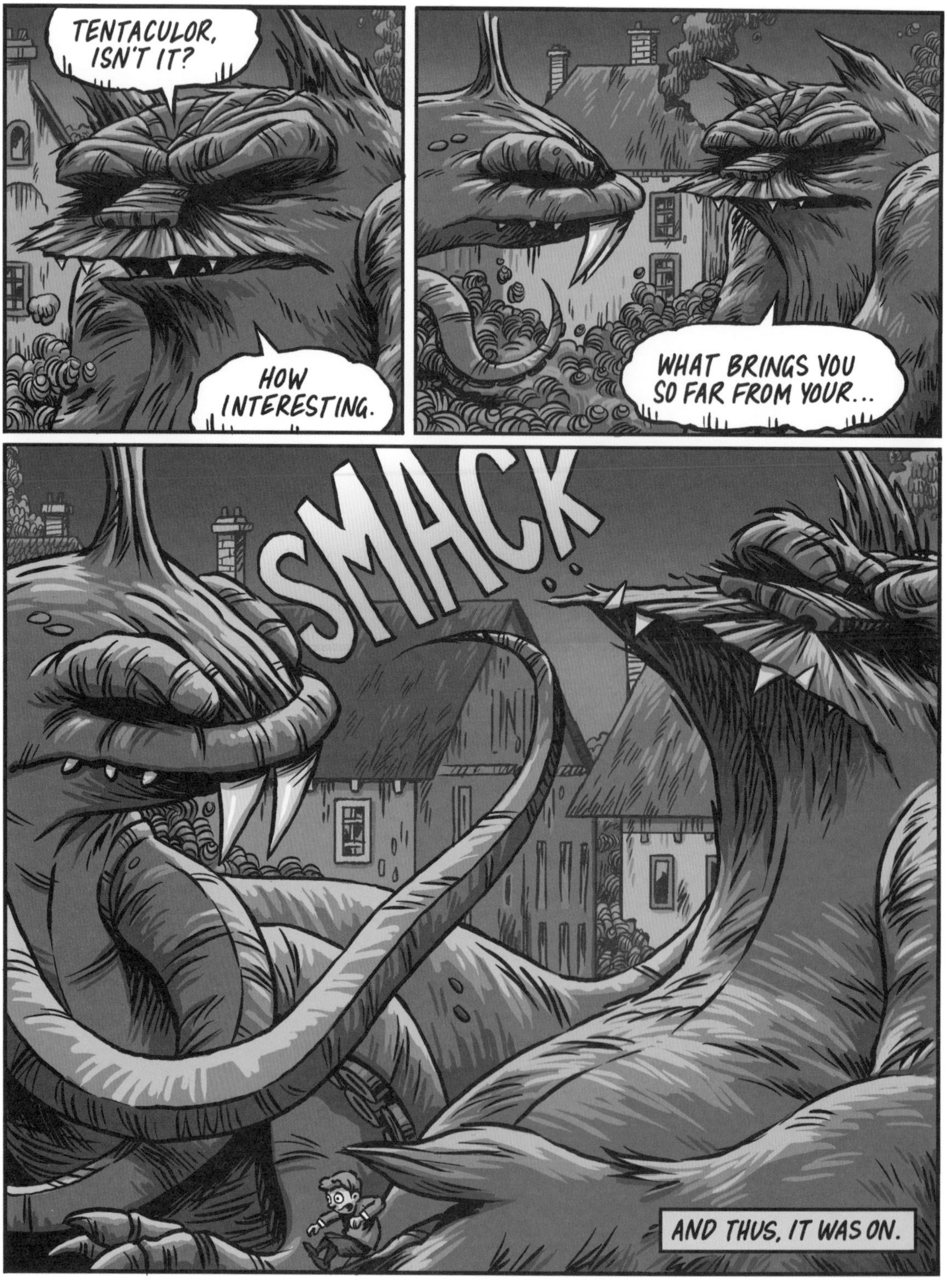
TENTACULOR, ISN'T IT?
HOW INTERESTING.
WHAT BRINGS YOU SO FAR FROM YOUR...
SMACK
AND THUS, IT WAS ON.

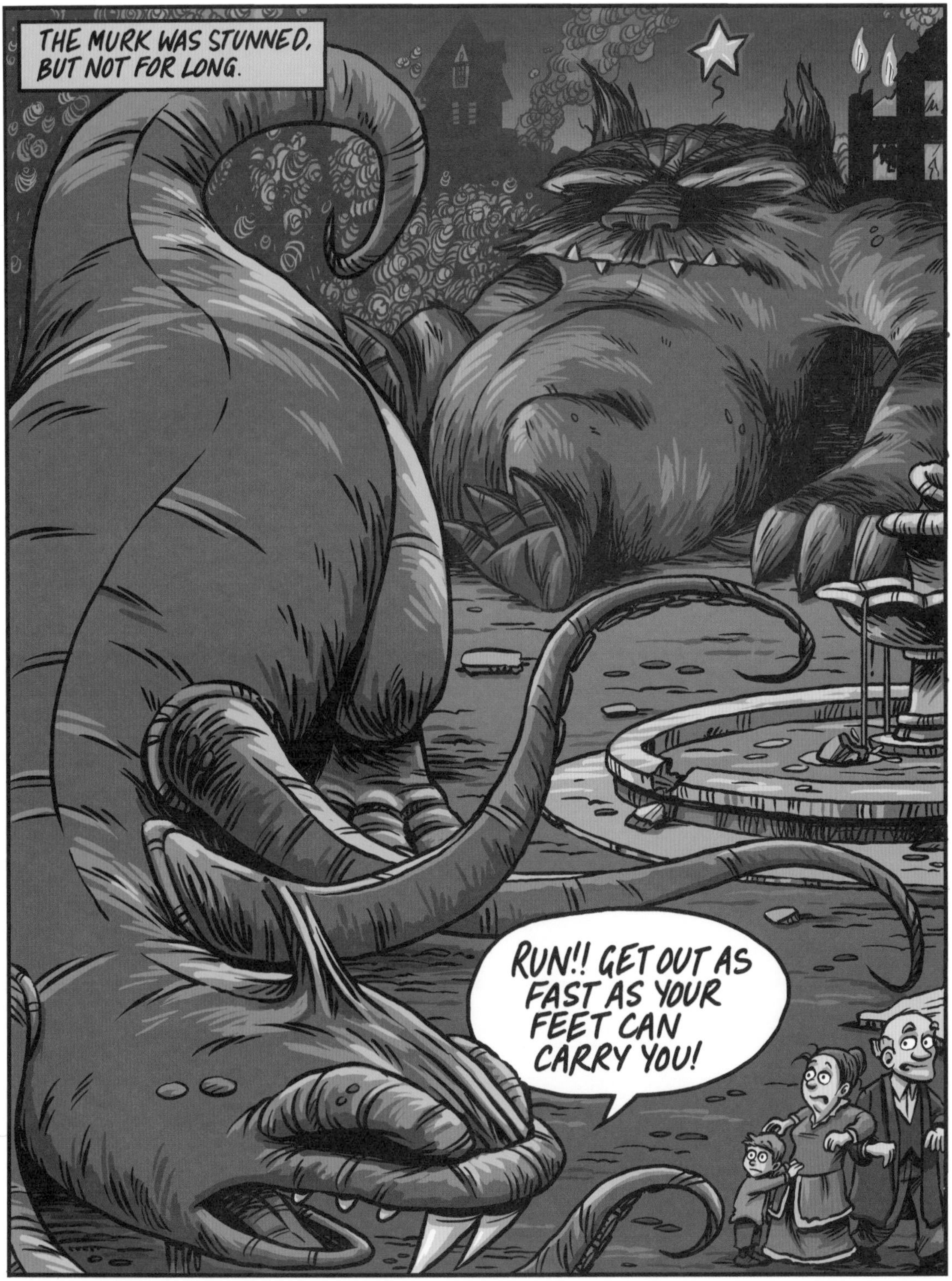
THE MURK WAS STUNNED, BUT NOT FOR LONG.
RUN!! GET OUT AS FAST AS YOUR FEET CAN CARRY YOU!

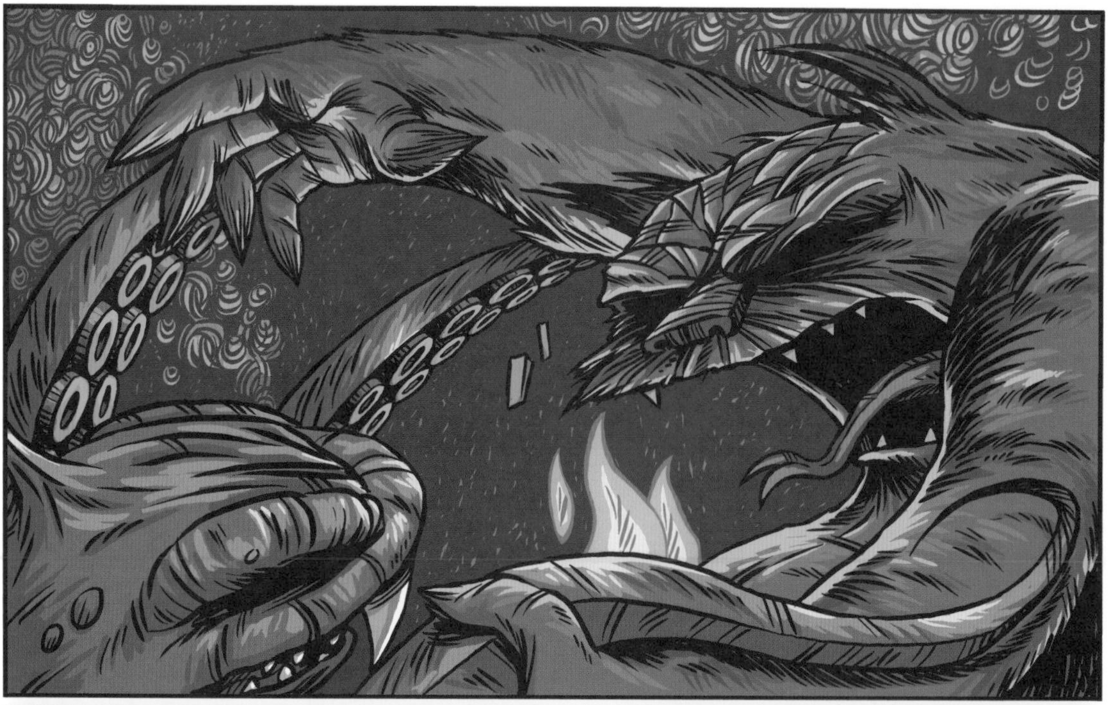

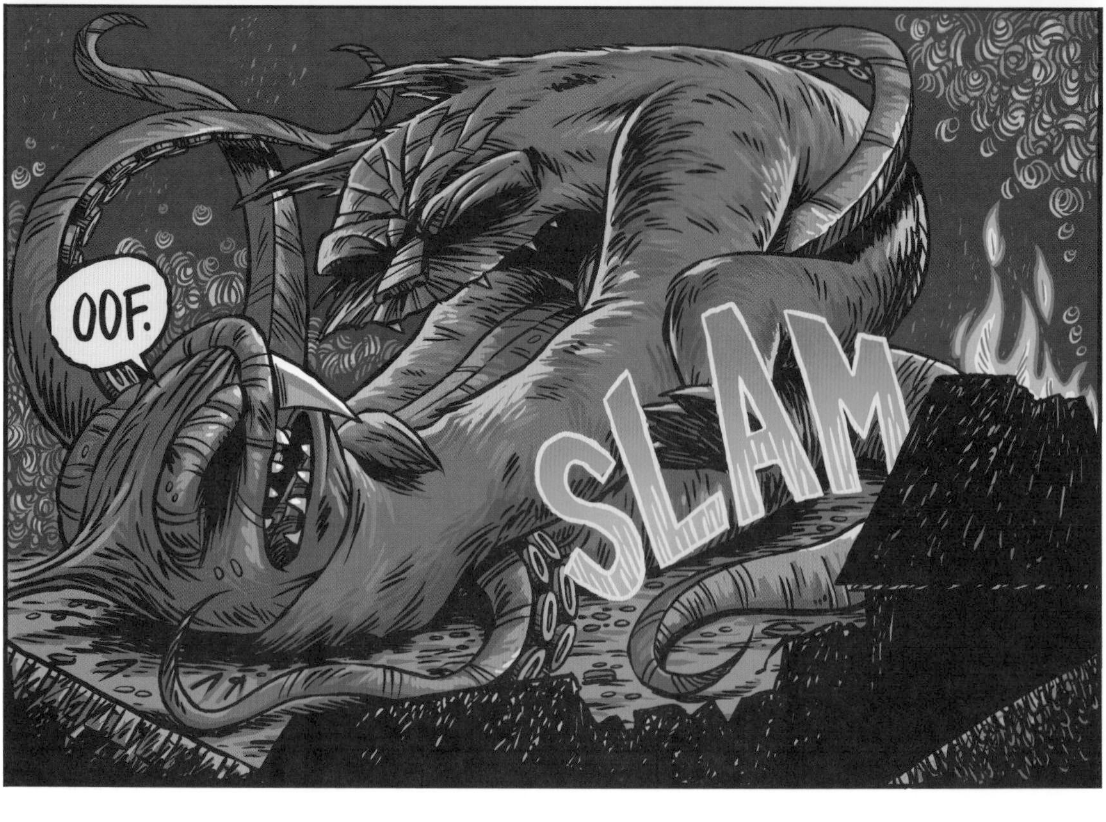
OOF.
SLAM

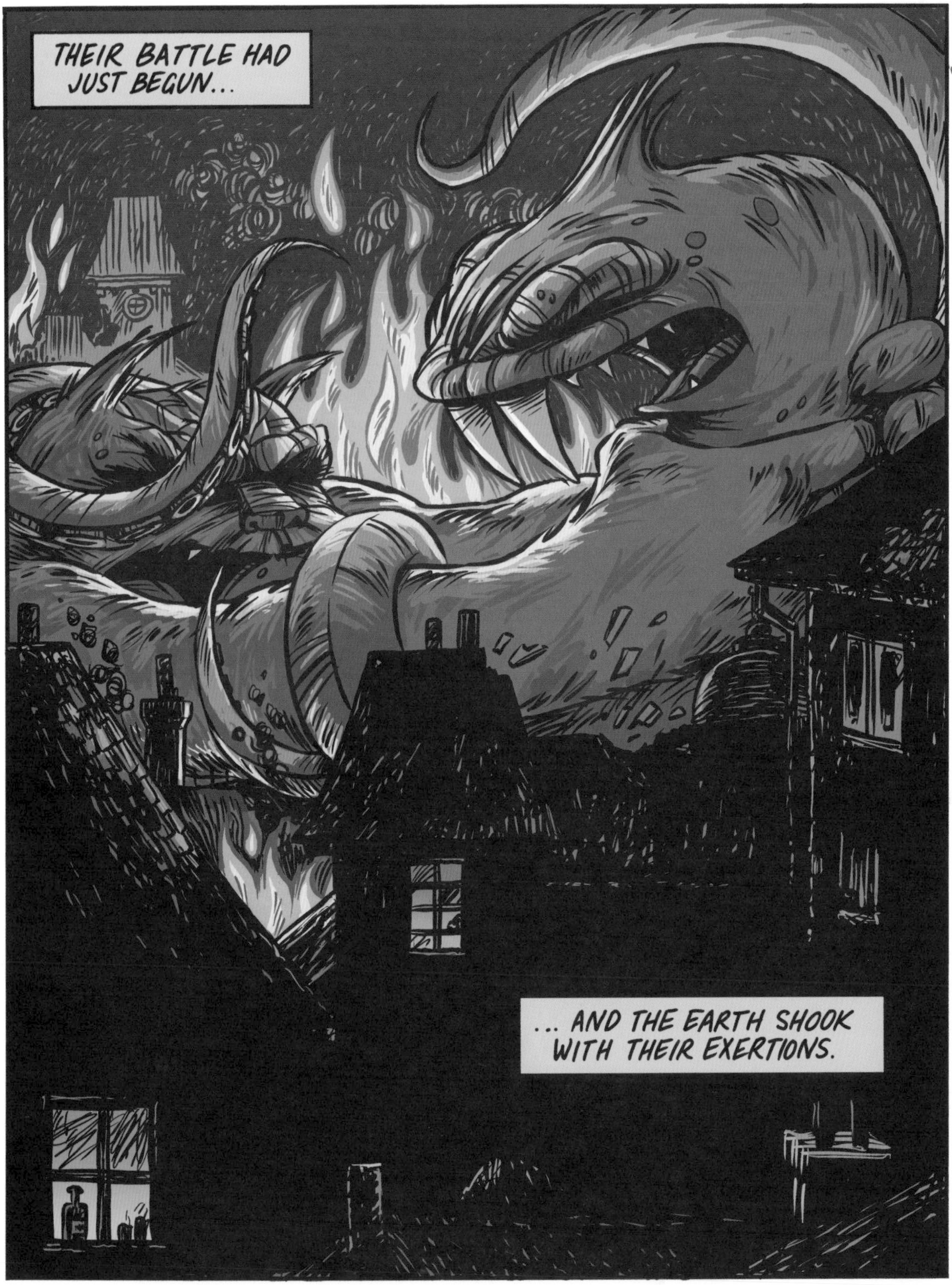
THEIR BATTLE HAD JUST BEGUN...
... AND THE EARTH SHOOK WITH THEIR EXERTIONS.

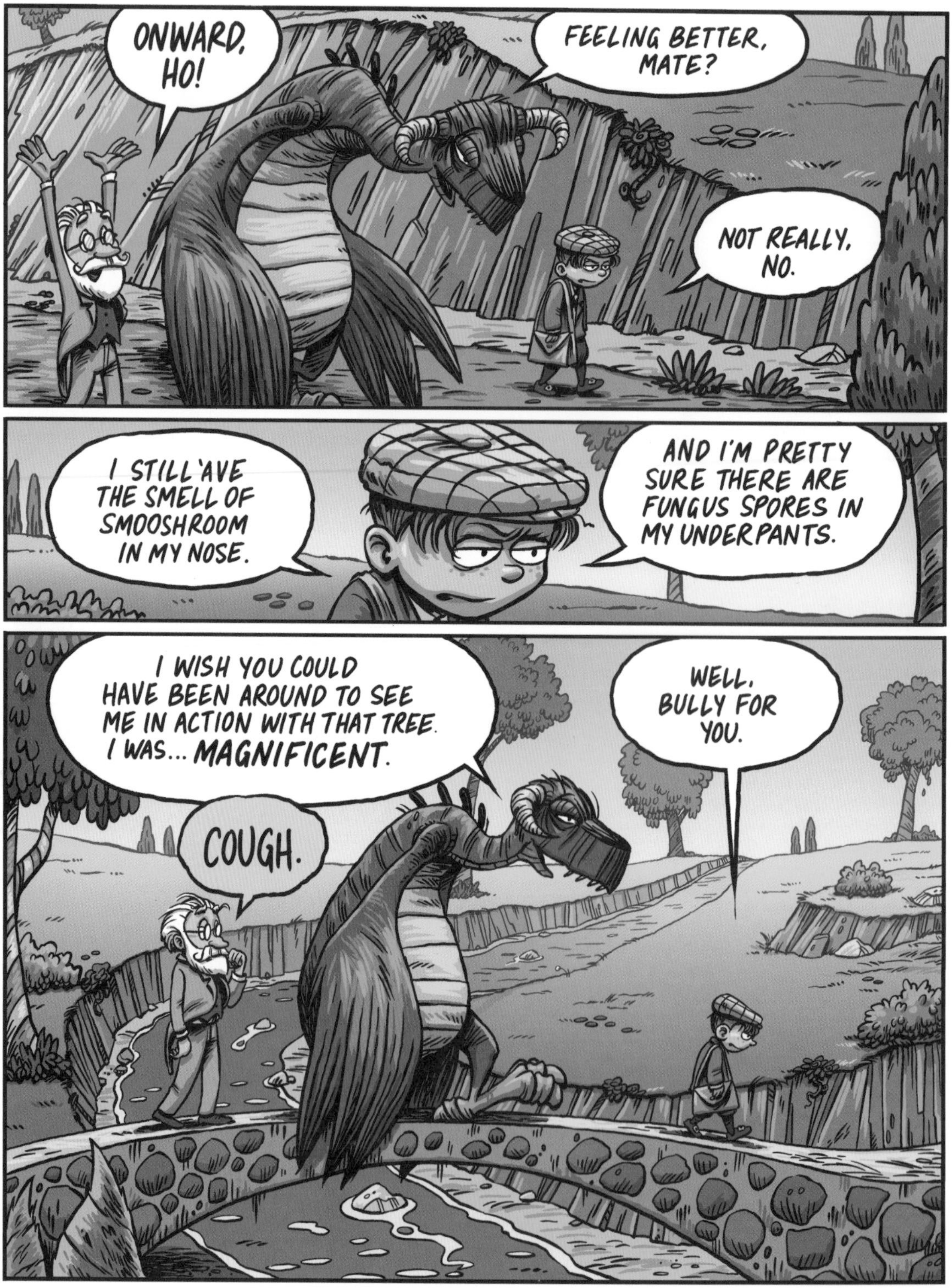
ONWARD, HO!
FEELING BETTER, MATE?
NOT REALLY, NO.
I STILL 'AVE THE SMELL OF SMOOSHROOM IN MY NOSE.
AND I'M PRETTY SURE THERE ARE FUNGUS SPORES IN MY UNDERPANTS.
I WISH YOU COULD HAVE BEEN AROUND TO SEE ME IN ACTION WITH THAT TREE. I WAS... MAGNIFICENT.
WELL, BULLY FOR YOU.
COUGH.

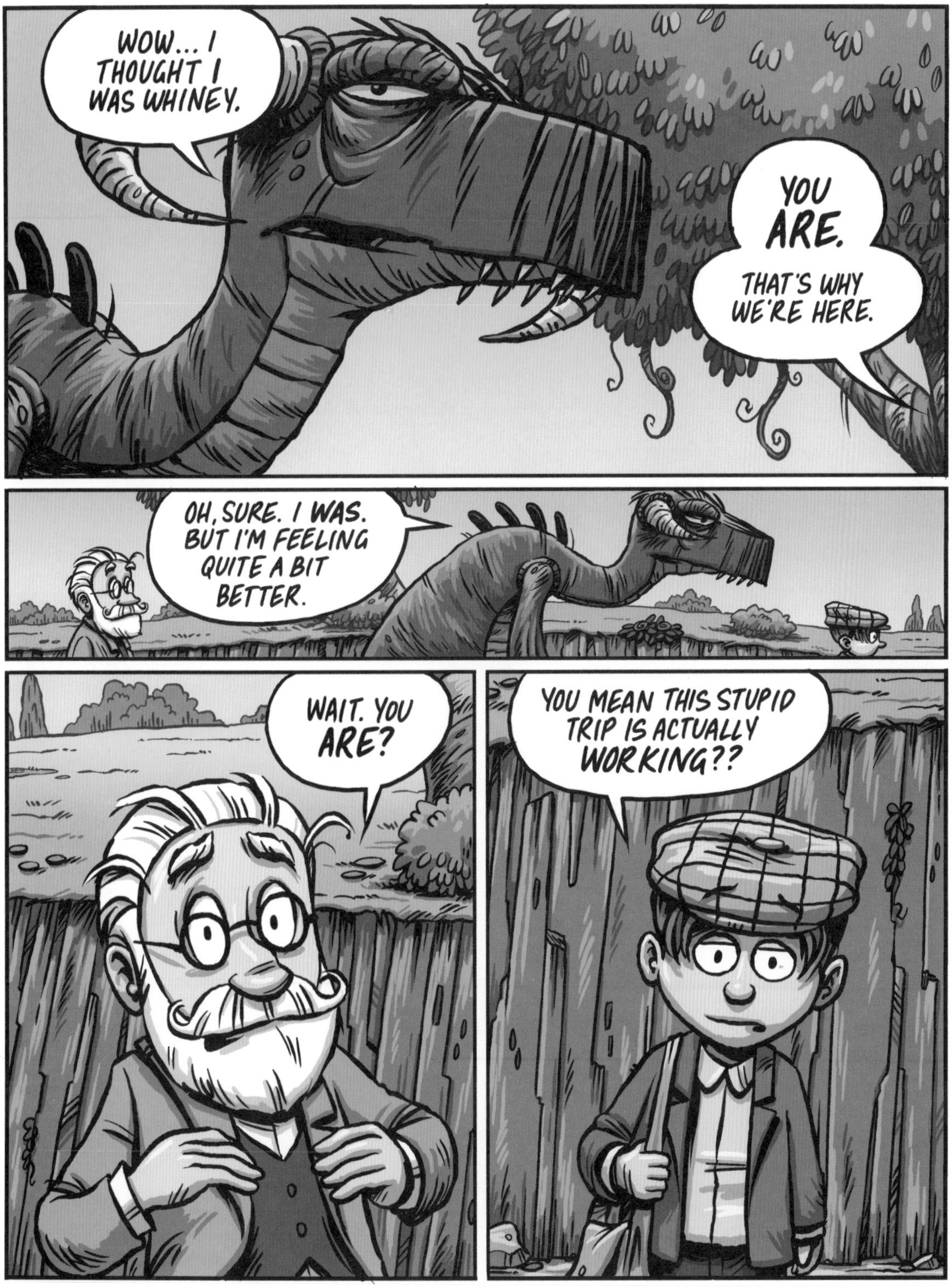
WOW... I THOUGHT I WAS WHINEY.
YOU ARE.
THAT'S WHY WE'RE HERE.
OH, SURE. I WAS. BUT I'M FEELING QUITE A BIT BETTER.
WAIT. YOU ARE?
YOU MEAN THIS STUPID TRIP IS ACTUALLY WORKING??

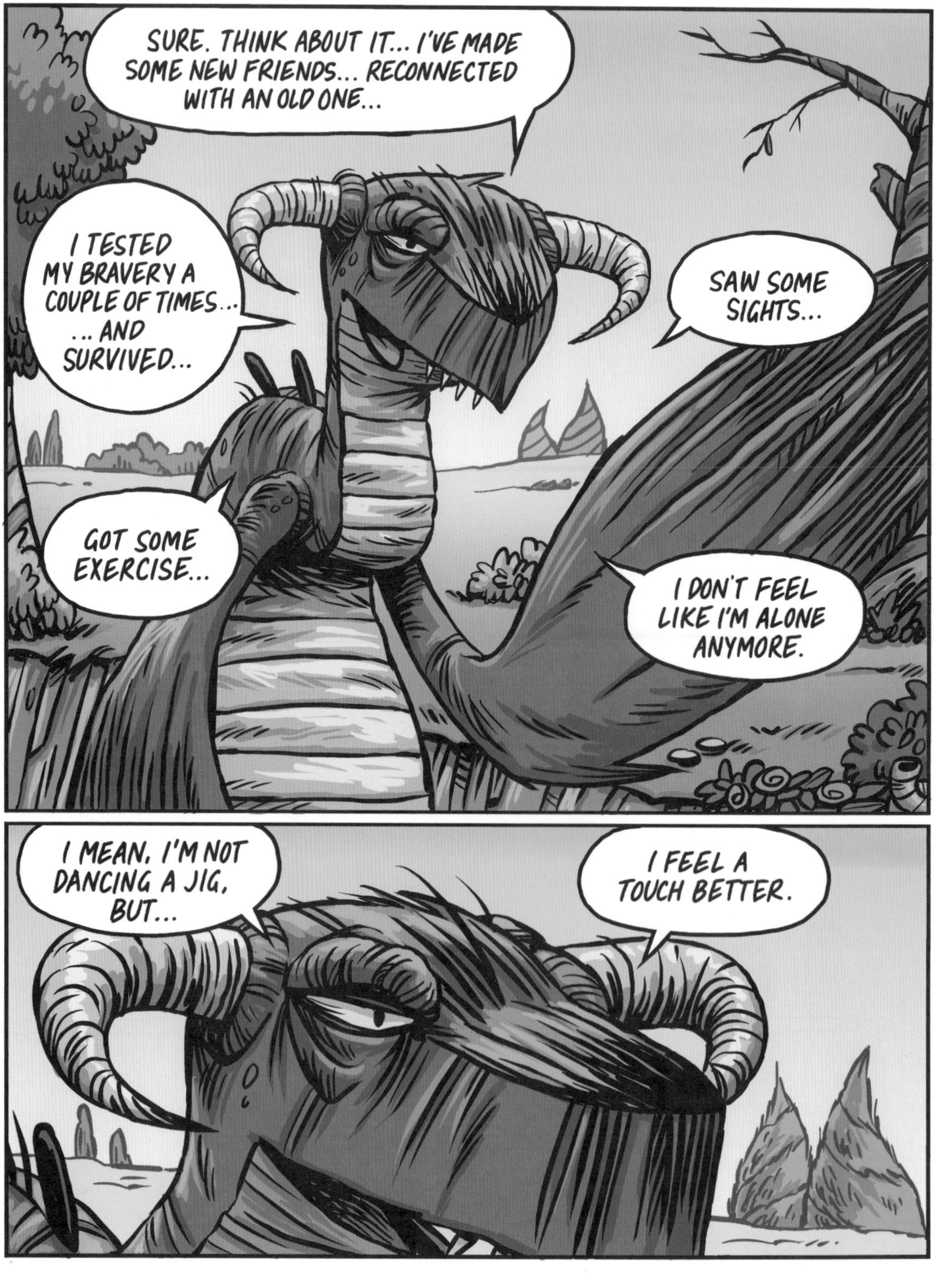
SURE. THINK ABOUT IT... I'VE MADE SOME NEW FRIENDS... RECONNECTED WITH AN OLD ONE...
I TESTED MY BRAVERY A COUPLE OF TIMES... ...AND SURVIVED...
SAW SOME SIGHTS...
GOT SOME EXERCISE...
I DON'T FEEL LIKE I'M ALONE ANYMORE.
I MEAN, I'M NOT DANCING A JIG, BUT...
I FEEL A TOUCH BETTER.

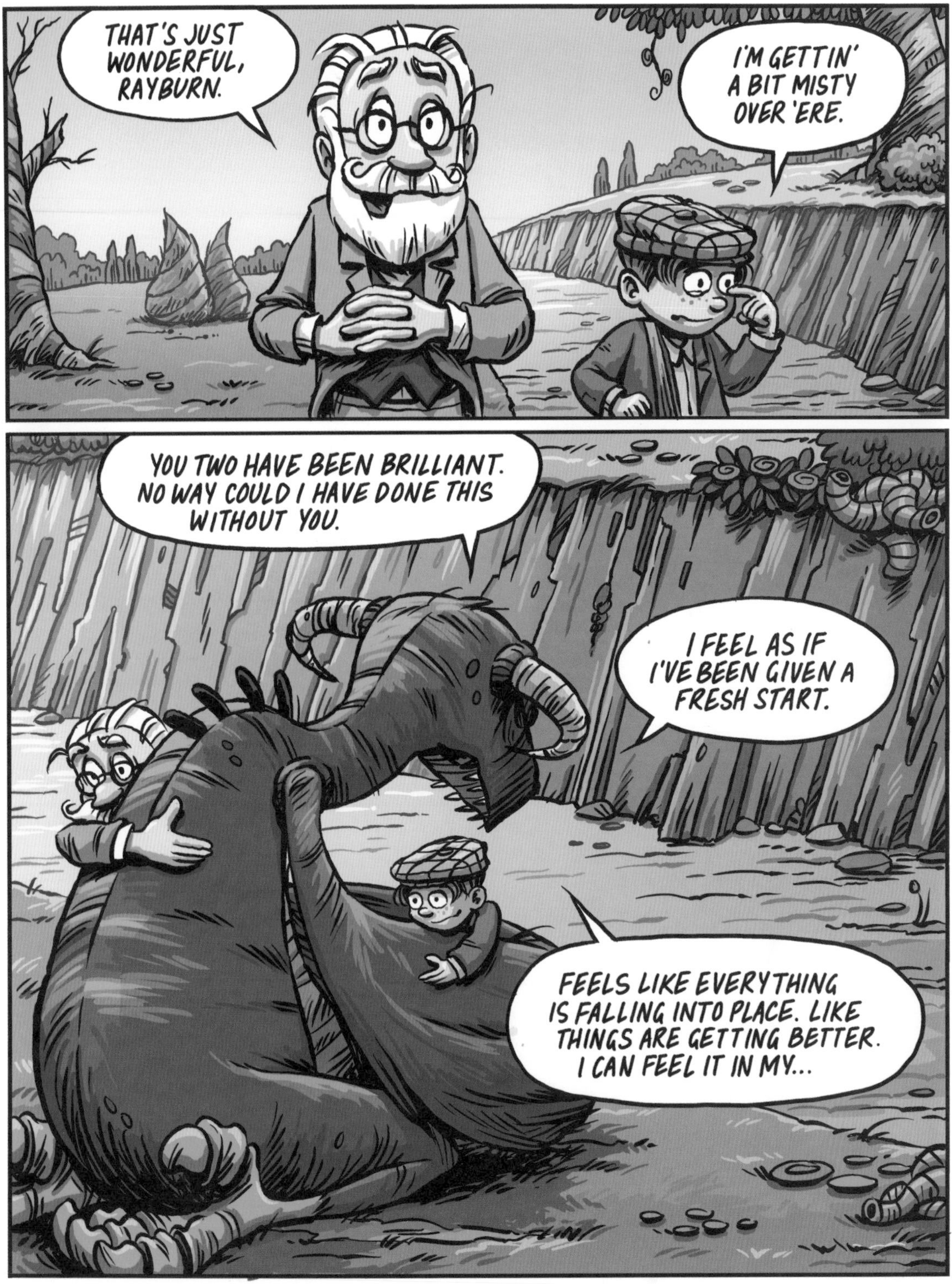
THAT'S JUST WONDERFUL, RAYBURN.
I'M GETTIN' A BIT MISTY OVER 'ERE.
YOU TWO HAVE BEEN BRILLIANT. NO WAY COULD I HAVE DONE THIS WITHOUT YOU.
I FEEL AS IF I'VE BEEN GIVEN A FRESH START.
FEELS LIKE EVERYTHING IS FALLING INTO PLACE. LIKE THINGS ARE GETTING BETTER. I CAN FEEL IT IN MY...

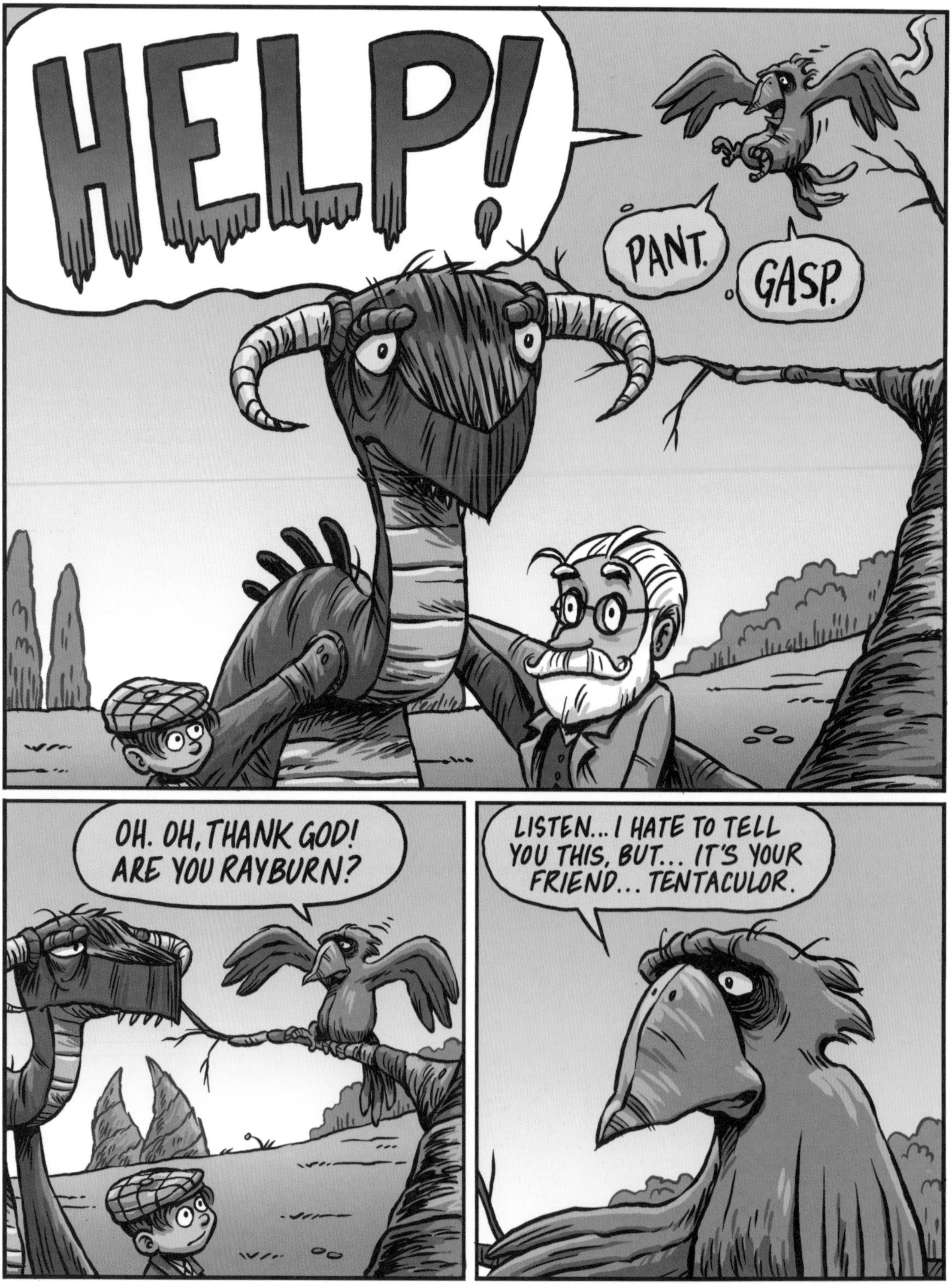

HELP!
PANT.
GASP.
OH. OH, THANK GOD! ARE YOU RAYBURN?
LISTEN... I HATE TO TELL YOU THIS, BUT... IT'S YOUR FRIEND... TENTACULOR.

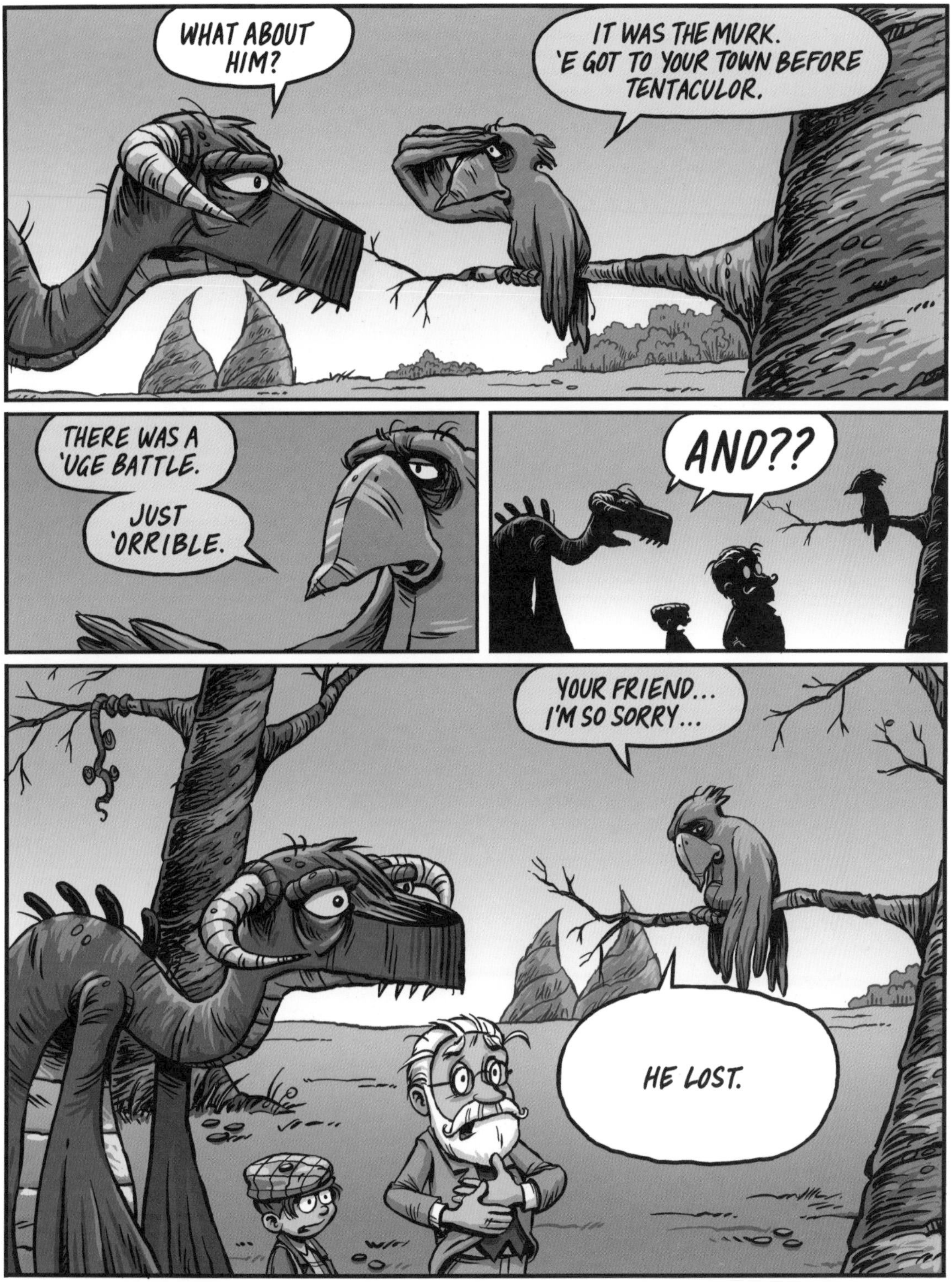
WHAT ABOUT HIM?
IT WAS THE MURK. 'E GOT TO YOUR TOWN BEFORE TENTACULOR.
THERE WAS A 'UGE BATTLE.
JUST 'ORRIBLE.
AND??
YOUR FRIEND... I'M SO SORRY...
HE LOST.

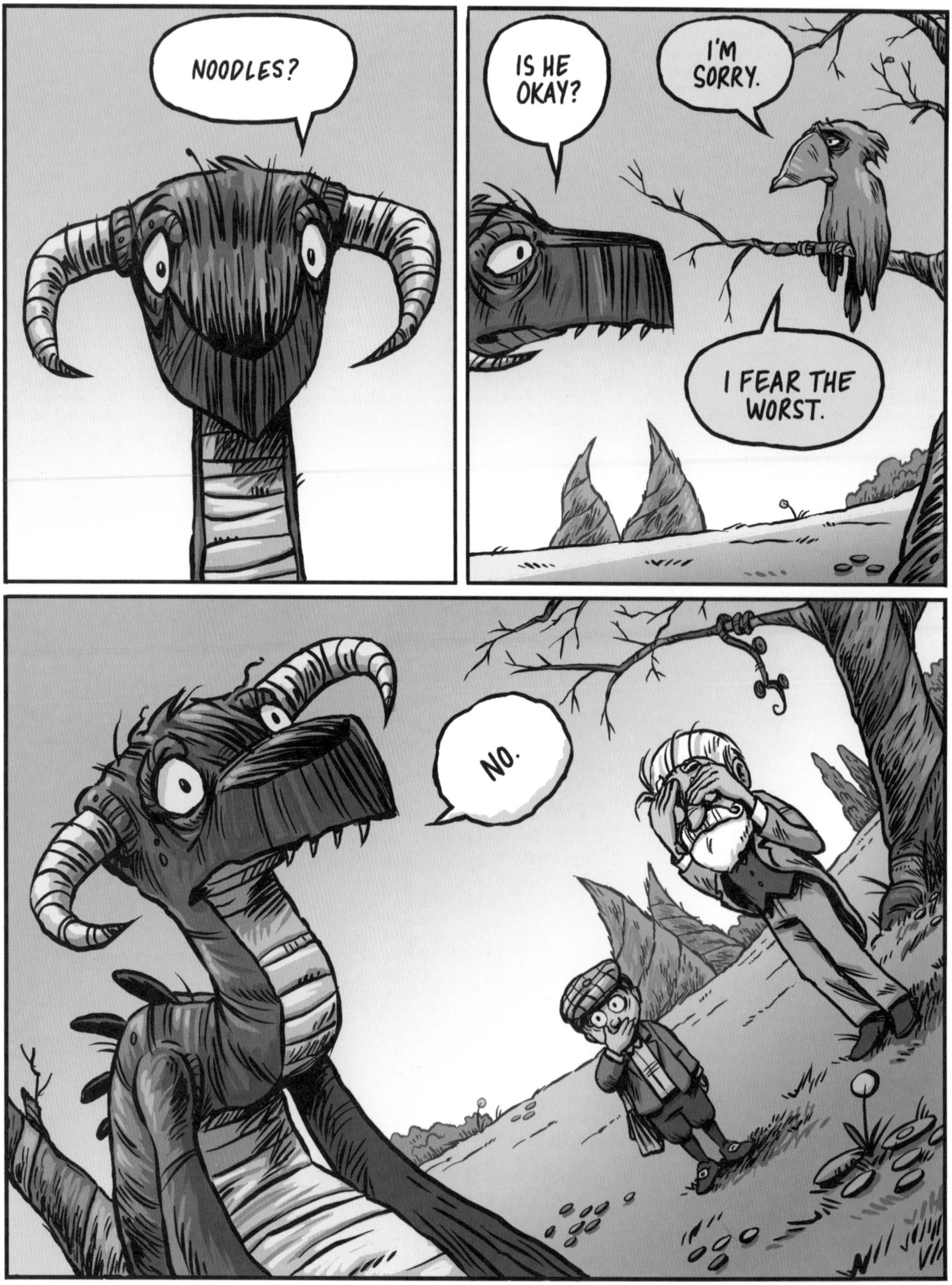
NOODLES?
IS HE OKAY?
I'M SORRY.
I FEAR THE WORST.
NO.

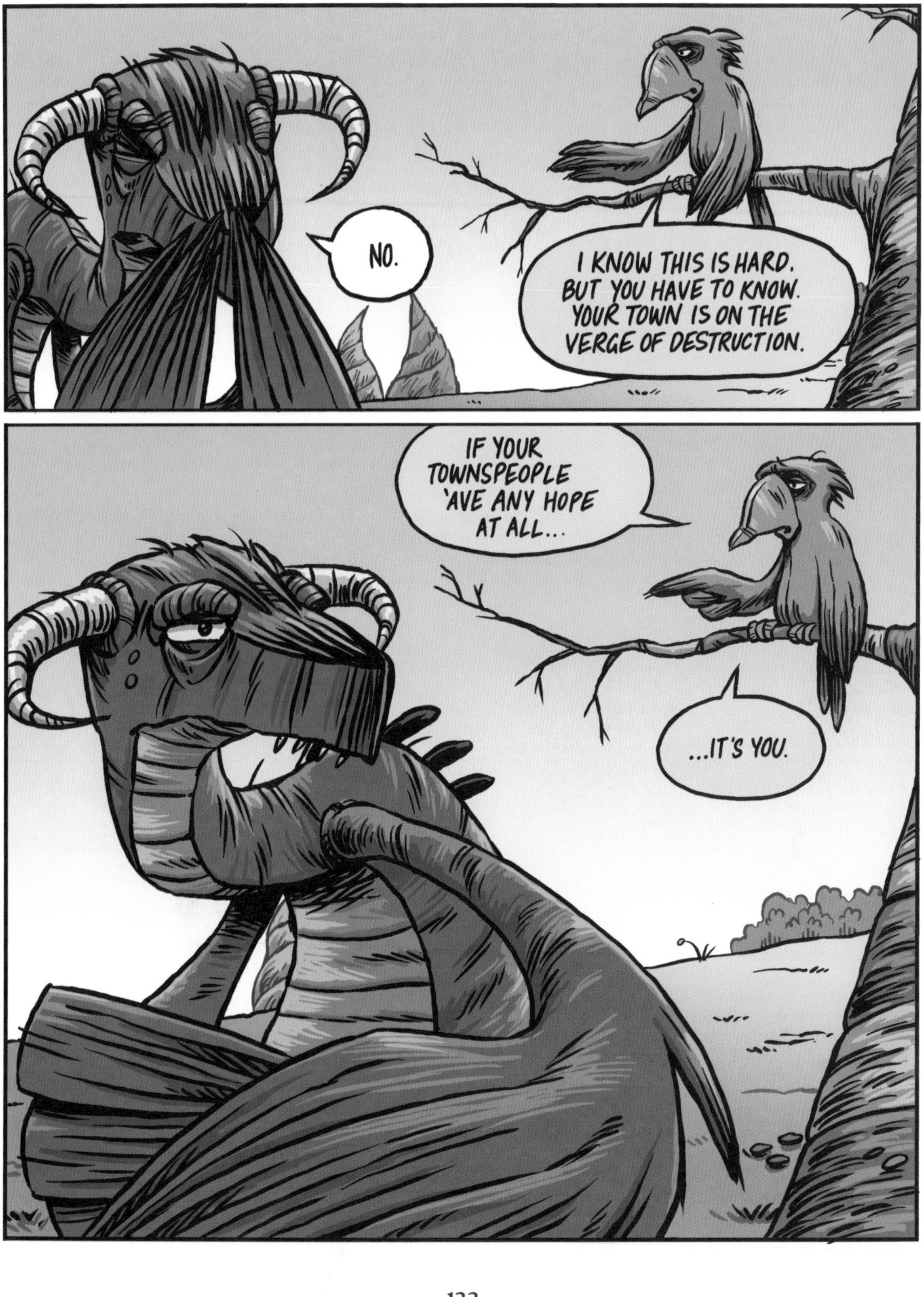
NO.
I KNOW THIS IS HARD. BUT YOU HAVE TO KNOW. YOUR TOWN IS ON THE VERGE OF DESTRUCTION.
IF YOUR TOWNSPEOPLE 'AVE ANY HOPE AT ALL...
...IT'S YOU.

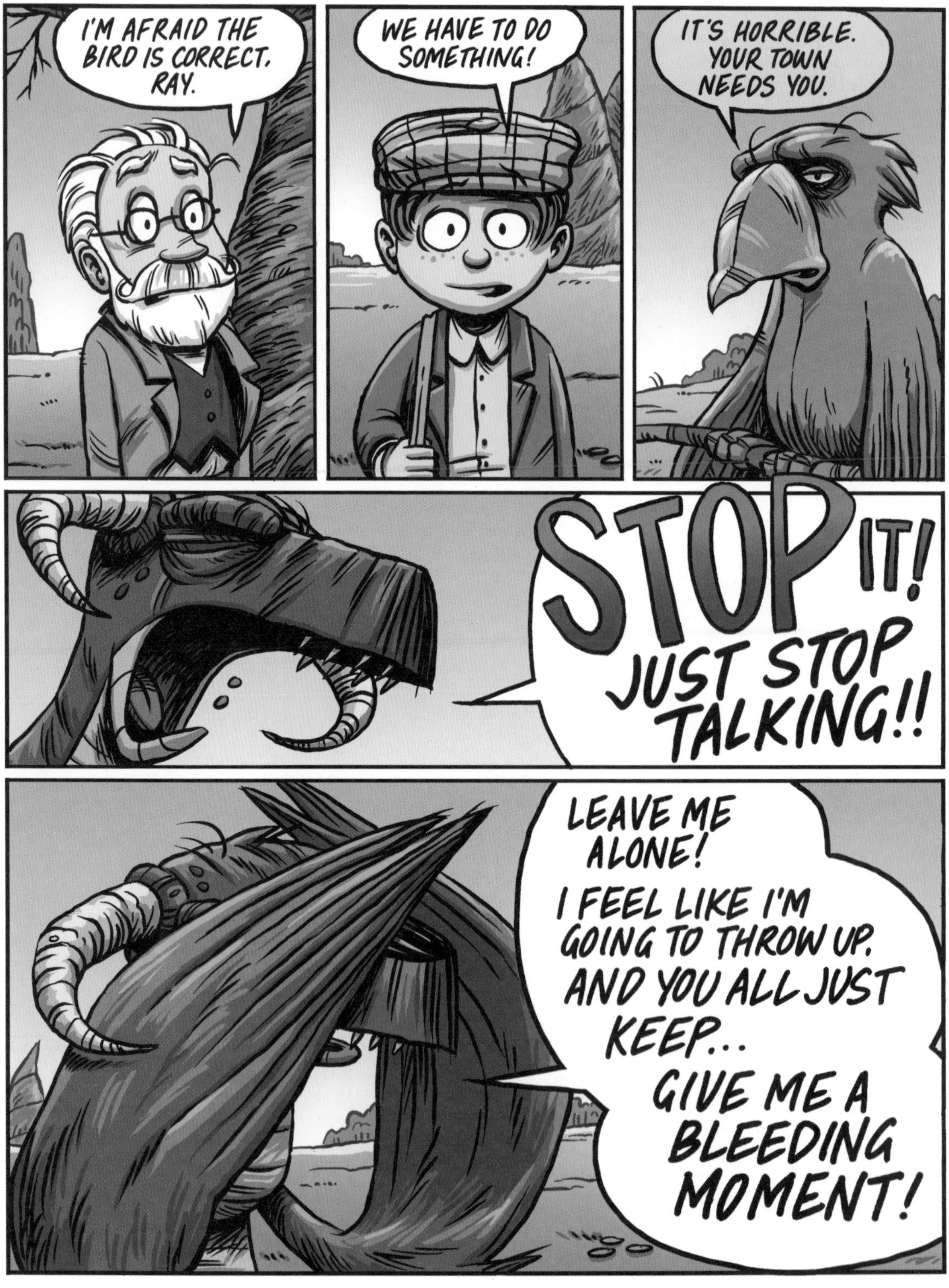
I'M AFRAID THE BIRD IS CORRECT, RAY.
WE HAVE TO DO SOMETHING!
IT'S HORRIBLE. YOUR TOWN NEEDS YOU.
STOP IT! JUST STOP TALKING!!
LEAVE ME ALONE! I FEEL LIKE I'M GOING TO THROW UP. AND YOU ALL JUST KEEP... GIVE ME A BLEEDING MOMENT!

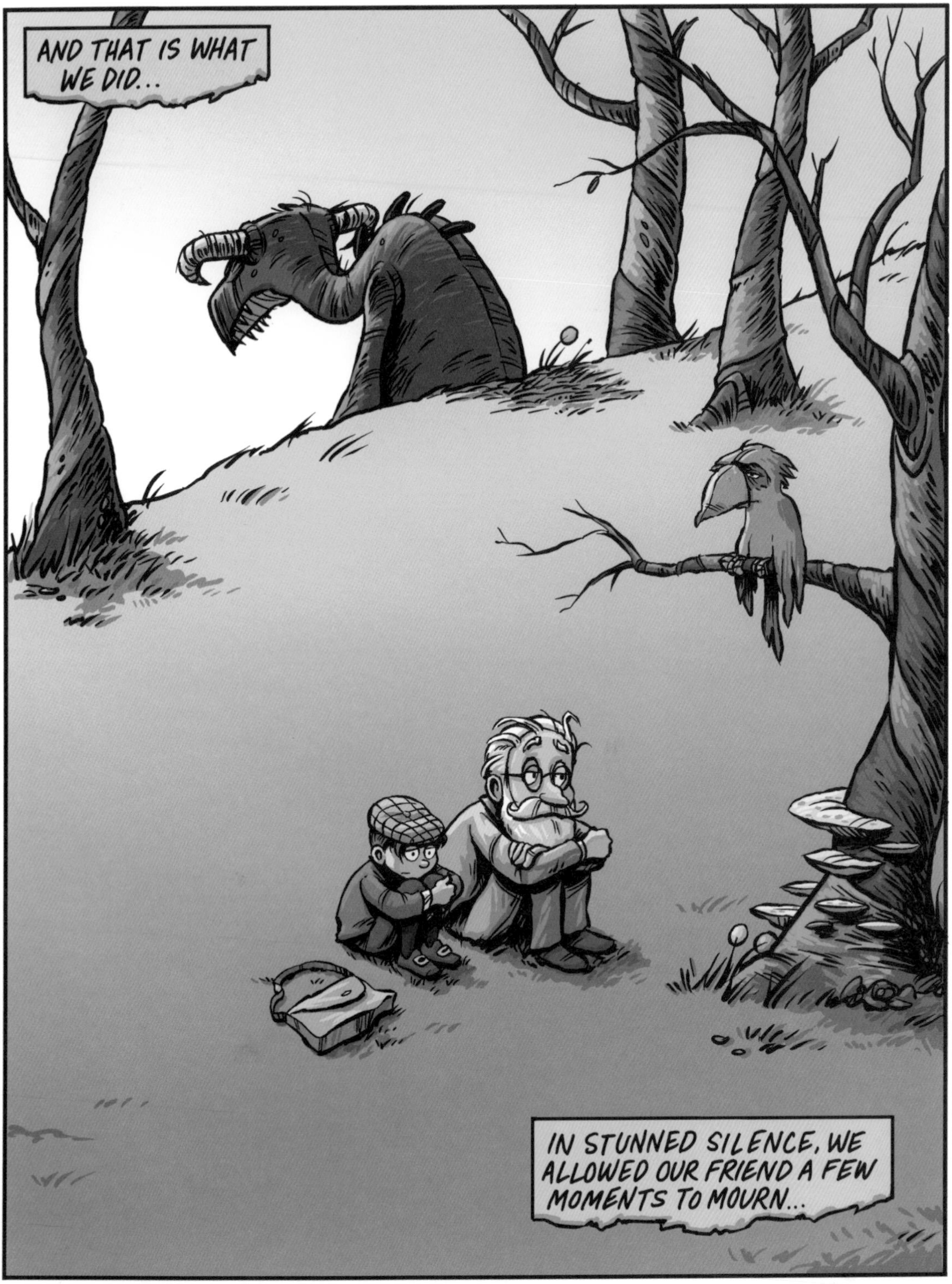
AND THAT IS WHAT WE DID...
IN STUNNED SILENCE, WE ALLOWED OUR FRIEND A FEW MOMENTS TO MOURN...

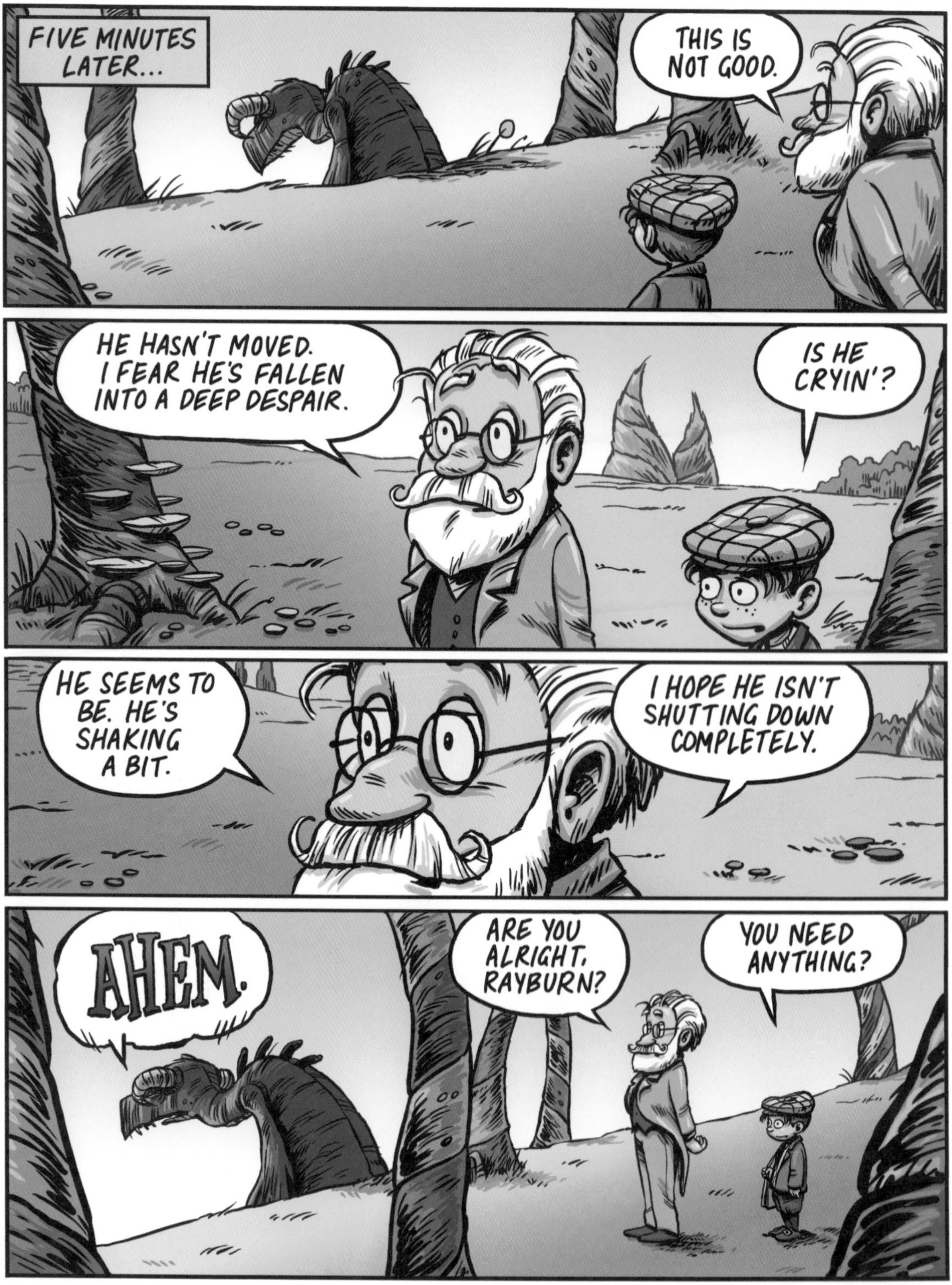
FIVE MINUTES LATER...
THIS IS NOT GOOD.
HE HASN'T MOVED. I FEAR HE'S FALLEN INTO A DEEP DESPAIR.
IS HE CRYIN'?
HE SEEMS TO BE. HE'S SHAKING A BIT.
I HOPE HE ISN'T SHUTTING DOWN COMPLETELY.
AHEM.
ARE YOU ALRIGHT, RAYBURN?
YOU NEED ANYTHING?

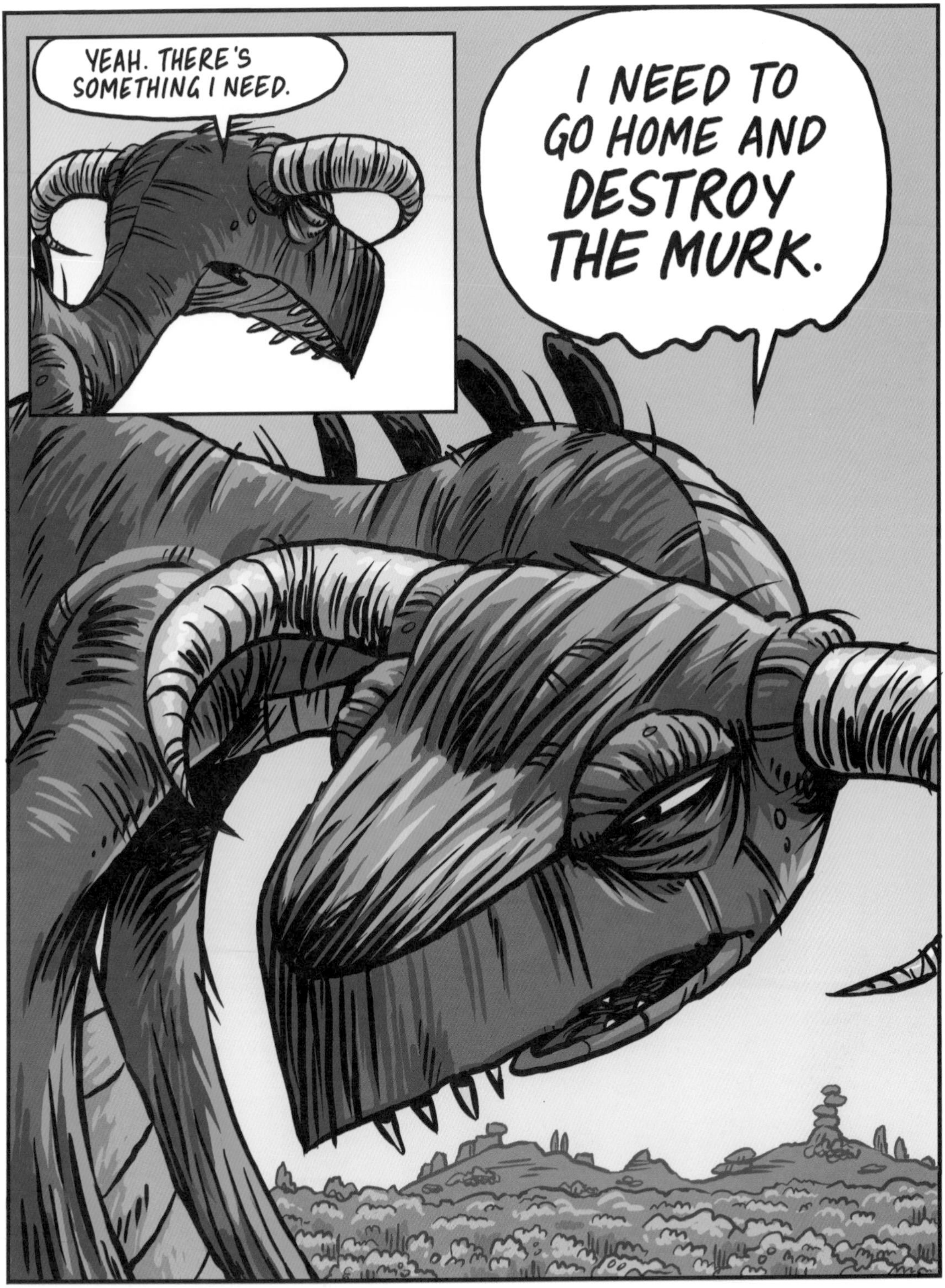
YEAH. THERE'S SOMETHING I NEED.
I NEED TO GO HOME AND DESTROY THE MURK.

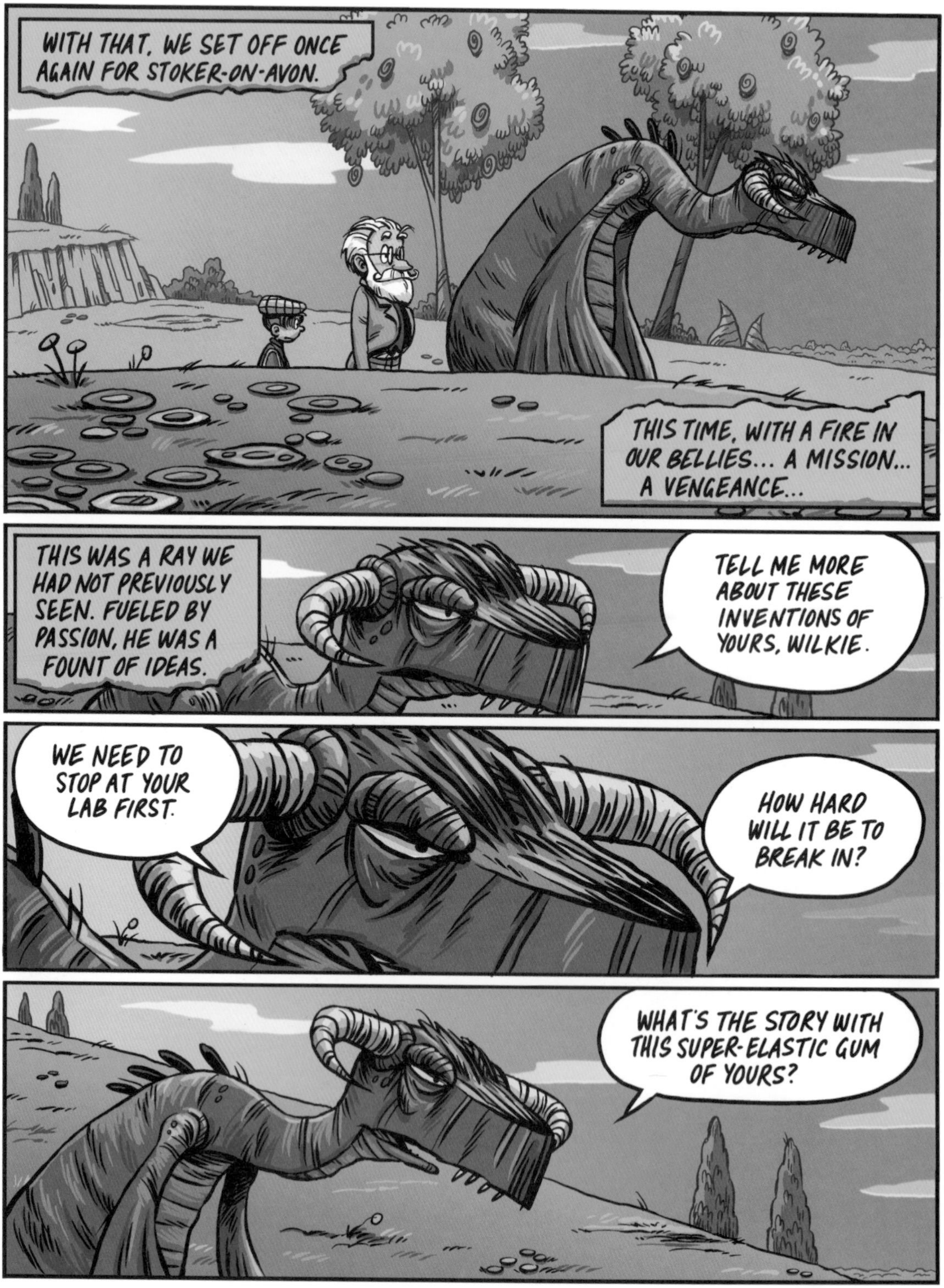
WITH THAT, WE SET OFF ONCE AGAIN FOR STOKER-ON-AVON.
THIS TIME, WITH A FIRE IN OUR BELLIES... A MISSION... A VENGEANCE...
THIS WAS A RAY WE HAD NOT PREVIOUSLY SEEN. FUELED BY PASSION, HE WAS A FOUNT OF IDEAS.
TELL ME MORE ABOUT THESE INVENTIONS OF YOURS, WILKIE.
WE NEED TO STOP AT YOUR LAB FIRST.
HOW HARD WILL IT BE TO BREAK IN?
WHAT'S THE STORY WITH THIS SUPER-ELASTIC GUM OF YOURS?

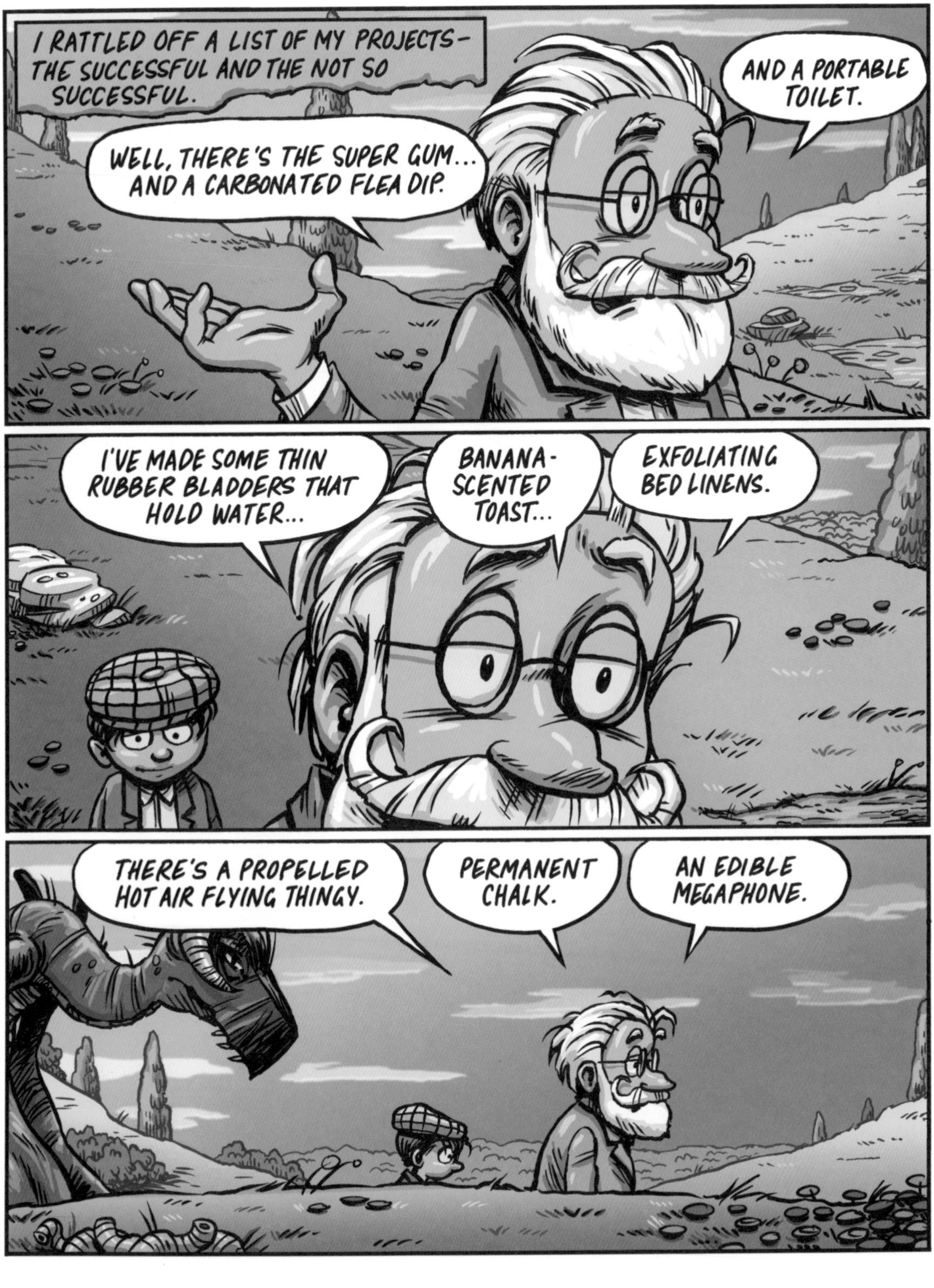
I RATTLED OFF A LIST OF MY PROJECTS-THE SUCCESSFUL AND THE NOT SO SUCCESSFUL.
WELL, THERE'S THE SUPER GUM... AND A CARBONATED FLEA DIP.
AND A PORTABLE TOILET.
I'VE MADE SOME THIN RUBBER BLADDERS THAT HOLD WATER...
BANANA-SCENTED TOAST...
EXFOLIATING BED LINENS.
THERE'S A PROPELLED HOT AIR FLYING THINGY.
PERMANENT CHALK.
AN EDIBLE MEGAPHONE.

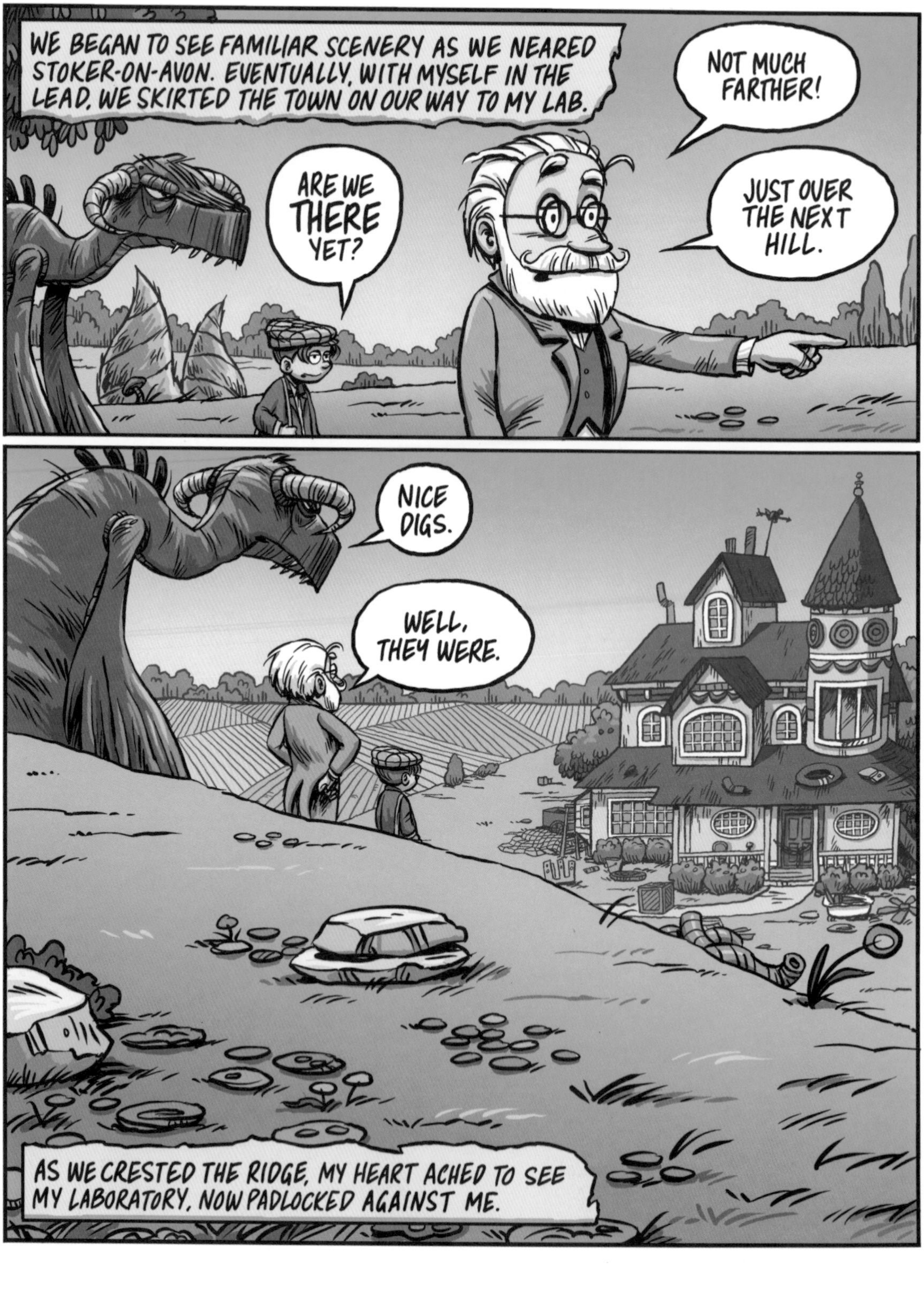

WE BEGAN TO SEE FAMILIAR SCENERY AS WE NEARED STOKER-ON-AVON. EVENTUALLY, WITH MYSELF IN THE LEAD, WE SKIRTED THE TOWN ON OUR WAY TO MY LAB.
ARE WE THERE YET?
NOT MUCH FARTHER!
JUST OVER THE NEXT HILL.
NICE DIGS.
WELL, THEY WERE.
AS WE CRESTED THE RIDGE, MY HEART ACHED TO SEE MY LABORATORY, NOW PADLOCKED AGAINST ME.

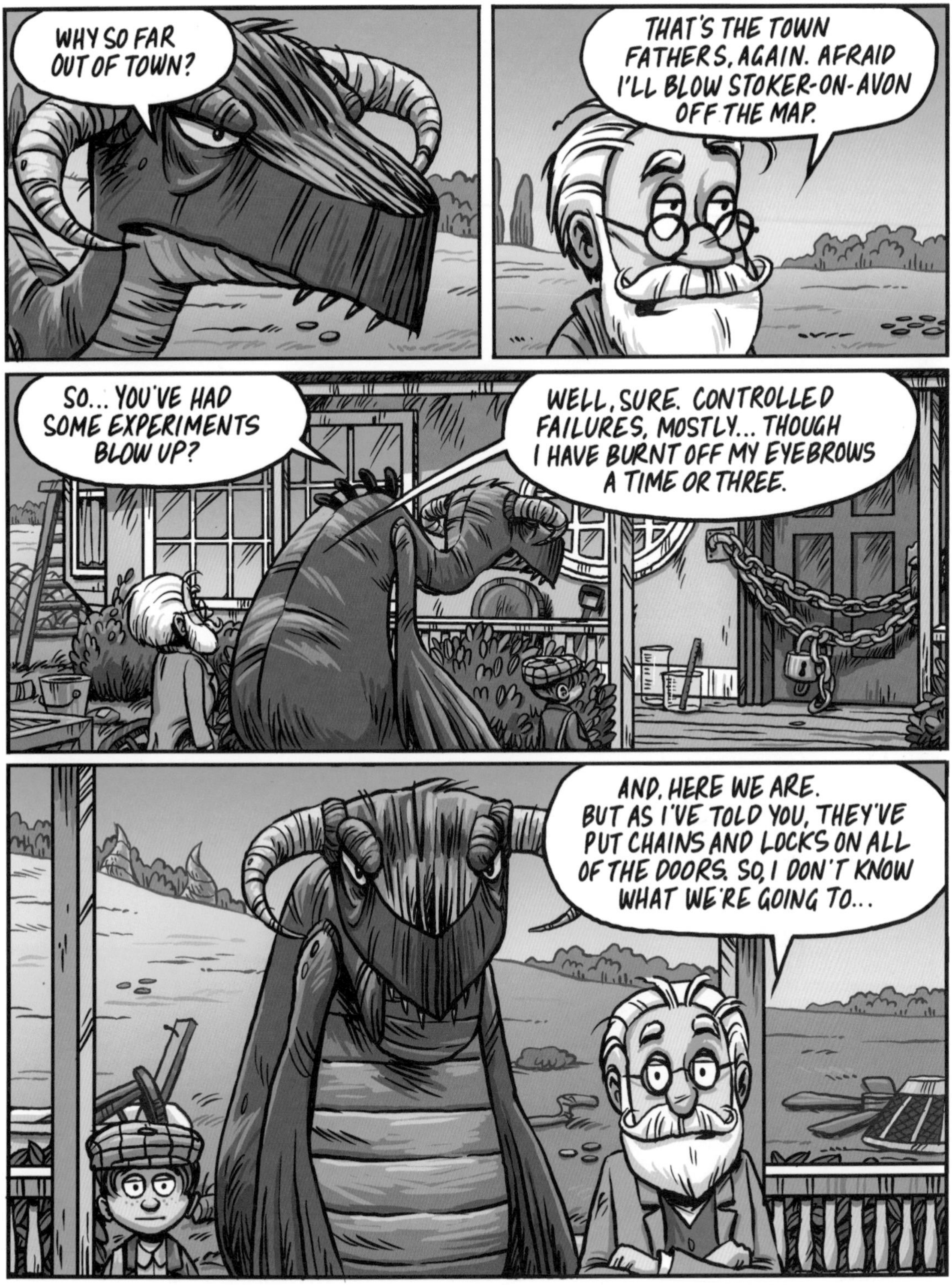
WHY SO FAR OUT OF TOWN?
THAT'S THE TOWN FATHERS, AGAIN. AFRAID I'LL BLOW STOKER-ON-AVON OFF THE MAP.
SO... YOU'VE HAD SOME EXPERIMENTS BLOW UP?
WELL, SURE. CONTROLLED FAILURES, MOSTLY... THOUGH I HAVE BURNT OFF MY EYEBROWS A TIME OR THREE.
AND, HERE WE ARE. BUT AS I'VE TOLD YOU, THEY'VE PUT CHAINS AND LOCKS ON ALL OF THE DOORS. SO, I DON'T KNOW WHAT WE'RE GOING TO...

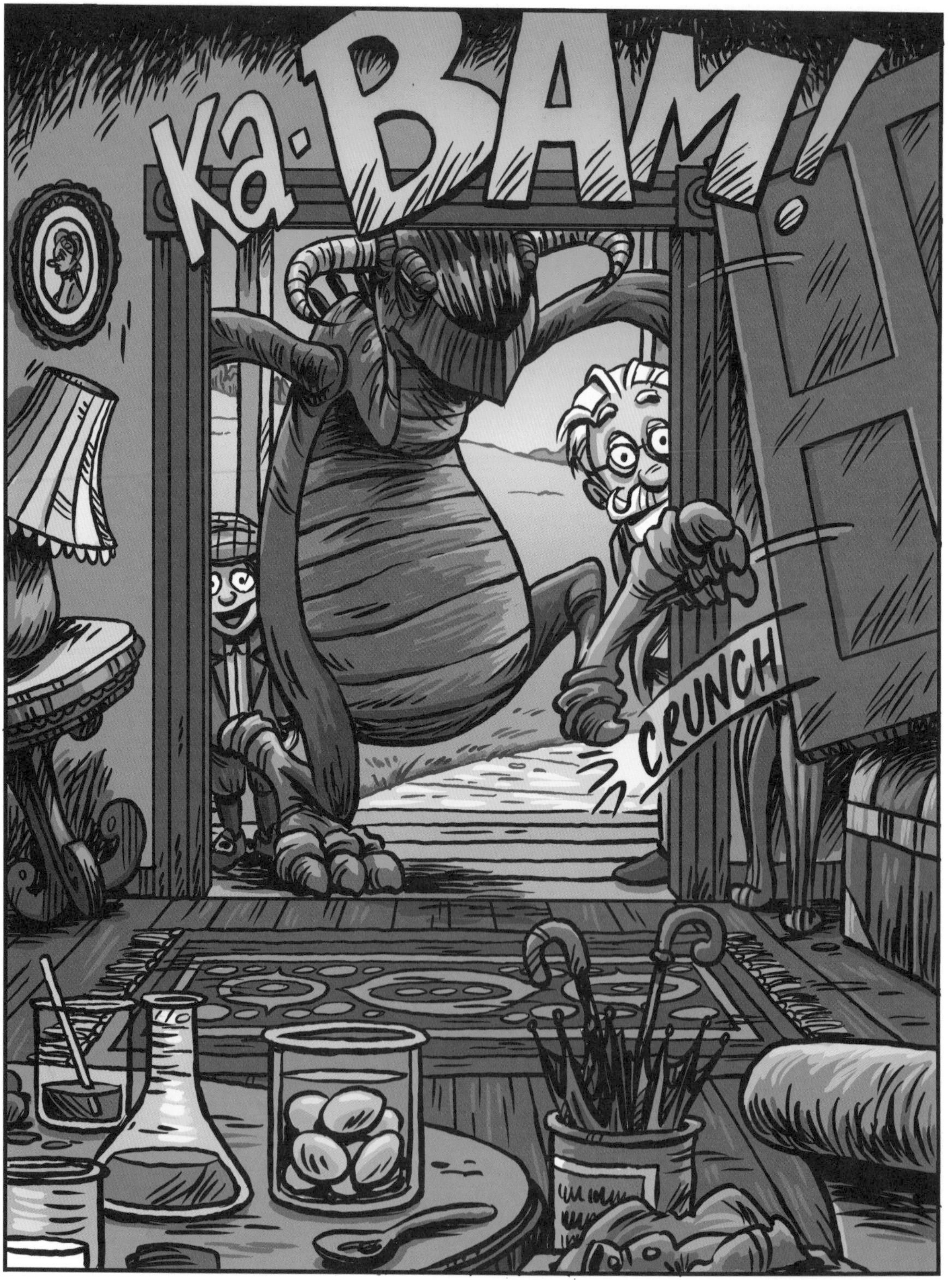
KA-BAM!
CRUNCH

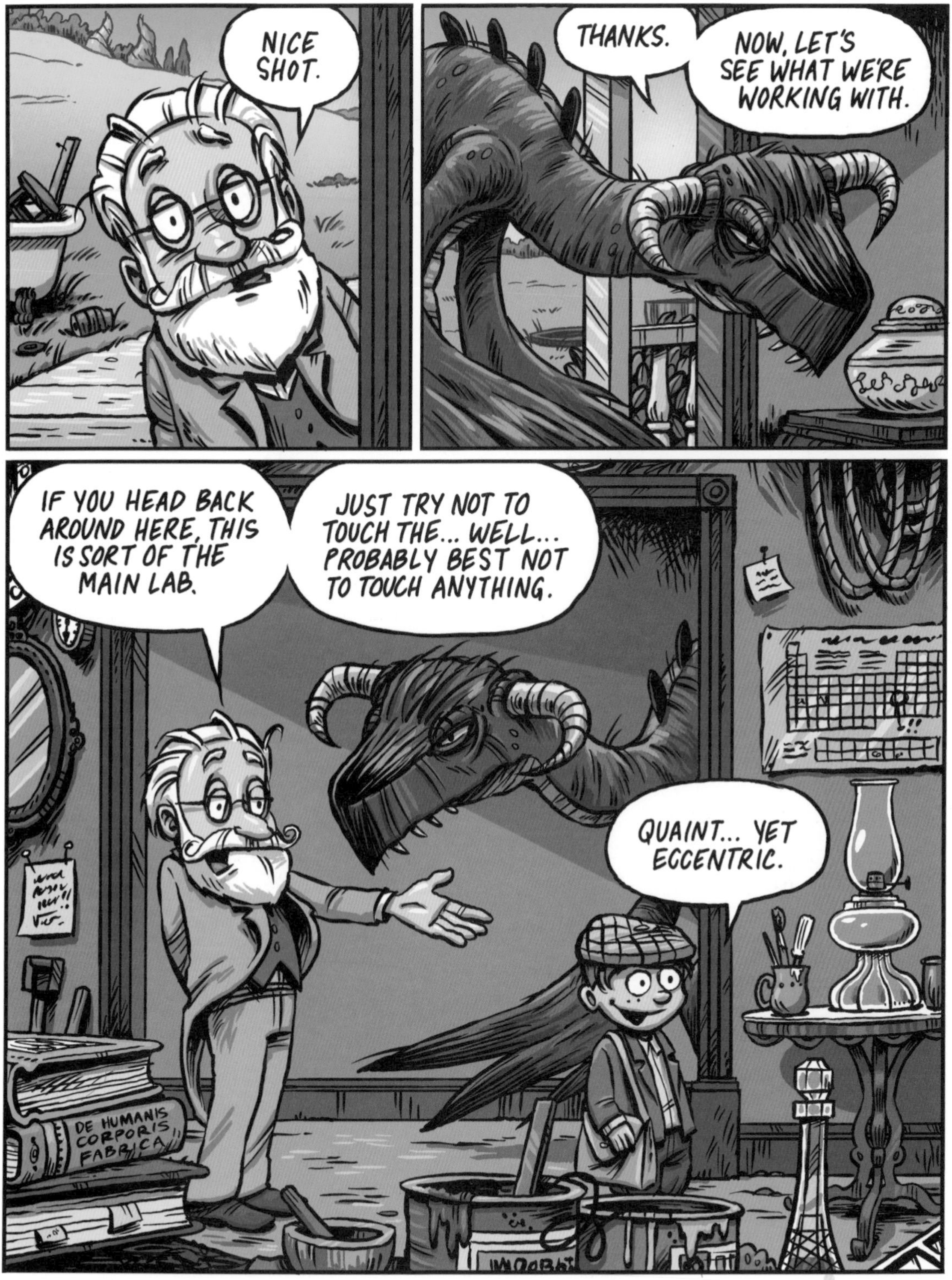
NICE SHOT.
THANKS.
NOW, LET'S SEE WHAT WE'RE WORKING WITH.
IF YOU HEAD BACK AROUND HERE, THIS IS SORT OF THE MAIN LAB.
JUST TRY NOT TO TOUCH THE... WELL... PROBABLY BEST NOT TO TOUCH ANYTHING.
QUAINT... YET ECCENTRIC.
DE HUMANIS CORPORIS FABRICA

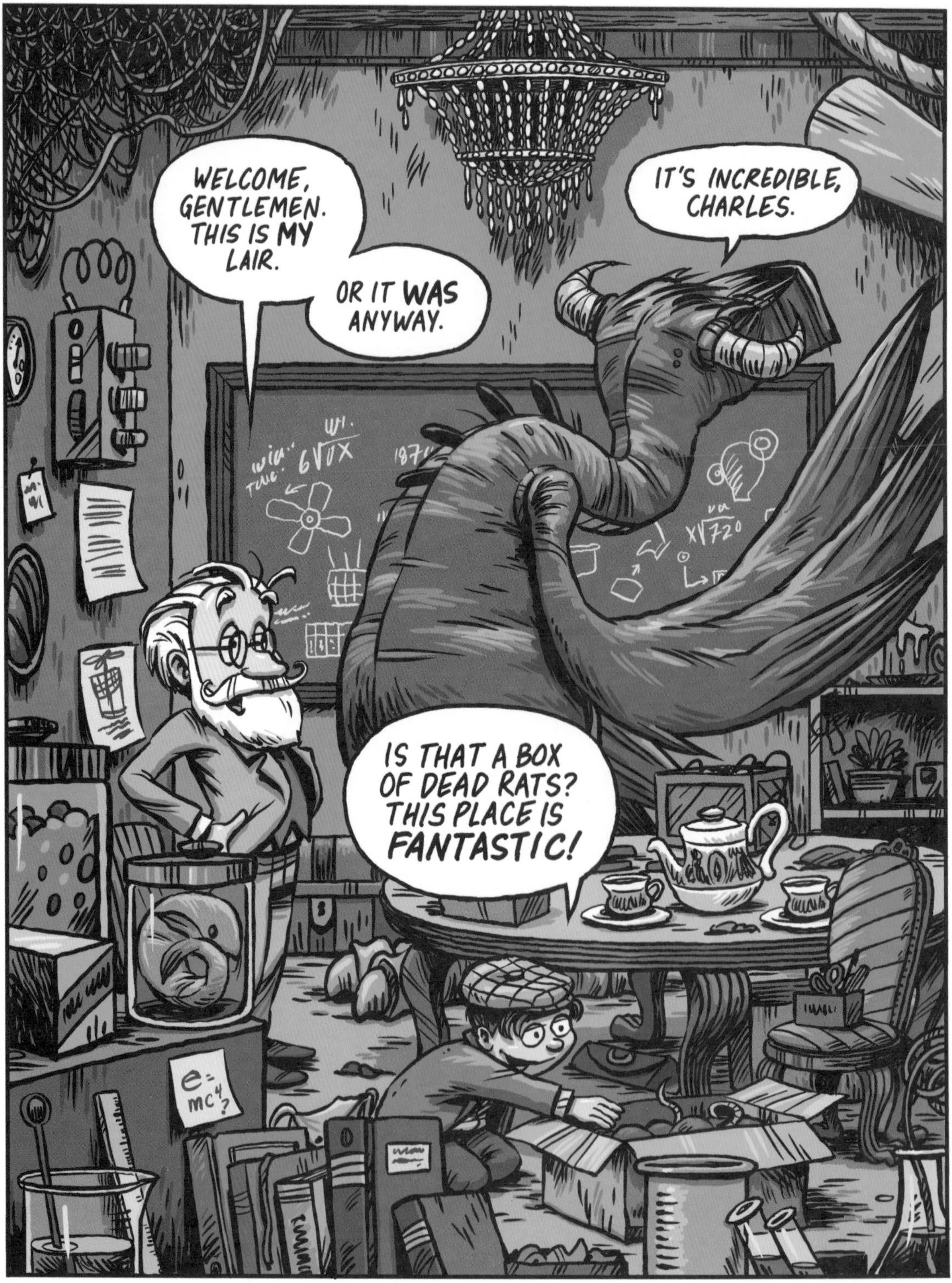
WELCOME, GENTLEMEN. THIS IS MY LAIR.
OR IT WAS ANYWAY.
IT'S INCREDIBLE, CHARLES.
IS THAT A BOX OF DEAD RATS? THIS PLACE IS FANTASTIC!
e= mc4?

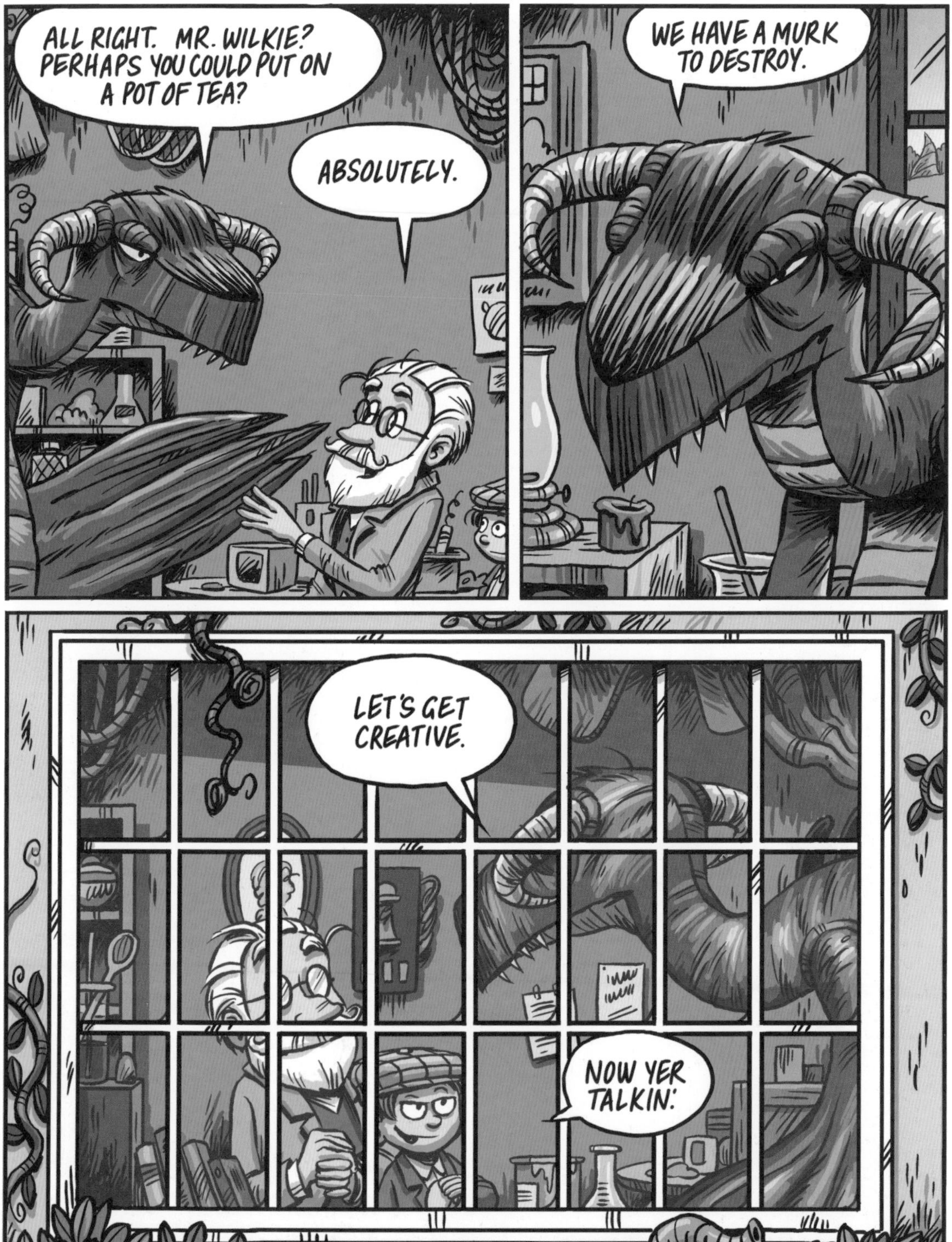
ALL RIGHT. MR. WILKIE? PERHAPS YOU COULD PUT ON A POT OF TEA?
ABSOLUTELY.
WE HAVE A MURK TO DESTROY.
LET'S GET CREATIVE.
NOW YER TALKIN'.

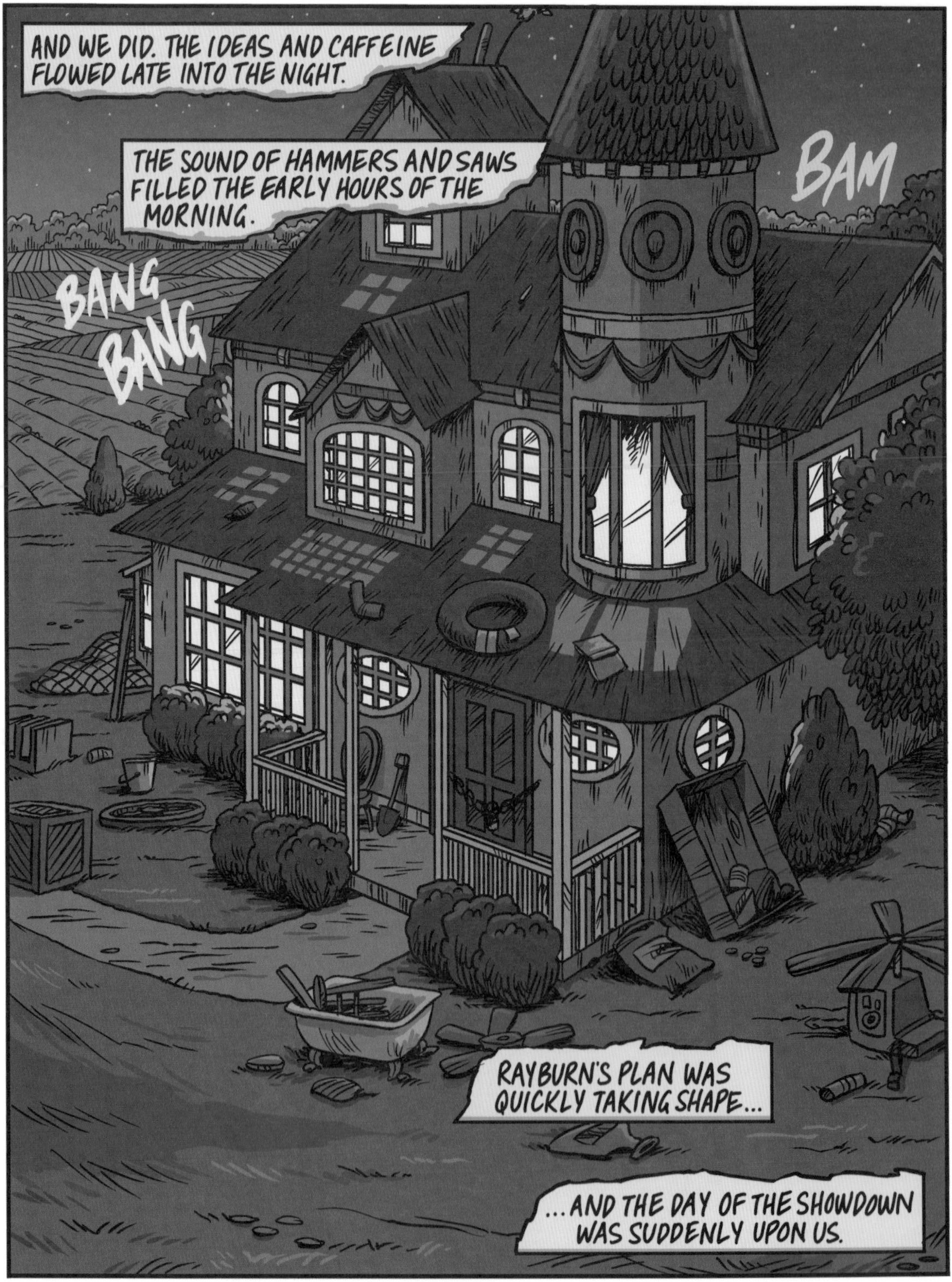
AND WE DID. THE IDEAS AND CAFFEINE FLOWED LATE INTO THE NIGHT.
THE SOUND OF HAMMERS AND SAWS FILLED THE EARLY HOURS OF THE MORNING.
BAM
BANG
BANG
RAYBURN'S PLAN WAS QUICKLY TAKING SHAPE...
...AND THE DAY OF THE SHOWDOWN WAS SUDDENLY UPON US.

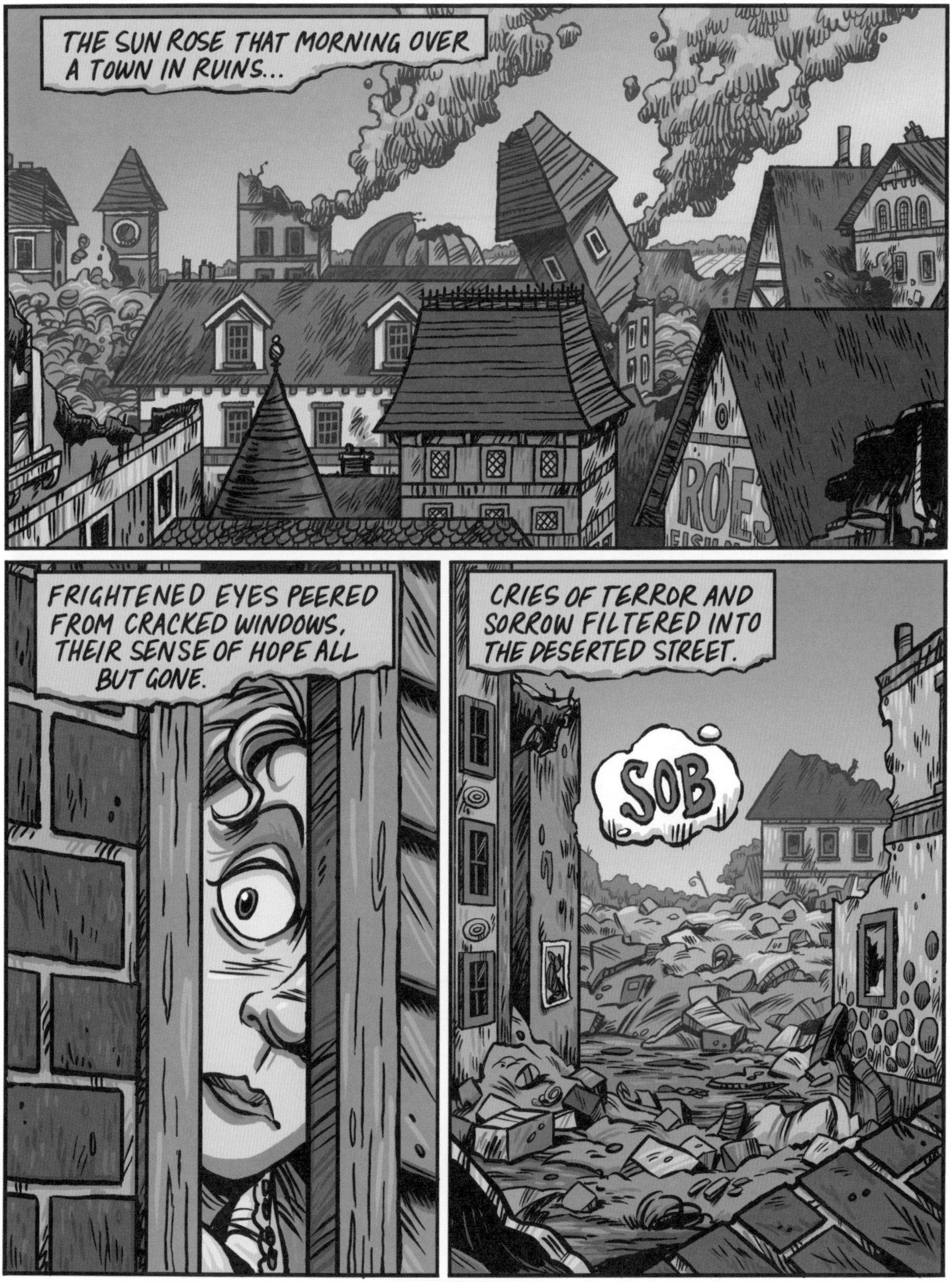
THE SUN ROSE THAT MORNING OVER A TOWN IN RUINS...
FRIGHTENED EYES PEERED FROM CRACKED WINDOWS, THEIR SENSE OF HOPE ALL BUT GONE.
CRIES OF TERROR AND SORROW FILTERED INTO THE DESERTED STREET.
SOB

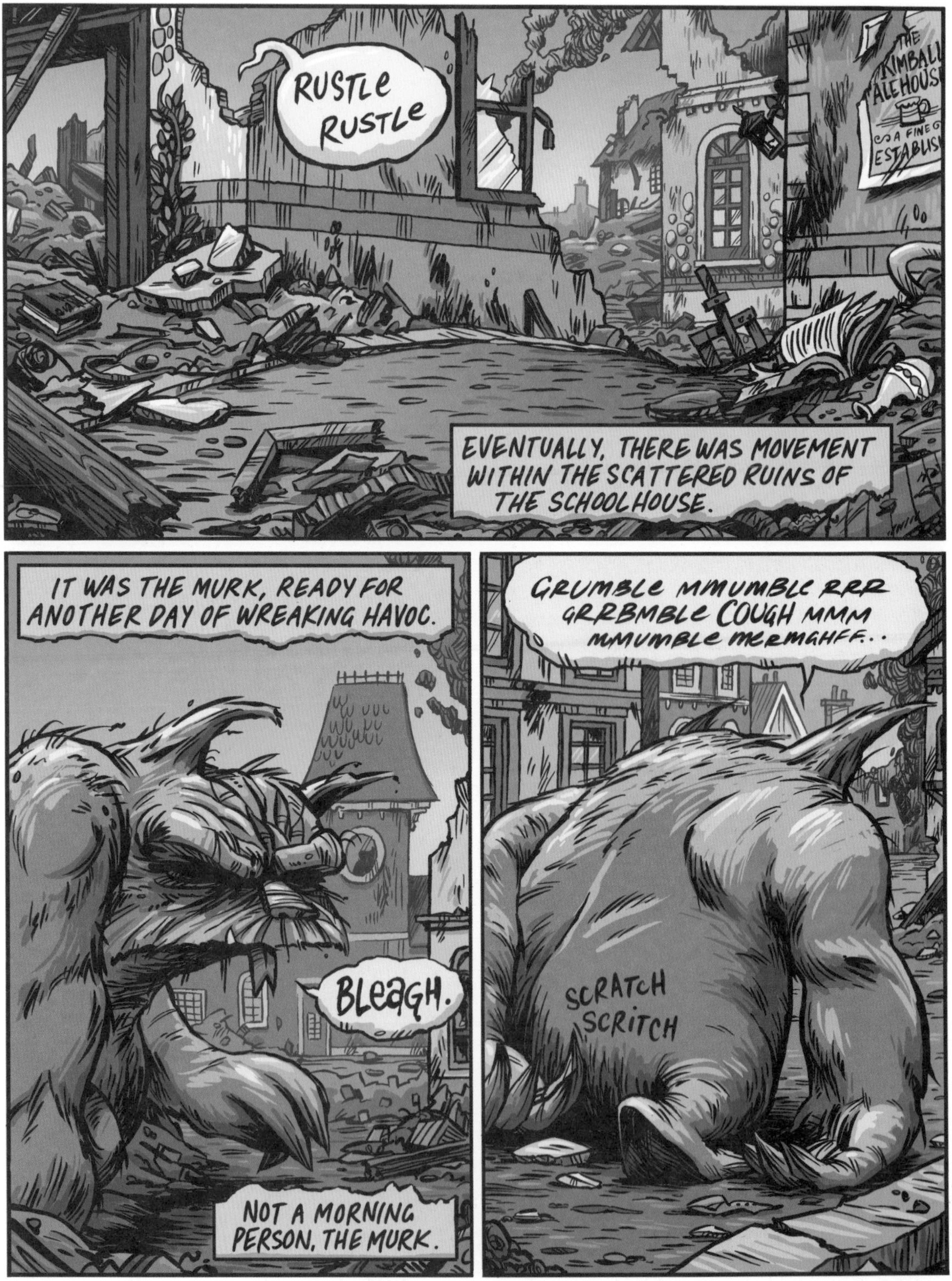
RUSTLE RUSTLE
THE KIMBALL ALEHOUSE A FINE ESTABLIS
EVENTUALLY, THERE WAS MOVEMENT WITHIN THE SCATTERED RUINS OF THE SCHOOLHOUSE.
IT WAS THE MURK, READY FOR ANOTHER DAY OF WREAKING HAVOC.
BLEAGH.
NOT A MORNING PERSON, THE MURK.
GRUMBLE MMUMBLE RRR GRRBMBLE COUGH MMM MMUMBLE MERMGHFF..
SCRATCH SCRITCH

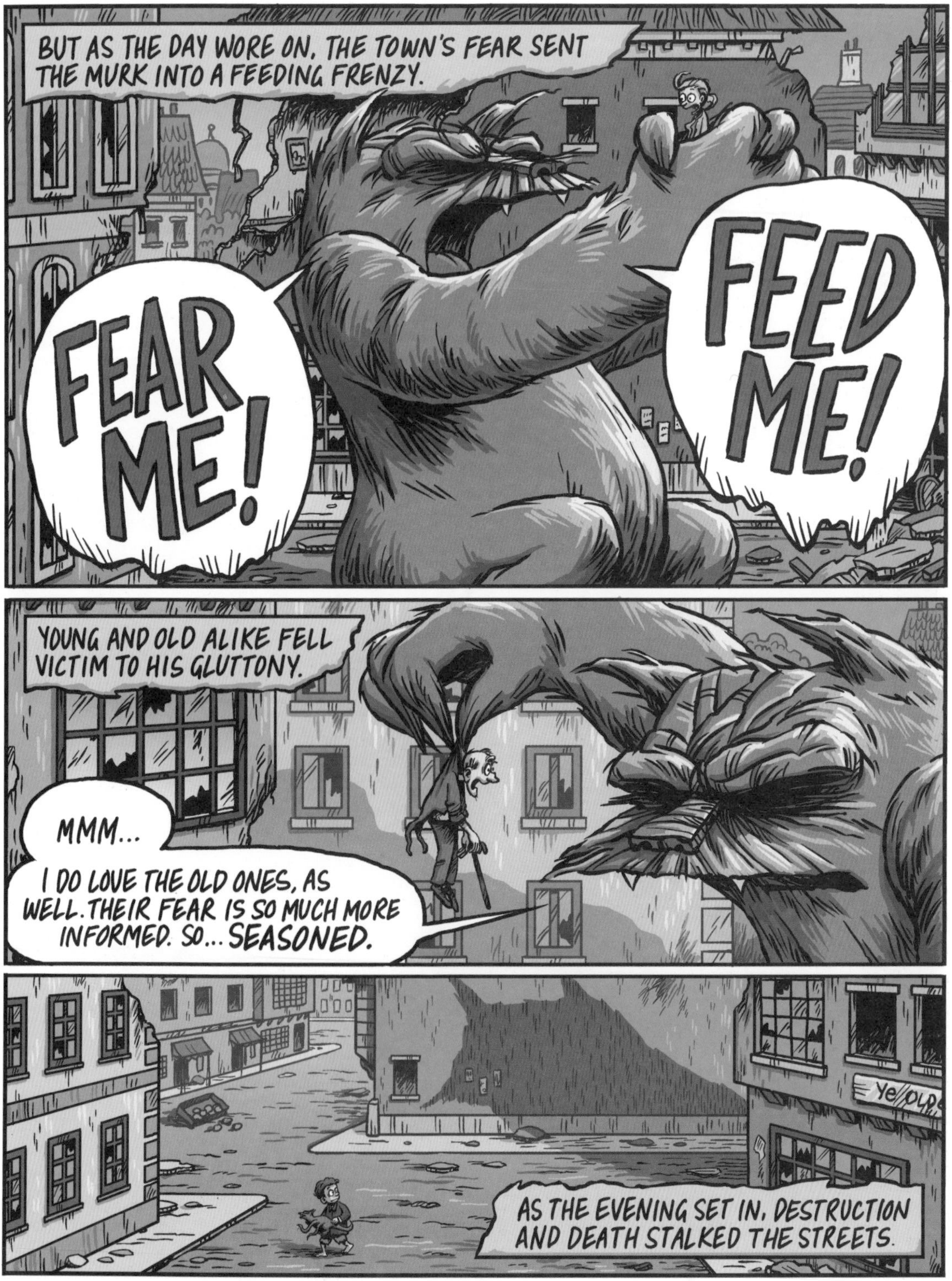
BUT AS THE DAY WORE ON, THE TOWN'S FEAR SENT THE MURK INTO A FEEDING FRENZY.
FEAR ME!
FEED ME!
YOUNG AND OLD ALIKE FELL VICTIM TO HIS GLUTTONY.
MMM...
I DO LOVE THE OLD ONES, AS WELL. THEIR FEAR IS SO MUCH MORE INFORMED. SO... SEASONED.
AS THE EVENING SET IN, DESTRUCTION AND DEATH STALKED THE STREETS.

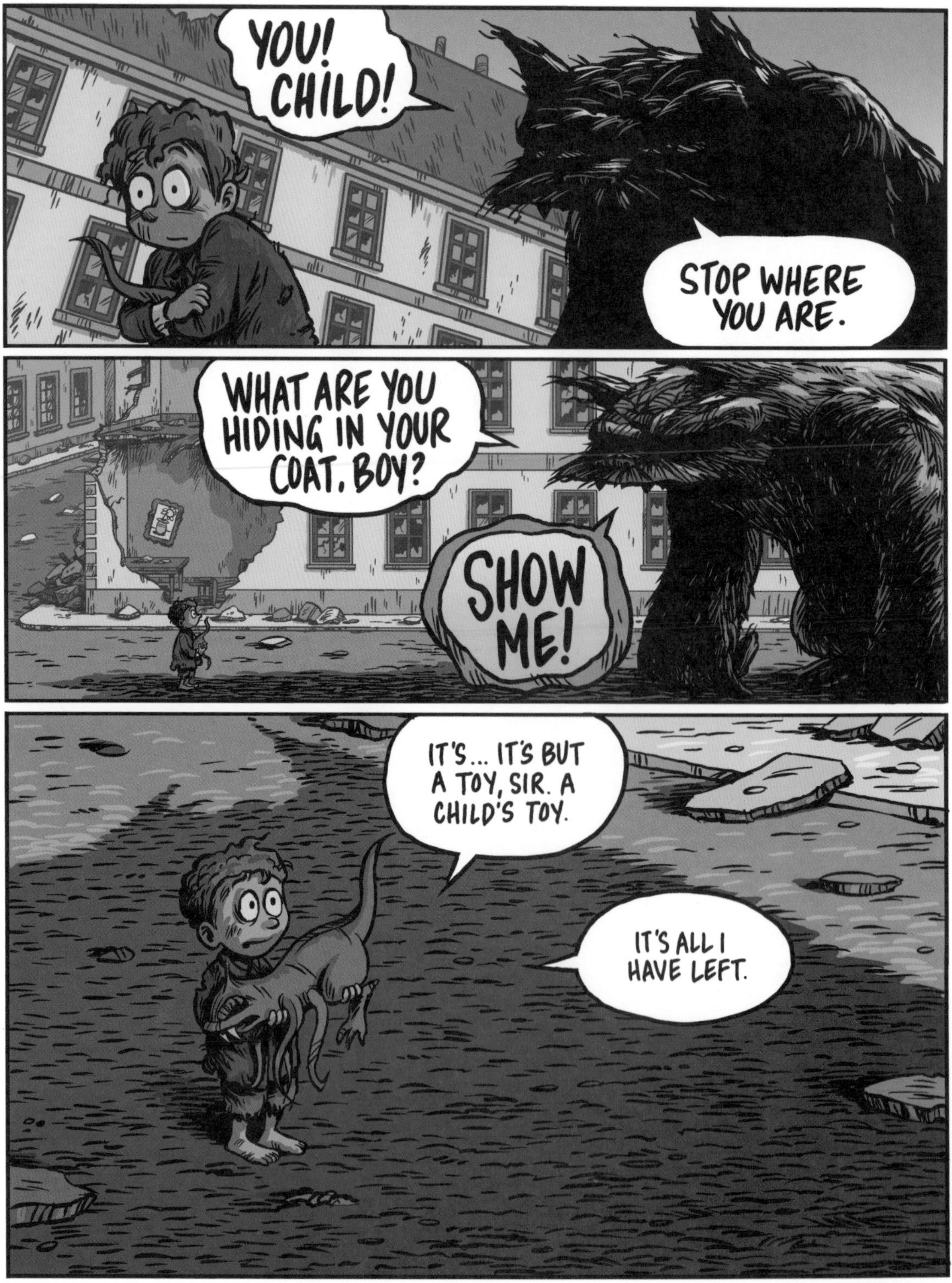
YOU! CHILD!
STOP WHERE YOU ARE.
WHAT ARE YOU HIDING IN YOUR COAT, BOY?
SHOW ME!
IT'S... IT'S BUT A TOY, SIR. A CHILD'S TOY.
IT'S ALL I HAVE LEFT.

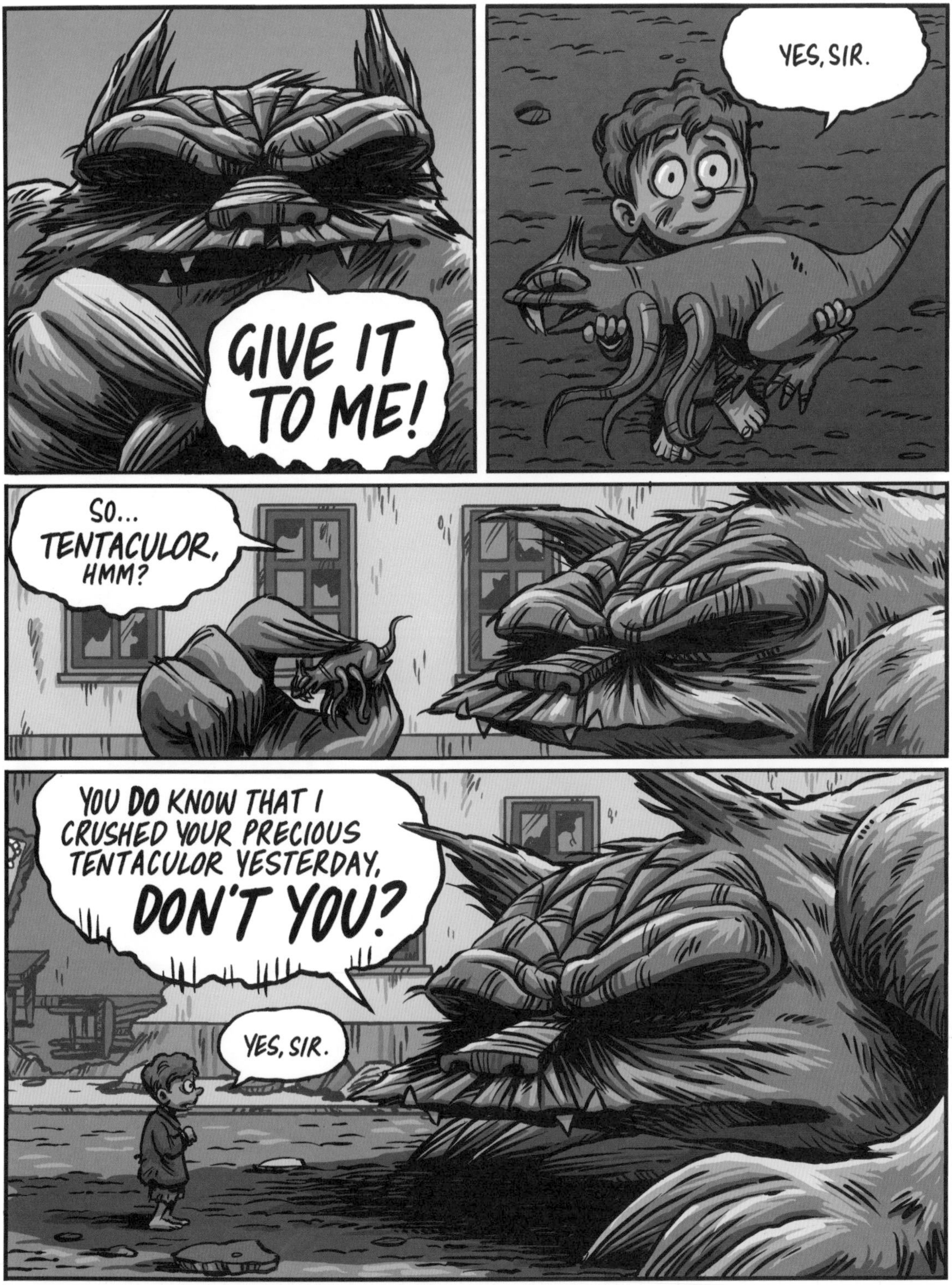
GIVE IT TO ME!
YES, SIR.
SO... TENTACULOR, HMM?
YOU DO KNOW THAT I CRUSHED YOUR PRECIOUS TENTACULOR YESTERDAY, DON'T YOU?
YES, SIR.

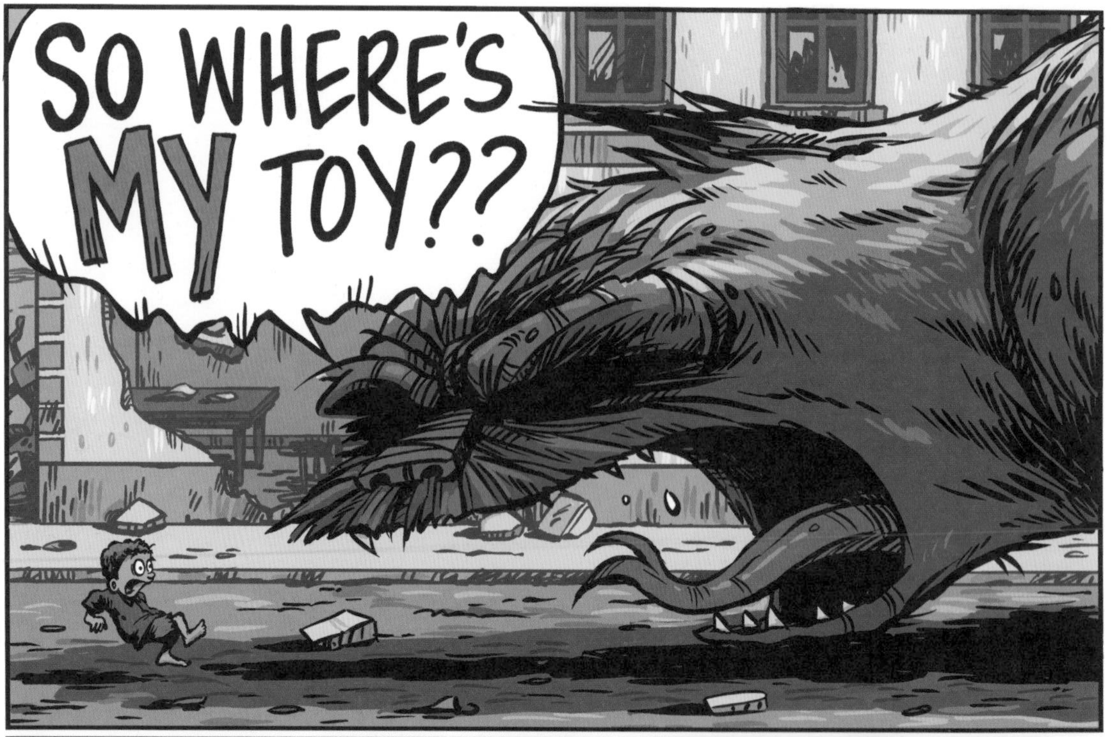
SO WHERE'S MY TOY??

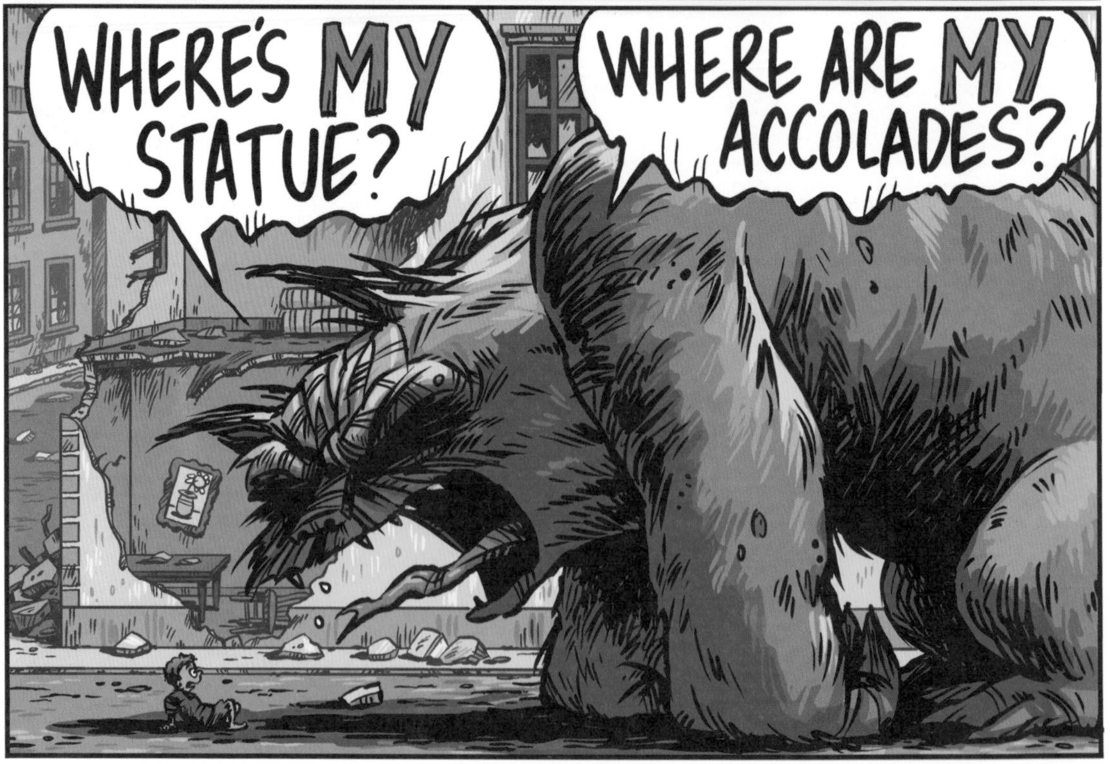
WHERE'S MY STATUE?
WHERE ARE MY ACCOLADES?

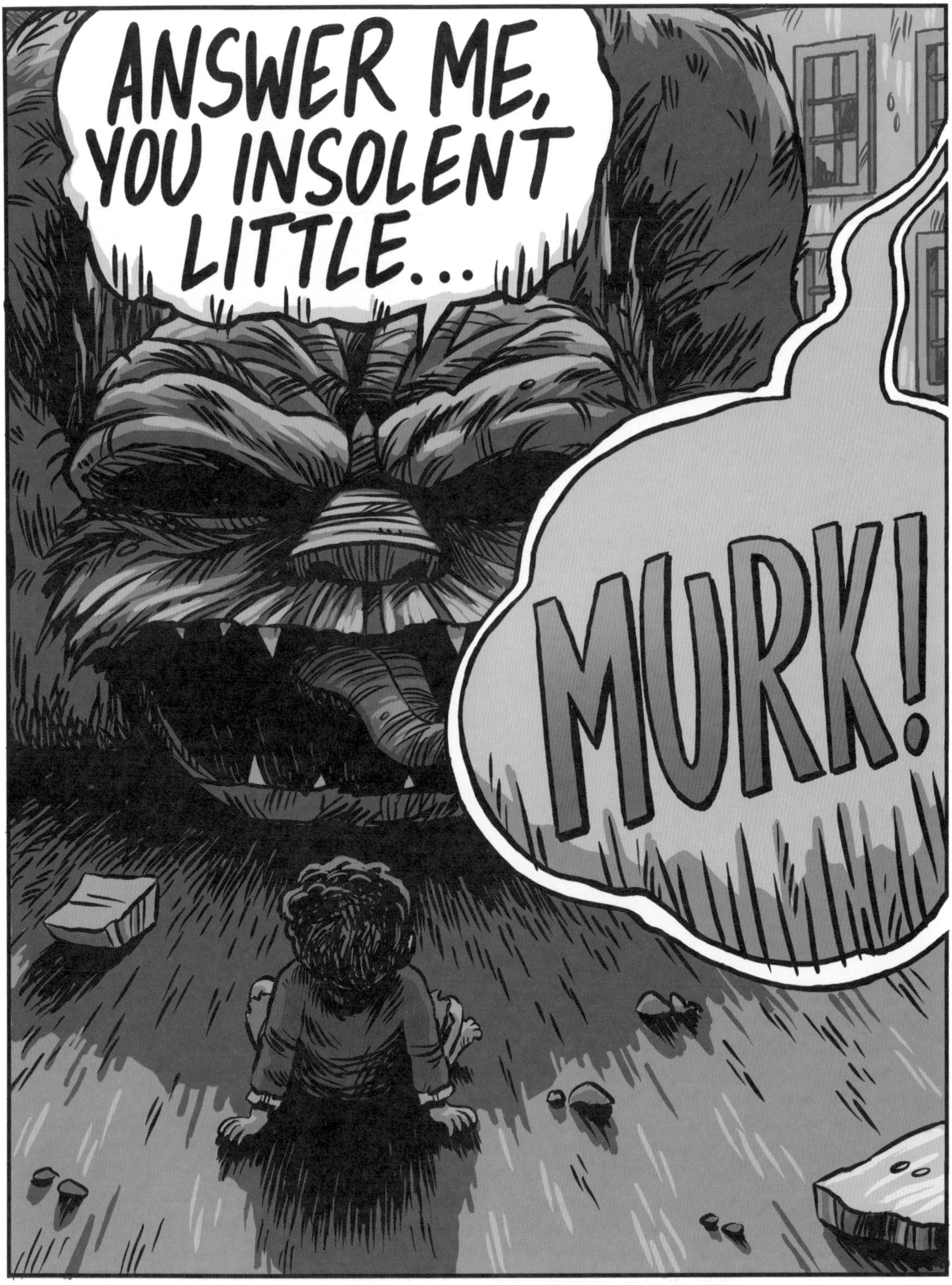
ANSWER ME, YOU INSOLENT LITTLE...
MURK!

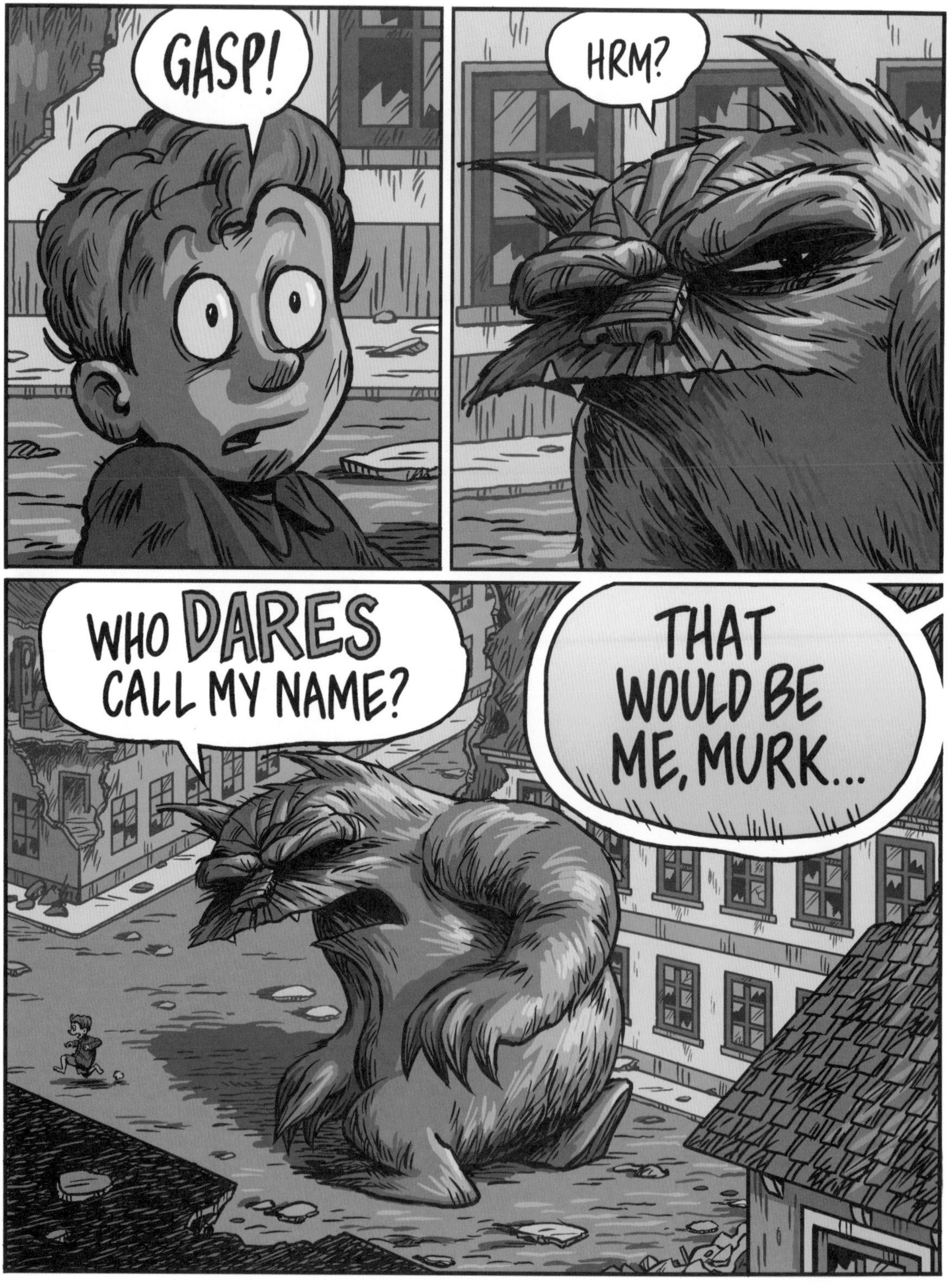
GASP!
HRM?
WHO DARES CALL MY NAME?
THAT WOULD BE ME, MURK...

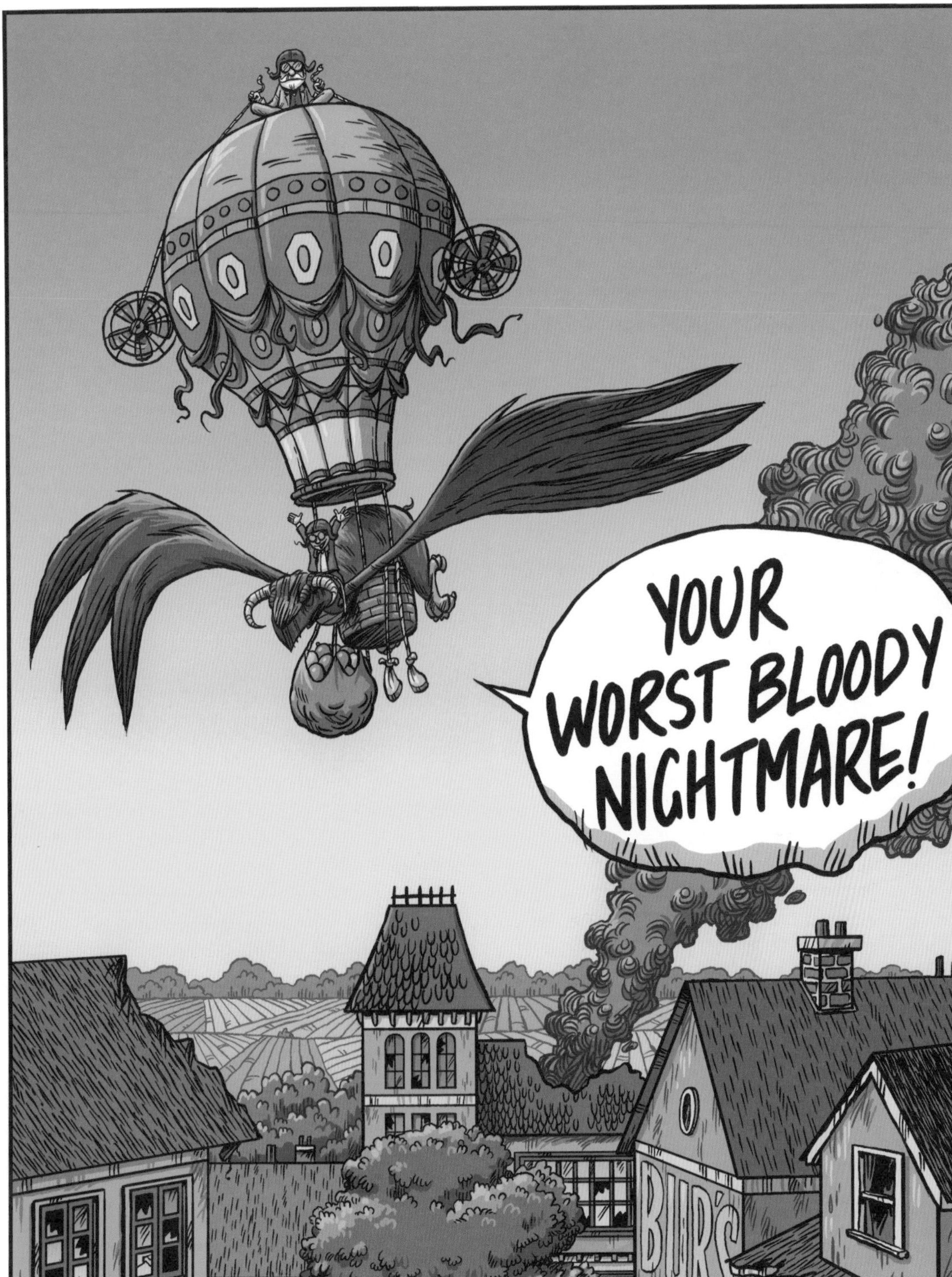
YOUR WORST BLOODY NIGHTMARE!
BUR'S

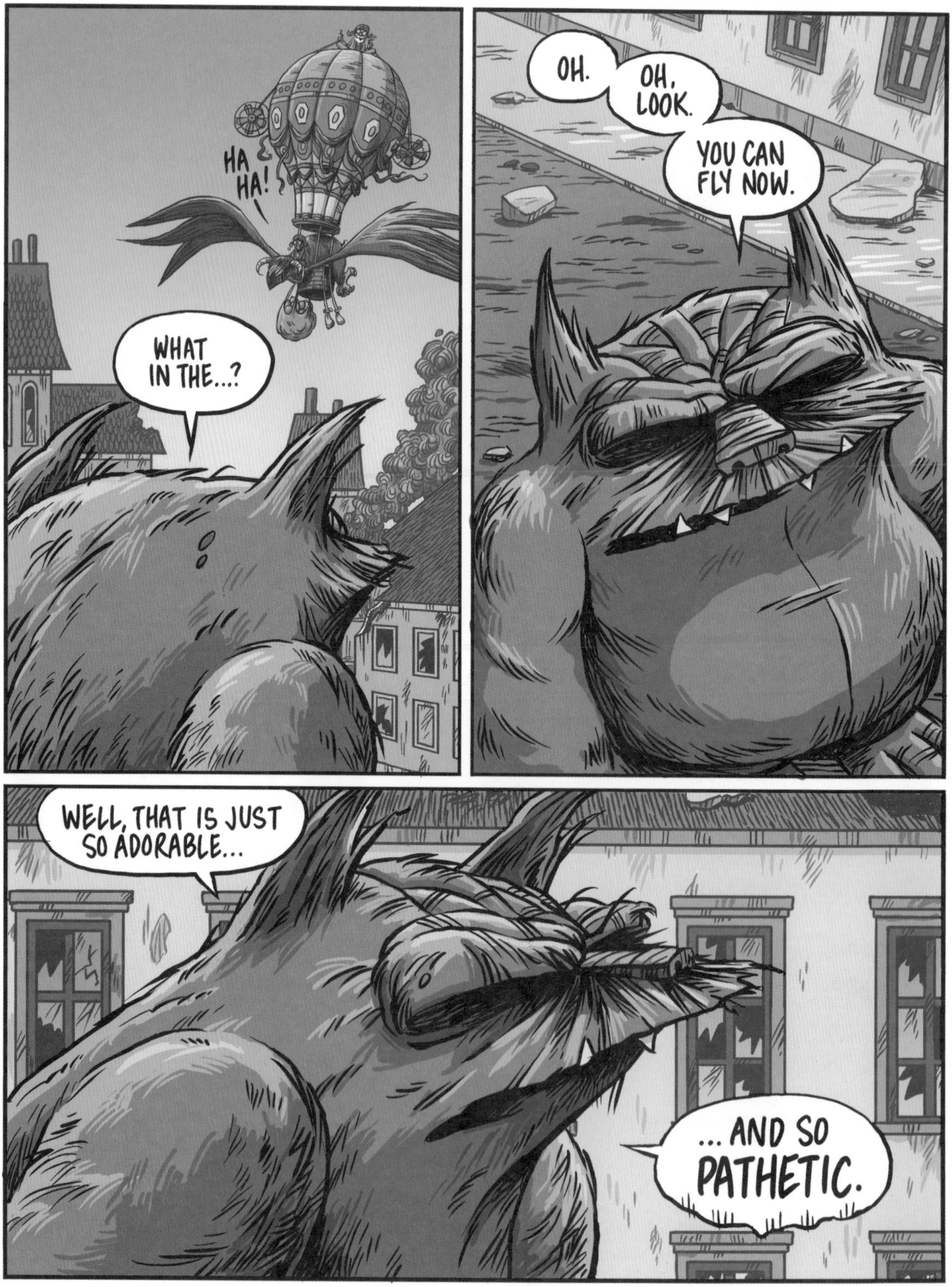
HA HA!
WHAT IN THE...?
OH.
OH, LOOK.
YOU CAN FLY NOW.
WELL, THAT IS JUST SO ADORABLE...
...AND SO PATHETIC.

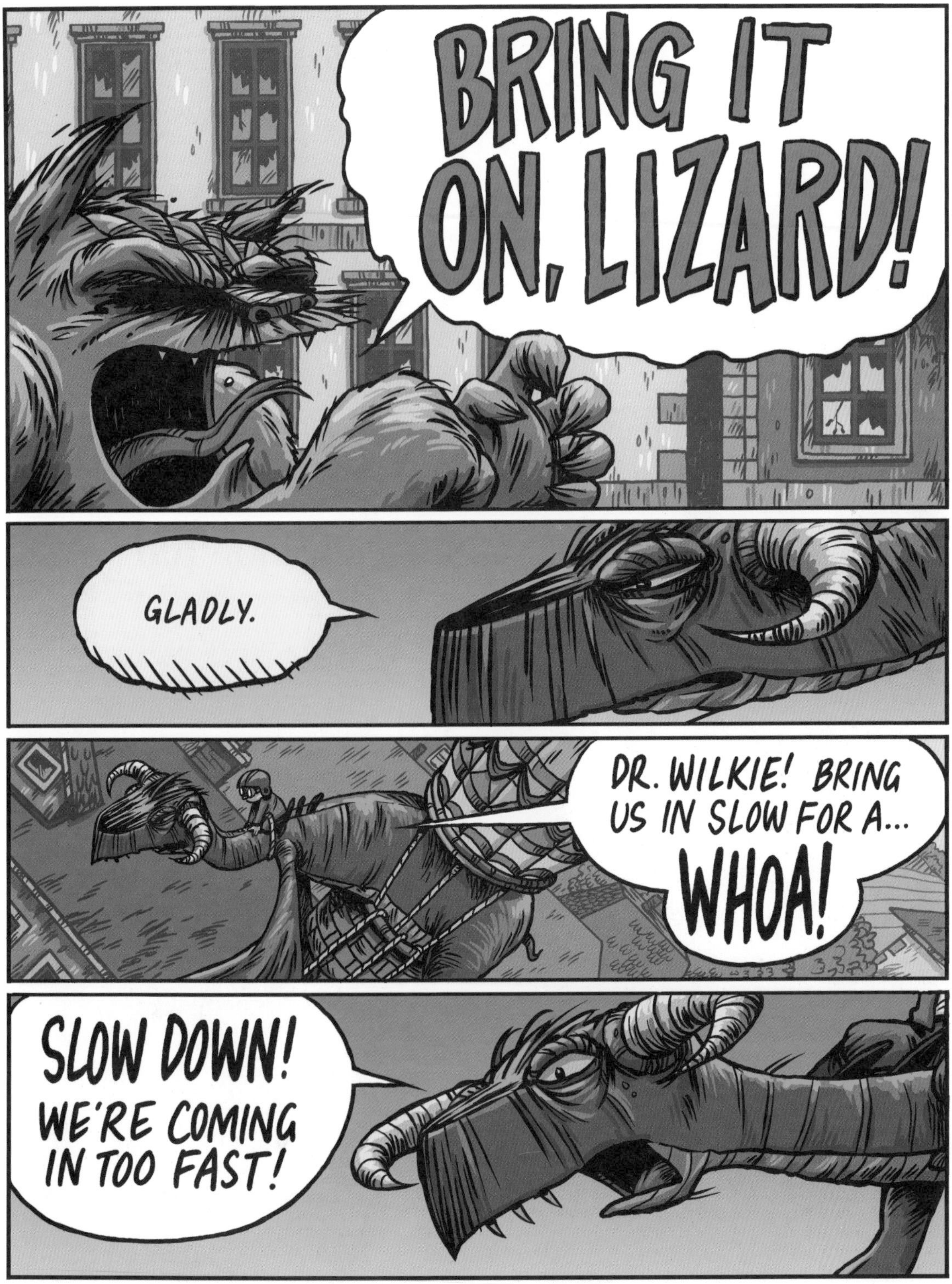
BRING IT ON, LIZARD!
GLADLY.
DR. WILKIE! BRING US IN SLOW FOR A... WHOA!
SLOW DOWN! WE'RE COMING IN TOO FAST!

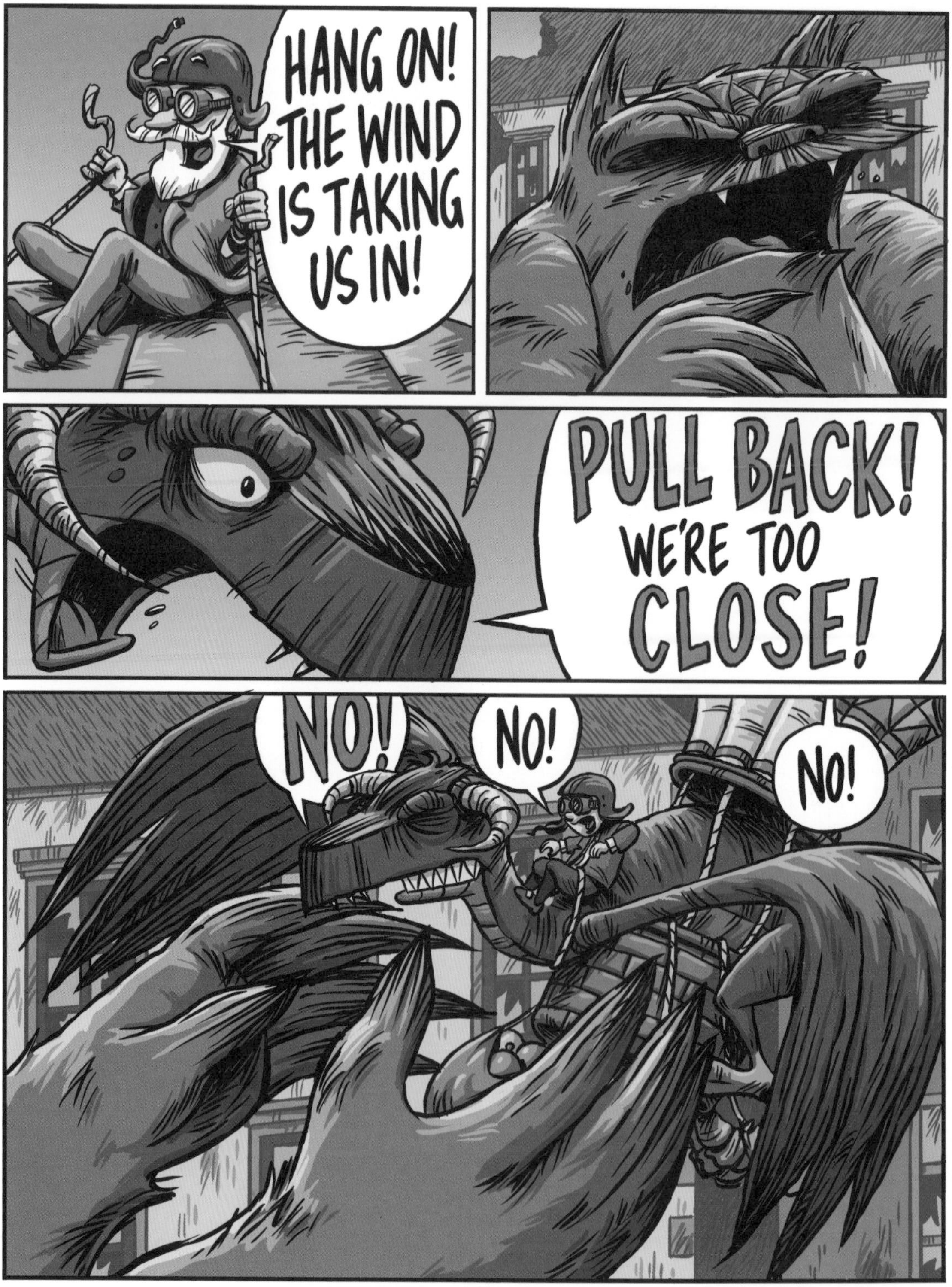
HANG ON! THE WIND IS TAKING US IN!
PULL BACK! WE'RE TOO CLOSE!
NO!
NO!
NO!

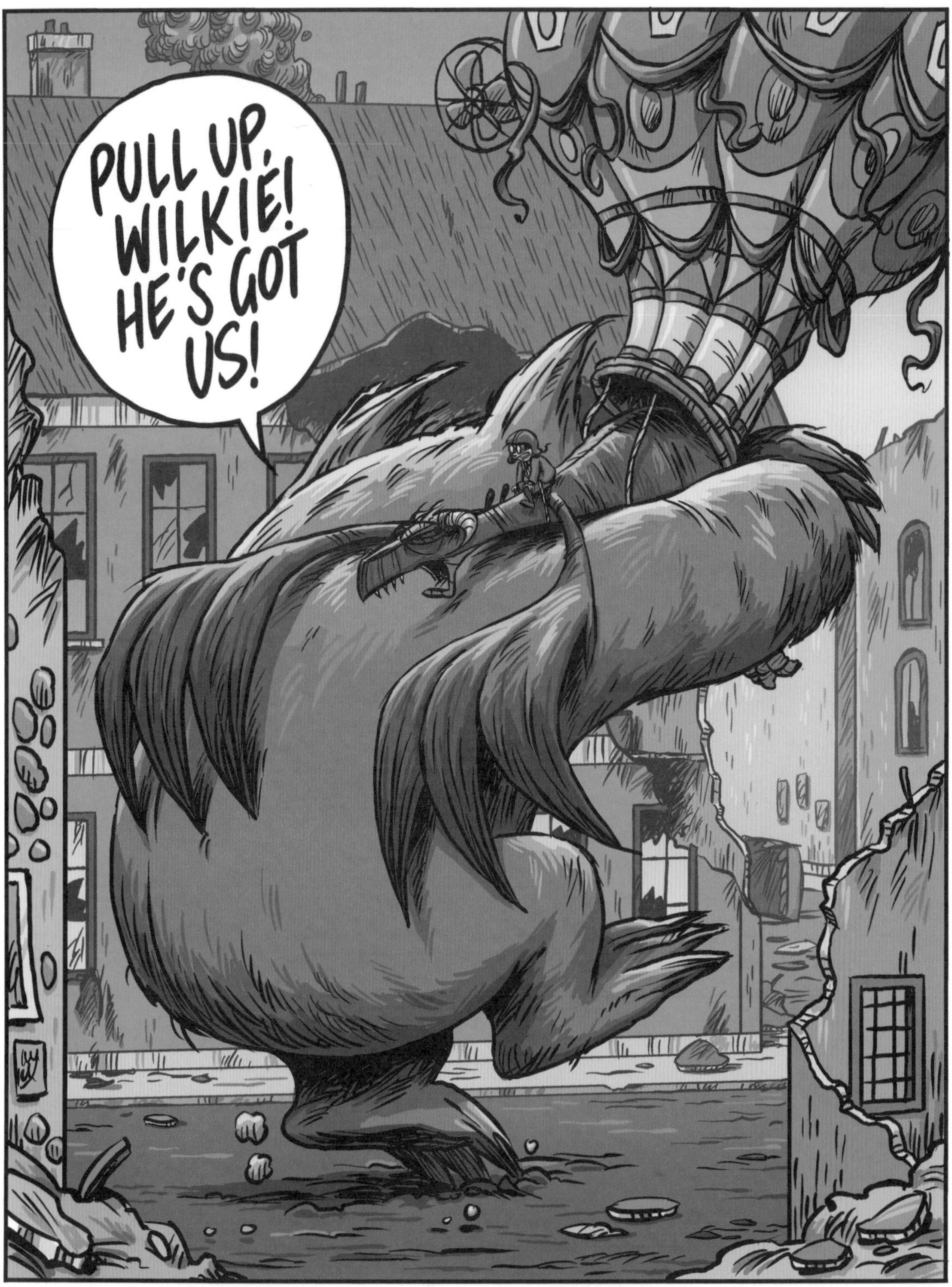
PULL UP, WILKIE! HE'S GOT US!

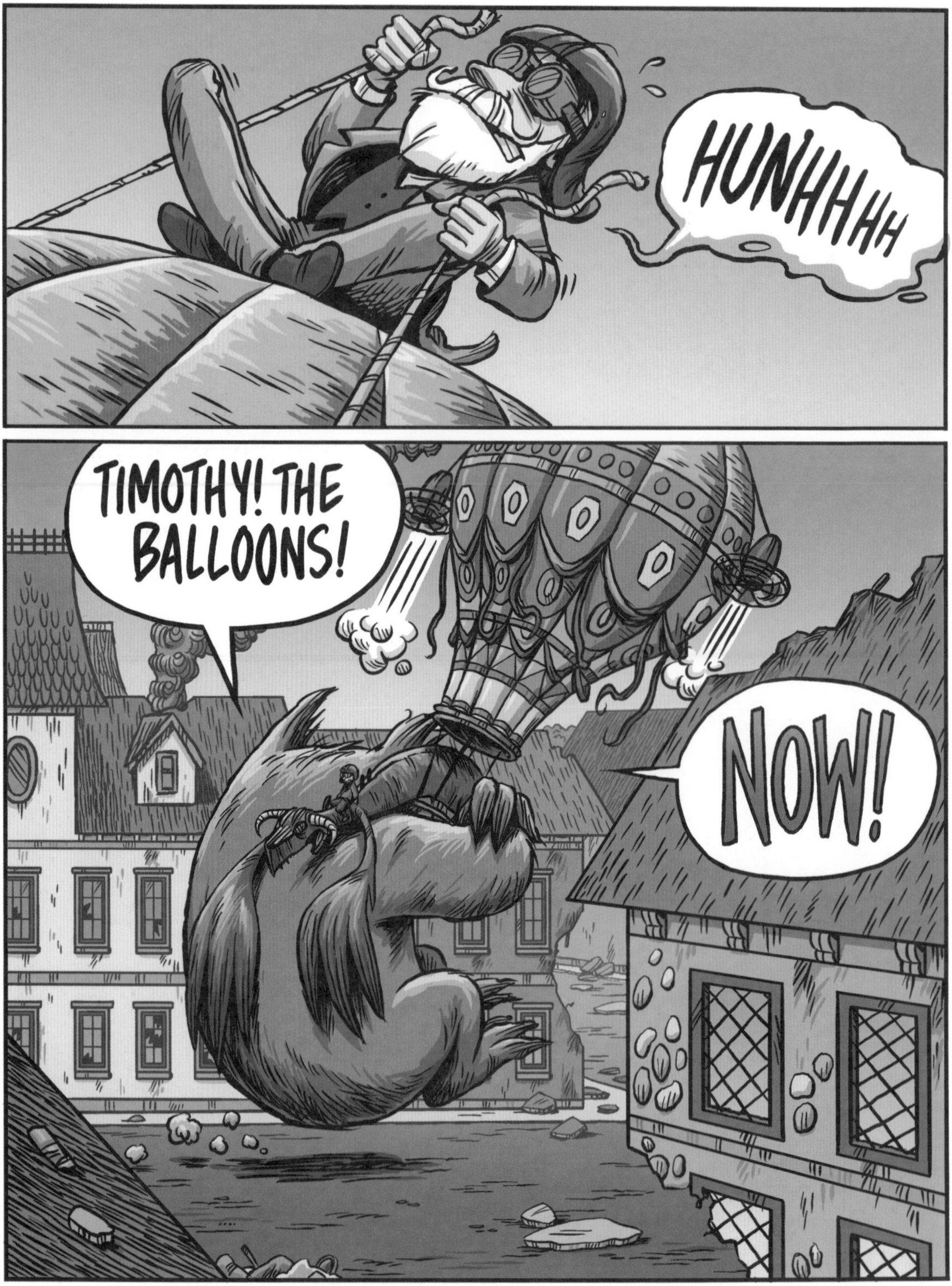
HUNHHHH
TIMOTHY! THE BALLOONS!
NOW!

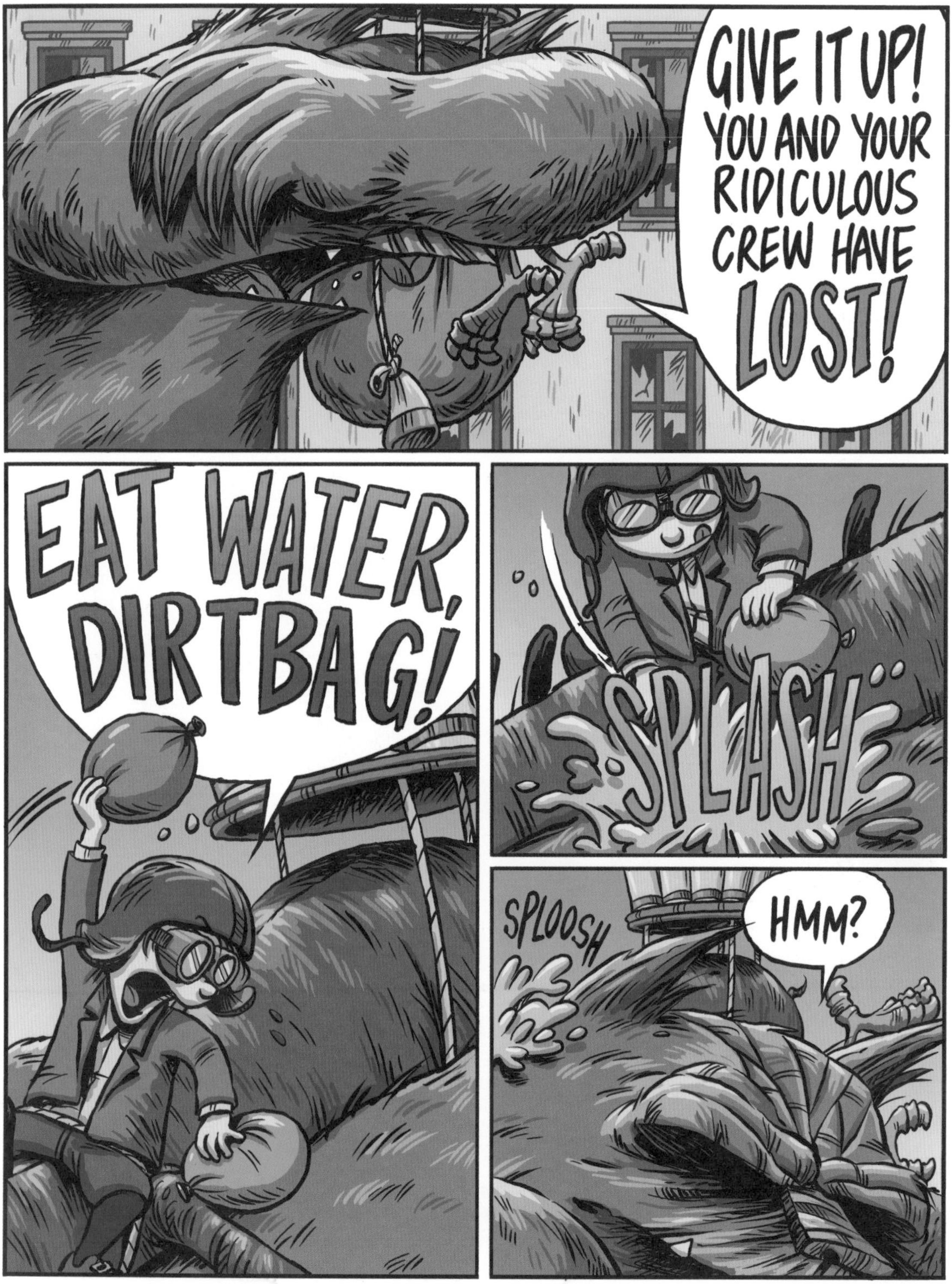
GIVE IT UP! YOU AND YOUR RIDICULOUS CREW HAVE LOST!
EAT WATER, DIRTBAG!
SPLASH
SPLOOSH
HMM?

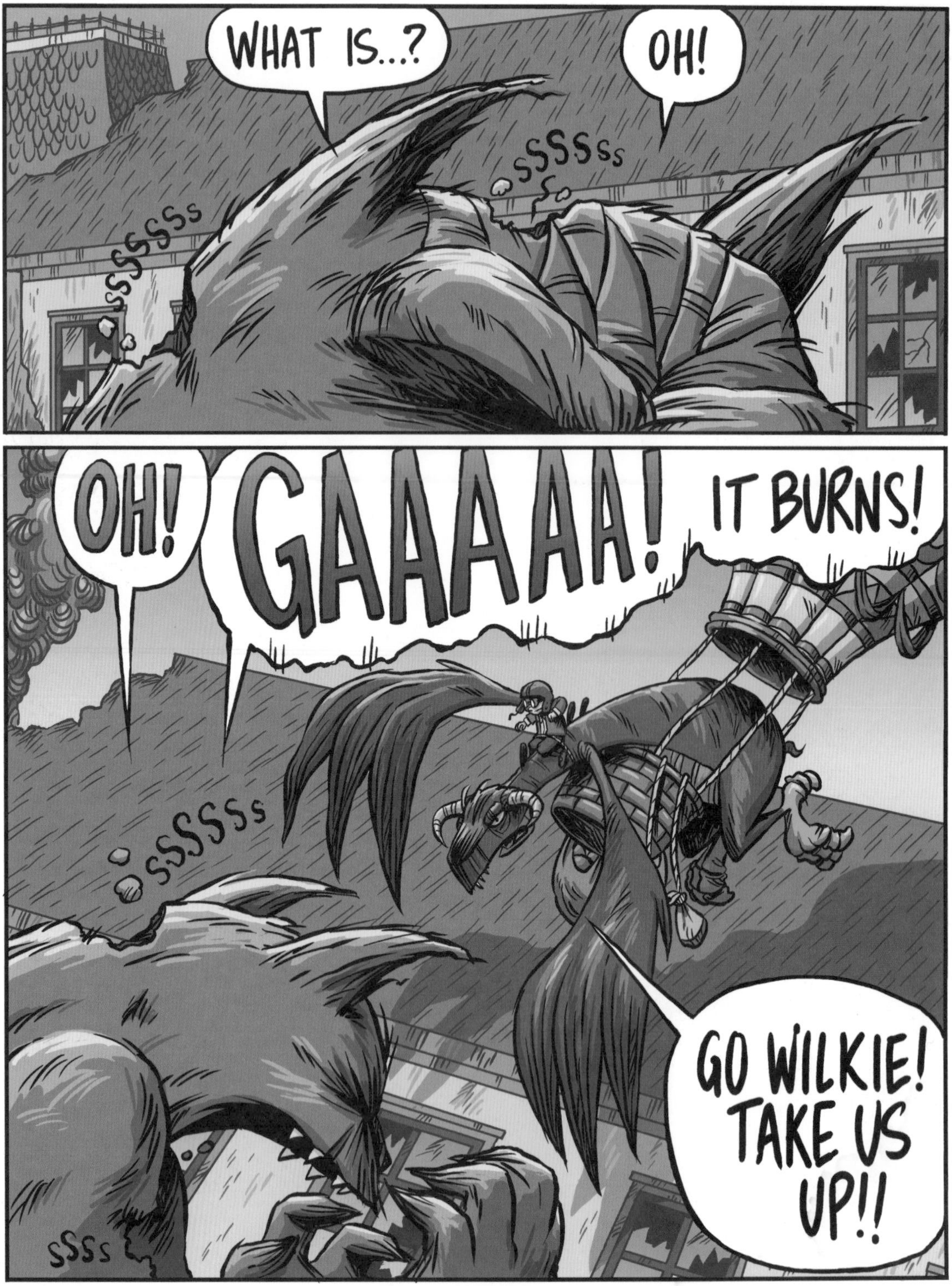
WHAT IS...?
OH!
sSSSSSs
sSSSSs
OH!
GAAAAA!
IT BURNS!
sSSSSSs
GO WILKIE! TAKE US UP!!
SSSs

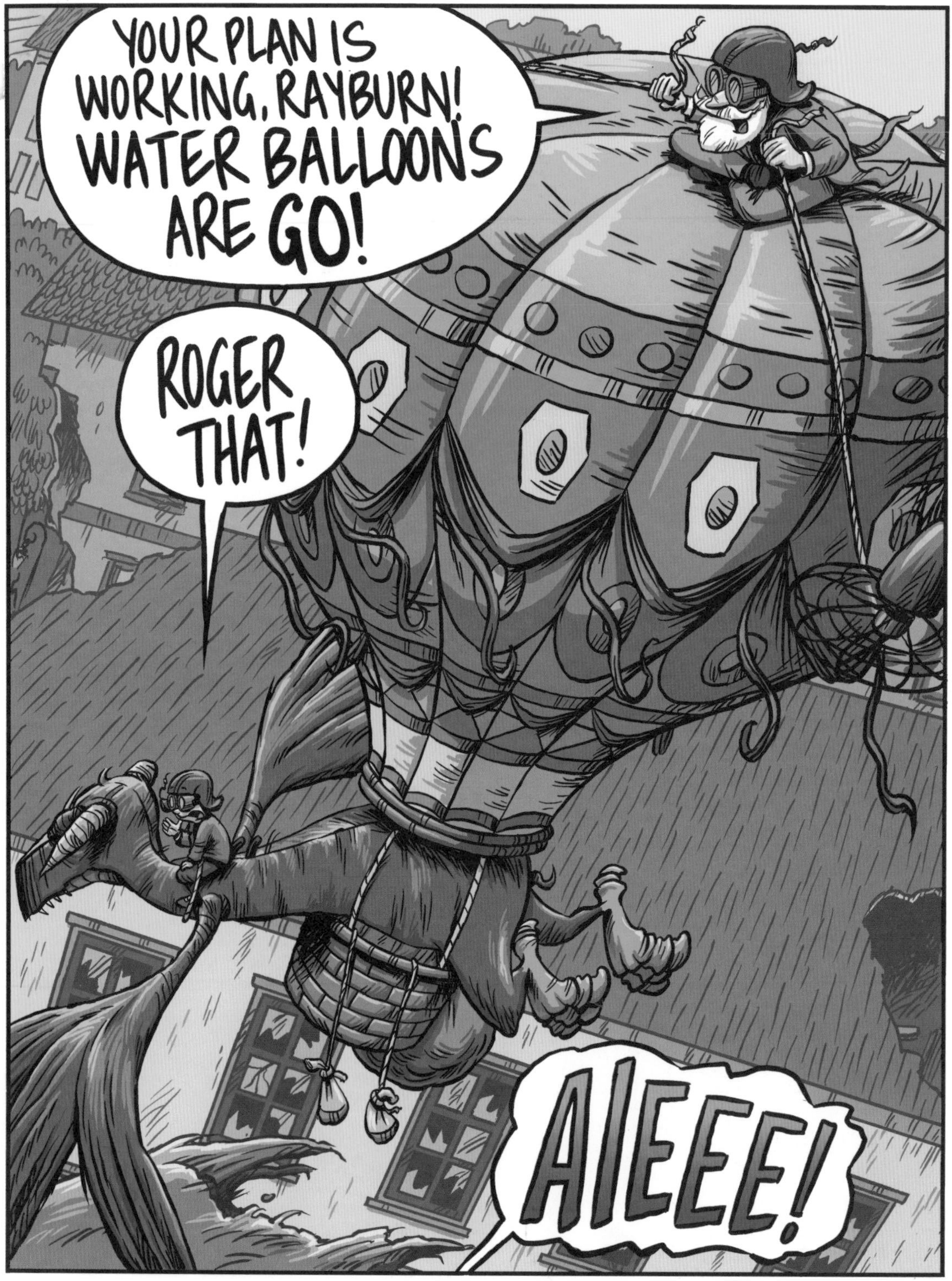
YOUR PLAN IS WORKING, RAYBURN! WATER BALLOONS ARE GO!
ROGER THAT!
AIEEE!

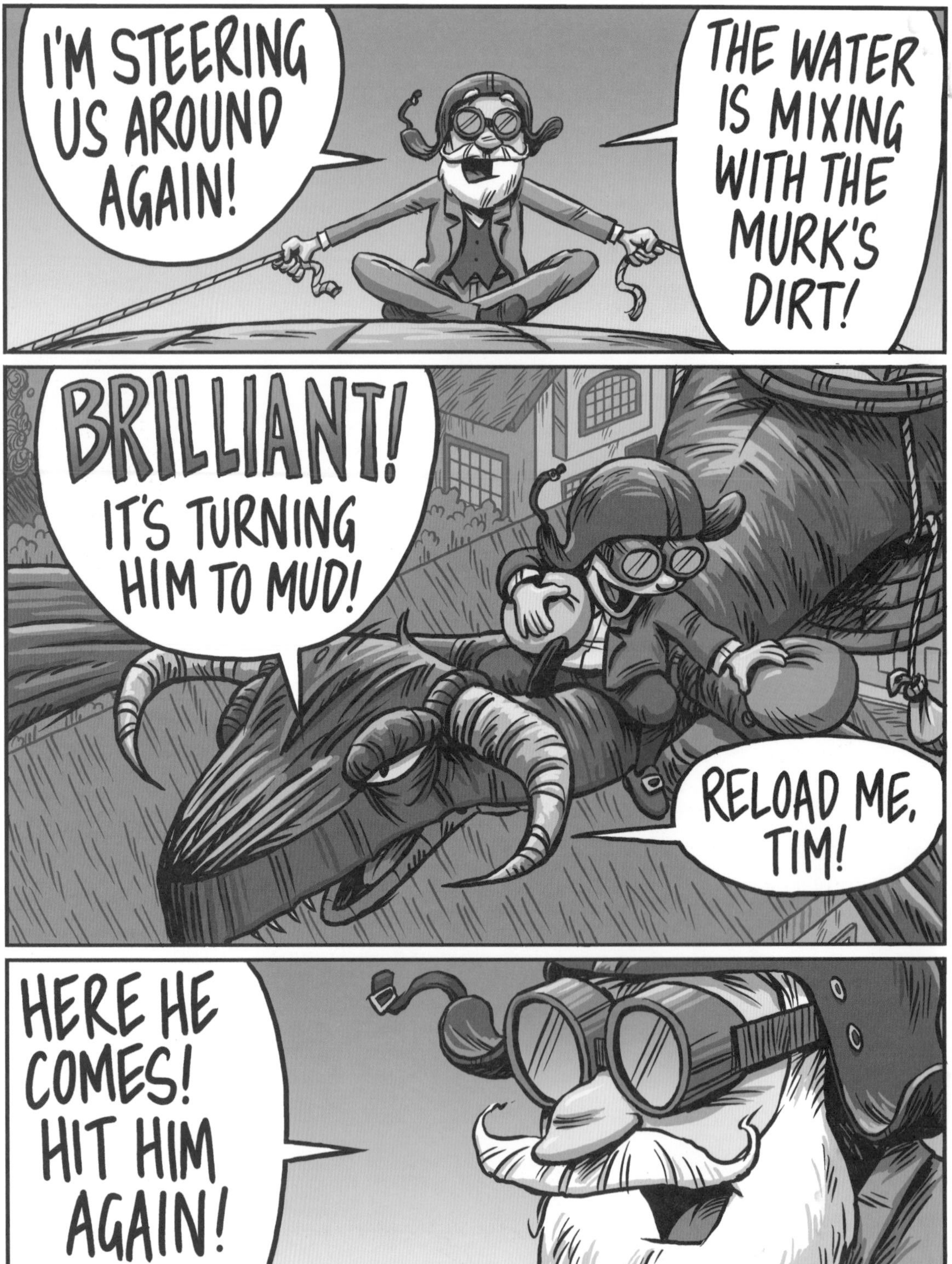
I'M STEERING US AROUND AGAIN!
THE WATER IS MIXING WITH THE MURK'S DIRT!
BRILLIANT! IT'S TURNING HIM TO MUD!
RELOAD ME, TIM!
HERE HE COMES! HIT HIM AGAIN!

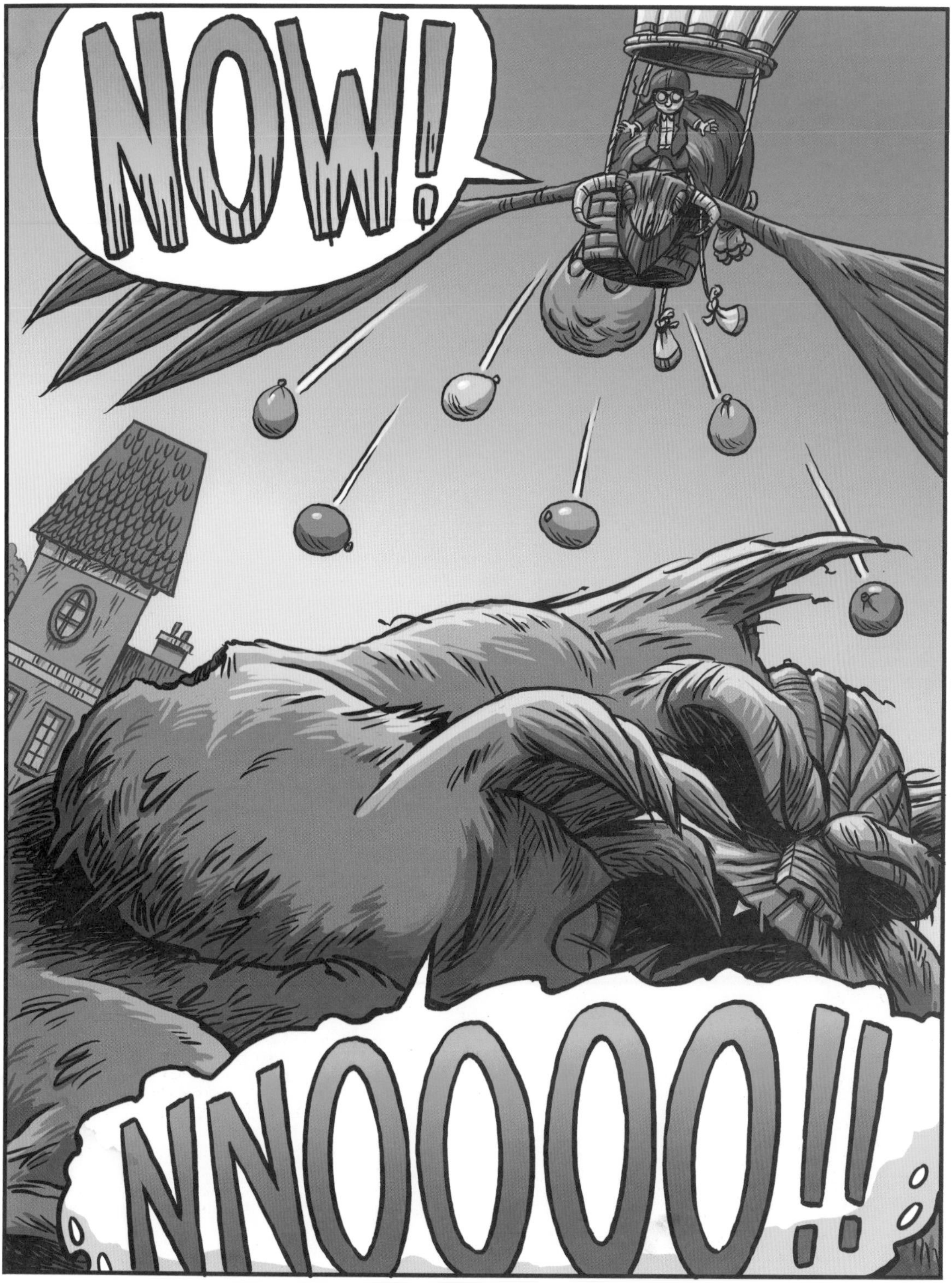
NOW!
NNOOOOO!!

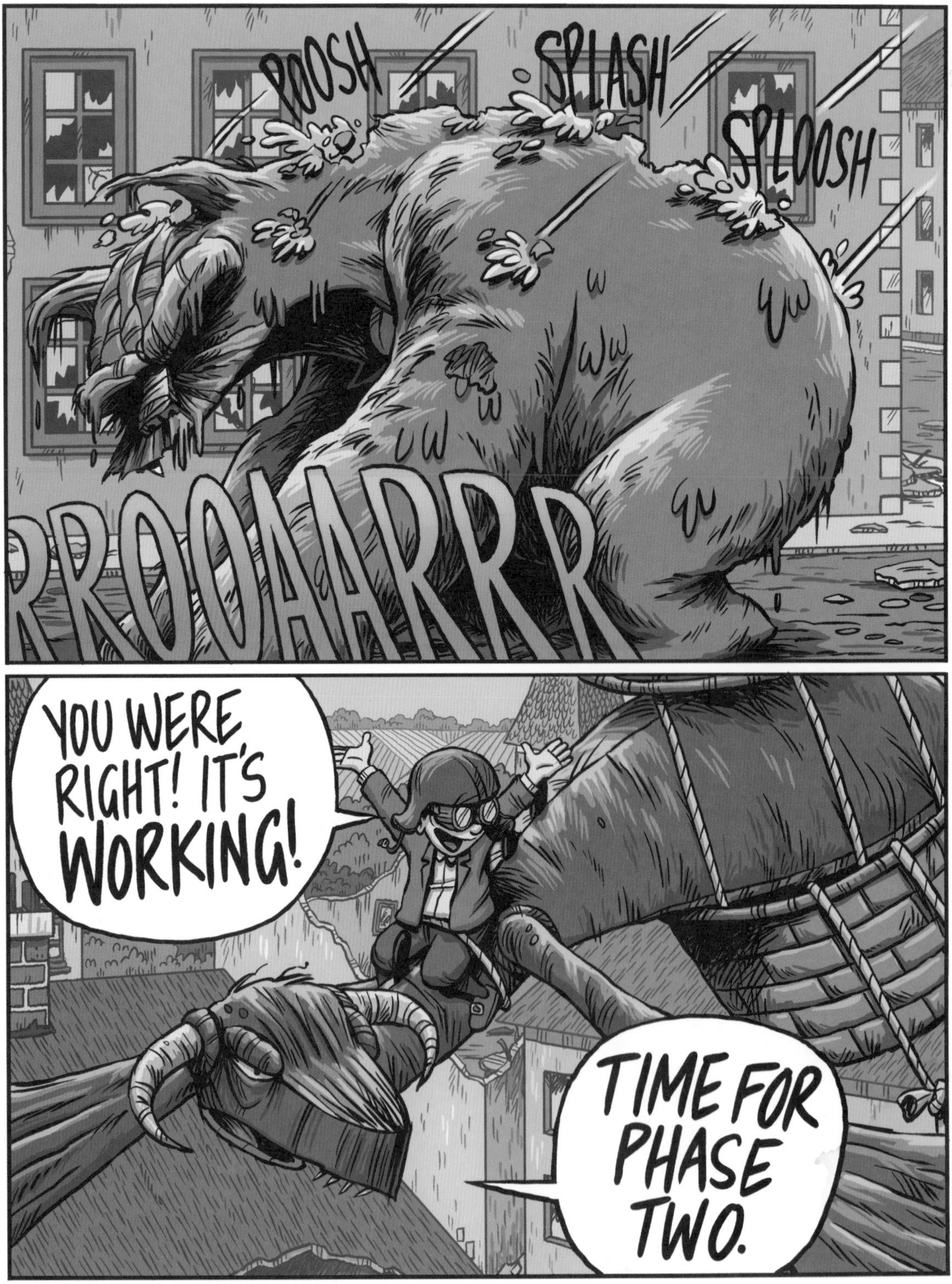
POOSH
SPLASH
SPLOOSH
RROOAARRRR
YOU WERE RIGHT! IT'S WORKING!
TIME FOR PHASE TWO.

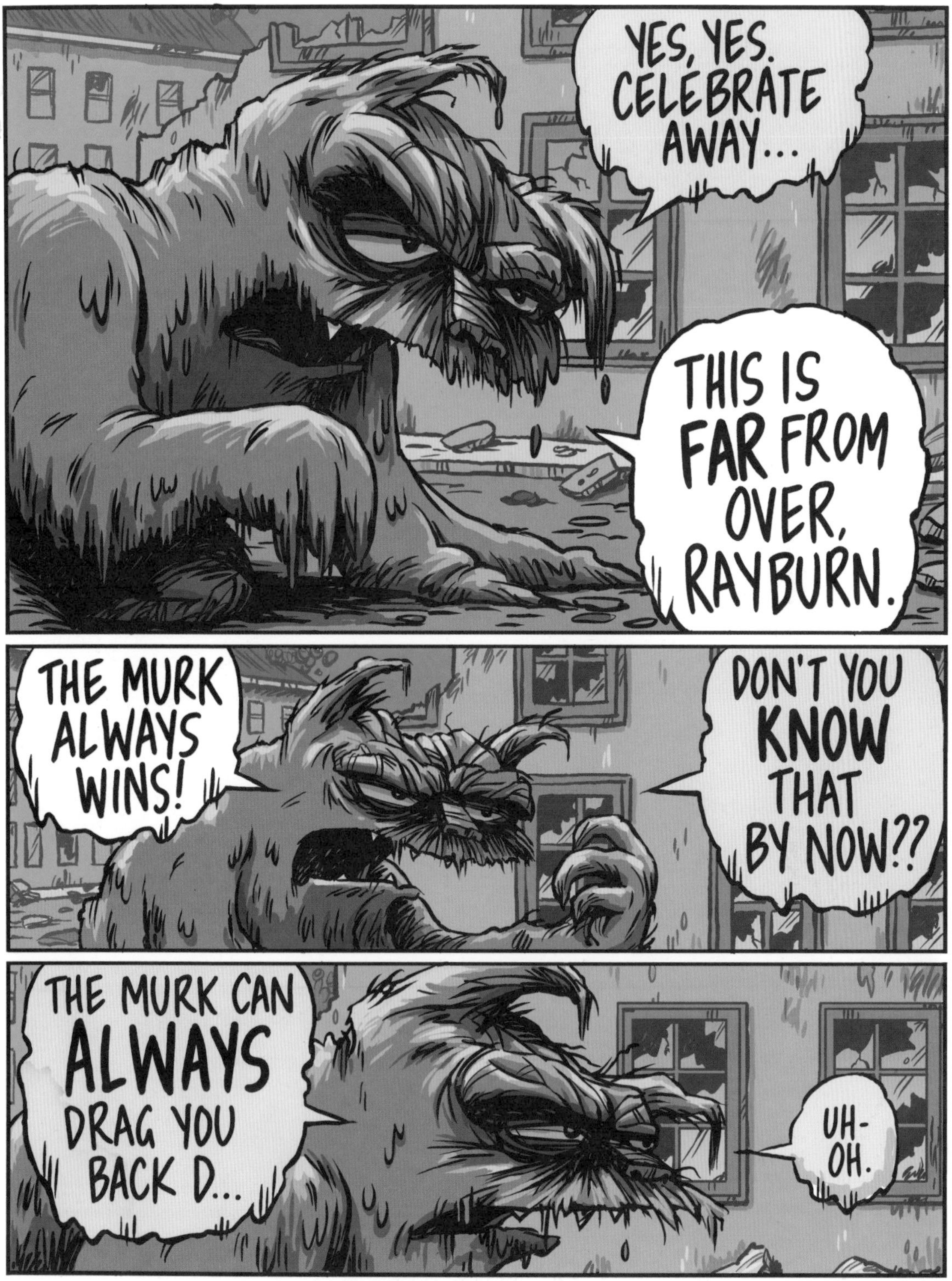
YES, YES. CELEBRATE AWAY...
THIS IS FAR FROM OVER, RAYBURN.
THE MURK ALWAYS WINS!
DON'T YOU KNOW THAT BY NOW??
THE MURK CAN ALWAYS DRAG YOU BACK D...
UH-OH.

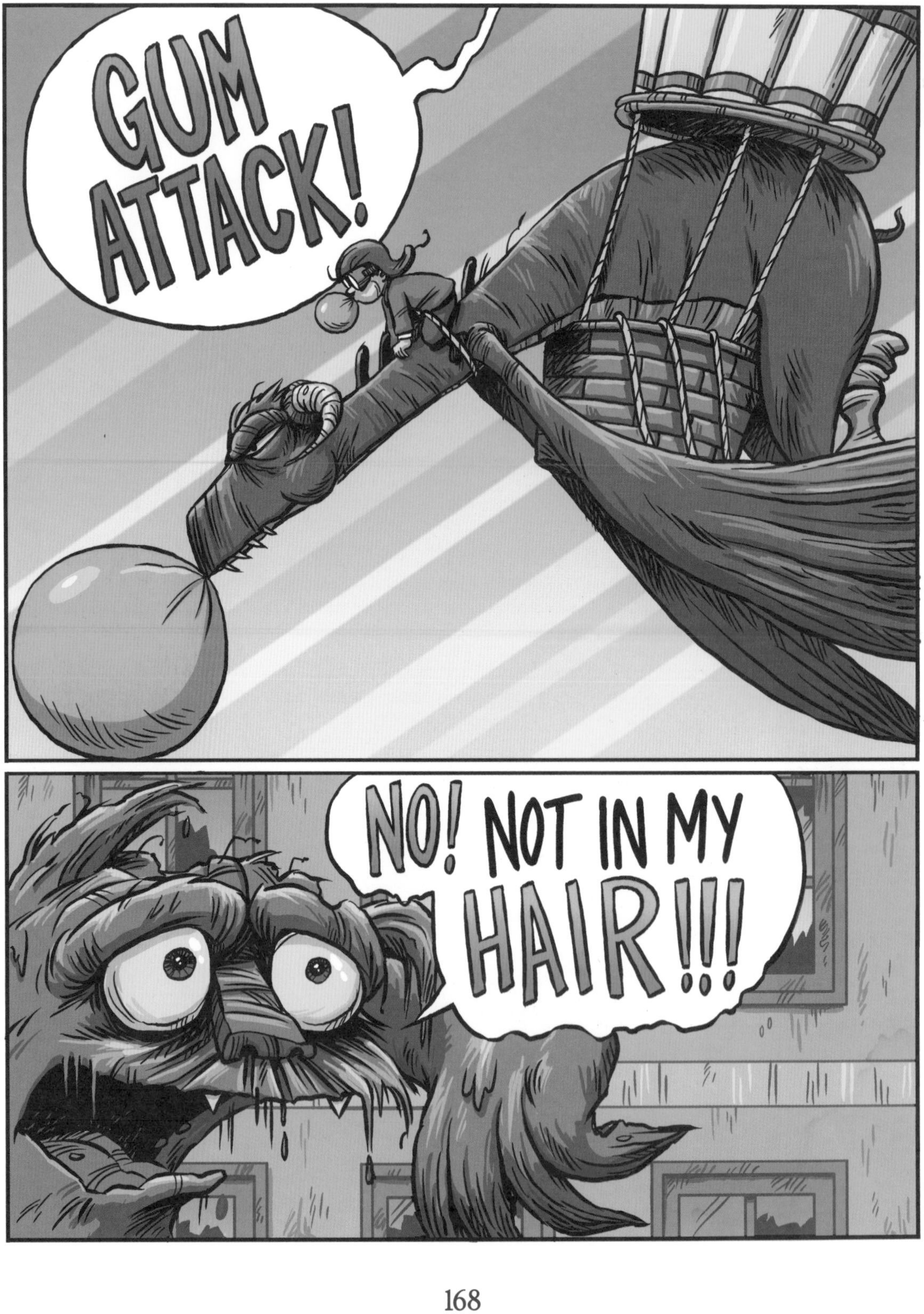
GUM ATTACK!
NO! NOT IN MY HAIR!!!

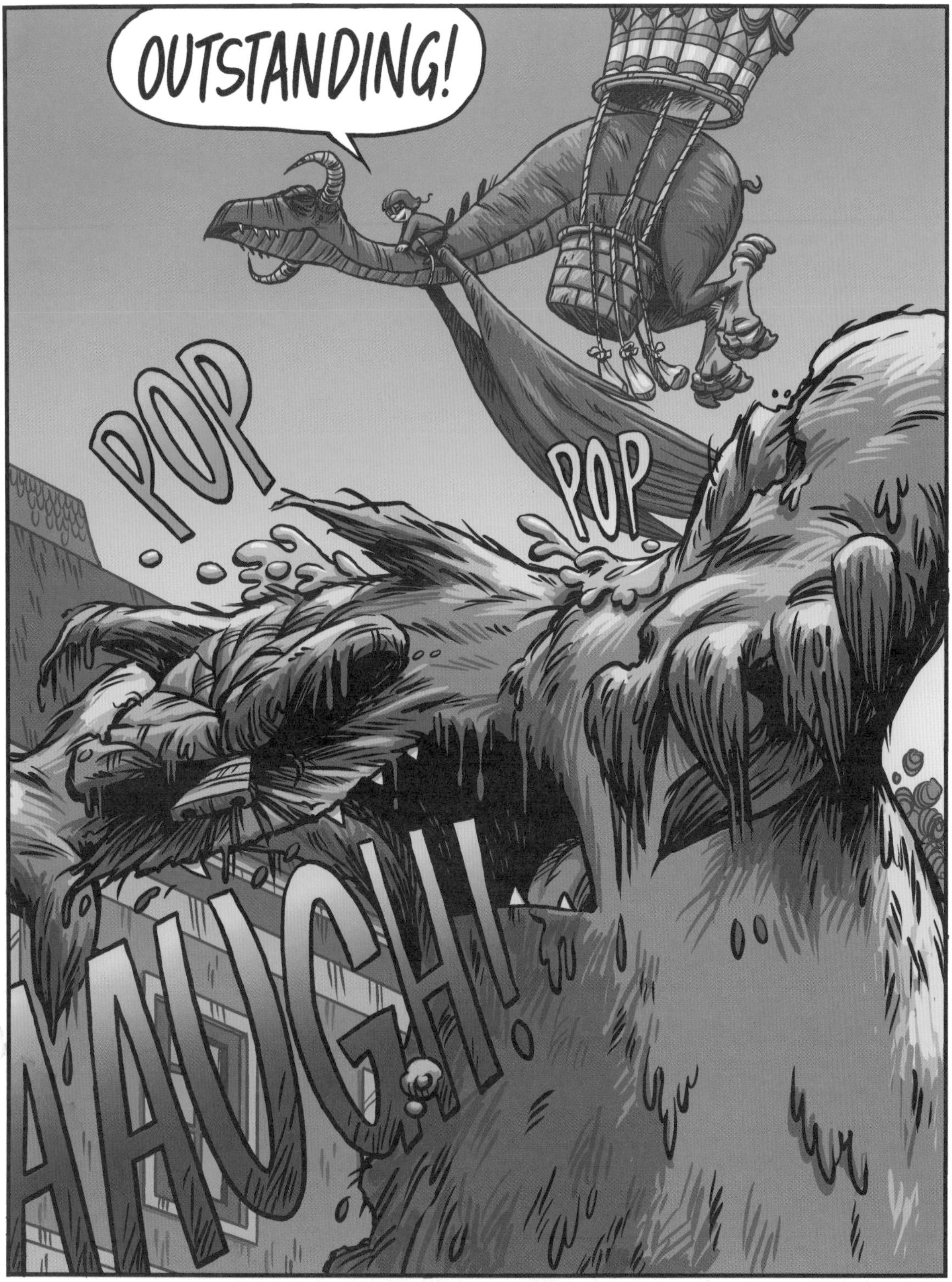
OUTSTANDING!
POP
POP
AAUGH!!

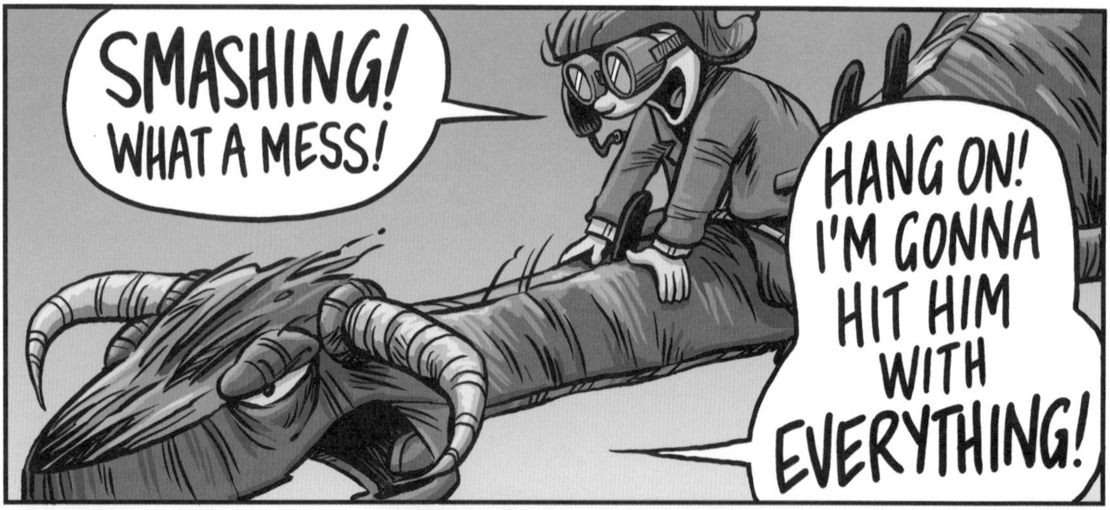
SMASHING! WHAT A MESS!
HANG ON! I'M GONNA HIT HIM WITH EVERYTHING!

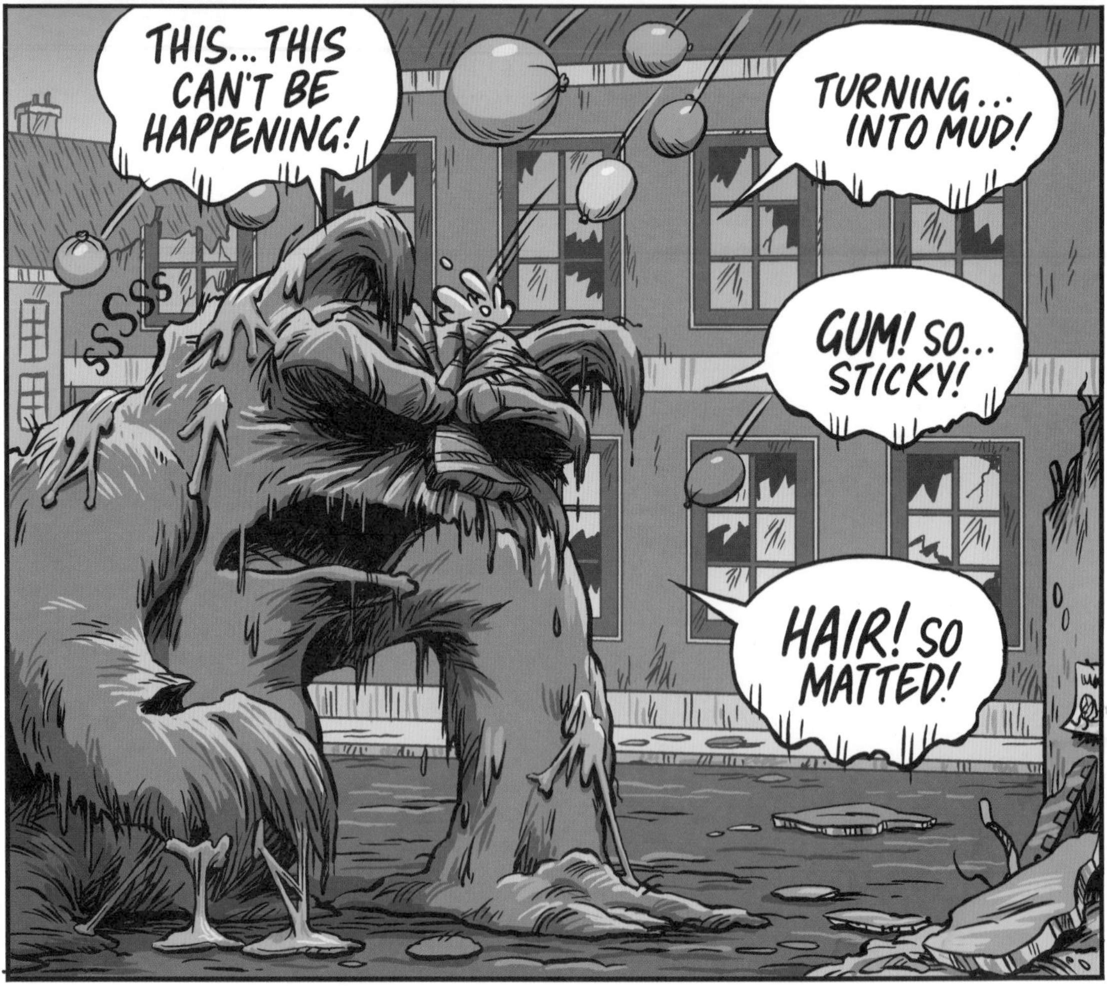
THIS... THIS CAN'T BE HAPPENING!
SSSSSS
TURNING... INTO MUD!
GUM! SO... STICKY!
HAIR! SO MATTED!

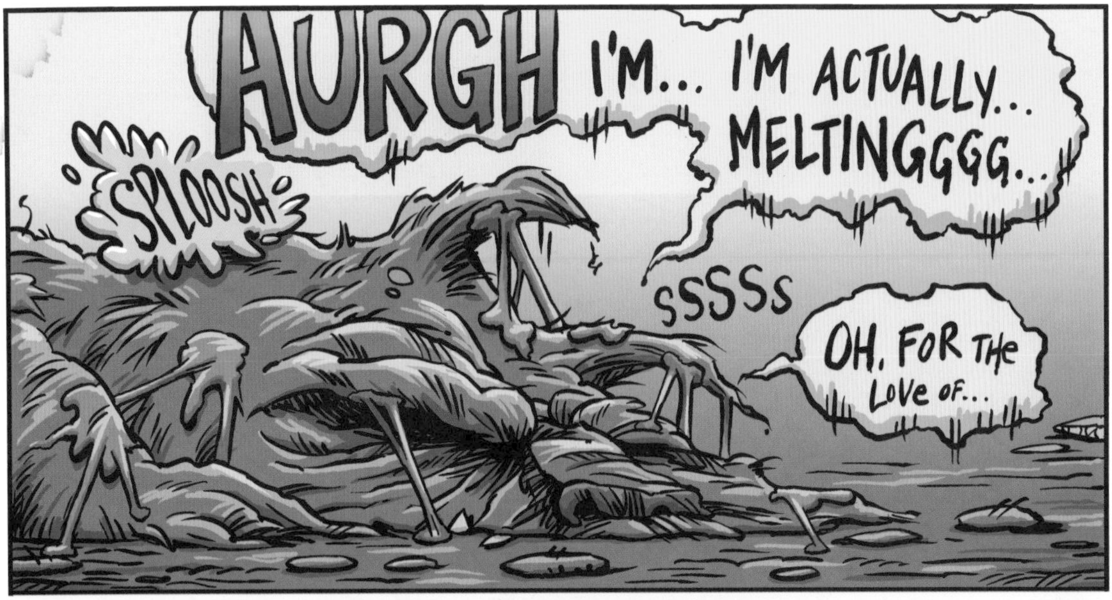
AURGH
I'M... I'M ACTUALLY... MELTINGGGG...
SPLOOSH
SSSSS
OH, FOR THE LOVE OF...

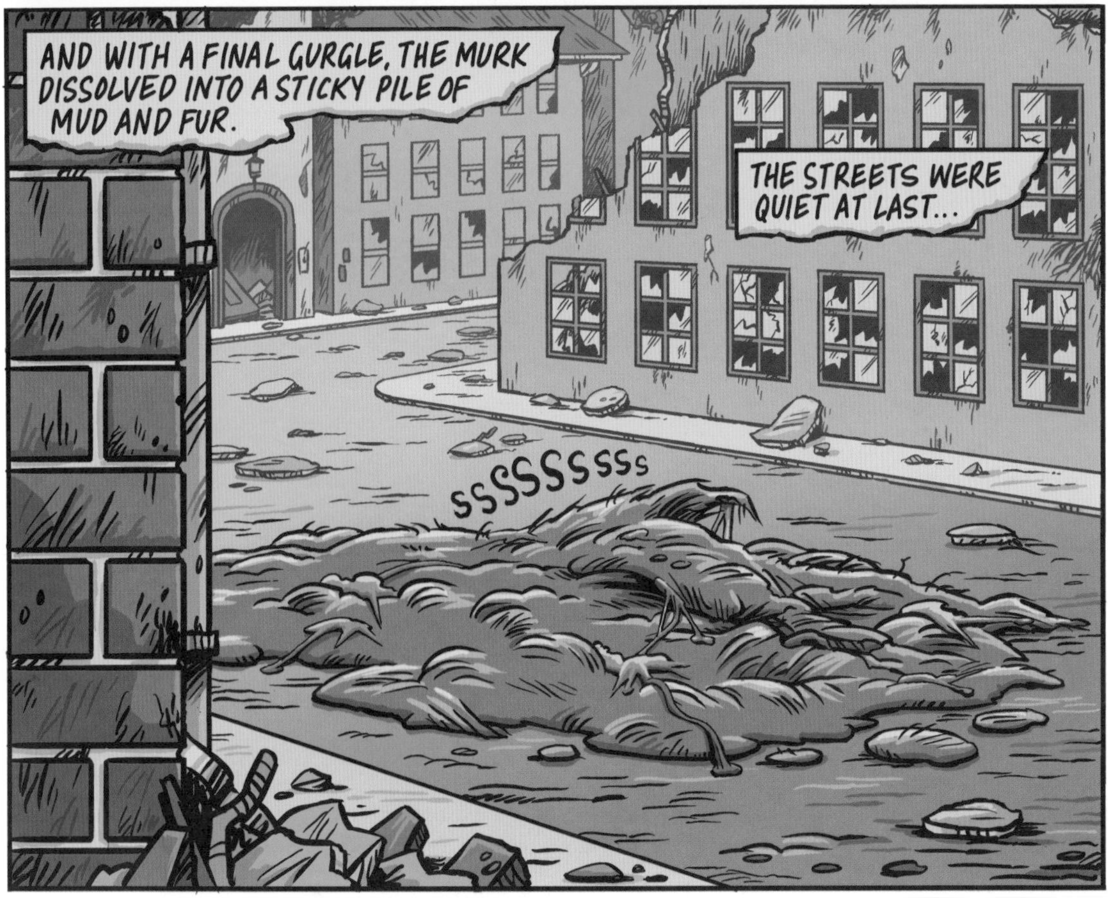
AND WITH A FINAL GURGLE, THE MURK DISSOLVED INTO A STICKY PILE OF MUD AND FUR.
THE STREETS WERE QUIET AT LAST...
SSSSSSSSSS

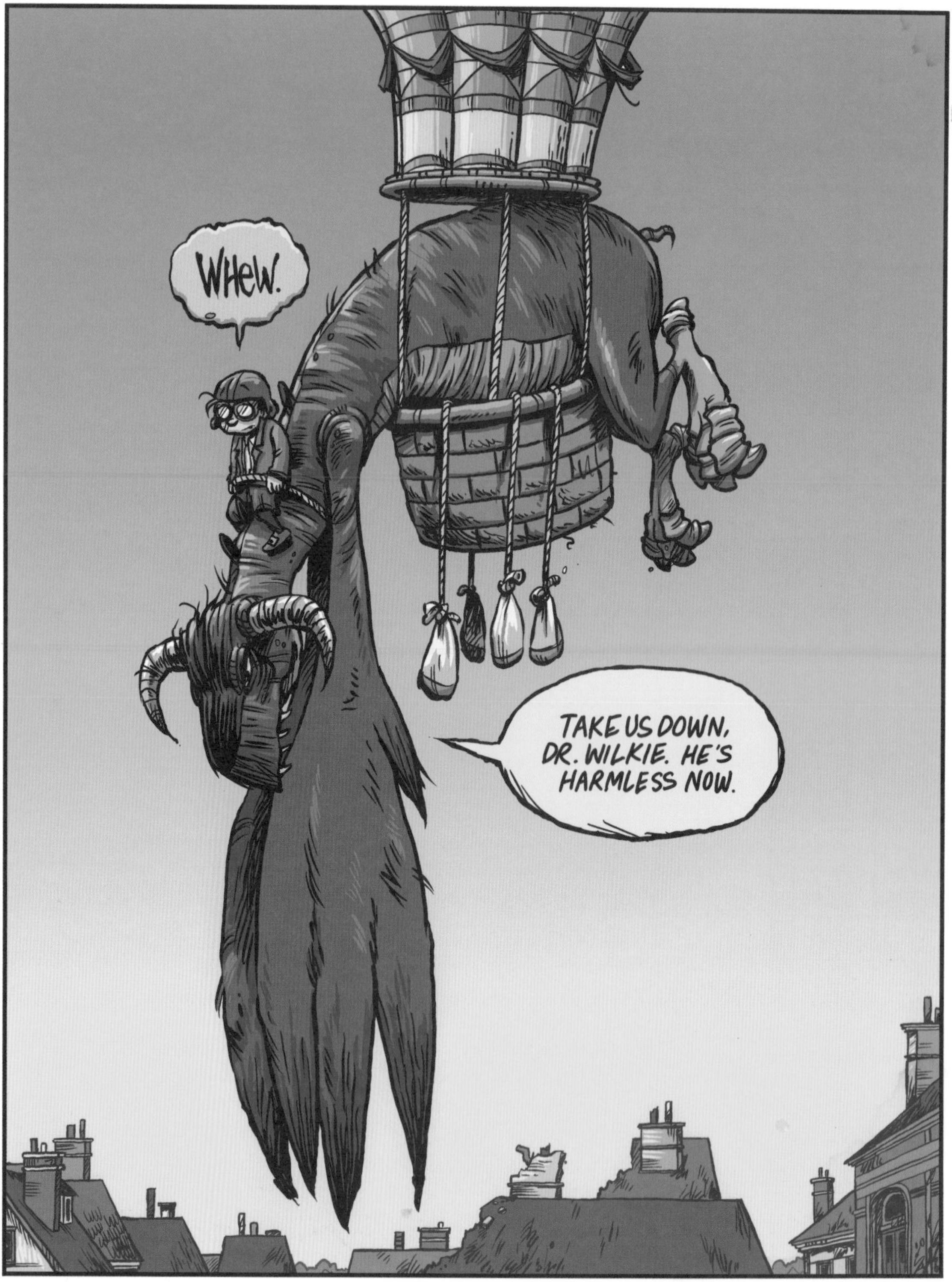
WHEW.
TAKE US DOWN, DR. WILKIE. HE'S HARMLESS NOW.

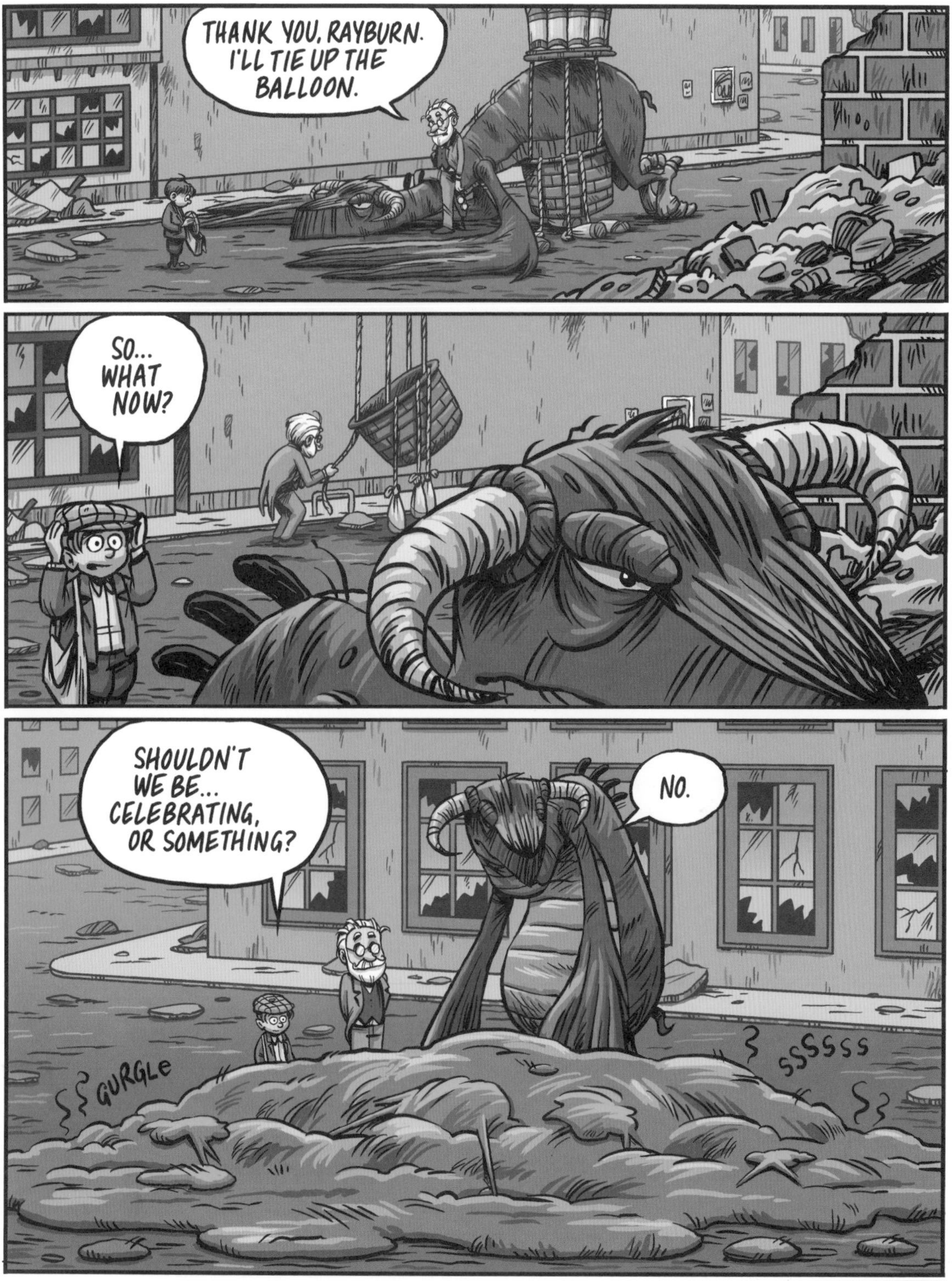
THANK YOU, RAYBURN. I'LL TIE UP THE BALLOON.
SO... WHAT NOW?
SHOULDN'T WE BE... CELEBRATING, OR SOMETHING?
NO.
GURGLE
SSSSSS

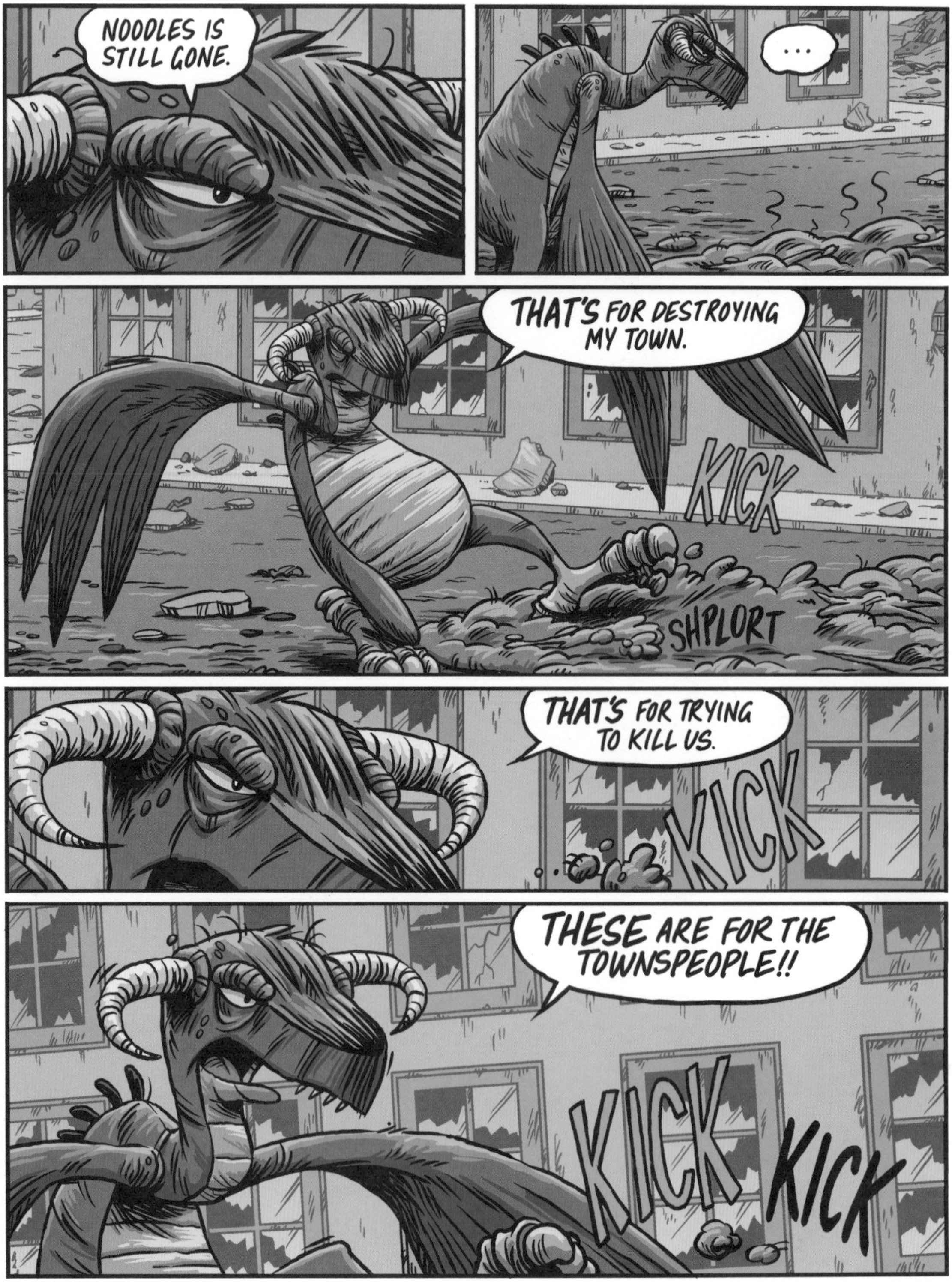
NOODLES IS STILL GONE.
...
THAT'S FOR DESTROYING MY TOWN.
KICK
SHPLORT
THAT'S FOR TRYING TO KILL US.
KICK
THESE ARE FOR THE TOWNSPEOPLE!!
KICK
KICK

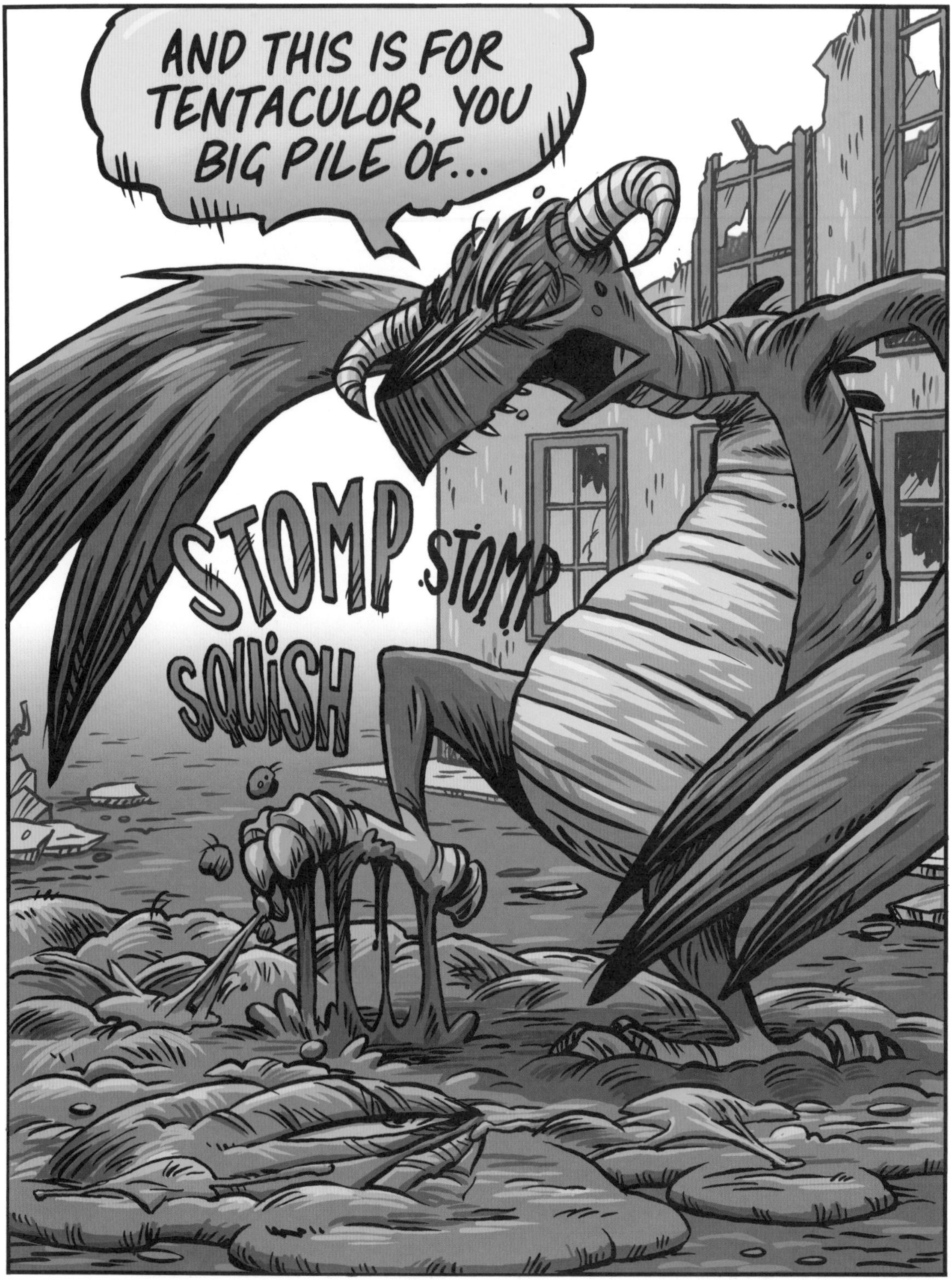
AND THIS IS FOR TENTACULOR, YOU BIG PILE OF...
STOMP
STOMP
STOMP
SQUISH

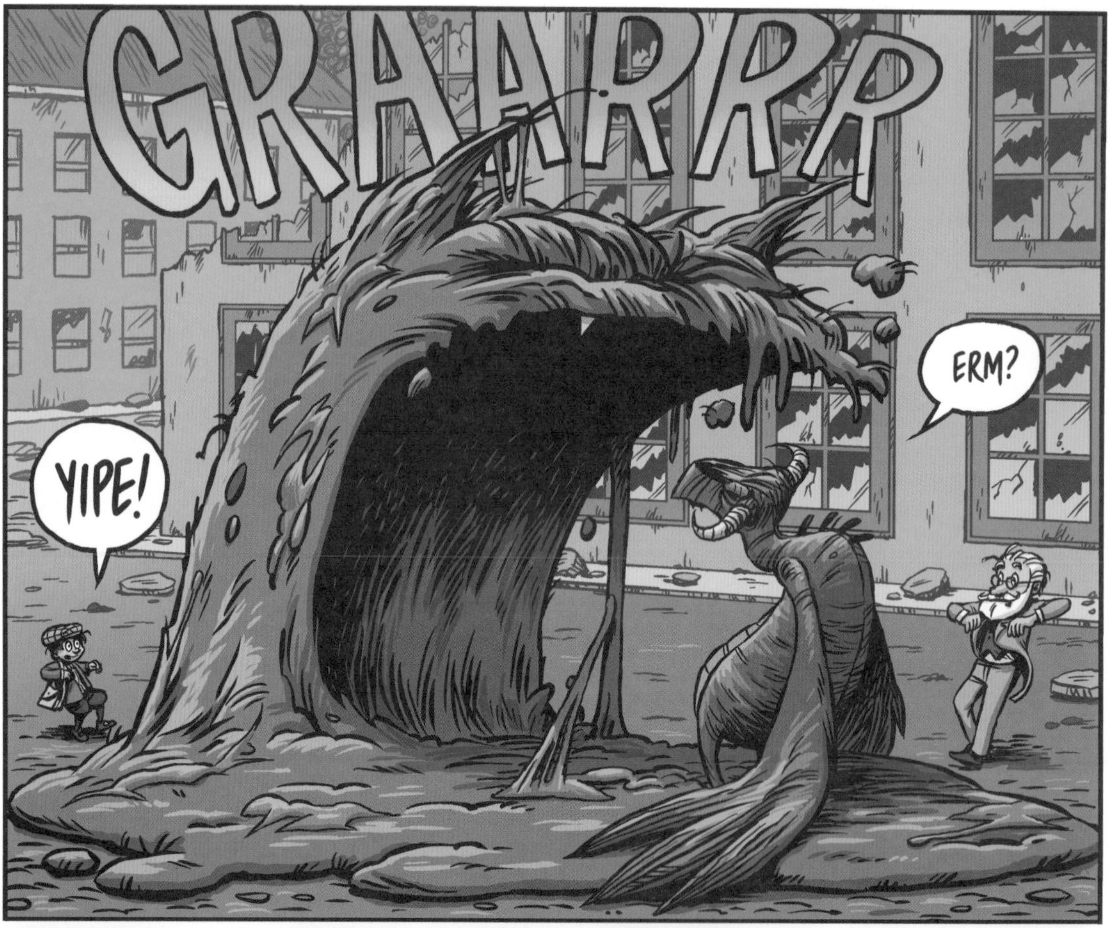
GRAARRRR
YIPE!
ERM?

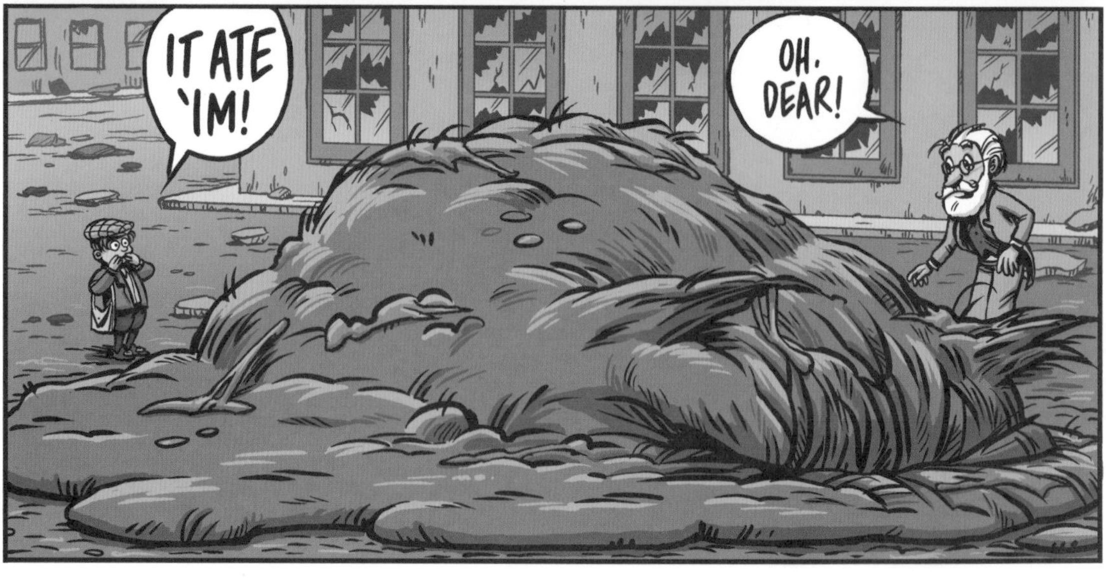
IT ATE 'IM!
OH. DEAR!

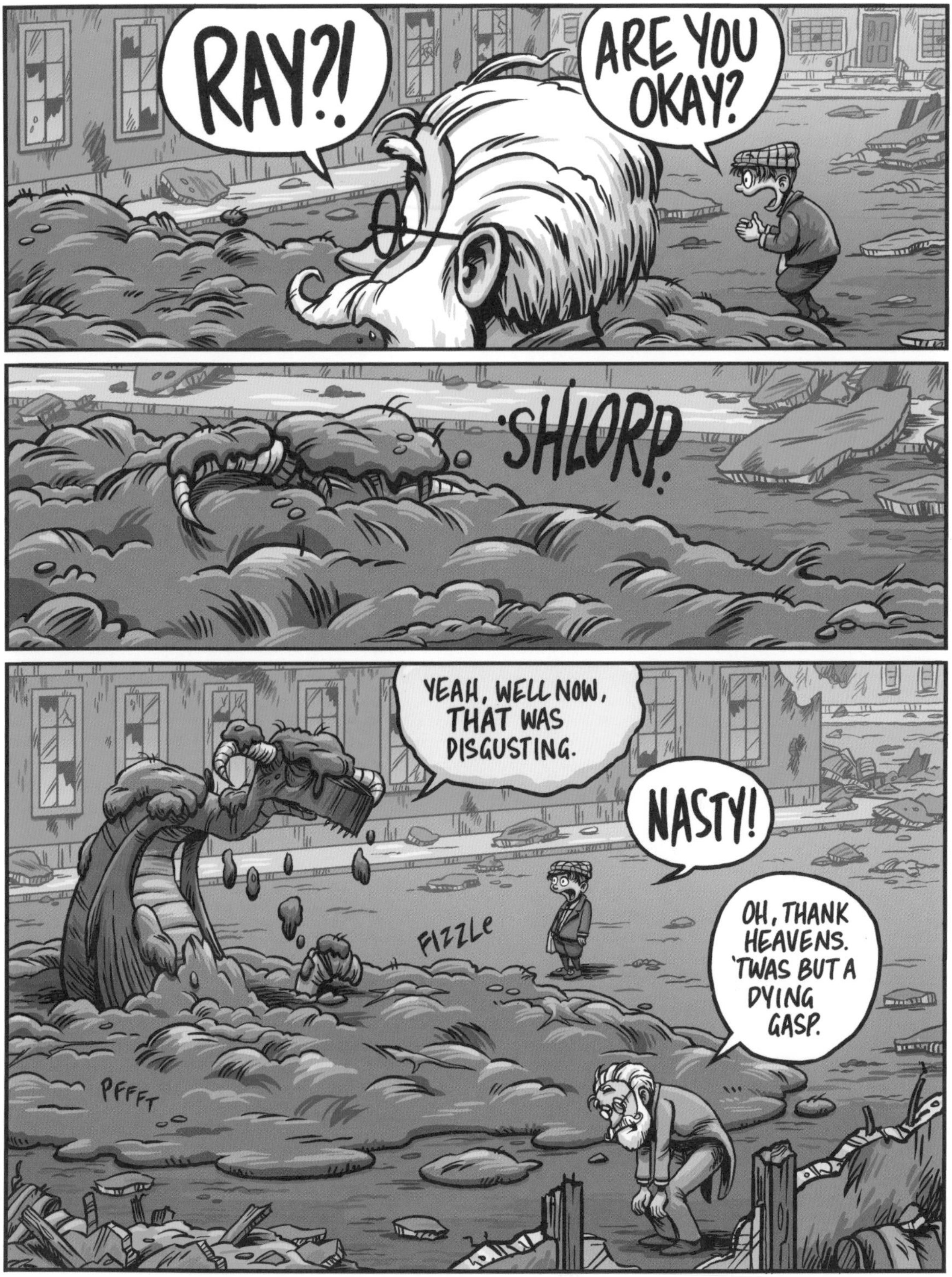
RAY?!
ARE YOU OKAY?
SHLORP
YEAH, WELL NOW, THAT WAS DISGUSTING.
NASTY!
OH, THANK HEAVENS. 'TWAS BUT A DYING GASP.
FIZZLE
PFFFT

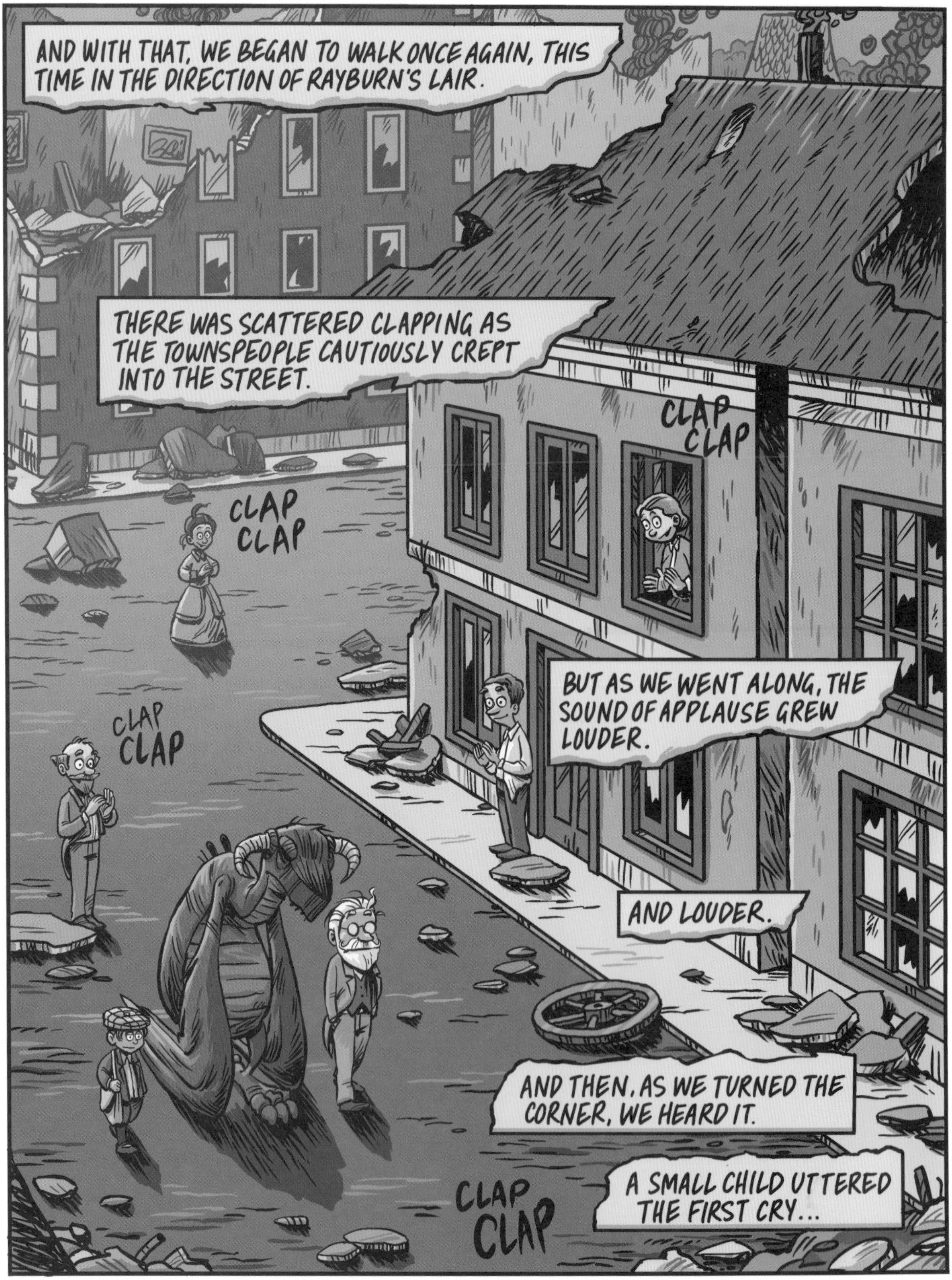
AND WITH THAT, WE BEGAN TO WALK ONCE AGAIN, THIS TIME IN THE DIRECTION OF RAYBURN'S LAIR.
THERE WAS SCATTERED CLAPPING AS THE TOWNSPEOPLE CAUTIOUSLY CREPT INTO THE STREET.
CLAP CLAP
CLAP CLAP
BUT AS WE WENT ALONG, THE SOUND OF APPLAUSE GREW LOUDER.
CLAP CLAP
AND LOUDER.
AND THEN, AS WE TURNED THE CORNER, WE HEARD IT.
CLAP CLAP
A SMALL CHILD UTTERED THE FIRST CRY...

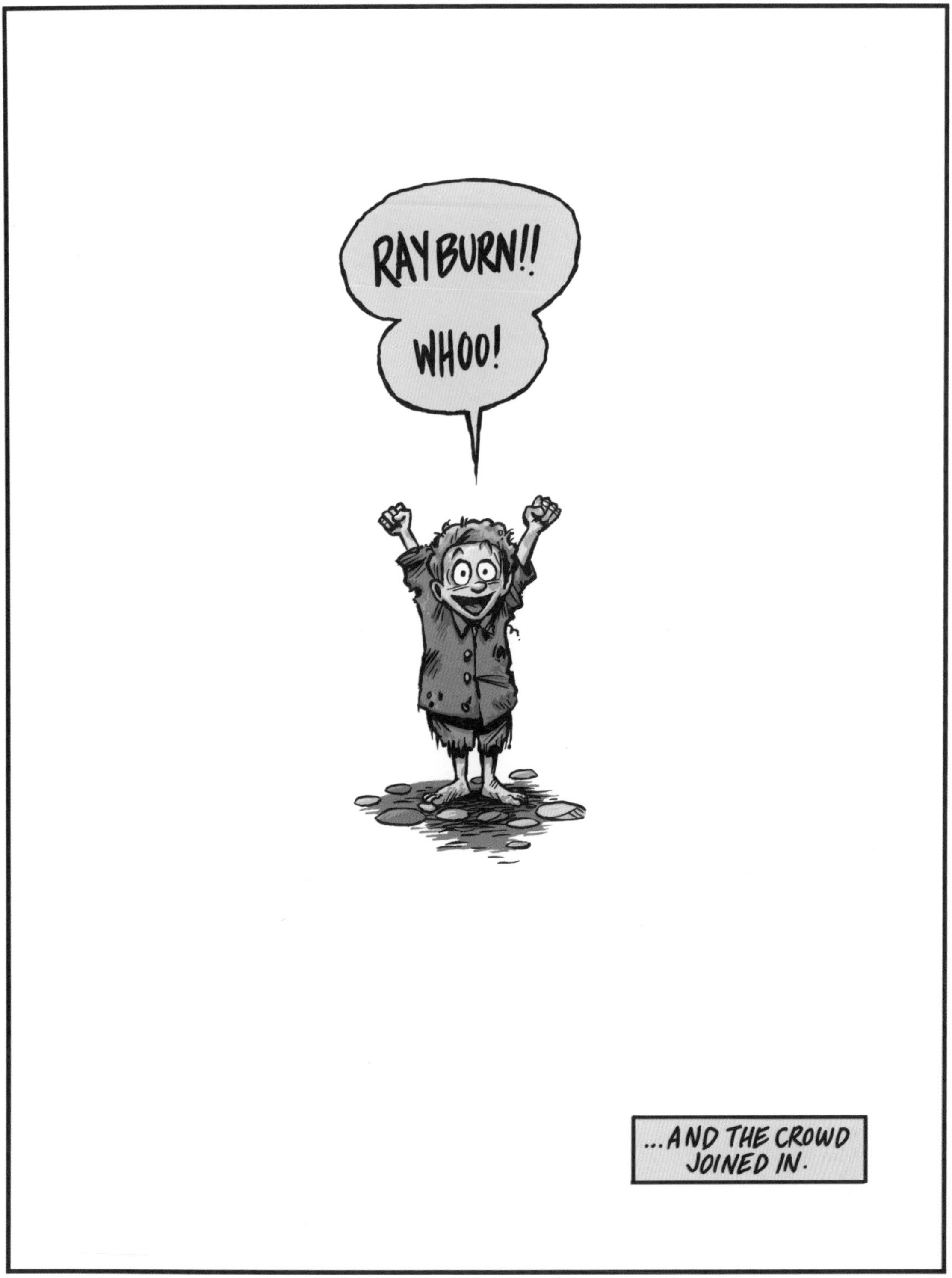
RAYBURN!! WHOO!
...AND THE CROWD JOINED IN.

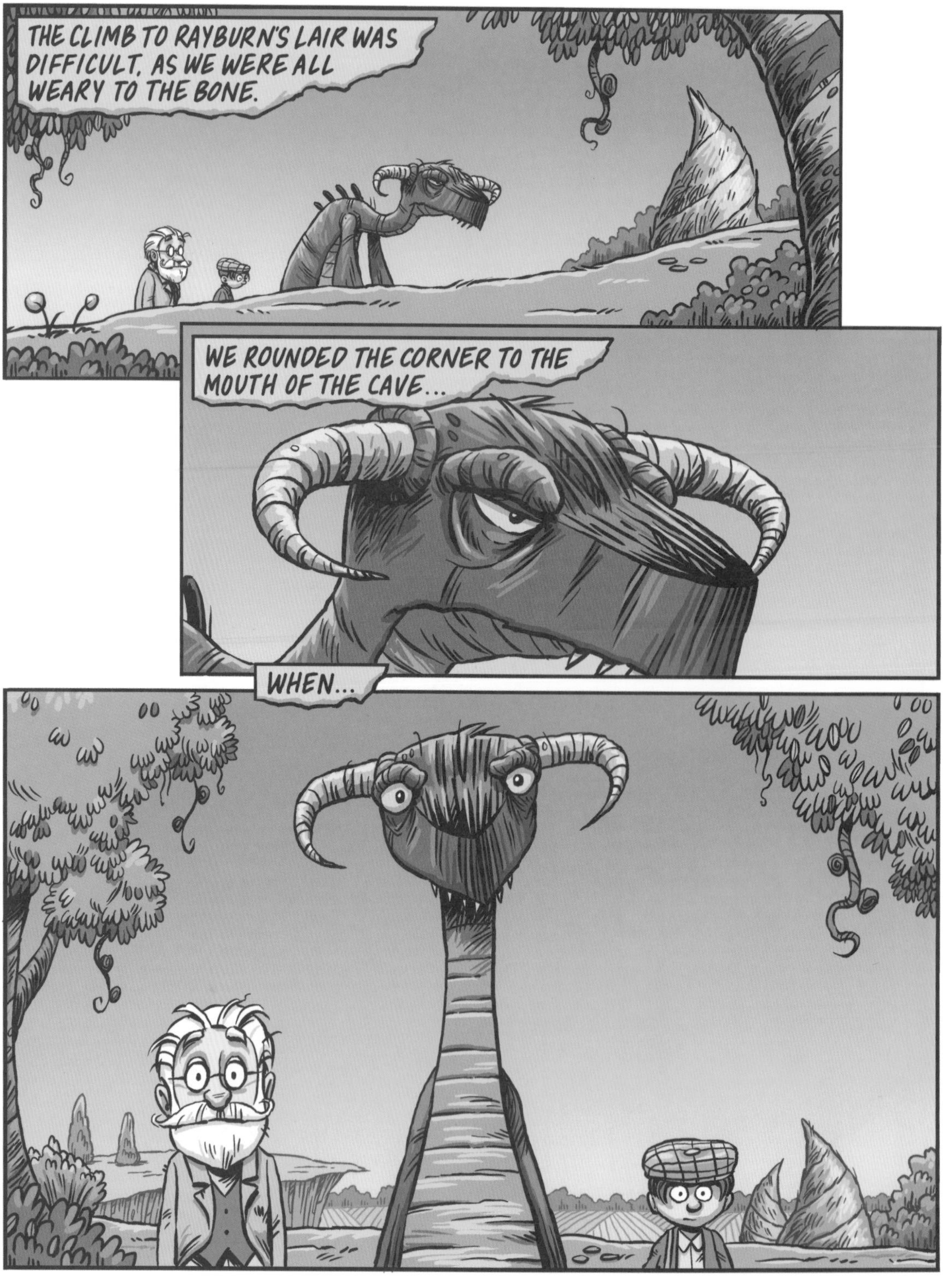
THE CLIMB TO RAYBURN'S LAIR WAS DIFFICULT, AS WE WERE ALL WEARY TO THE BONE.
WE ROUNDED THE CORNER TO THE MOUTH OF THE CAVE...
WHEN...

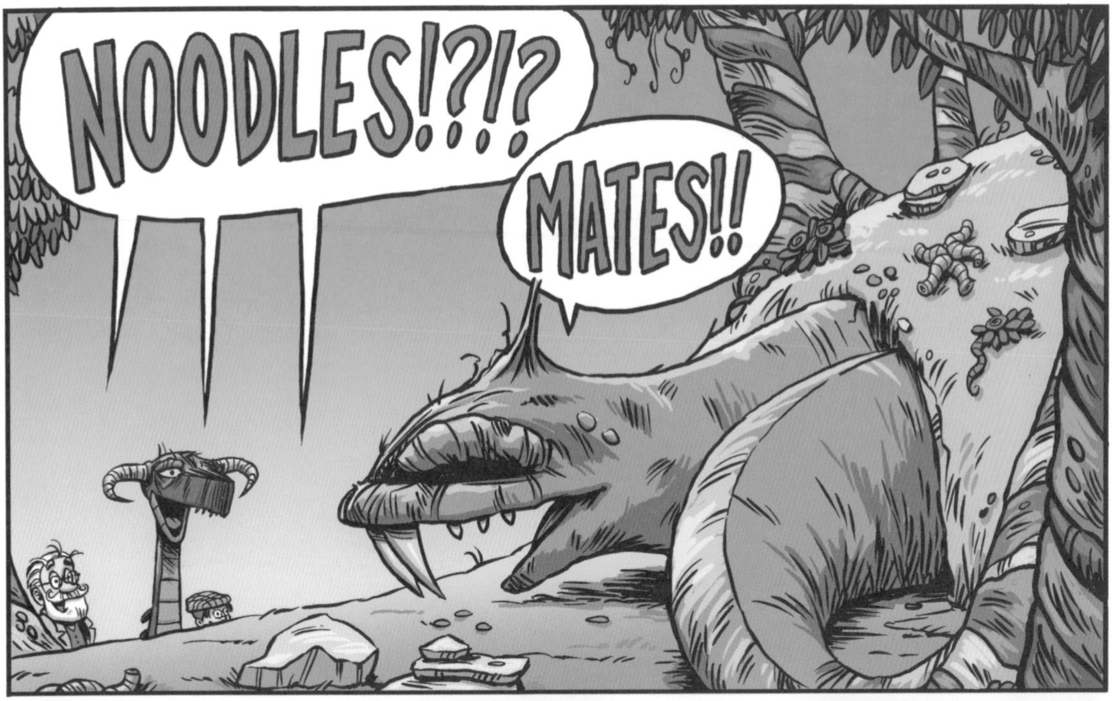
NOODLES!?!?
MATES!!

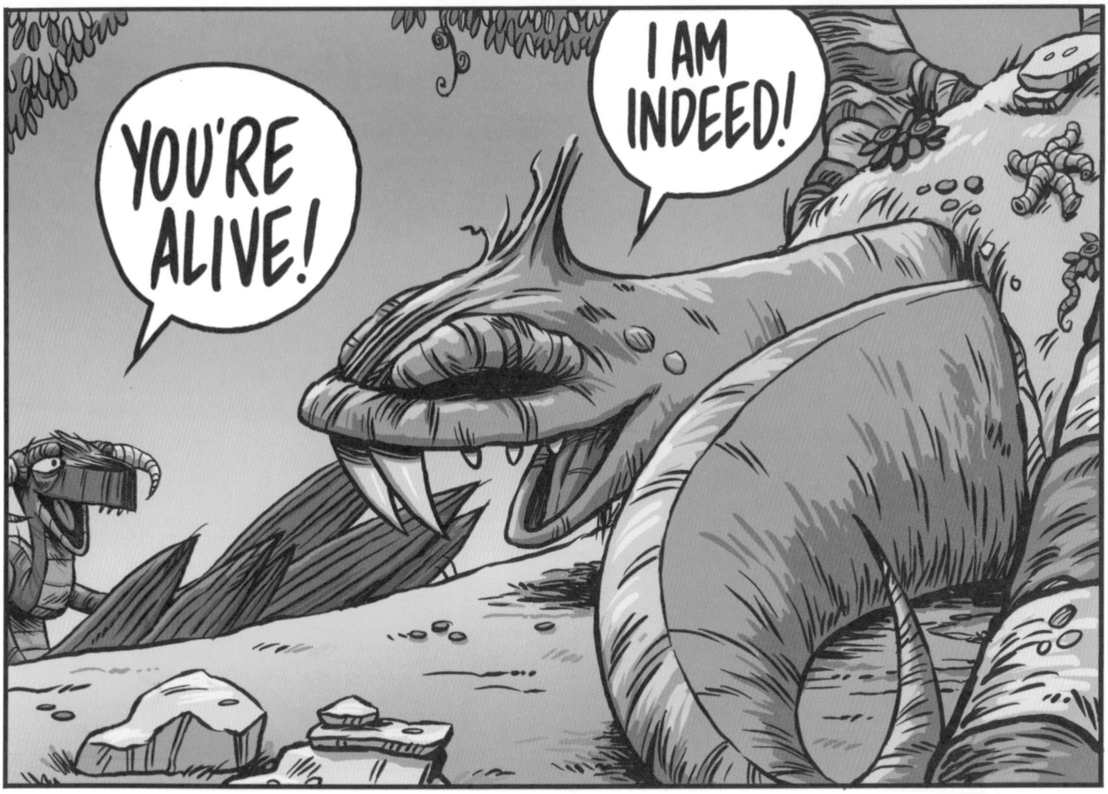
YOU'RE ALIVE!
I AM INDEED!

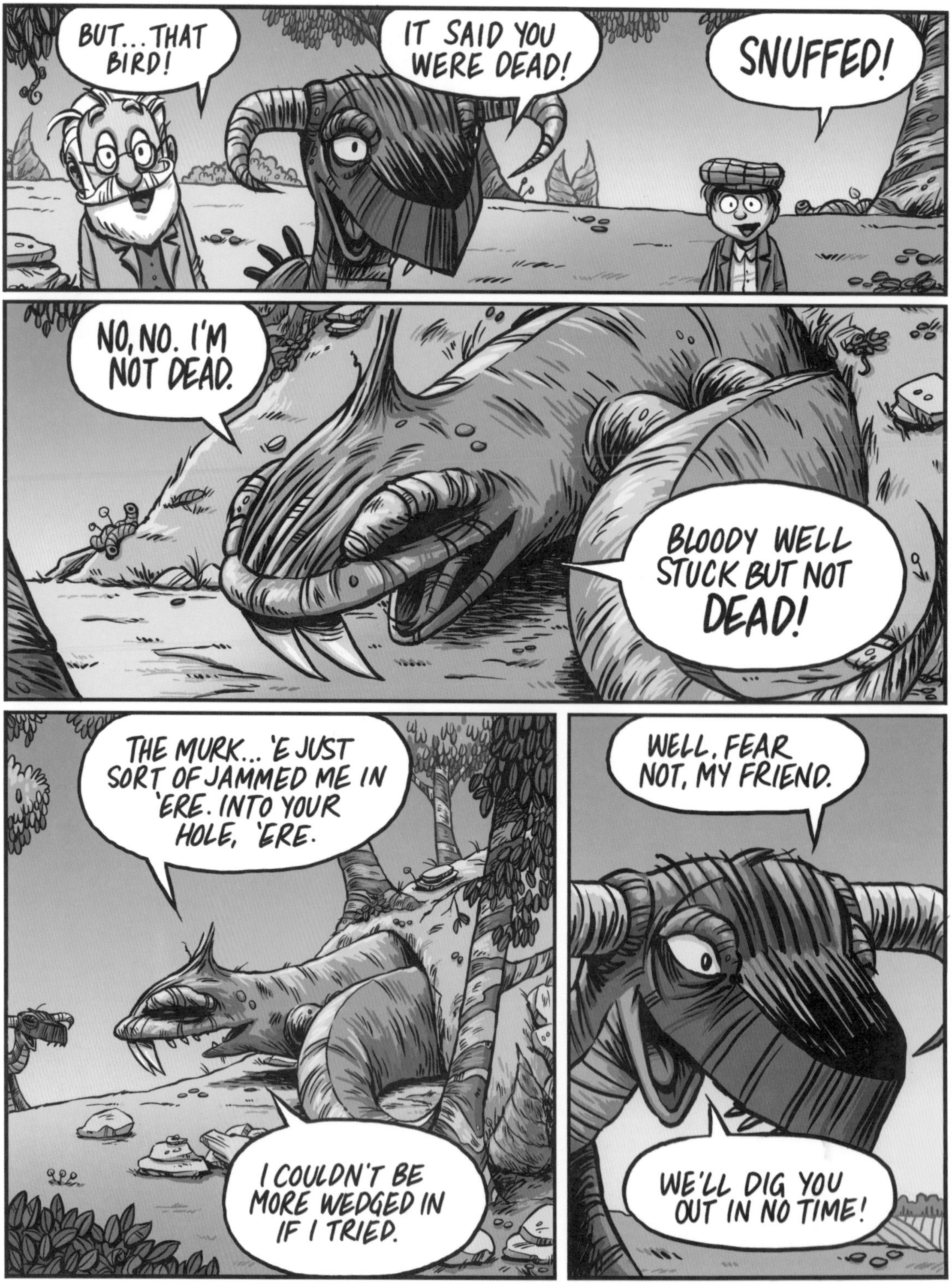
BUT... THAT BIRD!
IT SAID YOU WERE DEAD!
SNUFFED!
NO, NO. I'M NOT DEAD.
BLOODY WELL STUCK BUT NOT DEAD!
THE MURK... 'E JUST SORT OF JAMMED ME IN 'ERE. INTO YOUR HOLE, 'ERE.
I COULDN'T BE MORE WEDGED IN IF I TRIED.
WELL, FEAR NOT, MY FRIEND.
WE'LL DIG YOU OUT IN NO TIME!

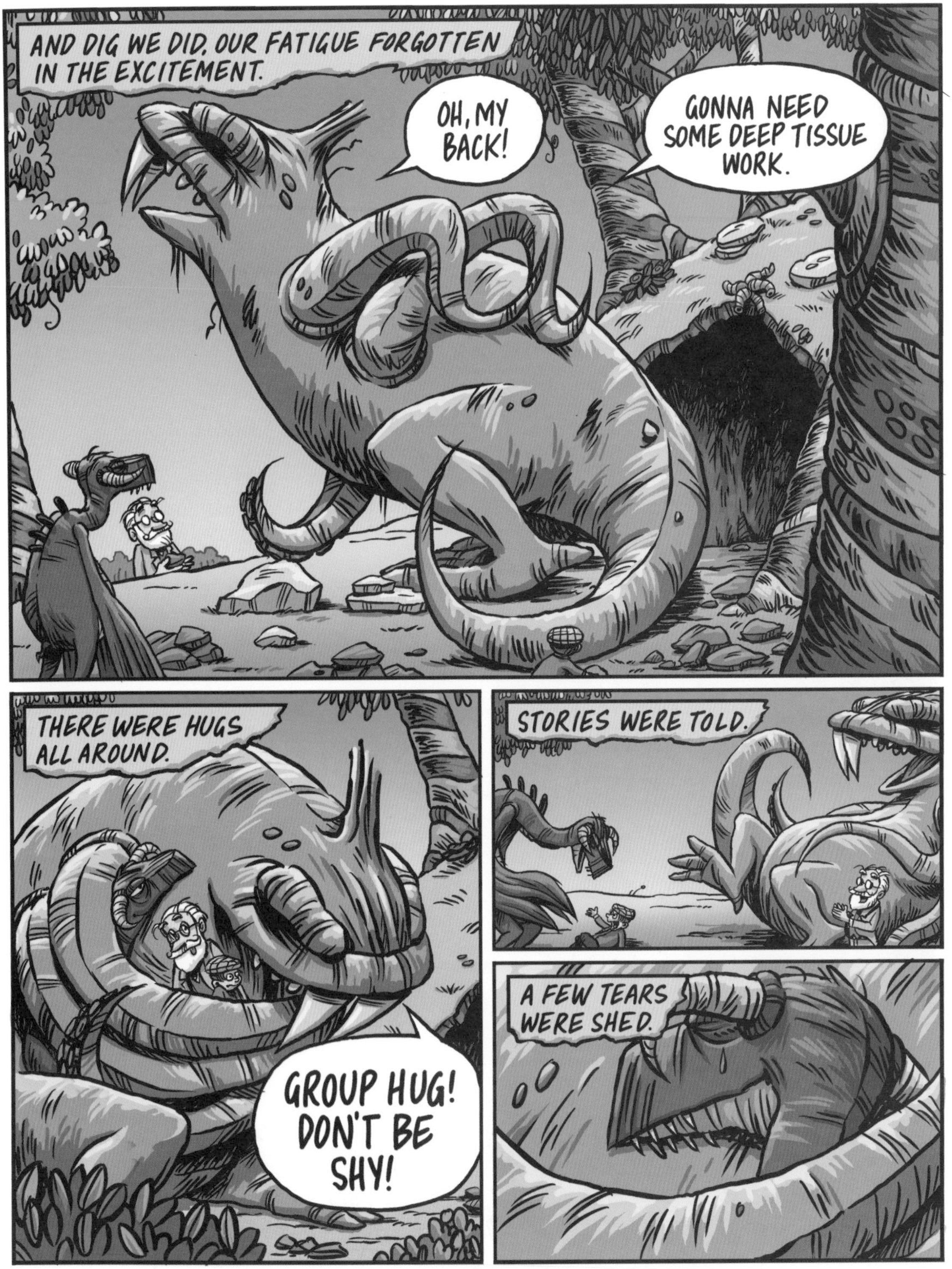
AND DIG WE DID, OUR FATIGUE FORGOTTEN IN THE EXCITEMENT.
OH, MY BACK!
GONNA NEED SOME DEEP TISSUE WORK.
THERE WERE HUGS ALL AROUND.
GROUP HUG! DON'T BE SHY!
STORIES WERE TOLD.
A FEW TEARS WERE SHED.

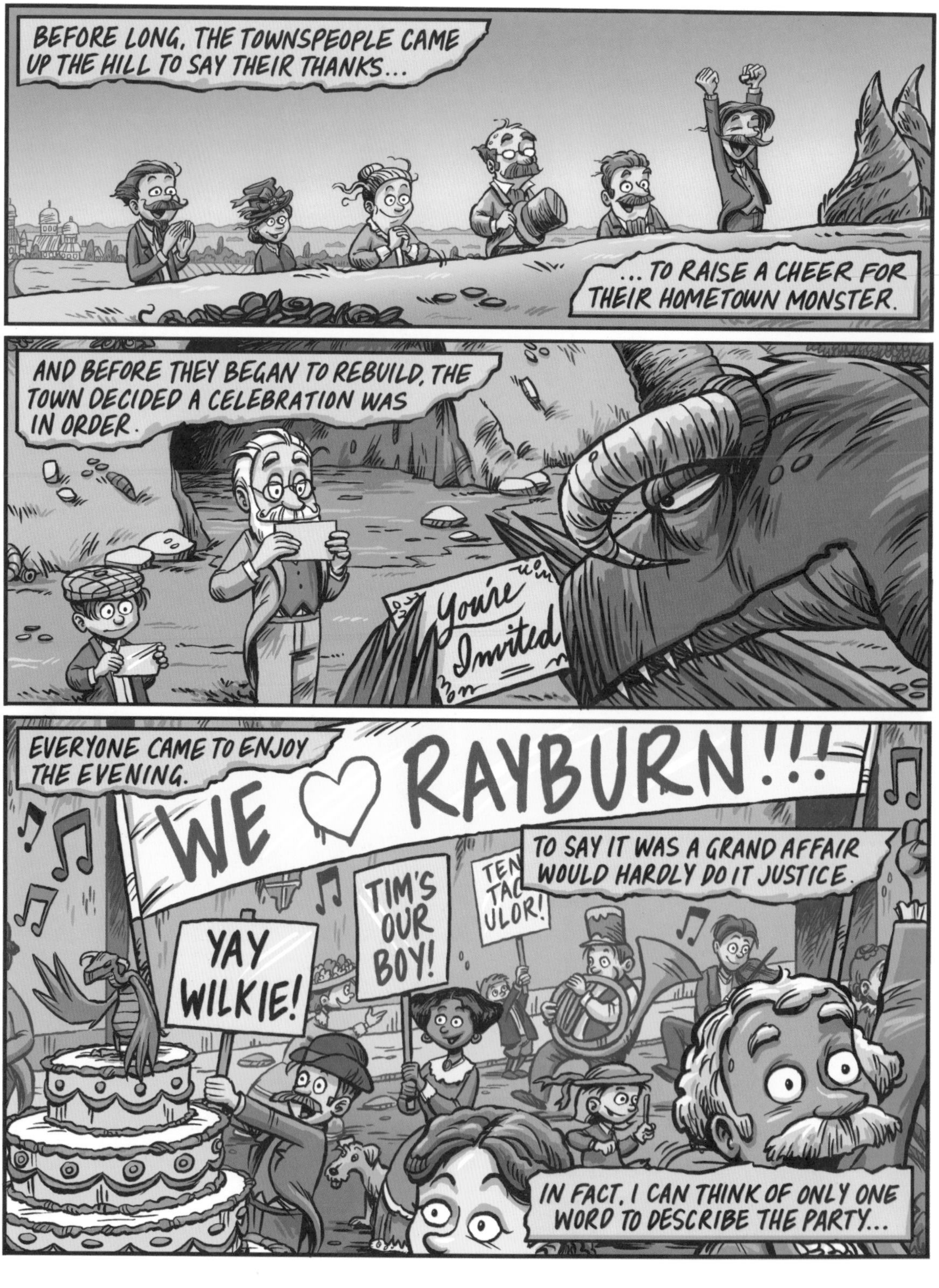
BEFORE LONG, THE TOWNSPEOPLE CAME UP THE HILL TO SAY THEIR THANKS...
...TO RAISE A CHEER FOR THEIR HOMETOWN MONSTER.
AND BEFORE THEY BEGAN TO REBUILD, THE TOWN DECIDED A CELEBRATION WAS IN ORDER.
You're Invited
EVERYONE CAME TO ENJOY THE EVENING.
WE ♡ RAYBURN!!!
TO SAY IT WAS A GRAND AFFAIR WOULD HARDLY DO IT JUSTICE.
YAY WILKIE!
TIM'S OUR BOY!
TEN TAC ULOR!
IN FACT, I CAN THINK OF ONLY ONE WORD TO DESCRIBE THE PARTY...

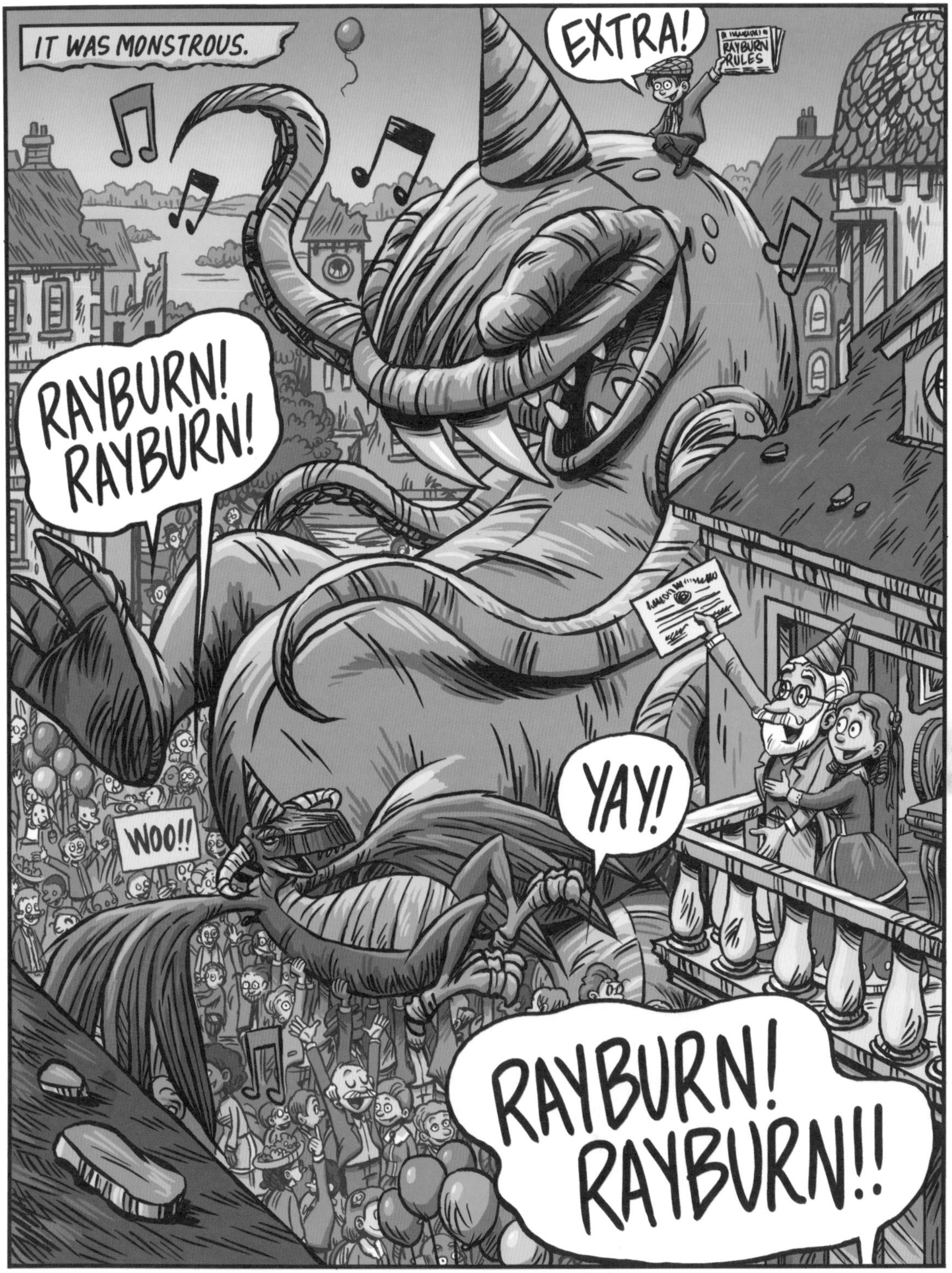
IT WAS MONSTROUS.
EXTRA!
RAYBURN RULES
RAYBURN! RAYBURN!
WOO!!
YAY!
RAYBURN! RAYBURN!!

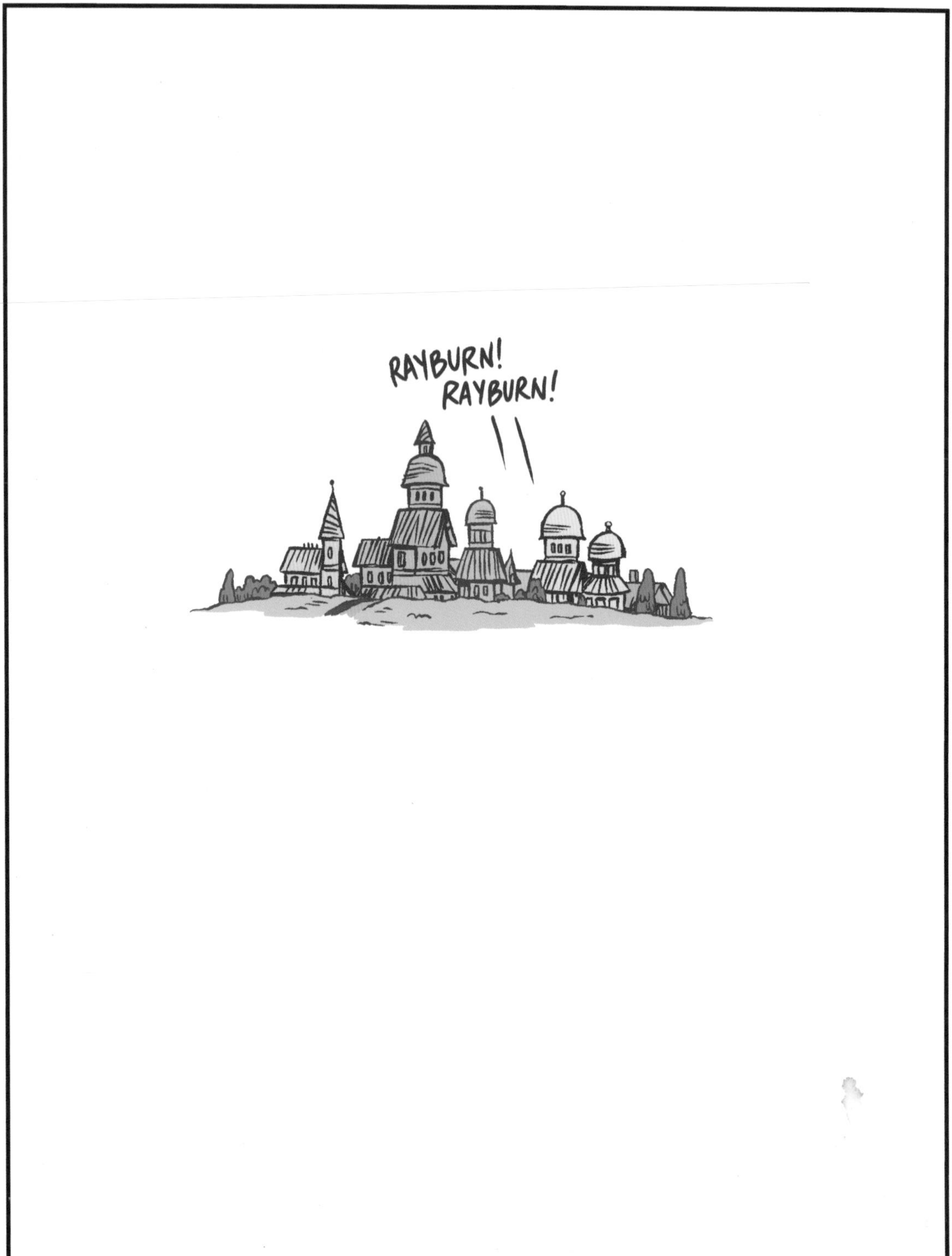
RAYBURN!
RAYBURN!

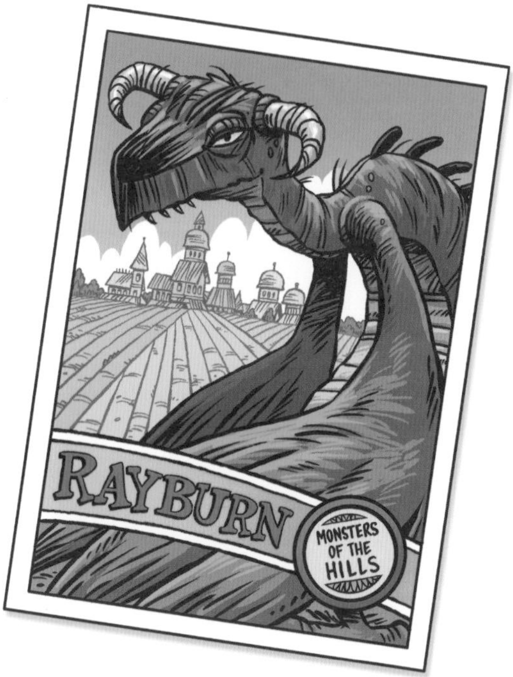
RAYBURN
MONSTERS OF THE HILLS

Acknowlegements

I would like to offer my sincere thanks to the following people for their help, support, and kindness: my incredibly patient family; my amazing and infinitely supportive wife, Amber; Chris Staros, Brett Warnock, Chris Ross, Leigh Walton, and everyone at Top Shelf; Jason Dravis; Josh Block; Jon Weed; Mark Pett; Team Dank; John Glynn and everyone at Universal; my amazing friends in Austin, Indianapolis, New York, and elsewhere; Bob Kingsley; and all of my personal Dr. Wilkies.

And finally, a special monstrous thank you to Wayne Beamer.

Born and raised in Bloomington, Indiana, Rob Harrell created, wrote, and drew the daily comic strip *Big Top*, which was syndicated internationally from 2002–2007 and collected into a book by Andrews McMeel. Currently, he draws the popular strip *Adam@Home*, appearing in over 140 papers worldwide. His paintings have been shown in galleries across the country, and his illustration clients include *Mad Magazine*, Simon & Schuster, American Greetings, Time Inc., and Volkswagen. He lives on a hill in Austin, Texas, with his wife, Amber, and their dogs, Cooper and Kasey.

Visit him online at www.robharrell.com.